Black Sparrow

Black Sparrow

A.J. Griffiths-Jones

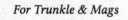

For Trunkle & Mags

FRIDAY 4PM – FARIDA RAFIQ

Staring at my reflection in the bus window, I hardly recognise the dark eyes gazing back at me. They look like deep pools of water, bottomless and cold. Where is my soul? Have I lost all emotion? It's hard to believe that I'm only forty years old and in what they call the prime of my life. There are a few tell-tale signs of tiredness on my face, lines by the corners of my eyes – crow's feet, I think the English would call them – but I have neither the money nor the inclination to buy expensive creams to try to stop them from creeping up on me. My hair has lost its lustre and there are a few stray white hairs poking from underneath my polyester headscarf like thin, ancient wires.

I move my head away, partly because I can't bear to look at myself but also due to the bus stopping, which means more commuters are cramming themselves inside the double-decker.

I don't mind using public transport, it's the only way I can get around, but sometimes the heat and crowded space make me feel sick. There's an odour on the bus today, unwashed coats and sweat mingled with stale cigarettes and greasy food, not pleasant by any means.

I've had a very enjoyable afternoon chatting with Shazia, who always takes such a keen interest in what I have been up to, but our tea went on for too long and now I find myself rushing home to prepare the meal for my family. I dare not be late, my husband would have something to say if I were.

As the bus makes a sharp turn into Kilburn High Road, I grab the handrail on the seat in front of me, accidentally brushing my fingers against the fur hood of a teenager who turns sharply and mutters something at me under her breath. After twenty-two years of living in this country, I still haven't got used to it. People aren't as friendly as at home in my native Pakistan. Yes, I still think of it as my home; after all, it's my motherland, the place where I was born and brought up, a place steeped in rich history and religion. I have a good life here, though. I live in a comfortable house with modern amenities, I have two clever and beautiful children and I have a husband with a good job. He is a difficult man, but we are married, and I am bound to him.

"Busy today isn't it, dear?"

There's an old lady next to me, peering up expectantly, waiting for me to reply.

"Yes, too busy," I tell her, trying to keep the conversation short. After all, I don't know her.

"Are you going far?" she presses, touching my arm with her perfectly manicured scarlet nails as she offers a pack of opened Polo mints.

"No, thank you. Just three more stops," I say, adjusting the heavy shopping bag on my lap which is giving me pins and needles in my thighs. I would eat a jelly sweet if she had one, but not a mint.

"I expect your family will be waiting for you to get home and cook dinner."

I let the comment hang in the stuffy air for a few seconds. She is, right of course. My family will be expecting a good meal, but also their clothes to be washed and ironed, the house to be tidy and their dinner plates cleared away as if by magic after they have eaten their fill.

"Will they?" the woman asks again, tucking the sweets back into her black patent handbag and snapping the clasp shut. "Be waiting for you, I mean?"

I nod politely. "Yes, I expect they will. Do you have family?"

"No, dear. I couldn't have children and my Albert has been dead these past fifteen years."

I don't know what to say. It must have been very hard for her in her youth, not being able to fulfil her role as a mother, so I mutter, "I'm sorry."

"Oh, don't be!" the pensioner says with a laugh, smoothing down her red and black tartan skirt. Then she lowers her voice. "If truth be told, I'm having the time of my life. I go to a couple of tea dances every week, lunch with my brother and his family most Sundays and I'm always out shopping. There's a lot to be said for arriving home with a new frock and not having to justify the cost to anyone."

I'm not familiar with the terms 'tea dance', or 'frock', so I smile politely, but a question leaves my lips. "Don't you ever feel lonely, being by yourself at night, or on cold, rainy days?"

I look deep into her watery blue eyes as she breaks into a smile. "Oh no, dear, not at all. I read a lot, listen to music and of course I have Bruce."

"Bruce?"

"My British Blue." The little old lady grins, taking out a photo of a very fat grey cat. "I love him to bits."

I don't like cats, they're selfish creatures in my opinion, but I've never actually owned a pet and I wonder how such a large, furry animal could possibly stir those sensitive feelings in her.

I see that we're coming to my stop and I pull my scarf tighter around my head, tucking the ends into my jacket so that it doesn't blow away when I go out into the windy street. After pressing the bell, I turn to say goodbye to the silver-haired woman.

"Excuse me," I say. "It was good to meet you, but this is my stop."

"Goodbye, dear," she says, smiling widely with her bright red lips and rouged cheeks. "Lovely to chat with you. Have a good evening."

I push my way to the exit, still sensing her beady little eyes watching me like a crow.

4

I walk along the damp pavement in my sensible loafers. It's been raining again today and I'm glad that I put my waterproof jacket on, although I'm aware that it's probably not the most fashionable item to wear with my pink shalwar kameez. Nobody takes any notice of me, anyway. The other pedestrians are too busy hurrying home out of the cold breeze to their warm and comfortable homes. I used to be like that, when I first married Jameel, but it's funny how things seem to change over time. I wonder if all marriages are like mine. Do couples lose interest in each other with the passing of years, or am I the only unhappy woman in London? Maybe it's natural to feel like this.

I still remember the buzz of being newly married. Everything felt exciting to me then – living in Britain, learning how to take care of a modern house, lying next to my husband every night, waiting for him to climb on top of me and take what now belonged to him. Before Uzma was born, Jameel would come home with a small treat on Friday nights. Sometimes it would be chocolate or a metre of fabric for me to sew into something to wear and he'd have big plans for the weekend. Once, we went to Madame Tussaud's Waxwork Museum and Jameel laughed as I stared at the model of the Queen for ten whole minutes. I didn't recognise even half of the celebrity figures on display, but they were so lifelike that it was quite creepy walking around in there. I couldn't bring myself to enter the dungeon so my husband went on ahead alone, leaving me to drink a cup of peppermint tea in the café.

In those days, unlike now, Jameel had never made excuses about having to work at the weekend or late in the evening. He was around much more then, and I seem to recall him being happier, too. Of course, he's not a bad man but things are different now. Jameel is much more serious these days, providing for us all, guiding us, but nowadays always stressing about something. I think part of the problem is his work. As a solicitor, he has a lot of cases on his mind, but maybe some of it is me, although I couldn't even begin to describe where things went wrong.

I've reached the corner of Appledore Gardens. This is where I live. I can feel the weight of my shopping bag pulling at the muscles in my shoulder. It's far too heavy for a woman to be carrying. The late afternoon breeze whips around the bottoms of my traditional Asian trousers and I remind myself to find my thermal underwear, as my friend Shazia said that temperatures will fall by next week. I still yearn for the heat of Pakistan, even after all this time, and recall sitting on my grandfather's porch with the sun on my face, eating fresh watermelon with my brothers to keep cool.

Number seventeen, this is my house. I need to balance the heavy bag now in order to dig in my handbag for the keys. I can't put it down as the driveway is wet, so I struggle for a minute or so. Our home is a nice place, detached like most of the properties in the cul-de-sac, with a neatly clipped front lawn and hanging baskets either side of the front porch, although the flowers have long since died and just a few stray brown leaves can be seen sprouting up from the soil inside. There is nothing to signify that there is a Muslim family living here; no tell-tale signs, just an ordinary place.

I turn slightly to rest the bag on my knee as I slip the key into the front door and see the old man who lives opposite peeking out from behind his net curtains. He always seems to be watching and waiting for a visitor who never comes. Maybe he's lonely. Maybe he doesn't have a cat like the old lady on the bus, although I'm still not convinced that having such a big, sharp-toothed pet in the house would be a good idea.

I'm inside now and can finally put down my burden. I slip off my shoes in the porch, glance up at the golden, star-shaped clock in the hallway and shake my head before taking off my wet jacket. I need to hurry if I'm to have the meal ready for six o'clock as Jameel will expect. Tonight, there will be a delicious mutton biryani with paratha bread, my favourite, although I know I shouldn't indulge, as the heavy quantities of ghee required to fry the flatbread are already beginning to show upon my once slender hips.

Still, my family will be content. They always appreciate my cooking, if little else. And there will be plenty of food should any of my husband's friends or colleagues decide to grace us with a visit. I hope that Jameel has eaten a respectable lunch, something

7

substantial to fill him during his working hours. I meant to prepare him a hot breakfast this morning, but he left the marital bed before the sun rose, fumbling around in the dark for his fresh cotton shirt, and before I had even boiled the kettle, the front door slammed shut and he was gone. No goodbye, just a grunt and a wave. I went back to bed for an hour but couldn't sleep.

I put away the groceries and wash my hands before carefully dicing meat into small cubes. I have a few good tricks to make the lamb go further, such as bulking up my dishes with vegetables and heavy sauces, which saves me a few pounds every week out of what Jameel calls my 'housekeeping money'. I do the same frugal shopping with packet and tinned goods, buying dented cans at reduced prices or taking the bus to bargain stores where I can make the pounds go further. I've been doing this for a long time now and, as far as I know, my husband has no idea how much money I have saved. It's quite a sum, tucked away in a bank account that Shazia helped me to open, and it's staying there, for now.

We had a good chat this afternoon, Shazia and I. She's my only real friend and I trust her. Today, we talked about our daughters, always a worry for an Asian mother in Western society. Shazia's daughter, Maryam, is training to be a nurse in a local hospital. She's been there since finishing her exams at school and will continue until a suitable husband is found for her when she's twenty-five. I think Jameel has the same plan for our daughter, Uzma, but I doubt whether he will discuss the matter in detail with me. He believes that the men in the family take care of such arrangements, no matter if it's the right thing to do or not. He's already regretting his decision to allow Uzma to go on an art course in Paris last summer. I think Jameel felt it would help to rid the girl of her ambition to become an artist – you know, shock her into realising how hard it would be to actually earn a living from selling her paintings. If you ask me, the plan back-fired, as she's been sullen and withdrawn since her return, spending hours alone in her room drawing, or on that computer of hers.

I remember the day that Jameel relented. Uzma was biding her time, making her father a drink, asking him about his day and rolling her eyes at him as she handed over the leaflet about the course. I sat in my chair watching, pretending to darn a pair of socks and occasionally popping a sweet gulab jamoon into my mouth, as she excitedly explained the details of what she would learn in the French city. I was surprised when, only three days later, Jameel wrote out two cheques, one for the art teacher and one for the lady whose house Uzma would lodge in for the duration of her stay. I said nothing, although I feared terribly for my daughter, but everything was settled, and she danced with delight.

The phone in the hallway is ringing, sending a loud echo up the staircase, so I slowly slide the pan of siz-

9

zling meat off the heat and walk down the hall to see who could be calling at this time of day.

"There you are," the voice on the other end states curtly. "You took a long time to answer."

"I'm preparing dinner," I say. "Mutton biryani."

My husband gives a short cough, clearing his throat and then continues, "I won't be home until eight. You'll have to hold dinner."

I note that this is more of an order than a request and suck in my breath, but at least I now have a few hours' grace. "Yes, of course. Is anyone joining us tonight?"

"No, not tonight," Jameel tells me, "but you'll need to ensure that the spare bedroom is prepared as we're having guests tomorrow. I'll explain later."

I want to ask who, as it's rare that anyone stays overnight, unless it's relatives visiting from overseas or another part of England, but the other end of the line has already been disconnected and I return the phone to its cradle.

I look at my reflection in the mirror on the wall, the second time today that I've taken notice of myself, and prod at my thickening waistline. I look alright for my age, I think, although Jameel wouldn't agree. Maybe I've spent too many afternoons eating sweet treats with Shazia when I should have been out walking or doing housework to burn off some calories instead, as my tunic is beginning to look tight.

Returning to the kitchen, I turn off the stove and reach for the kettle. I can afford to sit down with a cup of peppermint tea now, just for a while. A sharp twinge shoots up my spine as I lower myself into my leather armchair. That's all I need, the beginnings of sciatica! I flick through the TV channels, pausing at a shopping channel where a slim white woman is running briskly on an electric treadmill, her high ponytail swinging to and fro as she pounds the rubber. I glance up at the only family portrait that we have and see a younger, slimmer self, smiling back at me.

Uzma had been just six years old, and Khalid three, when Jameel had announced that we were taking a trip to the local photographic studio. He'd even encouraged me to buy a new sari for the occasion. Afterwards, he took us for ice-cream at a local Italian café, the first and only time that Jameel had taken us there.

I remember accidentally dripping chocolate sauce onto my sari and that was the very first time that I noticed the way Jameel looked at me. It was a condescending look, as if I, too, were a child who had misbehaved, causing him embarrassment as he quickly glanced around to see if anyone had noticed his clumsy and irresponsible wife. It wasn't long after that that the days out had stopped, Jameel blaming his workload and me blaming myself.

I still have that beautiful turquoise outfit embroidered with gold, but now it lies wrapped in tissue paper in a drawer under our divan. Maybe one day, when I've lost enough weight, I will be able to wear it again. Although, as long as Jameel is alive, I doubt whether we'll go to a function together unless it's a community or family wedding. I think Jameel would rather not have me in his life now, although I know he dotes on our children.

When I became betrothed to Jameel at eighteen, coming over to Britain as part of a traditional arranged marriage set up by my parents and their second cousins, I realise that I was very naïve. My mother had taught me well, so I knew how to cook decent meals and clean the house, but I wasn't prepared for the life that was waiting here for me, thousands of miles from my home. Jameel is six years older than me and he had already passed his law examinations before our wedding. I have to admit I was quite overwhelmed by the tall, dark man who wore Western suits and drove a big saloon car.

When my father told me that Jameel Rafiq was planning to buy a house for us to live in, I was so happy. It was everything I could possibly wish for. My parents were so proud – and they still are, although I seldom get to visit them now – and I was just glad that my older, more beautiful cousin was already married so that she couldn't be the one to move to London and live in luxury. In hindsight, I was a fool.

I pick up the remote control and press it to find another channel. Something about serial killers pops up on the screen and I leave it on for a few minutes. The man speaking talks too fast and has a heavy American accent but, from the feed at the bottom of the screen, I can read that a woman has been accused of killing a group of old people in the nursing home where she works. There's a picture of the home and a photo shot of the woman, who looks quite normal in my opinion. I learn that she's been giving them extra medicines mixed in with their meals, but I've never heard of the names of the drugs that she used. They must have been quite tasteless for people not to notice.

After a few more minutes, I switch off the set and get up, realising that I've been sitting down for nearly half an hour and my tea has gone cold. I wonder if the old lady who was on the bus is sitting down watching her favourite programme right now; what must it be like to have nobody else depending upon you to wash, cook and clean? She certainly wouldn't ever have to wait for the bathroom to be free every morning. I realise that I'm actually jealous of a grey-haired pensioner, although I still wouldn't have a cat.

Back in the kitchen, I sift flour onto the marble work-surface. Jameel is always scolding me for making such a mess in the kitchen but this is the traditional way to prepare the paratha, the way my mother taught me. It tastes better mixed in this way; using a bowl forces the air out.

My thoughts turn back to the woman on the television as I pour warm water into a little well in the centre of the flour. For a split second, I wonder if there's anything in our medicine cabinet that could be used to poison my husband; perhaps, by slipping it into the bread, the taste would be masked. I catch my breath. What a wicked thought! God will see my terrible deed and take me to task on judgement day.

I bow my head and repeat the words from our Holy Quran: "*If they pay no heed, God knows the evil-doers.*"

The house is incredibly quiet for a Friday afternoon. By now, Khalid is usually here, hungry as all teenage boys tend to be, and then Uzma should arrive soon after her brother, running upstairs before I can see the lipstick and eye make-up that she wears to college each day. She thinks that I disapprove, but I don't, really. It's Jameel that she should worry about. If he caught her coming home in her tight t-shirts and covered in make-up, he would take her out of college without another thought. I think that my daughter is pretty enough without having to use make-up, but I'm willing to let her have a bit of freedom before she settles down.

Personally, I don't think it will be long before Jameel starts thinking about a match for Uzma. In fact, perhaps we should think ourselves lucky that she hasn't shown any interest in boys yet. I wonder where my children are. They're both late.

I go out into the hall and pick up the phone, punching in my son's mobile number which I know off by heart. It rings six times.

"Hey, Mom," my seventeen-year-old yells over a noisy background. "What's up?"

"What time will you be home?" I shout into the receiver. "Your father will be late, dinner is at eight."

"It's okay, I'll get something out."

I immediately worry that my son will be eating greasy chips and fried chicken.

"Where are you now? I can hardly hear you, Khalid."

"At the arcade," he tells me, raising his voice so that I can hear. "Listen, I'm going to stay over at Ali's house tonight, we're going to watch some films."

Ali's parents are good people. I don't mind, so long as I know where my son is. "Have you checked with them? Khalid? Khalid?"

The noise level has risen to such a pitch that I can no longer make out what my boy is telling me and we cut off the call at the same moment. I'm exasperated that I can't make myself heard and I expect Khalid has better things to do than to listen to his mother.

Immediately afterwards, I try Uzma's phone. It rings and rings, but she doesn't pick up. I'm not too worried about her yet, as she often goes to a coffee house after college on a Friday, although lately she's been coming straight home and going to her room.

Jameel thinks that our daughter spends far too much time on her computer and wants her to limit herself to an hour every day. According to Shazia, every young girl is the same, so I try to divert Jameel to another topic whenever he brings the subject up. I don't lie for Uzma. After all, how can I when I'm not sure what she's looking at on the internet? But I trust my daughter to make the right choices. She's a good Muslim girl and knows right from wrong. I expect she's looking at fashion or chatting with her friends on that Facebook thing that everyone seems to be talking about. All these social network sites just confuse me. I can just about find the right button to switch the computer on!

With the house still empty, I go back to my cooking, deep in thought about Jameel's comment. He said guests are coming tomorrow and I'm intrigued to know who and how long they're staying. It's been a while since anyone has stayed in our back room and I must try to remember to air the sheets first thing in the morning. Perhaps one of my husband's cousins is coming down from Coventry. We haven't seen either of them for over a year now. They are solicitors, too.

I go into the laundry room, pick up a pile of folded clothes and carry them upstairs to put away. On top are Khalid's black t-shirts, so I push open his bedroom door and put them on top of the untidy duvet, still balled up from this morning as he left it. I tell my children that they are old enough to clean their own bedrooms now, but it seems to go in one ear and out the other. This boy will be the death of me. There are two empty glasses on his bedside table, both thick with orange juice at the bottom, which look like they've been here for days. Crisp packets and old magazines fill the waste paper basket.

I close Khalid's door and take Uzma's pale blue shalwar kameez to her cupboard. She wore this with a patterned cream scarf last weekend to attend the Mosque and the colour really suits her. The wardrobe is half empty. I blink twice, wondering if my eyes are deceiving me. No, I'm not seeing things. Uzma's traditional Pakistani outfits are all here, hanging neatly side by side, but all of her Western clothes, jeans, shirts, jumpers, dresses, are missing.

I sit down on my daughter's bed and take a deep breath, staring at the closet, wondering what this means. Suddenly, a thought strikes me, and I get on my hands and knees to look underneath the bed. Uzma's black suitcase has gone. I cry hot tears of anger and grief, I don't know what I should do.

I'm back in the hall, phone fixed to my ear but there's still no reply from Uzma's phone. It goes to voicemail and this time I leave a message, although afterwards I wonder if it sounds garbled: "Uzma, where are you? This is Ammi, Mum, please pick up your phone, I'm worried about you."

I don't know what else to say and let the receiver slip back into its cradle, only to snatch it up again seconds later. I need to phone my husband and I look in the little blue phone book for his number.

No response, only the familiar beeping of the message machine. Of course, Jameel has gone to play badminton, or so he says. I rarely call him, and it feels quite unnatural to be doing so now, almost as though I'm intruding upon a part of my husband's life that I know nothing about. I wonder whether he will ring back when he sees the missed call on the screen. Probably not. Perhaps he will think his stupid, forgetful wife is going to ask him to pick up something from the shops. No doubt the phone is in his sports bag anyway, buzzing away while he runs around the court, red-faced and sweating.

17

My gut instinct tells me to sit down and wait. I have no idea what to do and wouldn't have the first clue where to start looking for my daughter. Wherever she has gone, it was planned. I can see that much. Why didn't I see any signs? I'm her mother. My hands are shaking, I should drink a cup of water.

In the kitchen again. I feel the intense darkness from the early evening creeping across the window like the wing of a giant bird as I run the cold-water tap. No matter which way I look, all I can see is my own reflection, our back garden shrouded by the night. The water slips down my throat and makes me gag, it's too cold. It's getting chilly out there, too and I wonder if Uzma is wearing her winter coat. I trot quickly to the closet under the stairs where we hang our outerwear and see that her padded jacket is still here. Uzma will be cold, wherever she is. I remember her telling me that it was an unfashionable thing when I bought it from the market some weeks ago, and she's only been out in it a couple of times.

Tears roll down my face. I reach for a tissue from my pocket and wipe at them, soaking the flimsy material after just a few dabs. I'm frightened that my daughter has run away from home but I'm also afraid of Jameel's reaction. He will blame me for not noticing the signs. I am her mother, after all.

Back in the lounge. I stare out through the huge bay window. Across the street, I can see the shape of the old man sitting next to a tall lamp reading, his body hunched over as though he's studying something intensely, rounded shoulders and a hooked nose. I wonder if he saw my daughter come home this afternoon and take her suitcase of clothes, but I can't ask, we've never spoken. Perhaps she ordered a taxi to take her wherever it is she has gone to. Jameel will have to go over there later.

I want to ring Shazia, but I know that this will cause her to start calling our other friends. I'm not ready for that yet. I'm ashamed of myself. Why couldn't my own daughter just speak to me? What has happened? Perhaps there is a very simple explanation and I'm getting upset over nothing, but my mother's intuition tells me that something is very wrong. Uzma, where are you?

FRIDAY 6PM – UZMA RAFIQ

I've got two hours. Enough time to check-in and have something to eat before my flight, although the airport is really busy this afternoon and people are rushing around like crazy. The Tannoy announces flights departing to Berlin, Venice, Budapest. I wait in line, pulling my black nylon suitcase behind me. I'm already tired from struggling on the underground with my luggage. Trust me to travel in rush hour. I did plan my time carefully, though, making sure that I went to college this morning as usual. Having left my packed clothes under the bed, I returned for them at lunchtime when Mum was out at Aunt Shazia's. She's so fixed in her habits, it's easy to work out when the house will be empty.

I was really flustered at breakfast. Mum was asking me all sorts of questions about which classes I had today and where I would be having lunch, but my mind was just about as far away as it could have been. I could feel myself blushing guiltily as she talked. Mum has this habit of trying to brush my hair at breakfast; she doesn't understand that having it loose and a bit messy is fashionable. I think I was a bit sharp with her this morning. And now, here I am, ten hours later, preparing to fly to France.

The couple in front of me are arguing. It sounds petty. The woman is griping about who should take care of the passports and boarding cards. She's pretty, with straight black hair and is wearing a heavy sheepskin jacket. They look like newly-weds, too young to have been together long but both wearing sparkly gold wedding bands. The bickering is in hushed tones, but both are glaring at each other. In my opinion, it's simple – look after your own documents.

The queue moves forward and another desk opens but it's for Business Class passengers only. There's only one older man over there, standing bolt upright in his dark pin-striped suit, a typical city gent holding a black raincoat over one arm. I imagine that he smells of mothballs and whiskey like a lot of old English men. He must be quite rich if he's travelling business class on such a short flight, or maybe the company he works for has paid for it. I'd love to be able to travel to Paris in style, I bet he'll even drink champagne. I sigh and wait.

Today, I'm starting the life I've always dreamed of. I'm going to become an artist in Paris. If you'd told me six months ago that I'd be here today, escaping to live with my French boyfriend, I'd never have believed you, not in a million years. I'm scared, of course I am. But the six weeks that I spent learning from the street painters in Montmatre were the best of my life. And, of course, I had the best tutor in the world, Sylvain. We've only known each other for a few short months but it's as though he's switched on a light within my soul. I can finally feel passionate about my artwork and it also helps that he's drop-dead gorgeous. Sylvain has thick dark curls that brush against his collar as he works and a deep tan that suggests Mediterranean roots. I asked him about his family, but he just laughed, said his mother was a gipsy and his father worked in a travelling circus, so I didn't know whether to believe him.

When we met, it was purely a student and teacher relationship but, after a week of working closely together, everything changed. I stopped looking at his brushstrokes and focussed instead on the rippling muscles beneath his tight white shirts, inhaling his heady cologne as he stepped behind me to appraise my work. I was so scared that Sylvain wouldn't want me in the same way... afraid that he would think me a foolish, infatuated young girl. I needn't have worried, though. After eight days, he looked me straight in the eyes and I knew, from a smouldering look that made me melt. From then on, we were a couple. Sylvain is so talented. He's wonderful at charcoal sketching and watercolours and one time he persuaded me to let him sketch me on top of the bed wrapped in just a thin cotton sheet. The drawing was incredible. I treasure it and have brought it with me.

As my suitcase trundles down the conveyor belt, disappearing through a dark hole in the wall, I notice that my bright pink luggage tag has fallen off. It wasn't expensive but it makes my bag easier to identify, so I try to get the flight assistant's attention, but she's busy talking to an old lady with lots of bags. I leave it, can't be bothered, it should be okay.

I pass through Security quickly as I've put all my make-up and electrical items into my suitcase, so there is only my mobile phone to place in the plastic tray. It's unbelievable how many people are messing around, looking for clear bags to put lipstick in or a bin to get rid of bottles of water. Don't they read the signs? Passport Control is a longer wait. There are lots of families travelling together tonight; maybe they're having a weekend break in a warmer country. I smile to myself, thinking that nobody could imagine the adventure that I'm going on.

I have mixed feelings about dropping out of art college, I've been getting along so well with my coursework and it'll be two years of study down the drain, but there's nothing like hands-on experience and, if I'm honest with myself, it might have taken me another two years to hook up with a gallery in London, although Dad would probably have supported me until I found work. I keep telling myself that this sudden decision to leave isn't just because of Sylvain, but I know it is, mostly. Besides, he manages to sell his art to tourists and makes good money tutoring in the summer, so we'll be fine.

I doubt whether my father will be alright about it, though. He put such trust in me to finish college and get my degree, I bet he'll wish he'd never paid for me to go to Paris last July now. I love my dad, he's a strict but loving man, although I don't know whether he loves my mum any longer. They're a strange match. Thank goodness Dad hasn't got any ideas about fixing me up with my third cousin from Pakistan, or the son of a friend or an uncle of our family doctor. I'd die. I don't want to turn into Mum.

Finally, I sit down in a café. It's busy and I opt for a high stool, tucked under a counter at the window. The other occupants are either engrossed in books or staring at the Departure board. Nobody notices me sit down, nobody even looks up. For the first time today, I think through my actions. If I get on that plane to Paris, there's no turning back. I'm going to be in so much trouble when my dad finds out where I am. Hopefully, it will take him a while and by the time he starts ringing around, I'll be with Sylvain in his apartment. My head's wrecked. I've tried to cover my tracks, I haven't left any clues at home and only Maryam knows about my plan and I trust her not to tell. I really want to ring my mum, but she'll only start crying and beg me to go home. Maybe in a few weeks, when I'm settled.

She's also going to go crazy when she finds out that I've taken money from her bank account. I didn't have a choice, really and I hope she'll understand why I did it. Mum thinks her bank account is a big secret. I'm pretty sure Dad doesn't know about it, but she told Aunty Shazia, who's such a gossip. Maryam told me about the money and it wasn't difficult to work out where Mum would hide her bank card. It was in the bottom of the box where she keeps all her family letters from Pakistan and she even had the PIN number stuck on a Post-It note on the back. I wonder whether Mum will ever enter the twenty-first century. All my own savings are gone, I had to use them to buy my flight ticket and some new clothes. Imagine if I'd rocked up in Paris with just jeans and t-shirts! I needed some sophisticated outfits and so I bought them.

I finish my warm caramel latte, the froth momentarily sticking to my top lip and creating a sugary foam, then dispose of the remains of my chicken sandwich. I quickly look at my phone. I can't call Sylvain to tell him I'm coming as I don't have his number. We usually communicate by Skype, but my laptop is now on its way to the plane inside my luggage. It's been three days since we last spoke and he seemed a bit stressed about something last time I went to the Internet café to contact him. I'm not worried, though. I know he'll be excited to see me.

I close my eyes for a second or two, remembering the way that he would cover my face with soft, delicate kisses. I love him so much. Everything that I'm about to do is totally against my family and religion, but how can something that feels so right be wrong in the eyes of God? I've read enough magazine columns to know that sometimes you only get one shot at happiness and this is mine.

I don't care about the age gap. Ten years is nothing if you truly want to be together, and we're kindred spirits connected by our love of art. Still, I feel sick at the thought of leaving everyone, even pain-in-the-butt Khalid. I love my little brother but sometimes he can be such a nuisance, always borrowing stuff and sneaking around when I'm on the phone to Maryam. Maybe he secretly fancies her. I guess he's still a kid really, only seventeen, but I've heard it said that men mature later than women. Must be something to do with hormones, I guess.

As I walk away from the café, I think about all the questions that my best friend has put to me over the past few weeks. Maryam insisted that she wasn't trying to be negative about Sylvain but was just making sure that I'd thought things through carefully. At first, she was worried that he was some kind of con-man trying to extract money from me, but I assured her that my Frenchman took care of all the costs at our hotel and my only spending was for dinner sometimes.

I admit Sylvain does like to drink good quality wine with his steak and I did use a lot of my savings over the summer break, but I never would have expected him to pay for everything. I'm lucky that my father has a good profession and gives my brother and me a healthy allowance. Sometimes he asks what I'm spending my money on, but I tell him books and art supplies; never do I mention make-up and underwear. He'd have a fit!

I don't know why, but I find myself standing outside a door that says *Prayer Room*. Maybe I need to absolve myself. Perhaps I'm looking for answers, but I have no idea what the question is. All my life, I've followed tradition and never questioned my faith. There has been no need to. But today, I feel like I need something else, maybe a sign that I won't be condemned if I stray from the path.

I'm wearing a long black scarf under my denim jacket and I pull it over my head as I enter the inner room. The air is cool and I slip off my footwear. Not many people are in here and it's easy to find a mat on which to kneel. Closing my eyes, I take a deep breath and ask Allah for forgiveness. Words from the Holy Quran enter my mind: *God has sovereignty over the heavens and the earth. God has power over all things.*

I hope that God has the power to allow my parents to forgive me. I don't want them to be ashamed. It's not as if I'm trying to forsake my roots, I'm just choosing an alternative lifestyle and pursuing the career that I've always dreamed of. May Allah help them to see the light and forgive me if I have caused pain. Sometimes, in order to be happy we also need to be selfish, I tell myself.

Over in the newsagents, I pick up a glossy fashion magazine, something to keep my mind occupied on the flight, and go to the automatic pay machine. I feel as though I have a huge beacon on my head, flashing

27

Runaway, or *Bad Muslim*, but nobody looks at me. I'm just another customer.

I check my flight number on the boarding pass and start walking down to the gate. I pass one of my favourite shops and stop to gaze at a pair of red boots in the window. They're amazing, but I need to keep back as much money as possible to buy paints and canvas for when I start work.

I'm wearing black Converse trainers on my feet for practicality tonight, my good boots are packed. I'll have quite a walk when I get to the Metro in Paris and I need to be comfortable. These will also be great for when I'm hauling my canvasses around the city or visiting galleries. Sylvain told me that my paintings are amazing. He says I have a real eye for detail but maybe it was just flattery. I go red, feeling the warmth rising in my cheeks as I think of him.

Tonight, I'll be staying at the guest house in Montmartre, where I spent some nights with Sylvain. I picked up a card on our last evening there and rang the proprietor yesterday. Madame Joubert sounded very polite on the phone. She has a room and I wonder if it's *THE* room! I remember the bed sheets were crisp white linen, there were cushions embroidered with flowers and lavender coloured shutters at the window. The room was very clean. It smelled of citrus and fresh laundry. It was the place where I gave myself to my French tutor.

I remember that we left very early on the first morning, before breakfast, sneaking out into the street like thieves, with me returning to Madame Albert's house where I was lodging before she noticed I was gone and my handsome Frenchman disappearing into the dawn light to wherever he was staying with friends. Sylvain says it's the 'arty' area of Paris, but that the real artists can't afford to live here anymore because of the tourists. I'm not quite sure where he lives; he was between apartments when I was here in the summer, but my lover has a place now. That makes me smile. I'm twenty years old and I have a lover!

Sylvain isn't the first guy that I've slept with. I used to date a boy from my college last year and we, you know, did it in his car a few times. It wasn't amazing, and after a while it fizzled out as he was more interested in going out drinking with his friends than spending time with me. I don't drink; well, to tell the truth, I didn't. It's against my faith. But I have to confess that I had a glass of wine with dinner on two occasions while I was in Paris. The second time I drank was to pluck up the courage to spend the night in the guest house with Sylvain.

I wonder what Madame Joubert thought of us, arriving late in the evening with no luggage and paying cash, telling her that we wouldn't be staying for coffee and croissants in the morning? She didn't look at us with reproach or judgement, but a faint look of disapproval played on her lips and there was something very casual in the way that she dropped our room key into Sylvain's palm.

Something passed between them; a knowing look, I suppose. Maybe she had seen many couples come and go in her time. Perhaps she thought that our first night would be the only one but if she did, she was wrong. We went back two or three times a week until it was time for me to return home. Sylvain would never let me pay. He always told me to run upstairs and wait while he settled the bill with Madame Joubert. He must be making a lot of money if he can just get a room whenever he feels like it. It's the result of many paintings sold, and dozens of classes taught.

Will the guest house owner remember me? When I phoned, I didn't tell her that I'd stayed there before, and she didn't ask. I think it was the best option, though. I'll only need one night, just somewhere to sleep until I catch up with Sylvain tomorrow. My French isn't great, but I can get by; hopefully, I won't have to communicate with many people this evening. I remember that the hotel proprietor spoke excellent English, speaking to Sylvain in English for my benefit so that I could understand the conversation. She was very elegant, too, as middle-aged French women tend to be, her clothes simple but chic and her perfume expensive.

I've retraced my previous journey to Paris and I know where to get off the Metro to find Madame Joubert's place. It's only one stop away from the small college room where we had our classes with Sylvain. Tonight, I will try to have a good sleep and then dress in one of my new outfits tomorrow morning when I set off to meet Sylvain. I wonder if I'll be able to eat breakfast at the guest house this time, or will the butterflies in my stomach prevent me from eating anything?

I wish I'd carried my laptop with me now, instead of putting it inside my suitcase. I could have tried to Skype Sylvain again. Perhaps then he could have met me at Charles de Galle airport and stayed with me at the guest house tonight. It's funny how, in hindsight, people are always able to come up with a better plan than the one they're currently embarking on – although perhaps it's just as well. I bet I look frazzled right now and I'll certainly want to look my best when we reunite tomorrow. I've treated myself to a better brand of make-up than I usually buy and will put it on in the morning. I'm glad that I've stowed everything away, as, when I open my case later, there will be all my new outfits to try on, too.

I could spend so much money in this airport. The cash that I have on me feels as though it's about to burn a hole in my purse. I'm desperate for a bottle of perfume, Elie Saab or Marc Jacobs, and I'm toying with the idea of buying a gift for Sylvain, but I have no idea what he would like and everything that would suit him is incredibly expensive. I look at a watch in a retailer's window and suck in my breath as I see the price tag.

In the next shop, there's a cute beanie hat, charcoal grey and soft. I venture inside and pick it up, running my hands along the wool. I think this would suit my boyfriend. I close my eyes for a second, imagining Sylvain's thick curls billowing out from under the hat. Yes, it's perfect. It doesn't look like a luxury gift but it's a well-known British brand, so I hope he appreciates the thought.

"Would you like it gift-wrapped?" the cashier asks, and I nod yes, I do.

"Thank you," I say. Although I am handing over a quarter of my ready cash, I'm thrilled to have found something affordable for the man in my life. At least now his head will be warm this winter.

"Where are you flying to today?" the assistant asks, with a smile. "Off on holiday?"

"No," I tell her proudly, flicking my long hair back over my shoulder. "I'm moving to Paris," and as soon as the words leave my mouth, I feel that everything is real again. Here I am, actually going.

I sit at the gate and think about calling Maryam but when I check my mobile, it only has one bar and the signal is poor. Two missed calls from Ammi. There's a public phone on the wall opposite. I get up and reach in my pocket for loose change. Poor Maryam, she's my best friend and I know that Dad will be calling her later to find out where I am.

I can trust her not to tell. She's good at telling lies; not in a bad way, but Maryam has had to hide things from her family for a while. She's dating one of the white doctors at the hospital. He's a Catholic and al-though he's a professional, Maryam's parents would go mad if they found out. She has to keep this secret for me, as I've covered for her so many times in the past. But I owe it to her to call, even if it's just to let her know that my flight's due to depart on time.

"Hello?"

"Hey Maryam, it's me, Uzma."

"Uzma! Where are you? Why aren't you ringing from your own phone?" she asks, her voice tight.

"Listen, I haven't got much change," I tell her. "I'm boarding the plane soon. I'll call you from Paris."

"So, you're really going?" She sighs. I can hear the disbelief in her tone. "Are you sure about this?"

"Yes, absolutely." I nod, then realise that she can't see me. "One hundred percent."

"When are you coming back?" Maryam asks. There's an echo on the line. "Uzma?"

"I don't think I am," I confess, "I think this is good-bye. I'll miss you so much."

"Take care, my sweet Uzma, call me when you arrive. And let me know if you need me to..."

The phone beeps, its greedy mouth requesting more coins, so I drop the receiver and return to the gate. Phone calls to my family will have to wait. Eventually, they'll find the note. I haven't given too much detail, just told my family that I'm seeking job opportunities overseas... told them I've found a job in an art gallery in Germany. It was the first place that popped into my head. I think about Maryam, my beautiful, kind friend, and tears prick at my eyes for the first time today. Why am I crying for a friend, but not for what I'm doing to my family?

Maryam and I have been friends all of our lives. Our fathers knew each other when they were young and my mother and Aunt Shazia get along like sisters. We've been to more weddings and funerals together in our local Muslim community than I can count, always going through the excitement of choosing what to wear and how to do our hair, together. Maryam has three older brothers and I only have Khalid, so all the girly things that you usually do with a sister, I have done with Maryam.

I don't think Aunt Shazia has been as strict as my mother, though. My friend hasn't endured the endless cooking and dress-making lessons at home that I've pretended to enjoy to please my parents. My mum's not quite as Westernised as most Muslim mothers of her age, despite having lived in Britain for ages. She was so beautiful when she was young that my dad must have thought he was marrying the prettiest girl in Pakistan. My maternal grandmother is stunning, too, although I haven't seen her for about five years now. Dad always blames his work for not having the time to take us away and he won't let my mother travel alone with us. I think he doubts her ability to navigate airports.

I was so surprised when my father agreed to let me take the art course in Paris. I've been away on school trips to Europe before, but never alone, although Dad did insist on keeping tabs on me via the telephone, making me ring at seven o'clock every night and re-port back what I'd studied each day. Sometimes Dad would ring Madame Albert's house, checking up on me, but if I was out she'd always tell him I was ei-ther in the shower or asleep, bless her. I think the French are wiser than us when it comes to matters of the heart. I didn't tell her about Sylvain, but I think she knew. Every time he came to meet me in the café across the street, I would sense my landlady's net curtains twitching.

We're boarding! As I make my way down the aisle, I have a sense of déjà-vu as it's only four months since I was taking this same flight to start my art course. I feel more confident about flying alone this time, although my stomach is still doing cartwheels. I wish I hadn't indulged in that frothy coffee now.

Walking through Business Class, I notice the sixty-ish man from the check-in desk, He seems agitated but doesn't look up. I wonder, very briefly, why he's flying to Paris, but my curiosity soon vanishes, and I walk on to find my seat, 22A. Thankfully, I'm near the window and can watch London fading below as the plane climbs into the night. It also means that I can turn slightly, away from the snivelling child that sits between me and her mother.

Well, this is it; I can't change my mind now. How stupid I would look in front of all these passengers if I suddenly jumped up and asked to be let off the plane! I realise that, for the past two hours, I've been expecting a tap on the shoulder. Despite my careful planning, I can't help but wonder if my father has suspected anything... whether he's followed me to the airport or called the police. I breathe deeply, trying not to panic. I'm being stupid. The only person who might have seen me leave with my suitcase is old Mr Vronsky across the street. He's always peering out of his window, poor old guy. I doubt very much whether he'd tell anyone, though. I don't think he even leaves his house.

The little girl next to me fidgets as her mother fastens the seat-belt. She looks as if she's going to start crying again, until the woman produces a bar of chocolate. I smile at the child, and she eyes me warily, perhaps thinking I want to share her treasure. I hope the chocolate doesn't melt and get near my clothes. The little girl is cute, with big blue eyes.

"Wow, what have you got there?" I ask.

"Mine," the girl says, hugging the wrapper tightly and sticking out her tongue.

"Sorry." Her mother shrugs. "Helena doesn't like flying."

I nod and open my magazine, but the lights go off and we begin to taxi along the runway. Then we're up, the streets of London below looking like sparkling jewels in the night. I look down and wonder if my home can be seen from here. Mum will be wondering where I am by now. Dad's probably been trying to call me as he likes us all to sit down together for dinner. I think of my mother's cooking and my stomach rumbles. She makes the best samosas ever. How long will it be before one of them goes to my room and finds the note on my desk? Have they looked already? I'm tempted to check my phone but know it needs to stay off. Besides, the battery will die very soon. I need to try to relax, stop thinking about what I've left behind and shift my concentration to the exciting days that lie ahead of me. I'm twenty and have my whole life to live.

Closing my eyes, I try to imagine how our reunion will be. Sylvain has the softest skin, the colour of autumn leaves, and his eyes are so dark that you can almost see your own reflection in them. He's going to be so surprised that I've left home. Of course, we discussed me coming to Paris to be with him. He seemed concerned about living costs, but now I have almost five thousand pounds tucked into the lining of my suitcase. My dad always warned my brother and me about carrying too much cash in our pockets. He reckons that, by putting the majority of your money inside your luggage, there's less chance of it getting stolen. I've always taken that piece of advice. I did have two hundred of it here in my purse, but the hat for Sylvain cost me fifty.

A guilty pang shoots through me as I recall how I've had to steal and then replace my mother's card almost every day for three weeks, as the maximum withdrawal was £250 each time. Maryam told me that, according to her mum, my mother goes to the bank on the last day of every month to check her balance and pay in whatever money she has remaining from the allowance Dad gives her for groceries. That will give me a week's grace to write to her and explain, or to phone home to apologise personally.

I've never taken anything before in my life, but I wonder whether the money that my mother has saved is also classed as stolen; after all, it was earned by my father and given to Mum to spend on food. It's shameful that she has had to do this, and I have no idea what Mum was planning to do with her savings.

Maybe she is going to go back to Pakistan, where she could be happy again. When I start selling my paintings, I'll pay her back. Honestly, I will.

FRIDAY 8PM – COLIN FOSTER

Smoothing out the white paper napkin, I slide it alongside my unopened newspaper so that the edges are almost touching. That's how I like things; neat, tidy, aligned. It annoys me when the stewardess reappears and moves it back to its original place, putting a glass of orange juice on top. The bottom of the glass is wet and causes a yellowy circle to form on the napkin. I look up and my eyes connect with the air hostess just long enough for me to give a knowing look; not resentful, just reproachful.

I wait for her to move along to the row behind me, the rustle of her blue polyester suit irritatingly close. As I glance down, I see that she has shapely legs, but they appear a rather unnatural hue. I've often wondered why airlines insist upon their female members of staff wearing those diabolical 'American Tan' tights, a most unrealistic shade of flesh, as unflattering as a pensioner in a bikini. I can only take solace in the gratifying knowledge that this will be my last 'business' trip. Thankfully, the seats across from me remain unoccupied and I relax slightly. A trip is far more endurable if one is allowed to keep one's affairs private from roving eyes.

"Is everything alright, sir?"

Damn and blast it, she's turned back towards me.

I fake a smile and grit my teeth. "Yes, dear girl, perfectly satisfactory, thank you."

"Are you sure I can't get you anything?" she presses, leaning in to look at me. "Some nuts, perhaps?"

"I'm fine," I grunt, folding my hands over my stomach. "Thank you for asking."

Despite my irritation, etiquette has taught me to be polite and to avoid confrontation. In an ideal world, I would converse readily with anyone who might care to listen, but the sad fact of the matter is, I'm not entirely sure that I even like company any more.

For the past five years, I have hankered after solitude, watching my bank balance grow, one sizable payment after another, almost reaching a satisfactory amount, only for the obsessive compulsive inside me to move the goalposts and set an even higher target for my retirement fund. To tell the truth, I haven't yet determined where to go – now, how's that for indecision? – though I rather suspect that I shall end up somewhere tranquil and warm. In my younger days, I would have favoured the climes of Mexico or Cuba, digging my bare toes into the sand on some deserted beach with only a Wilbur Smith novel and a decent

Malbec to keep me company, although, if truth be told, one would undoubtedly miss the cricket. As the saying goes, you can take an Englishman out of England, etcetera.

I spotted the young Asian girl getting on a few minutes ago. I noticed her looking at me in the airport as I checked in my suitcase. I'm an expert at body language and there was definitely something amiss, almost as though she's running away, but with a hint of excitement, too. She's probably just a student on an exchange trip; looks about the right age. Maybe it's her first time abroad. People in general hold a great fascination for me, although, being a natural recluse, I'm not inclined to think about my fellow passenger for a moment longer. Her affairs don't interest me. One has far greater fish to fry in Paris.

Glancing backwards down the aisle, I scan the passengers for anything out of the ordinary. Habit, I suppose. Nothing catches my eye tonight. The curtain between Business Class and Economy is drawn closed, but the few passengers seated in my compartment appear to have little to hide. A peroxide blonde clutches the arm of her much older male companion as he pats her leg seductively. I'm guessing that the man is around my age, sixty, although the years have not been so kind to him and his thick, wavy hair is almost the colour of steel. I try to be discreet in my observations. I'm a master at looking casual and I look away before either of them turns their head my way.

In front, to the left, is a much younger gent. His suit has a definite Saville Row cut, expensive and stitched with great precision, not dissimilar to my own. The pink pages of the *Financial Times* lie open on the seat next to him, although his thoughts appear to be elsewhere. The man's body language, folded arms and crossed legs, suggest a disagreement or restlessness, but the gold band on his finger belies a deeper reason for his mood. I would put a wager on his wife causing ructions about her spouse flying to Paris for the weekend alone and who could blame her? What woman wouldn't want to join her beloved and browse the shops while he concluded his business? People-watching can be so eye-opening at times and, if I'm wholly honest, may well be the sole reason for my solitary existence to date.

I look away and scan the newspaper headlines, my new gold-rimmed spectacles perched upon the end of my nose rather precariously, and then turn to the weather section. Tonight, the forecast declares, it will be dry but there's a good chance of showers mid-morning tomorrow. I dislike rain, as I find it rather cumbersome to one's work which occasionally requires me to accomplish assignments outdoors at odd hours.

I suppose onlookers, my neighbours even, must wonder what on earth it is that I do, but it's complicated. I suppose the best way to describe my work is eradicating other people's mistakes, something which I take care of both quickly and professionally. I'm self-employed, in a fashion, although technically I do have a boss. The funny thing is, one has never met him. I receive instructions, via courier, I carry out the requirement and then I return home to wait for the next job. Simple. Although not just anyone could fill my position, it being one of great skill, discretion and trust.

For a brief second, I panic that I may have left my trouser press plugged in at home. Should that happen, it would no doubt overheat, cause an electrical fire and burn down the whole house. I breathe in and hold it for ten seconds, letting the air out through my nose. Of course I didn't forget to check everything before I left. Compulsion had me trotting up and downstairs like a whippet this afternoon, tightening the taps in the bathroom, examining wall sockets and locking windows. Goodness knows how many hours one spends in a day in this obsessive routine, not to mention the straightening of towels on the rail, alphabetically filing paperwork and music albums and lining up tins in the pantry. I try to push the nagging doubt from my mind. No, all was seen to, I hope, before I left my modest terraced house this afternoon.

Fastening the seatbelt around my midriff, I feel perplexed at how snug it feels. Have I been too indulgent since taking my last flight? Perhaps. It was three months ago, to Vienna if I'm not mistaken, affording the possibility that one might well have partaken of too many Weiner Schnitzels, accompanied by solitary bottles of Château Neuf du Pape. Still, what is the purpose of living if not to enjoy life? Perhaps upon retirement I should take up a sport. I've always rather fancied trying Tai Chi, as it requires little effort but centres upon one's core strength and inner balance. I am, however, in good shape for my age.

One of my guest rooms serves as a gym and every day, without fail, I run on my treadmill, followed by fifteen minutes on the rowing-machine. It's imperative that I stay fit, just in case one should happen to find oneself in a sticky situation that requires a sharp exit. I'm wholly satisfied that my facial features are ageing well, too. My greying hair is sophisticated, I'm told and the crow's feet around my eyes have a debonair charm. I wouldn't dare to describe myself as a good catch, although there are far less handsome men out there with beautiful wives. What harm does it do to dream?

As we take off, I find my fingers gripping the seat, the gold sovereign on my little finger chinking against the metal clip. I never have got used to this part of my trip, although one has taken dozens of flights and visited almost every country on our globe. As soon as the seatbelt sign goes off, I press the service button and order a mini bottle of wine. The choice of red is limited for my discerning palate and the taste lingers upon my tongue menacingly, a tinge of metal hitting my throat as I swallow. I look forward to sharing the vintage bottle that is carefully packed in a leather box in my suitcase, with my host tonight.

One would not normally bring a suitcase on such a short trip. A briefcase and a suit carrier usually suffice, but the decision to bring wine and additional clothing, should I decide to stay on for a few days, have caused excess bulk. I've been contemplating whether to disclose my decision to retire, for we have become almost friends these past twenty years, but I wonder if this might cause the dynamics of our concord to change. Perhaps a few extra days in Paris before my business is completed may hold the answer.

On occasion, I have toyed with the notion of a proposal, for the lady in question is a most elegant and sophisticated widow; but then, after much rumination, I have chided myself for such ridiculously indulgent thoughts. We share a mutual love of classical music and fine art, the topics of our many conversations over the years, and the dear lady is always careful not to pry into one's personal affairs. I don't recall her once asking about my business trips to Paris or what they might entail. The perfect companion, I tell myself, although the reservations are there, deep-rooted and prodding at me like a troublesome tooth. After sixty years as a bachelor, self-diagnosed with OCD at that, how would one cope with another person's foibles? One suspects that the experience would be intolerable at best.

I take out my pocket notebook, its black leather slightly worn, and turn to the back, where I keep a detailed record of my personal banking transactions. Every payment and withdrawal is listed down to the last penny, and it's there, with those bits of copper, that my frustration is so very often stirred. I like round numbers, you see. I have to see exact balances, no eighty-nine pence tagged on to my savings, just pure zeros. And so, every month when the interest is paid, I find myself standing at the counter of my local branch, asking for the excess to be withdrawn. My savings are healthy, four hundred and eighty thousand pounds, to be precise and by Monday night, upon completion of my final 'task', it will total a very respectable half a million. Upon receipt, I shall raise a glass in celebration and officially throw up my proverbial boots.

The only dilemma facing me thereafter shall be where to hang my equally axiomatic hat. Perhaps one should take a cruise up the Norwegian Fjords, or climb the foothills of Tibet, for it does appear that the world will quite literally become my oyster, albeit a rather lonely, single-shelled one. Who knows, perhaps, after the eradication of my professional life, a moment of bravado may fall upon me and cause one to whisk my beautiful French mademoiselle to paradise. If only one could be guaranteed her acquiescence!

Sitting here, reminiscing about my last trip to wonderful Paris, I can almost smell the delicate perfume that my charming friend wears dabbed behind her ears and upon her wrists... the tight chignon of her greying blonde hair, pinned up to reveal a slender white neck. It stirs the male instinct inside me and I discreetly place my newspaper upon my lap to hide the slight bulge in my trousers. Perhaps another glass of that diabolical wine is called for, to quell my overactive daydreaming.

There is a slight flutter of turbulence which shakes me from my reverie. I'm guessing that we've hit low cloud, but it doesn't warrant a message from the cabin crew and we're soon gliding along smoothly again. Checking my watch, I see that it's now a quarter to nine. I do hope that my arrival at Charles de Gaulle isn't delayed, as I was rather hoping to be in Montmartre by ten-thirty.

No doubt it will be too late for dinner but, on the occasion of me arriving after nine on my previous trips, my dear landlady has always provided a most satisfactory supper of cold meats and salad. I'm hoping that she has taken the very same initiative upon herself tonight. A distinct and very welcome aroma in her household is the delight of freshly baked baguettes. These suppers are always served on white china plates, the tablecloth as smooth as a newborn's behind and the butter just soft enough to attach itself to the tip of one's knife.

I relish the thought of such a supper tonight, sharing wine and making polite conversation whilst I no doubt childishly dance around the topic of my impending retirement. The beautiful guest house owner will smile politely, listening intently as she always does, interjecting with some witty remark and then laughing softly, revealing her perfect white teeth and soft pink tongue.

Tucking the worn diary back into its permanent home in my jacket pocket, I allow myself a momentary smirk of satisfaction; nothing enduring or conspicuous enough for the airline crew or my fellow travellers to notice, but the notion of such a milestone in one's financial circumstances is oddly comforting.

It's almost as though the notes were right here with me, begging to be spent in some frivolous way. It feels as though a lifetime's work has almost come to fruition, I just hope that I live long enough to reap the rewards.

This time next week, I may well be on a flight to Thailand or Australia – who knows where fate may find me? – but still the fear of growing into an old relic without companionship nags at me. The need or desire to share my sojourn is most definitely building within me and it is somewhat an entirely new sensation. All my life I've been alone, independent, never reliant upon a spouse, and yet here I am deliberating upon a union with a woman whom intimate relations have never been discussed, let alone embarked upon. Such is the new Colin Foster, retiree, affluent gent and intrepid globetrotter.

In the front of my leather-bound journal I have jotted the opening lines of *David Copperfield* by the rather brilliant Charles Dickens: *Whether I shall turn out to be the hero of my own life, or whether that station will be held by anybody else, these pages must show.* It is a quotation that has been copied from diary to notebook throughout my adult years; a reminder that I strive for achievement but can neither promise nor delude myself that the fruits of my labour shall lead to satisfaction. It yet remains to be seen.

The second glass of wine is slightly less offensive than the first, my palate now acclimatising itself to the unrefined origins of this ghastly offering and I begin to slip into a more tranquil state – although, due to the nature of my profession, I never truly lower my guard. My mother used to call me a difficult child. I suspect she never really took the time to penetrate the workings of my mind, and, growing up, solitude became my best ally. Perhaps it was simply a case of what one would call a chip off the old block. Rarely did she show emotion, unless it was a drunken rage, which only lasted as long as her next fix. Perhaps it is due to this experience that I am a somewhat cold creature, tepid at my best.

At school, during the later years when I attended without truancy, teachers found me impossible. They complained that my morbid fascination with dissecting insects in the playground disturbed them and that my curiosity was never quelled. It's perfectly true, of course. I distinctly remember finding ever more difficult questions to raise to my peers and would conjure up impossible equations in geometry that my masters would find frustrating and unsolvable.

My dear uncle told me not to worry, bowed to my genius and steered me towards making my natural talents lucrative, which of course I did. I was devastated when he passed away some fifteen years ago. He was the only male influence in my younger days and was my guide as I steered the tidal waves of maturity. Still, as I reflect upon the great man who taught me everything he knew and inspired me to achieve perfection in the few talents that he lacked, I'm unsure exactly of how we were related. With my mother being an only child, it could not have been a maternal link and naturally, this has opened up unanswered questions about my own origins.

Mother, through necessity, one supposes, worked throughout my childhood. In my early days, I was ferried between relatives and neighbours. I vaguely remember that six o'clock was the witching hour when my single parent would show up to collect me, hurriedly prepare some bread and jam for my supper and then promptly doze off in front of the television screen, leaving me to whatever mischief took my fancy. Naturally, with age, I became what was known as a 'latch-key kid', letting myself in through the back door after school, diligently completing homework alone and then going out into the streets, seeking stimulation in the form of the cinema, the library or the numerous city parks.

As money was always tight, I made my own ready cash by helping out in the East End markets on a Saturday, or simply just helping myself to whatever funds were ripe for the picking in other people's pockets. It's surprising how people idly stuff notes into a coat or shopping bag and expect them still to be there at the end of a journey. Although I'm not what you may deem a common thief, not having taken anything for many moons now, I did what was necessary in my youth to keep my belly full and my curiosity fired.

I remember my mother without a great deal of affection, I'm afraid. She was a thin, tall, dark-haired woman, aloof and prone to momentary mood swings which she doused with the contents of a gin bottle.

We rarely engaged in conversation, save for the most basic of exchanges, and my memory of her now is one of radical indifference. I know that she was employed as an operator at the telephone exchange, but beyond that, I can barely recall the colour of her eyes. My father, an unknown entity, was forever absent. The details surrounding my birth were never disclosed, nor did I venture to ask. I remain stoical in the resolution that, should I have raised the topic of my origins, my mother would have regaled me with her own rather distorted version of an immaculate conception.

I confess that, as a young boy, should a stranger meet my eye in the street, I would gaze at him intently, looking for similarities in our profiles; the high forehead, or the chiselled chin. Sometimes, in my naivety, I would imagine that my absent father was a serving naval officer and that one day he would come knocking at the door of our basement flat, searching for me, his heir.

I daydreamed of multi-coloured parcels, a new bicycle, a cricket set, a silver watch, but instead, at Christmas I got a small stocking filled with chocolate and nuts, and for my birthday a book – if, of course, Mother dear had remembered. She has been dead for a long time now. No doubt her remains are pickled for all eternity by the toxic cocktails imbibed over her lifetime. I did, however, afford her a respectable funeral in the end, albeit just the vicar and myself in attendance. God rest her very fragile and inebriated soul.

I began my adult 'career', the term being used loosely for want of a better noun, working in a rather distinguished Gentleman's Club in Soho. I forget the year, for it is now so many decades behind me, but let us say that it was sometime during the 1970s. An old uncle of mine first put my name forward for position of 'runner' at the establishment, which meant that it was my duty to hang around the lounge area where the hub of activity presented itself and make myself of use to anyone in need of assistance. On occasion, this would mean delivering personal messages to businessmen anywhere within the City of London.

My trusty steed was a bicycle in those days, which was quite safe as the traffic was nowhere near as brisk as it is these days. Should the need arise for my task to take me further afield, I would hop on the Underground. Other duties involved such menial chores as hailing a taxi for a drunken Lord, or venturing out to a department store for purchases when some butterfingered diner had spilled egg on his tie. Nothing mind-numbingly challenging, but it provided a regular income and the means to squirrel away the plentiful tips bestowed upon me by grateful and intoxicated toffs.

Those days served me well in the refinement of one's own mannerisms and etiquette. I would return home and mimic the sipping of tea with a pinkie raised, or the effeminate action of tugging at one's shirt cuffs to bring them an inch below a jacket sleeve. There was so much to be learned from those wealthy gents and I found myself absorbing every detail like a dry sponge. My accent also changed over a period of a few short years, straying far from my Cockney roots to a voice barely recognisable as my own, with its crescendos and grammatical perfection.

Yes, service at the club certainly lent itself to notions of ambition, albeit far above my station to entertain them. I fear I should have ended my days in such a way, too, pandering to the endless needs of others, had it not been for the events and circumstances of one particular cold winter afternoon.

Lord Darlington was a permanent fixture at the club, having no daily business to attend to save for his occasional presence in Parliament, and a great fondness for the Highland Malt kept specifically for his quaffing. I'm guessing that, at the time, the old man was an octogenarian, nearing the latter days of his life, and it was due to the melancholy nature of his daily habits that a certain occurrence arose.

It was common knowledge amongst both members and staff that at around 2pm, having partaken of a satisfactory three-course lunch and a bottle of finest claret, the aged Lord would become slightly fuddled, gradually nodding off in a wing-backed leather chair at the fireside. Instructions from my superiors were to leave him be until a chauffeur appeared to collect his lordship, who would be gently woken and whisked away home to tea. However, on this day, a rowdy bunch of bankers, newly enrolled into the Club membership scheme, were celebrating some lucrative financial deal and took it upon themselves to challenge each other in a bet.

Unfortunately, or perhaps in hindsight as luck would have it, I found myself at the centre of their dare and had little choice but to oblige with what was being asked, which was to pick the pocket of Lord Darlington as he slept, attempting to extract the old man's heavy gold pocket watch without being detected, which I duly did with the successful deftness of a seasoned professional. It was only due to the high volume of 'Hoorahs' from the young rascals that Lord Darlington awoke, unaware of the mischief which had befallen him.

I can now categorically state that it was the euphoria surrounding my triumph that led me to push the boundaries of my capabilities and, perhaps taking foolish risks, to concede to my next challenge, which was a far more serious and irresponsible risk. Still, it opened up doors of opportunity that may well have remained closed had I not risen to their bait and I dare say that I might well have found myself in a rather dull and unambitious profession, had I not been so young and foolhardy.

However, enough of my reminiscing, I tell myself sternly. The weekend desires me to stay sedentary and sharp-witted, therefore further fanciful reveries must be stored away into my mind's recesses until my current 'task' has reached completion. As per usual arrangement, I'm not entirely certain when details of my task will arrive. However, I do know that business will conclude some time before Monday afternoon, giving me almost two days to enjoy the city and muster up courage to test the water with my elegant mademoiselle before catching my return flight to London.

There is little preparation for me to do beforehand, as the tools of my trade will be delivered together with my instructions, although I'm rather hoping to enjoy at least one decent dinner before putting my 'professional' hat on, so to speak. From there, it will be back to London to begin packing up my belongings and give notice on the house that I currently rent. No doubt my landlord will quickly find a new tenant – after all, it is rather a splendid period property – and won't be unduly put out by my leaving. The biggest question, though, still remains. Where am I headed and who shall accompany me?

I momentarily close my eyes and list the possibilities: will it be the lure of the South Pacific, with its azure seas and raven-haired women that pull me close, or am I destined for a life of anonymity and seclusion in the French countryside, surrounded by lavender fields and splendid vineyards? One certainly hopes that one shall not die alone, for loneliness is a man's worst enemy and, in turn, an enemy's greatest ally. And when it comes to enemies, I have many.

The lights of my favourite European city are twinkling below. No doubt I shall have time to visit the galleries of the Louvre and sip coffee in view of the Eiffel Tower. During summer months, I like to stroll the river banks and take in the gothic grandeur of Notre Dame, but I fear that the November temperatures will be too chilly for such an excursion this time. Perhaps I should take this weekend trip as an opportunity to shop for travel wear. It's been nigh on forty years since I first donned my smart business suits and trusted overcoats. They've almost become the uniform of my trade, although one very much doubts whether the boutiques of Paris will stock Panama hats and boat shoes at this time of year.

As the seatbelt sign comes on, together with the captain's brief announcement that we shall be landing shortly, my thoughts rove once again to the lady whose guest house I shall be staying in. The rooms are so perfectly maintained, with chic décor and the freshest of cotton bed linen. I rather fancy that she suspects my obsession with neatness, as the bathroom towels are always aligned properly, the soap dish is placed parallel to the tiles and the runner on the bed is straight and perfectly smoothed. Unless I am mistaken and the delightful woman in question possesses the exact same compulsions as I! Could one really be so lucky?

I do rather wonder whether she would consider selling up and coming with me on my future travels. I see nothing to keep her in Paris, unless she has a suitor, of course. I must proceed with caution. There could well be some minor royalty or oil tycoon waiting in the wings to whisk the dear lady away. One wonders whether it's pertinent to ask, although

I fear our closeness has not reached its peak, and such probing may push her farther from my reach.

The crunching of the landing gear dropping from the plane's undercarriage jolts me and I snap out of my reverie. I spot the young city gent shrugging on his suit jacket in preparation to exit quickly, while the mismatched couple behind me no doubt have thoughts only for each other, although, by the look on the young woman's face, she also has eyes on her companion's wallet.

I ask myself whether I would swap places with that chap. Would I be flattered to have a pretty young gold-digger on my arm? There would certainly be no harm in it, but I fear that my miserly selfishness would put the dampers on any such liaison. I do not fear loneliness, for now I have money, and wealth can buy one almost any trifle that the heart desires. Although I doubt that Madame Joubert, the apple of my eye, would want me for my half a million, she strikes me as a woman who is already comfortably off. The very thought of her once again stirs something within me and the hairs on my neck begin to prickle.

You're not as young as you once were, Colin, old boy, I say inwardly. *Tread gently, dear chap, tread gently.*

FRIDAY 10PM – UZMA RAFIQ

Phew! We're here. It's a bit of a scramble to get off the plane, so I wait patiently in my seat until the aisle has cleared. The child next to me is pulled out of her seat by the impatient mother and leaves a trail of melted chocolate on the seat behind her. I check that none of it has got onto my jacket. I only have to carry my handbag and watch the other passengers for a few minutes as they struggle with carry-on luggage and heavy coats. It's incredible how much people take on a short flight, but I suppose it's to save the hassle of having to retrieve a suitcase, like I will have to do.

It wasn't a bad flight, although I'm really hungry now and tired, too. I must have dropped off for about twenty minutes, which I think is worse than having a proper sleep as it's made me feel sluggish. As I finally get out into the aisle, a passenger in front of me swings his sports bag up onto his shoulder and knocks my arm.

"Sorry," he mutters, looking straight at me.

I just shrug. It doesn't matter and I'm not in the mood for chatting to strangers.

"Are you going into the city?" the man asks, smiling and showing crooked teeth. "I can give you a lift."

I shake my head. "No, thanks. I mean, it's kind of you to offer, but my boyfriend is meeting me."

He almost looks disappointed, which causes me to smile, and turns to walk off the plane. The man had a French accent. It seems to me that European men are much more forward than English guys. I could never imagine someone at home offering a lift to a complete stranger. He must have fancied me. In other circumstances, I might have taken more notice of him and even made more of an effort to chat. I'm also shocked at how easy it is to lie, albeit a little white one. *My boyfriend is meeting me,* indeed! Where did that come from?

Inside the terminal building it's hot, stuffy and much busier than I expected. A lot of flights have arrived at the same time and we have to queue for quite a while. I spot the child and mother who sat next to me and the little one is now having a temper tantrum. The mother produces more chocolate and I wonder if the child will be sick soon.

Slowly we move forwards, but at a snail's pace. This gives me time to think about what might be going on at home. I know that Dad will be furious, but he'll be worried about me, too. I hope that my note is enough to prevent him trying to find me. I made up a story about getting a job in a gallery in Germany; they know my passion for art, so I hope the lie will give me time. I'll phone them in a few days. I just need to clear my head and get settled with my lover.

My mum is probably phoning Aunty Shazia right now, to see if Maryam knows anything, but I can count on her to keep quiet. I bet my brother is enjoying every minute of the drama. He's such a tell-tale, no wonder I never confide in him.

That old man, the one in the pin-striped suit who was in business class, is at the front of the express line at Passport Control. I guess you are entitled to priority treatment when you buy a more expensive ticket. He's got his overcoat folded over his arm and carries a small briefcase. He looks very serious and I wonder what brings him to Paris. A minute passes and then he disappears, walking stiffly with his shoulders back, no doubt off to collect his luggage. It's funny the different people you see at airports. If I had my paints and easel here, I'd quite like to capture the rainbow of colours that catch my eye, like a sea of silver fishes with the odd tropical beauty swimming amongst them.

The butterflies in my stomach are doing somersaults now and after having my passport checked, I find myself rushing to the nearest toilet. I don't know whether it's excitement or nerves, but I feel a little bit nauseous and slightly dizzy. I tell myself that I'll be fine once I've made contact with Sylvain. Looking at myself in the mirror, I see that I look tired and washed-out. I wish now that I'd kept some of my make-up in my handbag as some lip gloss and mascara would freshen me up. Running a brush through my hair, I try to relax and, before leaving the washroom, I splash cold water from the tap onto my face. I need a drink and will find a vending machine to get a bottle of juice soon.

By the time I get to the luggage carousel, most of the bags have already been claimed by their owners. There's one lone black suitcase going around, and I guess that it must be mine although, as I lift it off the conveyor belt, it seems in better condition, not so scuffed. I look around but only see a green rucksack and a red hard-shelled case left on the rotating rubber belt. There are no other bags for this flight.

I glance up at the overhead screen; yes, this area is definitely for the London flight. Perhaps I'm just tired and have recalled the look of my suitcase incorrectly. It's certainly the right make and size, so it must be mine. I look at the handle, to where the bright pink label with my name should be, but then remember that it fell off straight after check-in. I'm going crazy. This is my case.

Extending the handle on my case, I pull it behind me and walk out through the exit, looking at the sea of faces expectantly awaiting their loved ones. For just a second, I scan the crowd for Sylvain, but it's a pointless motion as he couldn't possibly know that I'm here. Just as well really, I think, as my denim jacket is crumpled from sitting in that cramped seat on the plane, my make-up has disappeared, and I must look like a frightened rabbit in headlights, coming into this arrivals hall with all the noise and excitement.

There are lots of people shouting "Taxi!" over by the entrance, but I can't afford to waste money on transport. What I have will have to last and it must be at least forty Euros to Montmartre from here. I'll be okay. I just need to find the sign for the Metro and from there, I can get to the guest house. It will cost me a fraction of the taxi price but I'm well aware that it's going to take me much longer to get to my destination.

It's easy to locate the Metro station and the platform that I need is just an escalator ride down. It's very clean everywhere, but there's still that smell of stale body odour and urine lingering in the air that all stations seem to have. I struggle a bit with my suitcase but refuse help from a passer-by in case they decide to run off with my belongings. You hear such terrible stories about theft, so I try to be cautious. It's only now, sitting with my hands gripping my suitcase, that I wonder if I'm being a fool coming here unannounced.

Maryam has spent three days trying to talk sense into me... or at least that's what she called her advice and non-stop questioning. She asked if there was a chance that Sylvain might have someone else, but I told her not to be ridiculous. She's never met him so it's easy to point the finger, I suppose. If she had, Maryam would see what I see, an honest, talented, kind man.

My friend also tried to convince me to wait a while, perhaps ask Sylvain to come to London. I did ask him, but he's so busy all the time with his art and tutoring that it simply wasn't possible. In all honesty, I don't think I could have waited another week to be with him. My heart is telling me that it will break if we're apart any longer, and once Maryam sees how happy we are together when she comes to visit, she'll know that I've done the right thing.

As the train gathers speed, the carriage rocks slightly and my stomach lurches again. I don't think I'm going to be sick, but I wish I'd stopped to get some plain biscuits or a coffee, as it's been a long time since I last ate or drank anything. In fact, I can see by looking at my watch that it's about four hours, so I'm probably dehydrated. I meant to look for a vending machine, I suddenly remember, but I was too preoccupied with finding the right train.

I recall that there was tea and coffee in the bedrooms of the guest house in the summer, so hopefully I'll be able to have something before bed. If I were at home, Mum would be making herbal tea around now. She's obsessed with the stuff, ever since Aunty Shazia introduced her to the new wholefoods shop in the high street. She's so funny, my mother; she believes everything that people tell her, no matter how ridiculous or unlikely. She's always on one fad diet or another, trying to lose weight, but then she forgets about all those sugary jellies that she eats in the evening while watching television.

The train lurches on. I think I remember the guide book saying that it takes nearly an hour to get to my destination from the airport. It was easy when I arrived in July, as there was a driver waiting for me and another student and he took us by mini-bus to our lodgings. The next day, I was picked up again to go to the academy where our tutor held his classes. It's much simpler finding your way around a strange city when there's a group of you and it was fun exploring. Being on a budget then, we did eat quite a lot of fast food, and I'm looking forward to Sylvain taking me to some proper local restaurants.

I think I must have sighed out loud, because an old man looks up from his newspaper quizzically. He's wearing a beret and looks an arty type. He must sense that I don't speak much French as he just shrugs and goes back to reading. I suppose I will have to take lessons once I've sold a few paintings, or maybe my lover will teach me. I can feel my eyelids starting to droop, but I must stay awake, otherwise I could accidentally miss my stop.

I glance around the compartment and then drop my gaze to my suitcase. Shit. It doesn't look at all like my suitcase now. The wheels are hardly scratched, and I know that mine were getting pretty worn from being dragged around. Perhaps Mum gave my suitcase a good polish and clean after I returned from Paris a few months ago. Yes, that will be it, although I have to admit that I didn't notice earlier. The silver badge says *Globe*, and that's definitely the brand of

luggage that Dad buys. I need to stop being so para-
noid. This trip is making me freak out.

To take my mind off the strange feeling that I have
about my luggage, I reach into my handbag and peek
at the soft woollen beanie that I bought for Sylvain.
I pull off the price tag and slip it into my jacket
pocket. He probably won't even care that it's a designer brand, but I hope he'll wear it, anyway. It's
not much but, as Dad has always told me, it's the
thought that counts.

As we get closer to the city centre, more and
more passengers climb aboard the train. Some of the
women are dressed in thick woollen coats, earrings
dangling like mini chandeliers and their coloured
evening dresses peeping out underneath. They're accompanied by smart, handsome men, and I suppose
that they've all been out to dinner or the theatre. The
couples seem very affectionate towards one another,
laughing and joking. Perhaps they're drunk, or just
buzzing after a really enjoyable night out.

In a few days' time, that could be me and Sylvain,
I muse. Out and about in the city, enjoying ourselves,
carefree and just happy to be together again. I've
bought some lovely dresses and shoes, so hopefully,
my man will appreciate the effort that I've gone to,
although he seems to favour the Bohemian cafés and
local bistros to anything more flamboyant and expensive. I'm looking forward to cooking for Sylvain,
too and, thanks to my mother, I can prepare a decent
meal. We'll be a proper couple.

I look up at the French women and marvel at how amazing they look. I wonder if they wake up looking beautiful, too, and imagine myself jumping out of my lover's bed first thing in the morning to put on my make-up and artfully dress my hair. I feel very scruffy all of a sudden, despite wearing my best jeans. Nobody seems to take much notice of me, though and I lean into the plastic partition all the way to my stop.

We're here! I rush up the steps and out into the open air as fast as I can, my heavy suitcase slowing me down slightly. The wind is whistling through the trees and the temperature has dropped considerably since I left the airport. I pull my scarf up around my neck and fasten my jacket to the top. From here, I know I can find the side street where Madame Joubert has her guest house, although everything looks different now that it's dark.

I check my watch again; it's really late. I hope the hotel owner won't be annoyed at me arriving so late. I forgot to warn her. Pulling the case carefully behind me, I set off along the road, looking for where the cobbles begin, as it's down there that the pretty little boarding house sits, set back slightly from the other buildings. I know I'll recognise the beautiful shutters and the window boxes, I just pray that the lights will still be on.

As I get closer, I let out my breath, which I realise I must have been holding since I stepped down here. The lights *are* on and faint music is coming from the sitting room at the front of the building. I raise my hand to press the buzzer and pause. I hear laughter, Madame Joubert's, I think. I don't want to disturb her but I have to go up to my room. I'm exhausted, starving, cold and incredibly tired.

I ring the bell.

FRIDAY 10PM – COLIN FOSTER

It was quite a smooth flight, by all accounts. Now to get myself through Arrivals before the economy class passengers come stampeding down the aisle. I only have my briefcase and overcoat to carry and my passport is already tucked safely in my jacket pocket with my mobile phone for easy access. Being a seasoned traveller, one is used to the rigmarole of airport security and I go about shifting myself without fuss. Thankfully, the stewardess has not yet opened the partition curtain to let the others push their way through.

Having reached the Passport Control area without being buffeted by the crowds, I sincerely regret having had that second bottle of wine for my bladder is urging to release itself. I quickly pop into the gents' washroom and exit again minutes later, momentarily reflecting that a younger man might well have been able to hold his water for a good while longer. Still, I am entitled to exit through the VIP gate and do so within a few minutes. Glancing back at my fellow passengers from the London flight, I can see how they may well feel frustrated at the lengthy wait ahead. It seems that several planes have arrived in succession, causing long queues and irritated security staff. A quick glance into the tiny recognition camera on the desk and within minutes, I'm on my way to the baggage claim area.

My suitcase is one of the first to come tumbling down the carousel and, from what I can see, it's looking rather worse for wear. The sides are battered and the wheels terribly scuffed, although the lock seems secure. My blood pressure rises marginally as I remind myself that this item of luggage was a recent purchase, especially intended to last a few years. Whether its current state is the result of mishandling by the baggage staff, or poor quality manufacturing, one can hardly tell, but it seems that I may find myself purchasing an elite brand for future travels. Pulling the case from the conveyor belt, I look down at my dismal black shell of a bag, wholly unsatisfactory for a man of means. As I pull it towards the exit, a customer service desk catches my eye and I wheel my baggage over to see what can be done to compensate me for the damage.

"*Bonsoir*, Monsieur," I begin, catching the sleepy attendant's eye. I see a worn paperback copy of *The Count of Monte Cristo* next to him. In French, of course.

He stops shuffling documents and looks at me wearily. "*Oui*, Monsieur?"

The attendant has a sullen look about him, as though he were enjoying a rest and I have intruded upon his tranquillity, although how one could relax in this busy environment is beyond comprehension.

"*Mes bagages, c'est...*" I start to explain in my less than perfect French, but the telephone rings and the man holds up a finger to stall me while he picks up the receiver.

I feel frustrated but strive for patience, knowing that it is the way of the French to take care of tasks in their slow-paced fashion. While he speaks to the caller, I amuse myself by watching the arriving passengers.

The conversation is a dull one, at least the parts I can comprehend, but the man starts to write on a notepad and I fear that he may take longer at his task than initially anticipated. The tip of his pencil breaks and it's another minute before he can find a replacement, stalling his progress and adding to the frustration that is by now beginning to rise in my alcohol-induced impatience.

Passengers are starting to fill the baggage claim area now and I fear that, at this time of night, taxis may be less plentiful than at other hours of the day. Glancing back at the desk attendant, it seems he is in no hurry to finish the call and I abandon my complaint, reluctantly tugging my battered suitcase towards the exit and out into the arrivals hall.

A thought suddenly strikes me. Perhaps, on this occasion, one should have purchased a small gift for Madame Joubert, for this will be the last occasion on which I shall visit Paris in a business capacity. But at this late hour there is insufficient choice of trinkets and one can hardly arrive with an offering of *macarons* or jellied fruits, which is all the small kiosk has to offer.

Outside in the fresh, breezy night air, I begin the short stroll to the taxi rank. There is but a small queue and I am soon settling myself into the backseat of a comfortable saloon.

"*Ou allez-vous?*" the driver asks, looking at me in the rear-view mirror. He has what one would call a distinctly French look about him, dark hair, drooping moustache and a striped sweater. One almost wants to gift him a garland of onions to complete the ensemble.

I tell him the address of my guest house and we speed out onto the main road.

As we traverse the highway, now pitch dark apart from the oncoming headlights of traffic from the opposite lane, I feel my stomach give a slight rumble, a reminder that one has eaten not a morsel since the ham salad for luncheon at one, although the sound of my intestinal complaints are muffled by the pop music playing on the taxi radio. I have always found music whilst travelling soothing for one's mind. However, it does deter one from conversing with the driver, which on this occasion seems to suit him fine. The man appears both consumed with paying atten-

71

tion to the tarmac before him and absorbed by humming along to the tune blasting out from the speakers.

I sit back and close my eyes, reflecting once again on my omission to choose some small token for my female friend. Of course, one should have taken the opportunity to browse the Duty Free goods at Heathrow earlier in the evening instead of heading to the lounge. Perfume is far too personal to buy for a person that one is not intimate with and I can only imagine Collete Joubert having tastes that would run into hundreds of Euros. A pretty scarf or box of chocolates might have been in order – although, being French, the dear lady probably has a closet full of such accessories and is watching her weight. One has very little experience in courtship, the majority of my 'liaisons' being meaningless and brief, but one hopes that Collette may hold the key to companionship in my fading years. There could be far worse endings to one's life than having a like-minded beauty at one's side.

I let out a sigh and the driver looks up.

"*Fatigué?*" he asks, glancing at me and then shifting his eyes back to the road.

"*Oui,*" I tell him. I am indeed tired, but underneath there is also a kind of trepidation brewing.

"*Montmartre est vingt minutes,* Monsieur."

I don't tell the driver that I'm aware of how far my destination is, having travelled this route more times than I care to recall, but I nod appreciatively at his concern and thank him. At least I shall reach

Madame Joubert's before the hour strikes eleven, but it is still an inconvenience to the dear woman, having to wait up for my arrival. In booking a later flight, it was quite remiss of me to have forgotten that she rises early in order to prepare breakfast for the various guests. How dreadfully selfish one has been.

Upon reflection however, with it being November, there might well be fewer residents at this time of year, which is all the better for affording one some privacy. Last time I was here, it was Easter and the little guest house was teeming with tourists, all paying through the nose to stay in the fashionable area of the city and tumbling into their rooms at all hours, excited by the heady romantic air that Paris tends to wash upon its visitors. A smile plays on my lips. Perhaps the *amour* of the city will affect me once business is taken care of. Who knows what this sojourn holds?

As we leave the main concourse and begin the short distance down a cobbled side street, I feel a distinct shift in my demeanour, more relaxed, alert and expectant. The tall townhouse is just as chic and resplendent as I remember it to be. So, too, is the proprietor who is waiting at the open door, dressed in a black cashmere sweater and a long camel-coloured skirt. Madame Joubert must have heard the taxi approaching and I'm mildly flattered that she is there to greet me.

Rapidly paying the driver, and tipping him far more than the man expects, judging by the look of surprise on his face, I take my luggage from him and watch while he closes the boot of the car. I hear a faint "*Au revoir*" and an arm waves from the driver's window as he gently pulls away, leaving me standing like a shy public schoolboy in front of the elegant madame.

"Monsieur Foster." She smiles, kissing me on both cheeks in traditional French custom. "How was your journey? Please, come inside, I have prepared a light supper."

Her softly accented English sends shivers down my spine and I realise that I have been looking forward to this trip far more than I've allowed myself to admit.

"Madame Joubert, you are too kind," I tell her, playing the game of formality, as we always seem to do until we begin to relax over wine. It's always the same, using titles until we're sure of each other, almost as though we are both afraid of being spotted by intrusive eyes. It's our little game, you see.

We ascend the staircase, my host going ahead, swaying her hips slightly as she moves upwards while I clumsily follow, lugging my suitcase with difficulty. The camel skirt is long, but I catch glimpses of slender ankles as I follow her steps. Collette's stockings are the old-fashioned type, with seams running up the back of the legs. To my mind, they are at once both sophisticated and seductive, and I briefly imagine a lacy suspender holding them in place at her thigh.

Leaving me to settle into my room while she prepares refreshments in the communal lounge, my host disappears in a flash, only dallying for a moment to sweep her smoky grey eyes over the room, no doubt ensuring that everything is perfect for her fastidious guest. Of course, as always, the room is immaculate; crisp sheets, fresh flowers, soft towels and the faint aroma of lavender. My weary head will have pleasant dreams upon that pillow, rest assured.

I take off my suit jacket and drape it around the arms of a chair, then lift up my suitcase onto the ottoman at the end of the bed. Now, something strange occurs. As I lever the digits into their correct formation to release the security lock, I find that it won't budge. I haven't changed the code since buying the case last week and I distinctly remember the sequence as 000. Being highly organised, I still have the security code from the purchase inside my wallet and quickly produce it to check if I am mistaken. The figures are as bold as day, just as I thought, no error.

What the blazes is going on? I wiggle at the lock to see if it might be stiff, but nothing gives. It's only when I look closer, at the scratches on the handle, that I see a set of initials: *U. R.*

Darn and blast it! In my haste, I've gone and picked up the wrong suitcase. Unbelievable! In all my years of traversing the globe, this is the first time that I've made such a stupid mistake. No wonder the case looks in such poor condition for one purchased so recently. And who the devil would have a name beginning with the letter 'U' except for a woman? Uma, Ursula? I'm hard pushed to recall a man's name, unless he is a foreigner. Umberto, perhaps? Why the hell didn't I notice this at the airport? Of course, my spectacles are tucked back in their case, where I secured them after finishing the newspaper.

Another, more worrying thought strikes me. Somewhere in the city, there's a traveller with my suitcase. What if he opens it? Is there anything incriminating inside that one needs to be concerned about? An involuntary shiver runs down my spine. There are certain items, apart from my personal clothing and toiletries, that don't belong in the public domain. One hopes that they are secured discreetly inside, as is my usual habit, but it's quite disconcerting to know that one's possessions are in an unknown location. Paris is a vast area, not to mention its outlying environs, therefore my belongings could be in any number of the multitude of hotels around the city.

Trying to calm myself, I take a deep breath. There is, of course, the chance that my suitcase is at the Left Luggage office. Taking out my phone, I quickly Google the Charles de Gaulle airport details and scroll down for the correct number. There are so many different departments, and each title is listed in French only, so it takes me a few minutes to locate the extension I seek.

Four rings, five rings, no answer. Glancing at my watch, I realise that it's now rather late and the attendant has, in all probability, gone home for the night to finish his novel. I save the number and curse. There is nothing one can do until the morning now and I dearly pray that the office shall be open first thing.

I'm most certain that in these circumstances, the fault being entirely my own in my eagerness to get to my destination, I shall have to make the half hour trip back to the airport in order to collect my belongings. That is, fingers crossed, if the dratted suitcase is there.

Washing my face in the en-suite, I prepare to go downstairs to where Madame Joubert has supper waiting for me. There's another thing; the wine that I had proposed to open tonight is also inside my case, no doubt getting far too warm for enjoyable consumption. In the mirror my features look taut, the stress giving itself away as it bubbles beneath the surface. This is not at all how one imagined the weekend to begin. It's a good job that we British are made of tough fibre. The unfortunate incident of my luggage is a mere blip – at least that's what I sincerely hope. I note that, in the heat of my anxiety, I have begun to perspire somewhat and, having no personal toiletries with which to freshen oneself, I shrug my jacket back on to cover the damp patches under my arms before stepping out onto the staircase to the rendezvous with my host.

FRIDAY – MIDNIGHT – COLLETTE JOUBERT

The Black Sparrow is sitting across from me, nibbling cheese and sipping slowly at the rich Merlot. I can tell that he's savouring the taste, deciding whether or not I have chosen a worthy beverage for his first night in France. I was careful to let it breathe for an hour after opening, so now it is just how he likes it, at room temperature.

His eyes are bright, like glistening marbles, and he watches me with interest, as though waiting for permission to speak. My guest is wearing a pin-striped suit which very much reminds me of those city bankers in London. Maybe that is the persona he is trying to bluff me with. My guest's hands are so delicate, his long fingers like claws, that I feel that my nickname for him is most apt. Of course, Monsieur Foster does not know that I have likened him to my least favourite bird, as there is a smile fixed upon my face, but I pray that my body language does not give away any clues.

"I must apologise," my guest finally says, carefully putting his glass onto the table and splaying his fingers. "I bought a most distinctive Malbec, jolly good vintage, too, but unfortunately it's inside my missing suitcase."

"Perhaps we can drink it tomorrow," I venture. "I'm sure your luggage will turn up."

"Mm," he mutters, unconvinced. "I sincerely hope so, my dear."

"How long do you expect to be in Paris this time?" I ask casually, changing topic and taking a long sip from my own glass, although I already know the answer. There is little about Monsieur Foster that I do not know.

"At least until Monday night," the Black Sparrow replies. "But, if I were to extend my trip for a few days, would that be a problem, Madame Joubert?"

"Of course not, the room is yours for as long as you need it. And please, Collette."

We have been playing our game of cat and mouse for a quarter of an hour, using formality as we chat, but now is the time to switch to first names, I feel. I always seem to have the upper hand, like the cat, but I'm careful not to underestimate my visitor. He's shrewd, I know that from past experience. Each trip is the same. I know that we do have a mutual fondness for one another, which is quite natural considering that we have known each other for over a decade, but still we dip our toes in and out of intimacy like children playing in a puddle. Something inside me desires this man, but I will never yield to those pangs of hunger.

"Of course, Collette." He says my name as though it catches in the back of his throat, which reminds me of a cat ridding itself of a hairball. For a handsome man, Colin Foster has no conversational skills with the fairer sex, although his roving eyes have already taken measure of my legs. And so he should. It was no accident that I just happened to be wearing silk stockings tonight. A couple of hours earlier and he would have found me in black trousers.

"The wine is superb," my guest says, picking up the bottle to scrutinise the label. "Smooth and fruity."

I raise an eyebrow anticipating more, but Colin is engrossed in reading the small print and firmly presses his lips together. At this moment, I wonder at how very different we are. He, with his very fixed set of life rules, and I like a caged bird, ready to spread my wings.

Being a generous host, I reach over and fill up his glass but not my own. I want to keep a clear head tonight. Tomorrow will no doubt be a long day.

"How will you amuse yourself tomorrow, Colin?" I ask. "Perhaps you would like to accompany me to the opera in the evening? *La Veuve Joyeuse* is on at L' Opera Bastille."

"Ah, *The Merry Widow*," he quickly translates, abandoning the wine bottle and grinning widely. "That would be most agreeable, *merci*."

The Black Sparrow's French has improved more than I realised, taking me quite by surprise.

"But alas, I may have to venture out to buy suitable attire, unless my suitcase shows up," he continues, re-iterating the fact that his luggage has gone astray, but still unwilling to admit that perhaps the misfortune was brought about by his own carelessness.

"Of course." I nod politely, hoping against hope that he won't repeat the whole scenario again. It's late and I fear my tiredness is beginning to reflect upon my mood. "Let's hope it arrives first thing in the morning. If not, there is an excellent department store, just one Metro stop away."

I pass a tray of fondants over to Monsieur Foster, knowing that he has a sweet tooth, and watch as he bites delicately, with his perfect white teeth, antici-pating the cherry liqueur filling at its centre. He is so, what, fastidious? Is that what a fellow English-man might call him? I know all about his humble roots, which makes this upper-class front quite in-triguing. Perhaps it is to rid himself of the stigma of poverty and an alcoholic mother, although I do be-lieve it could have more to do with wanting to fit in with his peers. The façade amuses me but doesn't de-tract from his natural magnetism.

I appreciate how good-looking Colin is. He seems to improve with age. Instead of his silver-grey hair ageing him, it has added a degree of sophistication that is quite appealing in older men. I notice, too, that his eyebrow hair is neatly trimmed and his finger-nails well-manicured. Some women may find Colin

Foster slightly effeminate, but the clues that signify a man who cares about his appearance are quite a charming quality, to my mind.

"Have you travelled much recently?" I press, trying to sound flippant but testing to see how much he will reveal. I enjoy putting him on the back foot.

"Not for a while," he considers, licking his lips with the tip of his cherry-liqueur-tinged tongue. "Just a couple of business trips, both within Europe."

Colin is expecting me to ask what line of business he is in, but there is no need. I never ask, as I have always sensed that he will not tell, but it doesn't hurt to push him with my teasing questions.

"And your trips were successful?"

At this point, I cross and then uncross my legs, revealing my slender ankles under the long skirt, an action which causes the man to open his mouth slightly.

Black Sparrow nods and reaches for another fondant, keeping his eyes upon me for every second. "Yes, not too bad. It pays one's requisite bills."

He briefly chuckles, finding his own rhetoric amusing, but I simply continue to smile.

"And here, Collette? Have you been busy during the summer months?"

"Oh, yes," I admit, "terribly busy, although you know I only let out half a dozen rooms at one time."

Colin ponders my response. I suppose he must be trying to figure out why I need so many rooms for my own quarters, most of which he has never seen, as I occupy the top floor.

"Have you thought about early retirement?" he says, completely out of the blue, catching me off guard. Of course, it's something that I think about every day of my life.

"No," I lie. "Have you?"

There's that glint in his eye again, as though he has something to say but doesn't know how.

"On the rare occasion, Colette. Although in my case, retirement may prove to be rather lonely. One senses that throwing in the towel and ceasing to work may cause undue reflection upon missed opportunity. I should imagine that it can be rather a sombre life, stumbling through one's latter years alone. Companionship, no doubt, would be a far more satisfying course."

The outside bell rings twice and I immediately think of the English expression, 'saved by the bell.' I don't know what Colin was implying but I sensed that he was about to venture into a course of conversation that he might later regret. Maybe the wine has clouded his judgement.

I excuse myself and go out into the hall, feeling the Black Sparrow's neck craning to see who might be arriving at this hour. I presume that he is also casting his eyes upon my retreating figure, which in truth I really do not mind.

Outside, waiting at the door is a pretty young Asian woman. I can see her shivering slightly as I briefly peer through the glass panel. She looks cold, hardly dressed for a chilly autumn night in her light denim jacket and jeans. I fix my smile and open the door.

"Miss Rafiq?" I ask, knowing full well that it couldn't be anyone else at this time. "I am Collette Joubert. Please come in."

The woman is shy and keeps her eyes low as she pulls her suitcase into the hallway. She has beautiful black hair and a slender figure. I detect something slightly familiar about her.

"Thank you," she says, following me to the reception desk and producing her passport for me to record the details. "I'm Uzma."

"Have you stayed here before?" I question, the words tumbling out clumsily before I can check myself.

"Yes," she says, blushing so much that her brown cheeks glow crimson. "In the summer for a few nights, with my, er, friend."

I stop writing in the register and look up, taking in the high cheekbones and full mouth. Now I know who she is. The art student.

I don't want to embarrass the girl by mentioning her romance with the Frenchman, so I nod politely and lead the way up to her room, chattering frivolously about anything that comes into my mind; the cold weather, busy Parisian traffic, breakfast time, keys. The poor dear looks exhausted, I think, as I open up a bedroom door and place the key into her tiny hand.

"Are you hungry?" I offer, thinking of the bread and cheeses downstairs, "I can bring something?"

84

I don't invite her to join Colin and me in the lounge, as what we share is not for public knowledge. Besides, I'm sure that our conversation would prove stifling to one so young.

The young woman shakes her head, her thick lashes flickering quickly over dark, molten eyes, "No thank you, I'm just really tired, so I'll probably go straight to sleep."

"If you need anything at all, please just let me know. There is tea and coffee on the table." I nod towards the corner unit. "You'll find some biscuits there, too. Sleep well, my dear."

"Thank you, Madame Joubert." She smiles wearily, watching me retreat into the passage. "Goodnight."

After closing her door, I stand in the hallway for a few minutes, sucking in my breath, before re-joining my guest in the lounge. Fancy that girl turning up here all alone! What on earth can she be up to? Uzma Rafiq, I roll the name around on my tongue a couple of times. It sounds delightful spoken with a musical French accent rather than her flat English one. On a serious note, I do hope the young lady won't bring trouble to my door. I need to be vigilant. It must be three months since she first arrived here to stay the night; could it be that she has come in search of a father for her unborn child? No, it would be far too early to tell, surely. I am jumping to unnecessary conclusions, although it's not an altogether unrealistic scenario. Let me hope that this is just a sight-seeing trip, although my feminine instinct tells me otherwise.

Back in the lounge, Colin Foster has almost finished the Merlot and appears to have no intention of retiring for the night. He is lounging back in the armchair whilst casting his eyes about the room, no doubt appreciating the new artwork which graces my walls. I offer coffee which he greedily accepts, sipping at the china espresso cup with his finger cocked, reminding me of a grand old Duke I once knew. Of course, I know how Mr Foster came across his impeccable manners, having taken it upon myself to find out everything there is to know about him. The one puzzle for me is why he never married. Good-looking, intelligent, smartly dressed, well-travelled and not short of a few Euros, I would have thought he could have his pick of the ladies.

"You have some fine pieces, Collette," he tells me, indicating the local scenes that sit proudly within his view. "I may well pick up some new works while I'm here. Perhaps you could help me to choose?"

"Sorry," I mumble, still preoccupied with the girl. "Of course, I'd be happy to."

I clear away the plates and stack them on a tray.

"Another guest?" he asks, jerking his head upwards and watching me refill his coffee cup for the second time. He must have sensed my distraction.

"*Oui.* I mean, yes." I hesitate, my French slipping into the conversation as my weariness begins to show. "A young Asian woman from London."

Colin nods as though he already knows, but he doesn't. He has no idea that the girl has been here before, sleeping in one of my beds with a man at least a decade older than her. Nor is he privy to the fact that they arrived late and left early like a pair of night stalkers, afraid to be caught in daylight.

"Is she on holiday?" Colin asks, rousing me from my reverie. "I suppose there are rather splendid deals on cheap flights available at this time of year."

I shrug my shoulders. "To be honest, I have no idea."

I feel it's impertinent of Mr Foster to mention budget flights, he who never has to travel economy class or sit amongst the crying babies and chattering tourists. In my mind, I see him as being a very aloof passenger, sitting back in his luxury seat sipping champagne and requesting caviar. Perhaps I am being too harsh. I check myself. For some strange reason, I feel a little prickly tonight. Maybe I just need some time to settle into my old routine with this particular familiar guest.

He's telling me a story about something that happened to him once on a plane going to Thailand, but I'm not really listening. Occasionally, I nod and make eye contact, but inside I'm wondering what has brought the girl back here. I noticed that she brought a heavy suitcase, although she has only booked to stay for one night. Perhaps she is meeting him, her French lover, tomorrow. I know that I won't be able to sleep until I know the full story. That is my way.

"Collette?" Colin is staring at me, his eyes quizzical and intense. "Are you alright, my dear?"

"Oh, I'm so sorry, Colin," I manage to say. "It's getting late and I'm afraid I'm not as young as I used to be. Perhaps we should retire to bed?"

For a second, there is something in his face that lights up. Does he think I'm propositioning him?

"I mean, we should…."

"Yes, yes, of course," he finally mutters, straightening his jacket and easing himself out of the armchair, embarrassed that such an improper suggestion might have crossed his mind.

"Goodnight, Colin," I tell him, kissing the man on both cheeks in friendship.

He looks at me closely, studying my face, waiting for a signal that there might be something more, but I am a strong-willed woman and will not tolerate such weakness in myself.

"Goodnight, Collette," he sighs and disappears out of the room and up to his chamber. He flits quickly, taking the stair treads two by two, as spritely as a man half his age.

The Black Sparrow has gone to roost, I think to myself, amused.

SATURDAY 2AM – JAMEEL RAFIQ

The sound in my ears is like heavy traffic rushing through a tunnel. I can see my wife's lips moving but my brain refuses to acknowledge that she is speaking. It takes all my concentration to banish my train of thought and look at her, and when I do, my anger rises up once again.

Farida is sitting opposite me, the coffee table a welcome barrier between us. She clings to a rumpled tissue in the palm of her hand, the same one that she has been holding for hours. I notice that her red nail polish is chipped from where she's been nibbling at her stubby fingers. Nothing about my wife is appealing any more. Her mouth is still opening and closing, up and down like a fish, and this time I cannot help but listen to the words that are tumbling out in a torrent of emotion.

"What are we going to do, Jameel?" she whines, like an old dog, moving all the responsibility to my already burdened shoulders. "Our daughter is out there somewhere, alone."

"What do you suggest we do, Farida?" I throw back, my teeth clenched so hard that they're making my jaw ache. "Clever wife of mine, come on, what's your wonderful idea?"

She flinches at my words and starts her incessant sobbing again, which only riles me further, so I get up from the sofa and walk along the hallway to my office, slamming the door behind me.

I sit down in the leather desk-chair and realise that I'm still holding my daughter's note. Her writing is neat and rounded. I read it again, scanning it closely, checking for clues.

Dear Abbu and Ammi,

I have gone to Germany. Yesterday, I got notice that I have been given an internship in a top art gallery. I applied for it a few weeks ago but didn't dream that I would get it. I also know that if I had told you both about it, you would have tried to stop me from going.

Everything will be fine. I just want to establish myself in the art world, you know that's my biggest wish and I'll explain more once I'm settled. Please don't be angry. I know that I can make a success of my life and I promise to make you proud. I'll phone soon.

I'm so sorry leaving without saying goodbye, please forgive me. I love you all very much.

Uzma

I know my daughter and I sense that this is not everything, but I have no idea where to start looking.

I have already checked the flights to Germany and there were several which would fit in with the time of Uzma's leaving, and there the puzzle lies; did she go to Cologne, Stuttgart, Berlin or Dusseldorf? And, of course, that's if she flew from Heathrow. What if she travelled to Gatwick, or Luton, or even took the Euro-tunnel to France and went on from there? My vulner-able, beautiful twenty-year-old could be just about anywhere. Looking for her would be like searching for a tiny ladybird on a thousand-acre plot.

Khalid tells me that he knows nothing about his sister's plans and I believe him. I have told him to come home first thing in the morning. He needs to be here to take care of his mother. There are no papers in her room to suggest where Uzma might have gone and I don't know where else to look. I phoned Shazia earlier, but she is adamant that she knows nothing.

Maryam is working a night shift at the hospital, so I guess we will have to wait until morning to see what she can tell us. Those girls were as close as sisters and I pray that Uzma has confided in her best friend. I feel so ashamed. Even telling Shazia has brought guilt and embarrassment to our family. I thought that we had shown our daughter how to live her life correctly and to respect her elders. What went wrong? And where has this sudden job offer come from? My gut is tugging, trying to get my full attention.

Sitting at my desk, I look at the photo on my right, the only one that graces my workspace. Uzma and Khalid are dressed in their best clothes, smiling for the camera, precious, wonderful children. I think it was taken two years ago at a family party, I don't recall exactly. Their mother is out of shot and, shamefully, it pleases me not to have to look at my wife's face while I work. Farida has become a burden to me. I cannot take her to official dinners or gatherings for fear that she might show her ignorance. My business partners have such glamorous wives, women who take care of themselves, who don't eat too much and who read the newspapers to keep up with current affairs. I couldn't even say for certain how Farida fills her days, but I know that she spends far too much time chatting with Shazia and not enough taking care of herself and our children.

When Farida was first introduced to me, I was a foolish young thing. I was mesmerised by her pretty face and trim figure. In those days, intelligence wasn't a priority in a marriage. I wanted a wife who I could brag about to my friends and relatives, someone who could cook well and was willing to take a back seat while I furthered my career. And here we are, twenty years down the road, hardly having anything in common and both as miserable as the other. Some nights, I lie awake listening to her snoring, her chest heaving up and down in bursts, and it's almost as though I'm in a stranger's life, just watching from the sidelines, willing myself to wake up and be somewhere else, all this just a bad dream. I wonder whether my marriage is the result of my own creation, or is Farida solely to blame?

Looking at the files that I carelessly dropped on my desk hours ago, I wonder how I am now going to manage to read through the papers before defending my client in court on Monday. My assistant has been a tremendous support in gathering new evidence in favour of the man's alibi and I'm anticipating the look on the prosecution's face when I reveal these new, undisputable facts. My delivery will be sensational. If only we can quickly resolve Uzma's predicament, then work can commence as usual, the wheels of justice turning once again. My career is tantamount to the family's well-being.

Before closing the door on my sanctuary, I glance once again at the photo, at the purity and innocence painted plainly upon my children's faces. Everything that I do in life is for them and my daughter's apparent disobedience is like a stab in the heart. I have to find her, while the wound is fresh.

I go into the kitchen and make myself a cup of strong black coffee. Farida comes shuffling in and I want to shout, to tell her to pick up her feet. The noise of her slippers on the linoleum is abhorrent. She is like some old, grumbling Naani who has accidentally entered my life by some stroke of dire misfortune.

"Do you want something to eat, Jameel?" she asks, her voice quiet and shaky, while her hands are busy lifting a wooden spoon and inhaling the aromatic spices. "I can warm this up."

I look over at the stove where the mutton biryani lies cold in its pan, congealed and hard.

"Throw it away, Farida," I tell her. "How can you think about food at a time like this?"

I know very well that she is thinking about her stomach. It's Farida's habit to eat when she feels vulnerable or upset. And I'm also glad to be able to prevent her from feeding her craving. She is stirring the pot under pretence of nurturing me, but I have the upper hand and point towards the bin. I will not allow my wife's hunger to be satisfied during a crisis, no matter how much she desires it.

"I worry about you," she lies, her head bowed while she slowly scrapes the rice out. "You ought to eat."

"Well, perhaps if you'd worried about our daughter and kept an eye on what she was up to, we wouldn't be in this mess right now. If you'd been home today, you might have seen her packing."

My words are unfair, but I can't stop them from tumbling out, although I do believe them. If my wife had been in the house, she would have caught Uzma coming back for her clothes, I'm certain of it.

"Where were you, huh?" I sneer, putting my face so close to hers that she can feel my stale breath.

I know the answer. Farida has already been interrogated and, as my daughter was preparing to leave, she was sitting on her fat behind drinking tea, eating gulab jamoon and gossiping with Shazia.

"Jameel, I didn't know," the shrill voice explains, but I'm not interested. Tomorrow morning, I will be humiliated even further when my brother arrives and that is something that I haven't yet explained to my wife.

Taking a sip of the hot coffee, I look at Farida. Her clothes are creased, and her face is tear-stained. A few strands of hair have come loose around her face and she looks incredibly tired. Heavy, dark rings now underline each eye, but I won't allow her to go to bed until we've been through the issue one more time. The slightest action may have a bearing on my daughter's well-being.

"Did you notice anything at all?" I press, letting out a breath to calm my tone. "What about when you were cleaning Uzma's room? Was there anything at all that didn't look familiar?"

Farida shakes her head, but at least now she looks as though she's thinking carefully. Her brow is furrowed in thought, her shoulders less hunched. She's still holding that piece of tissue.

"Any letters, or what about a diary, something about this job in Germany? Anything different?"

"Nothing." My wife sighs, dabbing at her cheeks. "I've double-checked, Jameel, really I have."

She's right, of course. I turned over Uzma's room myself earlier, with skill and precision, and there's nothing to suggest where she's gone. Our daughter's room is suspiciously void of clues. She has made a thorough job of covering her tracks.

"Farida, make yourself some peppermint tea," I suggest, "and then come into the living room. I have something to tell you about our visitors tomorrow."

She looks at me, wide-eyed, as though I'm going to reveal a big secret, which of course I am, but she has no idea. Obediently, and without question, she leaves the room. I can hear the chinking of china as Farida takes down a cup and saucer from the kitchen cupboard. I wonder if the woman might perhaps become more alert if she succumbed to the caffeine hit in a cup of coffee, but, heaven forbid, I wouldn't want her to form an opinion. Farida is a difficult enough woman to live with without having the audacity to speak out and I rarely give her occasion to express herself freely.

A few minutes later, she comes trudging back in, head down, a finger on top of the cup, making sure that she doesn't spill the tea. While my wife was in the kitchen, I tried Uzma's mobile phone again, but it went straight to voicemail, just like the other – what, twenty, thirty times that I've tried? This time I didn't leave a message and I even listened for the ring-tone, just in case her phone is still here.

Farida makes herself comfortable in an armchair, annoyingly rearranging the cushions as though she's settling in for the night, and looks at me expectantly. There's no easy way to explain this to her, so I jump straight in, trying my best to keep the details to a minimum.

"Tomorrow morning, I will be going to the airport to collect Ali and Tariq," I say, watching her face.

"Ali? Your brother?" she says, cocking her head to one side, a bad habit that she has formed, as it reminds me of the sun-darkened peasant women out in the fields in rural Pakistan.

"Yes, and Tariq's coming with him for a visit. We should welcome them warmly."

Farida nods but her face looks blank. "It's been such a long time, but yes, of course."

I watch my wife's hand shaking as she brings the tea-cup to her lips, her eyes fixed upon mine, waiting for more. She shows no emotion, but her eyes convey a hint of curiosity.

"Well, they will be arriving in the morning and plan to stay here for a couple of weeks."

"A couple of weeks!" Farida's voice comes out in a squeak. "But now is not a good time to have guests, not with Uzma gone. We need to focus on our daughter, Jameel."

She bites her lip, knowing full well that she has overstepped the mark, but I owe it to my wife to tell her everything. After all, if Uzma had heard me speaking on the phone to her Uncle Ali, it could well be the cause of her leaving. I can be certain that Farida has no notion of our plans.

"Farida," I begin, "Ali is bringing Tariq here for a reason. Just try to understand."

My wife stoops forward in her seat, her face taut, waiting for me to go on.

"We've arranged for Uzma to be married, to Tariq. The wedding will be in one week's time."

"But..." Farida starts, putting down her tea, "why haven't you mentioned this before? Surely I should have been consulted. Uzma isn't ready to be married."

I can't help myself from sighing loudly. It's under-handed of me not to have discussed this with the mother of my children, but Farida is so naïve and doesn't realise how being in London is affecting our only daughter. Uzma is becoming interested in boys, and we have to stop it, before it's too late.

"Listen to me," I explain. "You were younger than Uzma when we married. Her being at college, well, it's bound to give her ideas. She interacts with young men and sooner or later, something will happen. It's far better she accepts the traditional ways and takes a husband while she's still... well, pure."

I stumble on the last word. I don't want to spell things out to Farida. She still thinks our daughter is a child and treats her as such. I watch my wife closely as her lips tremble.

"It's too soon, Jameel," she finally says, her scratchy voice an octave higher than normal, and then her eyes widen, as a thought pops into her head. "Is this why our daughter has left home? Did she find out what you were planning?"

I shrug. I don't honestly know. I thought I'd been so careful, only phoning Ali from the office and asking the Imam to be discreet. How could Uzma have found out?

"I don't think she could possibly have known about it," I confess, angry that my wife is looking to put the blame on my actions. "I have been very careful."

"But not even telling me, Jameel!" she cries, raising her arms in distress, "How could you?"

Looking at the woman in front of me is like gazing at a stranger. I am unable to predict her next move and feel like I'm on the verge on losing a grip on my control. I have to take it back, quickly.

"Go to bed, Farida," I instruct the woman, as I feel bile rising. I can no longer look at her. "We will decide what to do in the morning, but first, we both need to rest. I'll stay down here, just in case."

"In case of what?" she dares to question, snapping at me like a viper, her pink tongue shooting out.

"In case our daughter phones, of course!" I shout, wagging my finger relentlessly.

My wife knows her place and retreats upstairs, probably in tears but that is none of my concern.

Left alone, I make another coffee and then go up to search my daughter's bedroom again. The curtains are still open and I close them against the outside world, fully aware that the neighbours may wonder why my daughter is not sound asleep at this time of night. Or is it morning? The hours seem to be slipping by and nothing has been resolved as far as tracking her down is concerned.

Uzma's laptop has gone, including the power cables, and so has her phone charger. Flipping open the wardrobe doors, I look inside and see, as I did earlier, that most of her clothes have gone but she has left behind the four traditional shalwar kameez that she wears for our Muslim festivals and celebrations. It's almost as though she's left her Pakistani self behind, shedding its outer layer and taking the inner Westerner with her.

There's a jewellery box on her dressing-table, which plays a tune as I carefully lift the lid. It's empty apart from two pairs of cheap, brightly coloured earrings. The gold bracelets, handed down from my mother, are gone but I have no idea what other pieces would have been in here. Does she have other items that she could cash in if she needs funds, I wonder? What does that say about how well I know my daughter?

Checking under the bed, there is nothing to see except a small amount of fluff between the bed-frame and skirting-board. I must remember to tell Farida about her poor housekeeping skills in the morning. Uzma's bed is neatly made, the pale pink duvet pulled up over the pillow, which I briefly push aside to look underneath. This might be a good hiding place but unfortunately there is nothing to see. A copy of *The Alchemist* sits on the bedside table, a bookmark inserted one-third of the way through. An unusual choice of literature for a young woman, I muse. For a second, I wonder why my daughter didn't take the book to read on her journey. Surely she would have time on her hands? But it's a ridiculously trivial question to ponder and I continue to look around.

Frantic at being unable to find anything that might lead me to Uzma's whereabouts, I glance again at the bookmark sticking out of the paperback. It's a postcard depicting the River Seine in Paris. The reverse side is blank, but this reminds me of my daughter's recent trip and I can't help but blame the situation at hand on my allowing her to go. Searching the bookshelf for something, anything, I find no more postcards. I know that I'm hoping to find a letter, a card, a diary, written evidence, but my clever daughter has left nothing. I look in the waste paper basket, its empty mouth gaping at me as though laughing at my grief. Not even a receipt or bus ticket to acknowledge that somebody has been here recently.

I get up, a cold sweat starting to ravage my bones and I panic.

"Farida," I call to my wife's sleeping form as I enter our room, "wake up!"

"I'm awake. What is it, Jameel?"

"Did you empty the bin in Uzma's room today?" I ask, irritated by the way she still lies there on the bed.

"Yes, this morning, why?" she replies sleepily, slightly tipping her head to look over one shoulder.

"Good grief, for the love of Allah!" I can't help but scold. "Perhaps there was something in it that might have given us a clue to her whereabouts! Have you even looked?"

"Oh, I didn't..."

I see my wife's hand go up to her mouth. She knows what I'm implying and is waiting for my temper to give way to a barrage of abuse. I am too upset to be near her and close the door, leaving the woman to think through her own stupidity. I will not go out to the dustbin at this time of night, but I'll make a point of telling Farida to do it tomorrow.

The living room clock is ticking, almost reaching the next hour. My head aches from thinking, planning, worrying. There is no point in ringing the police. As a solicitor, I know that they wouldn't consider my daughter a missing person until at least twenty-four hours has passed and as a Muslim, I don't wish to have the community hear of my family problems. Everything must be resolved quickly, but until I know exactly where my daughter is, I cannot begin to search.

Ping. My mobile phone judders as a message arrives.

I hesitate. Could this be Uzma? Is she sorry and ready to admit her juvenile mistake?

I look at the message, the device feeling warm against my cold palm.

Hope you're ok. S. xx

My heart skips a beat as I run the implications of this through my mind. How has my darling managed to slip away to text me in the middle of the night? Is she pretending to get up for a glass of water? And will she remember to delete the words from her outbox as I've so often warned her to do?

My fingers tap lightly on the coffee table before I give in to temptation and reply.

Yes. Just deciding what to do. X

I hear movement upstairs and roll my eyes towards the ceiling, but it's nothing of concern, just my wife rolling over in bed as she often does during the night. There is something quite liberating in being down here, sitting in silence, while she sleeps.

Take care, speak soon. Xx the next message says.

I want to pour out my feelings, tell my other woman how I feel. The loss of my daughter is melting me inside. The cold interior of Jameel Rafiq is beginning to thaw and the side that only my lover knows is bubbling to the surface. So many stolen moments together, forbidden love, yet none of it compares to the hurt that I am experiencing now. If Uzma set out to hurt me for arranging her marriage, my daughter's actions are certainly having the desired effect.

Closing my eyes, I imagine the scent of my beloved, the woman who bares her soul to me, the woman whom I should have married. But then I open my lids, realising the harsh reality of today. Whilst my daughter was running away, packing her bag and leaving my house, my wife was sitting drinking tea with my lover. Both women caught in a tangled web, but one oblivious and the other, Shazia, no doubt relishing the thought that she held a sordid secret that could never be revealed.

SATURDAY – 4AM – UZMA

I wake, cold but still fully dressed apart from my denim jacket, which lies discarded on the over-stuffed armchair in the corner, I'm even wearing my boots. As my eyes adjust to the strange darkness around me, I scramble off the bed, feeling my way to the wall and reach for the shutters. Faint light streams softly into the room from the ancient church across the square and then I remember where I am.

My bedroom is at the back of Madame Joubert's guest house, away from the street and facing a small park. I can just make out the benches, and the fallen leaves, blowing around in the wind like discarded wings. It's a tranquil place, a place for couples, lovers, romantics, the same place where Sylvain and I used to meet in the summer. We stole a kiss on the steps of that church, too, my lover looking furtively around in case any of the other students were watching, but he needn't have worried, nobody saw us.

The scene is different now. It looks more surreal at night, and the cold autumn breeze has stripped the flowers of their pretty buds. I have no idea how cold it gets here in Paris. I hope I've brought sufficient winter clothes with me. Maybe it's a bit warmer here than London. I hope so.

The house is deathly quiet and I'm guessing that everyone else is fast asleep. Quietly, I move across the room and open the door, peeking out into the corridor. There's a light on at the end of the landing where it joins an upper staircase and I can't help but wonder how many guests are staying here tonight. I'm afraid to go wandering around outside in the middle of the night, although I'm desperate to call Sylvain, and I silently close the door again.

My watch says four o'clock.

Switching on the bedside lamp, I go to the bathroom to pee and then pick up a bottle of mineral water that is on the side-table in my room. There's a small booklet next to it, house rules and local information. I'll read it properly in the morning, but I notice that breakfast is between seven and nine o'clock. The water is not particularly cold, but it quenches my thirst within seconds. Glancing back at the neatly typed notice, I realise that I haven't eaten anything for hours, but the excitement of actually being here in France, in Montmartre, seems to have overridden my hunger pangs.

I pull my suitcase towards the bed and kneel down beside it, jiggling the numbers around to unlock the catch. Nothing happens. Stopping for a few seconds to rethink whether I've recently changed the code, I try again. Still nothing. I check the zip that runs around the edge of the case and it's then that something very odd strikes me. This suitcase is new, in fact it looks brand, spanking new and hardly used at all. It's nothing like the scuffed one that I've been dragging around on my recent trip. Shit. Shit, shit, shit.

I sit on the bed, arms around my knees, gathering my thoughts, trying to decide what to do. My French isn't good enough to phone the airport and, anyway, there's another issue. Looking at my phone, I see that it's down to three percent battery life. The charger is in my suitcase, wherever my suitcase might be. I'll have to ask the hotel owner to help me. She seems kind and I'm sure she will. While I still have that remaining bit of life on my mobile, I quickly write down the telephone number of the college where Sylvain teaches. Without my laptop, I can't call him on Skype and I still don't have his new address.

Breathe, Uzma, I tell myself as I feel my heartbeat setting up a frantic thumping. *Everything will be alright.*

Pushing the suitcase against the wall, I go back into the bathroom and look at my dishevelled hair and tired face in the mirror. It's been the longest twenty-four hours of my life and I look as though I've been dragged through a prickly hedge. I start running hot water into the bath, adding some of the lavender salts that have thoughtfully been provided by Madame Joubert. Thankful to have at least put a hairbrush in my handbag, I tug at my tangled locks, cursing silently.

Slow down, I tell my weary self. *You'll look better after a bath and putting on a pretty outfit.* But, as I undress, I realise that I don't have any fresh clothes to change into. Everything I have is in my luggage; underwear, make-up, toiletries and clothes, my computer, even my Quran. Every aspect of my new life is in that case, together with the bulk of the money that I stole from my mother.

Another pang of guilt runs through me as I think about my actions. Not only am I a thief, I'm a thief without her treasure. *Don't panic*, I tell myself. *Whoever has your suitcase must be looking for their own. Everything will work out just fine.*

The water eases my tension – maybe it's the subtle aroma of the lavender – and I lie back, enjoying the sensation of my muscles relaxing fully while my mind still races at a hundred miles per hour. Of course, I'm still worrying about what's happening at home, too. I don't think that my father would have called the police, not yet, anyway, but I never can be sure. Sometimes he acts on the spur of the moment, but something tells me that he won't want to lose face in front of his Muslim friends and work colleagues.

I hope that he believed my letter, as that way, his thoughts will be turned towards Germany and my fake job, although the only way to be certain is for me to phone home at some point, to reassure my parents, and right now I'm unable to do that. Both because I don't have the means, and also because I'm not nearly brave enough.

This place, this guest house, feels safe. Even though I'm alone for now, I know that Sylvain is not too far away and as soon as I sort out my communication problems, we'll be together again. The look on his face will be priceless. I know we agreed to wait a while, but I don't see the point. If two people are meant to be, then one month, one week, one day, what's the difference? Why wait, when you could be enjoying life together?

There was a time some weeks ago when I doubted whether Sylvain loved me. He was making excuses to cut our calls short and asking me not to disturb him at the weekend. But all that has passed now. It turns out he was working on a special commission, a piece that demanded all his attention and would pay enough to put a deposit on the chic new apartment that he wanted.

There's a creak outside the door, as though someone with a light foot is passing. It stops for a few seconds and then carries on, probably trying not to wake the sleeping residents. Who would be up at this hour? Surely not the hotel owner? Goodness, I wonder if I woke someone by running my bath? Being an old house, the pipes clanged quite loudly as the hot water passed through them and anyone in the next room might have been disturbed. Still, whoever it is has gone downstairs as I heard the faint snap of the front door closing. An early bird gone out to catch the worm, as my father would say.

As I dip down below the water level, I think about our last conversation. The connection was bad and the line kept breaking up. I recall that I had to re-dial several times. I told my lover that I was coming here to be with him and he laughed. I know it was an excited reaction, He used to do that whenever I talked about our future. He had a funny mannerism, too, pinching the bridge of his nose whenever I tried to get him to commit to something.

It's not like I expect Sylvain to marry me or any-thing, although that would be great, but I just needed confirmation from him that we would be finding a place together and beginning a new chapter. I know that the studio where he was living was too small for the two of us and he must have been embarrassed, too, as he never took me there. No, it was here, in this pretty guest house, that we spent our most inti-mate times and perhaps that's why I feel so relaxed here now.

Sliding a hand down to my belly to soap myself, I close my eyes and drift to a place where Sylvain is touching me, his soft, huge hands caressing my skin and pulling me close. I felt tiny against his big, mus-cular torso, my face buried in his chest as we hugged after sex. I cannot wait for my darling man to hold me in his arms again. A few seconds later, I realise that my hand has moved downwards and despite be-ing alone here, I feel embarrassed. There's an over-whelming sensation of being watched and I quickly turn my eyes towards the open bathroom door and the outer one beyond. Relieved, I see that the key is still firmly in its place, blocking the view should anyone try to peep inside. Still, the moment of relaxation has gone now and the water temperature has dropped to lukewarm.

Climbing quickly out of the bath to avoid getting cold, I dry my wet body and sit on the edge of the bed, wrapped in the warm, fluffy towel. The shutters are still open but the windows themselves are closed and only the moonlight drifts in. It feels comforting, this lunar glow. I wish I had my paints here to capture the beauty of the night sky. I love the way that the church spire is silhouetted against it. I'd probably add a couple of bats, just to darken the scene even further.

There is so much to paint in this vast city and I cannot wait to get started. Sylvain's style is more geared towards the tourists; café scenes, street-life, multi-coloured layers depicting the city lights. It's what earns him his money, so he says, but I know that my own paintings will depict fantasy and gothic myth, something which I've become more attracted to since my schooldays.

The money in my suitcase is going to be vital to setting myself up, buying equipment and helping my boyfriend to pay for food, I just hope that it can be located quickly and that everything will remain intact. I have another tiring day ahead of me, not quite the welcome that I had in mind for my first weekend with Sylvain, but I have to stay calm and think rationally. I smirk, unable to help myself, as I think of how my mother would react in such a situation, where her luggage had gone astray. The image of her startled face makes me giggle out loud. I can't help it.

Poor Ammi, I shouldn't make fun of her but anything out of the ordinary, any slight domestic crisis, makes her panic. Perhaps right now she's lying awake worrying about me, wondering if I've arrived safely in Germany, thinking about how strange everywhere would be. I wish I could have told her my secret, explained the truth, but I know that my father would have forced it out of her one way or another and Mother would have been left at home sobbing while my father came to Paris looking for me.

Then suddenly, I feel myself scowling, brows furrowed together tightly as I look at the suitcase on the other side of the room, its zipped jaws laughing at my predicament. I want to know whether the owner of that case has equally important items that he or she is missing. Do they also have a secret stash of cash tucked inside the inner compartment?

Briefly, I wonder whether there might be some designer outfits folded up inside the luggage; now, that might be worthy compensation! Although, what use would they be while I had no way to earn money yet, or even make my first local call to Sylvain? I hope I will be able to return the case to its rightful owner and get my own back before anything goes missing. I don't know what would be worse; losing all that money, or being without my laptop, my connection to the world.

I slide underneath the covers on the bed, shivering slightly as I pull them right up over my head. The bedspread is so pretty. It's embroidered with delicate purple flowers which perfectly match the colour of the window shutters. I never noticed that until now. This place is amazingly calming, and I start to drift back to sleep, my head full of scenarios in which Sylvain and I meet again. He's smiling at me, a wide, handsome grin, showing his perfect white teeth, and holding a bouquet of wild flowers in one hand. I imagine that I'm dressed in a pastel shift, kitten heels upon my feet and my legs bare. It's strange, but in each scene it's summer, I just can't seem to reconstruct our meeting in the colder months, but no matter. Soon, I won't have to fantasise any longer.

As I fall deeper into slumber, I feel a warmth envelop me. Maybe it's just the blanket, or perhaps it's the vivid memories of the warm summer sun which are back with me once again. Deeper I go, unable to stop myself from falling now, my eyelids too heavy to open voluntarily. Everything is as clear as day; my journey, the phone call to Maryam, saying prayers in that hot, stuffy airport room, chocolate around a little girl's face and Madame Joubert looking at me in that odd way. It was as if she recognised me but didn't want to say. There was definitely something in her expression, it wasn't just a figment of my imagination. She looked friendly, but she also looked as though she shared a secret knowledge. Maybe she does remember me, after all, but she doesn't approve of me coming here.

I desperately try to erase all thoughts of the people who worry me, pushing my parents, my friend, my brother, and now Madame Joubert to the far reaches of my mind. Breathing heavily, I allow the warmth of the bed to wrap its invisible arms around me and, as the faint chirping of the morning chorus starts up so very far away, a smile plays upon my lips. Here I am, ready to begin my new life, but first I must sleep.

Although weirdly, that stranger also appears in my dream – the businessman in the pin-striped suit, hurrying along with his heavy black suitcase, like a little black bird dragging its meal to the nest.

SATURDAY – 6AM – COLLETTE

"Can you manage for a while?" I enquire of Maria, naturally speaking in French to my wonderful house-keeper. "I need to go out for a while, but I'll be back before breakfast."

"*Oui*, Madame," she replies, glancing up from lay-ing silver cutlery on the pristine white tablecloths, each setting looking immaculate as always. "Is ev-erything alright?"

Maria knows very well that it is unlike me to ven-ture out without at least two espressos inside me. Her face is showing the concern of an elderly aunt and I'm grateful for it. The woman is a godsend and without her, I would have given up renting out rooms years ago. Maria nurtures me, despite there being only a decade between us, but I appreciate her con-cern and would trust her with my life. She also ex-udes Continental chic. I'm aware that I do it effortlessly, but even Maria's plain black dress and starched apron have a certain fashionable quality to them.

I simply nod in reply and tie a silk Hermes scarf over my hair. Having taken time over it this morning, I don't intend to let the wind have its wicked way with my chignon. "Just getting some fresh air, Maria."

The ageing woman returns to her task, humming a hymn quietly as is her usual habit. She's such a blessing. Discreet, hard-working and loyal, everything a person could wish for in an employee. By the time I return, the dining room will be fit for a king, or even a Black Sparrow. The thought amuses me greatly, despite my sombre mood this morning, and an involuntary laugh escapes my lips as I pull on my winter coat and open the heavy front door.

Letting myself out onto the silent cobbled street, I head for the telephone box in the square. It's only just light and few people are walking in the area, just a couple of early risers in the park with their dogs, and the priest, hunched over with his head down, heading towards the church, no doubt with morning prayers weighing heavily on his mind.

The cold has abated for a while and behind the church of Saint Pierre, the sun is pushing its way out from between the clouds, slowly spreading its golden glow like magic dust, but still I can faintly see my breath blowing tiny circles as I walk. I love this time of day when it's so peaceful. It's the best time to be left alone with your thoughts, but alas, today I have no such indulgence. I have something to discuss with a certain young man and I fear that he won't be ready for my news. I must think of a way to soften the blow.

I quickly make the phone call, engaging in as little conversation as possible, and then push open the gates to the park, choosing a bench on the opposite side of the pond, away from any prying eyes that may be looking through the rear windows of my house. Both Monsieur Foster and the Pakistani girl, Uzma, have rooms on this side and the very last thing I need is either of them seeing me with the man for whom I wait. This side of the enclosed space is also where he will enter, and I want him to see me before he has a chance to hide the bravado that he wears so well. It has been four days since we last saw each other and every night has seemed longer than the previous one. I yearn to see him again but accept that it is not always possible.

I thrust my hands deep into the red woollen coat that I'm wearing, grasping for warmth, as, despite the presence of our solar friend, there's still a slight frost on the ground. A few curious walkers cast sidelong glances in my direction, perhaps wondering why a woman in her prime is sitting out here alone. I stoop to stroke a scruffy terrier that has lurched forward to greet me, its owner tugging gently on the lead. We smile, no words, just the silent acknowledgement of one animal lover to another, and then he is gone, moving swiftly away to begin his day. The solitude is liberating, a sensation hidden from my watchers, and it gives me time to consider the events of yesterday evening.

The Black Sparrow's arrival has forced me to put up my invisible shield, the defence that protects my romantic side, the part of me that is prone to give in to fancy and flattery. It happens every time he comes to Paris. He cannot stay elsewhere, there are several reasons why he would not even contemplate such a thing, and I'm torn between excitement and grief at having him here. I know to the exact date how long it has been since he slept in Room No. 3. It is the same bed-chamber that he requests every time, the one that I reserve for him without a second thought.

I have missed his very Britishness, the quirky mannerisms with which he avoids directly responding to certain queries, as though the question of whether he would prefer tea or coffee were as important as the Spanish Inquisition. I have never before encountered an Englishman with such impeccable manners and attention to detail, and at times I wonder if the Black Sparrow has a personal butler attending to his daily wardrobe and personal grooming.

The date of his arrival has been circled on my desk calendar for many weeks, and I have no doubt that Maria has sensed in me some subtle change as I prepare for Colin to open the door to my world. In some ways, Monsieur Foster and I are the same, independent, head-strong and lonely, but I have something that he does not. I have a past.

Imagining the Black Sparrow, his finicky ways and very precise routine, with a harem of women across the globe, is an idea verging upon the ridiculous. Could that man, undeniably good-looking and cul-

tured, function within the bounds of a normal relationship? It seems such a contradiction to his outer
shell, which presents itself as a nut, both colloquially
and quite literally, being hardened to change but also
absolutely crazy. The man has a very endearing way
about him and I am perfectly certain that he would
smother any wife of his with a generous amount of
affection, but it would be getting to that point, tiptoeing around the frivolities of love-making and such,
that would have him scarpering with his tail between
his legs.

I do know that he has never engaged in a long-
term relationship, for, when it comes to Colin Foster,
I am acquainted with just about everything there is
to know. I wouldn't call it an obsession, just a matter
of keeping myself acquainted with his 'comings and
goings', the expression Colin himself so often uses to
refer to his movements. Without even glancing at his
passport, I am able to recall the last ten cities he visited and I have no doubt that I could predict his next
move. Perhaps the conversation tonight will reveal
to me some intention that I wasn't yet aware of, but
I very much doubt that it will.

Once, I was married, to a man whom I dearly cher-
ished and who adored me in return. For over thirty
years, we shared everything and then one day, his
heart could go on no more and his life ended abruptly.
The wounds are still raw, too sore to contemplate beginning anew, and I feel it would discredit everything
that we had, just to tuck the memories in a drawer
and find new love. Even if it were possible, I have no

inkling as to whether Colin could be the one to help me recover my old self. His obsessive neatness, punctuality and control might stifle me. I would become the Black Sparrow's caged dove.

I sensed last night that there is something which he wishes to tell me, but hopefully, our theatre trip will put a stop to any notion he might have about discussing his future with me. Do I want to become a part of it, honestly? I fear we are too different, he and I; that we are fated to continue only as... what? What are we? Friends? Perhaps. We do share a connection. It would be impossible not to, given our continued companionship over the years. But maybe he does not realise where my priorities lie. Such a waste of a man, I think, financially comfortable, amenable and kind, but there it stops. There is no fire inside Monsieur Foster, no passion that is so necessary to us French. I am convinced that where my fellow Parisians are hot-blooded and passionate, Colin's veins are decidedly cold.

Leaning my head back, so that my head is tilted up towards the last few rays of morning sunshine, I realise that this morning I am dreadfully tired, having been unable to sleep last night as my mind whirred with notions. Each time my lids threatened to close, the Black Sparrow's face would be there, pecking at me to wake up, his beady eyes twinkling like polished stone. It felt as though he was there watching me as I lay upon my bed, although I know how ridiculous that might sound should I dare to speak my concerns out loud.

I cannot fully blame my newly-arrived gentleman guest for my sleepless night, for I am also concerned about the appearance of the girl and the trouble she might bring to my door. I curse myself for not having recognised the name when she booked the room. If only I had, perhaps I would have refused the booking, told her that the guest house was full – although sometimes these things are best dealt with when the Devil is at your door, so to speak. I heard her running a bath in the small hours, so obviously she was unable to sleep, too, unless her religion is the cause of such an early start. Perhaps there is some ritual that a Muslim has to perform before turning their thoughts to prayer.

She didn't go outside, of that I'm sure. My bedroom faces the front street and, in the hour that I stood smoking through the open window, I neither saw her leave nor return. Perhaps she has already informed her lover of her arrival. But then, why not go straight out to meet him? I consider the various possibilities. Young girls are so fickle these days. Maybe her being here is pure coincidence. That's a ridiculous thought, I tell myself with a sigh. She is here for one reason only and very soon, that cause will be coming through the park gates.

I sit on the hard, wooden bench for twenty minutes, the flaking paint as pink as my flushing cheeks where the morning air has been pinching them. Eventually, the tall, dark man appears. He is unshaven, and his unruly curls look as though they haven't seen a brush in weeks. I'm guessing that he has just rolled out of bed and I dearly hope that it was his own. Still, he is as handsome as ever, with smouldering looks and the most perfect of smiles. He's wearing a heavy grey jacket and faded jeans and could easily have just stepped away from a designer fashion shoot.

As soon as he sees me, his sombre mood lifts. There's a spring in his step and our eyes connect. In that split second, everything else is irrelevant. All around us, people are rushing to their work or their homes, tugging their dogs and looking at watches, but I am almost oblivious to everything else now that he is here. He takes long strides towards me, his broad shoulders looking as though they carry the troubles of the world upon them and I have to force myself to sit still when all I want to do is stand and embrace him.

He stoops, kissing me softly on both cheeks as is our custom, and then once on the top of my head, and in that moment, I can forgive everything. The feeling inside me is one of unconditional love.

"What's the emergency?" he asks, his voice deep and gravelly, no doubt dry from too much beer yesterday evening. He sits down at my side, looking worried. "Are you ill?"

I shake my head, trying to look stern, but a smile plays on my lips. With him, I can never be angry. I sense that he, too, has missed his morning coffee, his mood still very much in slumber mode.

"She is here, Sylvain," I tell him simply, although his almond eyes and dark face show no sign of knowing what I mean. "At the guest house. Did you know?"

"Who? What are you talking about?" He frowns, pushing his arm through mine for warmth, although I can see that my statement has grabbed his full attention.

"Uzma Rafiq," I mouth, almost in a whisper, raising my brows to show him that I, too, am surprised.

"Uzma? Here? You're joking!" He's genuinely shocked and releases my arm again to run both hands through his matted hair. "When?"

"She arrived late last night."

"Are you sure it's her?" Sylvain presses, rubbing his fingers across his beautiful soft mouth, enabling me to catch a glimpse of his perfect teeth. "It might just be someone who looks like Uzma."

"It's definitely her. Naturally, I asked for her passport details when she checked in."

I give him a moment to think through my words before voicing my burning question. "Did you encourage her to come? No woman would just jump on a plane unless she was certain that someone was waiting for her at the other end."

He shrugs, in the half-hearted way that he does when he's made a mistake, or has something he needs to confess. "We've been talking, but I didn't ask her to come. It was just a fling, something that got out of hand."

"Nothing more?" I have to ask, the possibility of a pregnancy having weighed heavily on my mind all night. At first, he doesn't register what I'm implying but, when he does, he is outraged.

"No, I swear! It was just a bit of fun. She's interesting, but there's no way I promised her anything. We had a good time. I thought that when she went back to London she'd forget about me."

"How could any young woman forget about you, Sylvain?" I tease, ruffling his hair, "When was the last time you spoke to her? Do you remember what was said?"

He sighs heavily, the burden of what he has to tell me like a sour taste on his tongue.

"Last week. We just chatted for a while on Skype. Yes, she said that she wanted to come here to be with me, but..." he looks into my eyes, pleading, waiting for me to say something scornful, but this time I allow him to continue, "... I told her the time wasn't right. I was trying to let her down gently. You know how it is with these girls. They get attached so easily and expect commitment."

"Did you give her any reason to believe that the two of you had a future together? Surely she wouldn't just come here without a promise or something?" I say, watching him avert his eyes. "Sylvain, I need to know, if I am to help you get out of this mess."

He spreads his hands wide, eyes pleading with me. "No, it was just fun, I promise you."

I have to believe him. I know the way that young girls throw themselves at Sylvain and sometimes it leads to complications. This time, I will help him, but it has to be his final mistake.

"This has to be the last time, Sylvain." The words come out harshly and I try to soften the blow by holding his hand in mine, stroking the rough, dry knuckles with my thumb. "Lie low for a few days and I will try to convince her to leave. Don't try to contact her, do you hear me?"

The man at my side nods, and I see the frightened child inside him, contemplating his actions and regretting each move. I have been complicit in his affair, allowing them to stay in one of my rooms, but how else was I supposed to know what he was up to? I would rather have my nose rubbed in his affairs than have him sneak around behind my back. I've been foolish to think that he would outgrow these sordid flings and it disappoints me to acknowledge that he will possibly carry on in this way.

"Do you think you can persuade her to go home?" he urges, his words choked and clumsy.

"I should imagine that she has left without her parents' consent, with limited funds and no way of contacting you at home. Therefore, it shouldn't be difficult to play to her weaknesses."

Sylvain leans back against the slatted wood of the bench, lets out a sigh of relief and kisses me once more. Our love for each other is what holds us together. Nothing can break that bond.

"Thank you so much." He smiles shyly, letting me see his soft side again. "I promise I've learned my lesson now. There won't be any more girls. It's time for me to stop playing around."

It's hard for me to believe him. Sylvain has been carrying on with young women since his college days and becoming a tutor has only opened more doors of opportunity, instead of dampening his fire. I can recall at least a dozen broken hearts in the past decade and there must be many others of which I'm unaware, but what can I do? This beautiful man is filled with passion and needs. Like a volcano on the verge of eruption, nothing can stop his desires. Not even me.

I will never desert Sylvain, he means too much to me and during my difficult years, after my husband passed on, he has been my rock. We share supper together once a week, hidden from the world and oblivious to anything else but the needs of each other. Perhaps Sylvain is the sole reason that I am reluctant to leave Paris, unwilling to admit that I could not survive without him. The more I begin to contemplate the questions that my Black Sparrow might ask of me tonight, the more I realise that, as long as Sylvain is here, this is where I will remain. To leave him would be like ripping out my heart, so great is my love for this man at my side.

We sit in silence for a while, each content in the other's company. My mind is racing, filled with thoughts, but it is calming enough to just be here, in this tranquil place, feeling each other's slow breaths as we think through the future. When Sylvain speaks it is with furrowed brows.

"I'm sorry that you have to be involved in this," he mutters, squeezing my hand tightly. "I'll make it up to you, truly I will. I can't believe that Uzma would just come here like this."

I give an involuntary shudder, recalling the many times that I've heard these pleas before, but today, instead of the arrogance and pomp, there is sincerity in his eyes and I roll over like a cat waiting to have its belly stroked.

"I am already involved, am I not?" I purr. "Who else can you tell about this? Besides, if she's in my house, at least I can be sure that the two of you aren't carrying on again."

He shoots me a sidelong glance. "I don't know what to say, really I don't, except sorry."

"Maybe one day you will grow up and realise that relationships are delicate. Young women are more vulnerable than you think and despite your obvious sex appeal, you are a dangerous man, Sylvain."

He nods slowly, the thick curls bouncing on top of his head, and I reach up to stroke them. The texture is as soft as goose down and I feel that I could quite contentedly sit here forever.

"Are you mad at me?" Sylvain asks, sitting up straight so that my hand slips back down to his shoulder. "I wouldn't be surprised if you are, I just don't know what gets into me."

"I could never be truly mad at you," I confess. "After all, I lived with a man for thirty years who had the same irresponsible nature, although I managed to tame him in the end."

We embrace, a natural, loving gesture, and I feel the eyes of passers-by watching with wondering looks at this woman in her more mature years with this handsome creature in her grip. We must look an unlikely couple, but I will not let go, not yet. It may be days before we have the opportunity to meet again properly and this morning deserves a proper departure, to let Sylvain know that I am still here for him and that I will do anything, absolutely anything, to help him out of this current mess. I hope the girl is ready to put up a good fight, for she knows little of what she's dealing with yet.

Suddenly, the bell-tower of Saint Pierre strikes seven and I know that I must return home. The guests will expect to have me there, overseeing their breakfast, making sure they have everything that they need. Maria is perfectly capable of taking over but I, too, need to oversee what my new arrivals have planned for the day. The responsibility of what lies ahead weighs heavily on my shoulders.

"I have to go, my darling," I tell Sylvain, disengaging myself from his grasp and brushing my fingers along his high cheekbone. "I'll ring you later, after I've found out what she's planning to do, and don't come around here again until I tell you it's safe."

I see a genuine sadness in his eyes. Perhaps Sylvain realises how much he has been hurting me. I long to believe that the trail of destruction, the disastrous affairs and the weeping women, will now cease, but if he is not somehow embroiled in some illicit union, this incredible man will turn his attention to drink. I have seen it happen so many times, and his artwork can testify to the shift, becoming dark and demonic, instead of the vibrant street scenes which I know and love so well.

"We'll sort this out and then perhaps take a trip to Bordeaux," he tells me, and his eyes are filled with promise. "I'll drive us down to Grandma's old cottage and we can get away from everything."

I know that he means it, and maybe we can get away together, but my instinct tells me that there are many demons looming on the horizon and the next few days are going to be filled with trials.

"That would be wonderful, Sylvain," I say, with a smile. "Just what we need."

He hugs me tightly one more time, as though this is the last time we are going to meet, although I honestly do feel that his gratitude is the reason for this sudden display of affection. I hang on to that moment of bliss for a few seconds more before straightening my coat and looking up into his amazing dark eyes.

"I love you," he says, bending down and softly whispering in my ear, so close that I can feel the warmth of his breath and the prickle of his unshaven chin. "Never ever forget that."

I can feel the tears beginning to prick at my eyes and I know that, if I don't leave now, I'll be unfit for breakfast conversation by the time the guests see me. I leave one parting comment.

"I know. I love you, too."

"Take care, Mama," my son says as we separate, "and thank you."

SATURDAY – 8AM – COLIN FOSTER

Descending the staircase, I am greeted by the unmistakable aroma of freshly ground coffee beans and warm croissants. I have forgotten how heavenly the breakfast here is and my taste buds are fired up before I even push open the door to the dining room. My usual table by the window is vacant and a copy of this morning's *Guardian* newspaper is folded neatly next to the side plate. It's the little touches that make coming here so familiar and one can't help but feel blessed at having such an accommodating host.

As soon as I sit, Maria is here with the coffee pot, pouring and chattering, welcoming me back but non-intrusive in her queries. I order my usual Eggs Benedict and peruse the front-page news whilst sipping the heady Colombian brew. Having slept well, one is ready for whatever the day might throw at one and that includes tracking down my missing luggage.

"Good morning, Monsieur Foster." Collette grins as she pushes open the kitchen door. "Did you sleep well?"

I briefly take in her black trousers and white blouse, form-fitting but not tight. She looks the epitome of elegance, although her eyes portray tiredness and worry.

"Absolutely," I enthuse. "A good six hours by my reckoning, Madame Joubert."

We keep up the ruse of formality for the few groups of tourists that are scattered around, eating breakfast. Old habits die hard, I suppose.

"I'm very glad to hear it," she says softly, brushing a hand against my sleeve as she retreats to the kitchen. "I'll see how Maria is getting on with your eggs."

As Collette slinks out of sight, I take a moment to watch, very discreetly, and something stirs within me. I wonder if our trip out tonight will find me plucking up the courage to divulge my plans. Before returning to my paper, I glance around the room. There are a couple of Japanese tourists, plus three middle-aged ladies sitting together, whom I guess hail from Germany considering their sensible walking shoes and collection of guide books. The Asian girl whom Collette mentioned last night is nowhere to be seen. Perhaps she is a late riser; after all, she arrived after midnight, one supposes.

Breakfast is an explosion of melt-in-the-mouth softness and textured crunch, thoroughly enjoyable and a fitting start to my busy day. I become aware of myself lingering far longer than necessary as I wait for Collette to finish giving directions to the Japanese visitors, smiling and laughing politely as she does so. The couple bow before leaving – such an odd habit, I've always thought – and their host reciprocates politely, bending her head and placing her hands together. This is a woman whom one could take to just about anywhere in the world and she would try her best to embrace local culture and tradition. Without a doubt, the perfect travelling companion.

"More coffee, Colin?" she offers, assuming informality after having seen the last of the guests out into the hallway. "I'll join you."

I nod in the affirmative and sit back in my chair, splaying my hands on the table in front of me. "Go on then, my dear, just one more."

If ever there was such a movement of graceful coffee-pouring, then Collette does it to a tee. Her perfectly manicured fingers hold the lid in place whilst the other hand tilts the pot, her delicate wrists so alluring that I find my mouth has opened involuntarily. I close it quickly and dab it with a napkin.

"I have taken the liberty of noting down the direct number for the luggage office at the airport," she informs me, sliding a piece of paper from her pocket and settling down on the opposite side of the table. "I do hope they are able to locate your suitcase."

"Most kind of you. Yes, I sincerely hope so, too," I tell her, quickly running through the scenario of someone else actually opening my case in my mind. "A most unfortunate predicament."

I omit mentioning that I already have the number, having tried to call last night to no avail, but I pick up the paper and politely pocket it.

"Do you have plans today, Collette?" I venture, watching her blow on the hot liquid before taking a sip.

She shrugs, in that very chic French way of hers. "Not particularly. Although I do need to select something special to wear for our theatre trip tonight."

"I'm very much looking forward to it. I'm sure that whatever you wear, you will look stunning."

Collette looks startled for a second and I wonder whether my compliment has unnerved her, but then she smiles broadly and throws back her head.

"Oh, you are such a flatterer, Colin Foster."

We sit looking at one another, both slightly embarrassed, heads dipped to drink our coffee.

"I should really go and help Maria," my host says, excusing herself. "I shall see you later, *oui?*"

The last word is a reminder of why I am drawn to this beautiful woman. It's the mystical foreignness of her accent and mannerisms that attract me, like a black widow tugging on her web.

"Indeed. And I, too, should run along," I confess and then, assuming an imitation of Hercule Poirot, "the case of the missing suitcase needs to be resolved!"

My jovial attempt at referencing Agatha Christie is lost on Collette Joubert and she wanders off to the kitchen, bewildered and shaking her head slightly.

I can almost see the shocking headline news should we ever enter into courtship: *Eccentric Brit Woos French Madame With Atrocious Poirot Impression.*

I leave the dining room and return to Room Three, intent upon tracking down my luggage.

After twenty minutes of waiting on the line while the assistant checks for lost luggage, and then another five minutes of arguing when they proclaim that there's nothing to be done until the person who has mistakenly taken my suitcase shows up with it, I put down my phone and sit on the edge of the bed. At least the kiosk attendant was astute enough to take both my number and that of the guest house, but it still doesn't quell my frustration. Where the hell can my luggage be if not with another passenger? And surely by now they should have realised the mix-up and contacted the airport?

There's nothing to be done for now it seems, although I'm still extremely concerned about the items that I have inside my case; things that I tend to carry everywhere with me. Should they get into the wrong hands, goodness knows what might happen. It's something I don't wish to contemplate.

I smarten myself up as best I can, despite having nothing else to wear save my pin-striped suit and yesterday's crumpled shirt. It's not something I had planned to do, but one must now go out shopping for clothing and toiletries. Being very particular about the brands which I use, I'm going to have to head for the department store that Colette mentioned last night. Really, this is all terribly inconvenient. The best possible scenario now is the speedy reappearance of my suitcase.

I go into the bathroom and splash a handful of cold water upon my face, followed by a gentle dab with the soft towel provided. Then, as is my usual habit, I begin straightening things. The swivelling shower head needs to be aligned with the line in the tiles, the bath mat straightened so that the longest edge touches the side of the bath, each bottle must have its label facing directly forwards and the toilet roll needs to be wound towards the lavatory with one single sheet hanging down. Once everything is ship-shape, I can venture out into the morning breeze and take care of my tasks.

Before heading to the nearest Metro station, I stroll over to the telephone box and dial the familiar number of my business contact here in Paris. The line buzzes three times before being answered.

"*Oui*?" a muffled voice says curtly.

"Foster," I tell the person, for no more needs to be imparted.

"Monday, 4pm. Instructions will be delivered."

"I'm at the..." I start to explain my address.

"We know." The line goes dead.

I hang up and lean my head against the cold pane of glass in the cubicle as the familiar thrill begins.

After a few minutes spent collecting my thoughts, I step back outside and look up at the imposing steeple of Saint Pierre. The church must be centuries old and the hideous gargoyles that loom down at me seem as though they will topple at any moment. I am not a religious man, but today would have been my mother's birthday and I step inside to light a candle at the altar in her memory.

It's still early and the vaulted ceiling and stained-glass windows do little to shed light onto the aisle as I walk. It truly is quite a remarkable place, extremely tranquil and the carvings most elegant. Upon reaching the candle box, I take one and light it from another, dropping a ten Euro note into the collection box nearby. If mother were alive, she would no doubt scoff at my charitable gesture and encourage me to spend my cash on a bottle of brandy to steady her nerves instead.

"Good morning." A voice intrudes upon my reverie. "You are saying a prayer for someone close?"

The man is speaking in English and one can't help but wonder if the cut of this suit and dark trilby earmark one as British. I turn and see a young priest, standing with his hands delicately clasped.

"No, not really," I lie between gritted teeth. "Just an old acquaintance."

"Still," the holy man goes on, gesturing towards the battered wooden box, "the church appreciates your generous gesture. I must say, I haven't seen you here before."

I shrug uncomfortably. These places aren't the most alluring at the best of times and I was under the distinct impression that it was solitude which visitors sought inside religious institutions. Perhaps this particular priest needs a lesson in decorum before he starts playing detective.

"Just enjoying a few days rest in Montmartre." I bite my lip. "Being an art lover, it's the ideal place."

"Indeed," he agrees, stepping forward. "The home of our Parisian painters. Are you staying locally?"

"With Madame Joubert, just across the square." The words tumble out before I can stop them. "A most comfortable and hospitable little guest house."

"Ah, the lovely Madame Collette." He smiles. "I happened to see her very early this morning."

The revelation surprises me and, for fear of showing too much interest, I say as casually as possible, "Perhaps she fancied a stroll in the morning air."

"Perhaps." He nods, raising his heavy dark brows. "Although she was heading towards the telephone box. I only remark upon it as I thought to myself that maybe the phone lines were out in her house."

"I really couldn't say," I tell the other man, concerned that my voice may have just raised a fraction.

"No matter." The priest shrugs, probably realising that there is no more information to be gleaned from me. "Have a good day, and I will say a prayer for your... old acquaintance."

As I navigate my slippery soles back down the damp steps of Saint Pierre, my curiosity overwhelms me and I can't help but look over towards the glass telephone cubicle on the edge of the square. What the devil was Collette doing out here so early? It must have been well before eight, as she appeared to have been busy in the kitchen for some time when I arrived in the dining room. I must remember to ask whether there is some issue with the phone line in the guest house when I return later. It must be a terrible inconvenience trying to run a business if indeed that is the case.

But who would Collette need to speak to so early in the day? I realise that I have been standing for some moments gazing upon the telephone kiosk, and propel myself into motion. So, too, am I reminded of my own brief conversation some short time ago, when I received my instructions from the powers-that-be.

Walking briskly towards the station, I dwell upon the sum that will be deposited into my bank account on Monday, after the completion of my task. No doubt the £20,000 figure is only half of the amount that will be transferred to my contact, but no matter; he is the one who makes the arrangements and is also the supplier of my equipment when the time comes. Now that the exact moment, four o'clock, for me to complete my part has been confirmed, I feel a switch turning on inside me. I am starting to come alive, the buzz I get from my work is starting to thrill me and next two days will be a part of an excruciating wait.

Having located the department store, I go about selecting appropriate garments to see me through the remainder of the weekend should my suitcase remain elusive. I choose shirts, a couple of ties, trousers, underwear, socks, some expensive after-shave and a gift pack of toiletries. My sensible black Oxford brogues will see me through for footwear, which is just as well, as the price of my goods in Euros is staggering.

Laden with bags, I nip into a nearby pharmacy and procure shaving materials before hailing a taxi to take me back to my temporary residence. Both the streets and traffic are starting to become insufferable and I feel relieved at having completed my purchases before the Saturday morning shoppers have descended in full force.

"*Anglais*?" the taxi driver asks, sniffing and lighting up a cigarette before offering me one. "*Fumer*?"

"*Oui, je suis Anglais*," I confess, putting up a hand to decline the smoke.

"Tom Jones," he chortles, manoeuvring the vehicle into the stream of heavy traffic.

"Yes, quite," I manage, grasping at my bags to prevent them from sliding off the slippery leather seat.

The man slips a CD into the dashboard console and immediately we are serenaded by Mr. Jones's rendition of *Delilah*, which the driver insists on singing along to in abominable English.

At last, we arrive back at Guest House Joubert and I reluctantly part with a two Euro tip. The ride was erratic and dangerous, but for entertainment value it was top notch.

"*Merci*, Monsieur," I hear, as the taxi pulls slowly away, its tyres crunching on the cobbles. "Anytime you need a ride, just ask for Toto. Everybody knows me."

The first thing that strikes me as I push open the door is Collette. She is standing at the reception desk, which is not such an extraordinary pose, given her profession, talking on the telephone. I hover for a few seconds, pretending to rearrange my shopping bags in my hands, until she is free. It seems that the call is nothing more than a booking confirmation and is concluded speedily and efficiently.

"Ah, Collette," I say, smiling and stepping forward as soon as the device is back in its cradle. "Glad to see the phone lines are working again. What a nuisance that must have been."

She is puzzled and her mouth parts, showing perfect teeth, but no sound escapes. After a pause she repeats, pronouncing the two words slowly, "The phone?"

"Yes," I continue. "The priest from Saint Pierre happened to mention that he saw you using the phone box in the square earlier. I do hope that everything is alright."

Something flits across her face. Anger? Embarrassment? I can't be sure.

"Ah, yes," she eventually tells me, although I know she is lying as her cheeks begin to glow. "Just a momentary problem with the phone, and the baker failed to deliver today. Everything is fine now. No need for your concern, but thank you."

I'm startled that Collette is capable of telling me such a bare-faced lie, for I saw the baker arrive through my bedroom window at seven and it was Maria who greeted him at the back door. My host looks down, obviously avoiding my eye, and starts to shuffle some papers.

"Well, I'll see you later then," I say politely, still wondering what on earth is going on. "I must go and hang up my purchases."

"Oh, a successful trip?" Collette suddenly asks, still blushing, her smooth cheeks glowing pink.

I nod and hold up the bags to waist height. "Indeed, a most fruitful expedition."

The door of the dining room opens, and a dark-skinned young woman appears. For a second, there is recognition in both our eyes, having seen each other somewhere before. She seems very casually dressed, in jeans and a black sweater, and wears scruffy training shoes on her feet. We both turn, the French-woman and I, to face the newcomer who has so rudely interrupted us.

"Thank you, Madame Joubert," the younger woman says, "I'm sorry to inconvenience you."

"Nonsense," Collette tells her, "You were only a few minutes late. Have you eaten enough?"

The guest nods shyly. "Yes, I have. Thanks again, see you later."

We watch her retreat upstairs, both noticing that she glances at me again before reaching the bottom step.

Madame Joubert raises an eyebrow inquisitively. "Have you met Miss Rafiq before, Colin? She seemed to recognise you."

I shake my head, pondering, but then suddenly realise that I have. "I believe we were on the same flight from London last night. By Jove, what a coincidence!"

Collette blinks, and gives a sweet but rather fake smile. "Oh, I see. How very strange."

I climb the stairs, feeling the most beautiful eyes in Paris watching me as I go. Although my mood now is much more sombre than when I arrived back here some minutes ago and I feel as though a dark gloom has descended upon me. Only a woman could affect me in such a way, I muse.

Strangely, my mind seems to have concluded that Collette Joubert has a lover. For what other reason would she need to lie about making phone calls outside the house? One cannot help but feel somewhat deflated at the thought of my host involved with another man. Perhaps I have been a fool to think that she has been saving herself for me. I admit that my trips to Paris have been less frequent than I would have liked, but one simply cannot choose where business takes one.

As I unpack the items and lay them out on the bed, I feel as if something inside me has deflated. My ego, no doubt, silly old fool that I am. To think that a woman like Collette would lock herself away from suitors until I was ready to pounce! She is far too great a catch for that. Had I not neglected my personal life to such a degree, she would have waited. I can't help but wonder if she's involved with someone younger, more virile, better looking. Maybe there is a certain stigma attached to her liaison and, for that reason, she keeps him away from her home – although it does seem extreme to not receive or make calls to a lover from one's own establishment when the woman in question is a widow.

And that Asian woman. Blow me, if that's not a strange coincidence! Fancy her turning up at the exact same establishment. I could have saved the poor woman some Euros had I known, by offering to share my taxi from the airport. Oh well, such is life, these things surely happen for a reason.

I resolve to employ myself in reading for the remainder of the day, keeping out of Madame Joubert's way until it's time for our rendezvous this evening. Perhaps, after dinner and some decent wine, she will reveal the truth behind her mysterious actions this morning. Having people lie to me causes a certain distaste in my mouth. It's been that way since I was a youngster and dear Mother would lie about her drinking, but it's especially nauseating when the one telling the untruth is the object of one's affections. I can only hope that, should Collette have met someone whom fulfils her, she will be honest with me. If only I had given her some inclination of my feelings towards her some time ago. Drat my stiff British upper-lip! She needs passion and extravagance, neither of which I am inclined to.

Sort yourself out, old chap, I tell myself, your main objective in Paris is to complete the small business matter. Anything beyond that must not, in any way, shape or form interfere.

To remind myself of the goal awaiting me, I open my pocket notebook to my accounts page and slide my finger down to the current balance. The next twenty thousand will bring me to my goal and after that, I can finally begin to lay plans for the future, with or without Collette Joubert.

SATURDAY 10AM – FARIDA RAFIQ

As soon as he hears me coming out of the bathroom, Jameel is upon me like a crafty snake, slithering along the landing and fixing me with his tired eyes, deciding how to force from me what he needs. He hasn't shaved this morning and greying stubble protrudes from his usually smooth chin.

"I've been thinking," he tells me, running a hand through his hair. "If anyone would know anything about Uzma's whereabouts, it would be Maryam, wouldn't it?"

"Yes, I suppose so," I reply after a slight pause, ashamed to admit that I am a bad mother for not sensing that my own daughter was planning something. "They're best friends, after all."

"So, you need to call her," Jameel insists. "Talk to her as an aunty, explain how concerned you are and that you just want some contact information for our daughter. If anyone, Maryam will confide in you."

"Jameel, I don't think she'll tell me anything..."

But he's not listening. Instead, he's bustling me down the stairs and over to the side table where the phone is. I'm not good at being subtle and I'm not sure what to ask, but before my bare foot touches the carpet, my husband has already dialled Shazia's number.

"Good morning Shazia," I say, as brightly as I can under the circumstances, keeping my tone even despite my lack of sleep. "Is Maryam awake? Can I speak to her please?"

My friend disappears for a couple of minutes and I'm left idly holding the receiver, desperately trying to avoid Jameel's glare. I can detect a spark in him, as he suddenly darts into his study and picks up the extension in order to listen in. Now I feel really uncomfortable, as though I'm betraying the girls, although I suppose he has a right to know what's being said. Perhaps he doesn't trust me to relay the conversation back to him afterwards.

After a while, a sleepy Maryam answers. "Aunt Farida?" She yawns loudly. "Sorry, I was on shift until late last night. Mum says you need to speak to me, although I don't really see how I can help..."

"Sweetheart, listen," I explain softly. "You won't get into trouble, I promise. I just need you to tell me anything you possibly can about where Uzma has gone. Her father and I are worried sick."

"I don't know exactly where she is," Maryam admits, after a few silent seconds. "I tried to phone her this morning and I've sent three text messages, but she hasn't replied."

"Okay, okay," I tell her, wondering how best to proceed. I have to be very careful with my words. "When was the last time you spoke to Uzma?"

"Just before her flight last night." Maryam sighs deeply. I can hear worry and concern in her voice but there's another sound, too; my husband breathing down the other line.

"And she was catching a flight to... where, exactly?" I prompt gently, crossing my fingers that Maryam will take the bait, and then, suddenly, when she does, I'm shocked.

"Paris, of course."

Both Jameel and I are taken aback. I can hear him sucking in his breath. According to the explanation in our daughter's letter, she has gone to Germany, not France.

"Paris?" I repeat, "Are you absolutely sure?"

"Yes, Aunty," the girl sobs, finally allowing her emotions to take over. "But I don't know whereabouts, I promise you. Uzma said she would call me when she's settled."

"Okay, thank you." I pause, thinking quickly before we end the call. "Maryam, did Uzma borrow money from you before she left? I'm just wondering if she has enough cash."

The question seems to startle Maryam for a moment and she's silent, so I repeat her name and wait.

"No, not from me," she tells me. "Uzma borrowed five thousand from your bank account, Aunty Farida,

147

but she said she's going to pay back every penny when she starts selling her art."

All hell is about to break loose in my house and I feel suddenly quite queasy. I sit down on the bottom step before my legs give way underneath me, but not before the raging bull comes charging out into the hallway, waving this piece of evidence at me like the triumphant lawyer he is.

"What does that mean?" Jameel sneers. "What account is she talking about, Farida?"

His face is near mine and I can smell the coffee and stale cigarettes on my husband's breath as he presses his fingers into my chin and turns my head towards him, catching my hair in his grip.

"What money do you have? Answer me!"

Despite occasions of mental cruelty throughout my marriage, my husband has never been physically abusive towards me, but I fear that today may be the first time for him to unleash his temper in a physical way.

"I have a little tucked away for a rainy day," I confess, my voice barely above a whisper. "It's really not much, Jameel, just a bit of savings."

"And seeing as how you've never worked a day in your life, it would be fascinating to know just how you've been able to accumulate these... *savings*," he goads, pressing my head against the wall.

"Really, it's just left over from the housekeeping money, just a few pounds here and there."

"How much?" he shouts, scaring me half to death. Cold sweat trickles down my back.

"I want to know exactly how much you've got hidden from me," Jameel presses, spittle on his lips.

"Twenty thousand pounds." I have to tell him, as Jameel will find out eventually and I'm too frightened to lie to him. I can sense that he's shocked by the figure as he stands there in disbelief, a look of sheer incredibility on his face. Now it's out and too late for me to deny anything.

"Twenty... thousand... pounds," he repeats slowly, shaking his head and finally letting go of me. "Get me the card and pin number. *Now!*"

I run upstairs as fast as my legs will carry me, glad for a moment's reprieve but dreading what will happen next. Oh Maryam, sweet child, why did you have to mention the bank account?

Fumbling in my little box, I lay my hand on the plastic card and hold it tightly for a few seconds before returning to my husband. My whole future lies right here in the palm of my hand and everything I'd ever dreamed about is now going to be obliterated before my very eyes.

It suddenly occurs to me that, should I have anywhere to run to, now would be a good time to make my escape. But of course there is nowhere for me to go except downstairs, to where Jameel is waiting.

"You bitch!" Jameel spits as we sit on opposite sides of the coffee table, "All the years I've worked to keep a roof over your lazy head and the way you repay me is by stealing from me."

"I'm sorry," is all I can offer, keeping my head bowed down as he would expect. From past experience, I know that it is sometimes best to keep my part of the conversation to a minimum.

"What were you planning to do with it?" my husband demands, tapping the card on the glass surface. "Are you planning to leave? Is that it?"

"Of course not," I lie, scavenging the corners of my brain for something, anything to tell him. "It was just rainy day money. I thought perhaps we could use it for a family holiday."

"Hah! A family holiday. Do I look like a complete idiot, Farida? Do I?"

I shake my head and reach for a box of tissues, afraid that once I start crying I won't be able to stop. Jameel hasn't taken his eyes off me once since he dragged me in here and I can't tell what he's planning to do. The fear of not knowing is making my hands tremble.

"I'm not happy." A tiny voice escapes from inside me and at first, I'm not entirely sure whether he's heard it, or if the noise was actually mine. But then a light switches on inside Jameel's brain.

"You're not happy," he repeats, following it with mocking laughter. "Well, poor old Farida. Perhaps you would like to return to that stinking hole your parents call a farm in Pakistan, eh? Or would you like me to buy you a world cruise to cheer you up? Would that be enough for my idle, good-for-nothing wife?"

Suddenly, my husband reaches across to the sideboard for something and I hardly dare to look. He opens up the door and pulls out his battered leather Holy Quran, carefully choosing a page. It's almost as though he's planned this moment for a lifetime. All I can do is sit as he reads aloud.

"Four-thirty-four. *Men have authority over women because God has made the one superior to the other, and because they spend their wealth to maintain them. Good women are obedient. They guard their unseen parts because God has guarded them. As for those from whom you fear disobedience, admonish them, forsake them in beds apart, and beat them. Then if they obey you, take no further action against them. Surely God is high, supreme.*"

When Jameel has finished quoting, I know where my fate lies and resign myself to what will follow. There is a smug, almost sadistic look upon his face and in those few seconds that I force myself to look, Jameel is almost unrecognisable as the man I've spent the last twenty years with. I will take my punishment for the sake of our children and because I believe that it will make me a better wife, although how I ended up arriving at this conclusion is beyond any reasonable logic.

The little pink bedside alarm clock says ten-thirty. I must have passed out for ten minutes or so without realising. Slowly, I uncurl myself from the foetal position in which I am lying but every single bone in my body feels like lead. It takes all of my effort to straighten my legs, pain searing through them as they touch the mattress. I'm afraid to look, but I need to know how bad things are... if anything is broken. I can already see bruising beginning to form on my arms where I've tried to defend myself against the blows, but the skin remains unbroken and if I'm lucky, there won't be any scarring.

I manage to slide myself off the bed and crawl on my hands and knees across the landing to the family bathroom, moving as quietly as I possibly can to avoid letting my punisher know that I'm awake. Warm water should help, I keep telling myself. Heat on the bones will bring out the swelling.

As I finally get the door shut, careful to pull across the bolt on the inside, I can hear my husband in the room directly underneath. It sounds as though he's talking to someone on the telephone, although his voice is low, perhaps deliberately so. I lie flat on the cold linoleum, my ear pressed to the floor, desperate for any clue that I can gain from his conversation.

"And she just told you this now?" Jameel is saying. "So who is this man? How did Uzma meet him?"

I stay perfectly still, afraid that the slightest movement may cause the floorboards to creak and give away my position as I eavesdrop. He must be talking to Shazia.

"I can't believe this. Okay, okay," he tells her, after a few seconds of silence. "Listen, I'm picking up Ali and Tariq from the airport at four, so I'll give you a call later. I'll ring your mobile. Don't phone the house unless you really need to, or of course if you hear from Uzma. Bye-bye."

I hear footsteps as Jameel leaves his study. He pauses at the bottom of the stairs before carrying on into the kitchen and only then do I let out a breath. Did I just hear correctly? There is a man involved? Surely not! And why would my husband need to call Shazia on her mobile phone? I wasn't even aware that he had her number. How odd.

I understand why Jameel doesn't want her to call the house. He's worried that I might answer and tell my friend what has just happened. Although in truth, I don't really know whether Shazia would believe me. Everyone thinks that I have the perfect marriage, a supportive partner who provides so well for his family. Who would believe that Jameel Rafiq is nothing but a bully and a bitter, hateful man?

I pull myself up into a sitting position and start running hot water into the bath, depositing lavender foam and Epsom salts into it until the room is filled with a steamy aroma. Only then do I slowly begin to remove my clothes, examining each limb for purple welts and punch marks, finding far more than I could ever imagine. There is not one single bruise on my face, for Jameel has been clever and knew where to avoid so that nobody would ever find out. Perhaps he has played out the scene of violence in his head one too many times, carefully plotting the moment that he would pummel his wife like a pillow.

I will forever hate my husband for what he has done today, but I have nothing in my own life to live for and would gladly take a hundred beatings if only it would bring back my beautiful daughter. I plunge beneath the hot water, closing my eyes and almost forgetting to breathe. It would be so easy just to opt out of living right now, but first I have to be sure that my Uzma is safe and a very important part of that is to make sure that she has a family unit to come back to.

Dressed in an old black sweater and loose trousers, I sit on the edge of our marital bed and wait until I hear my husband's car reversing out of the drive. I have no idea where he could be going at this time on a Saturday morning. I heard him telling Shazia that his brother arrives at four, but there are still many hours before it will be time to head out to the airport. I pray that my son will return home soon. I need him to be here and, with Khalid in the house, my husband might think twice before raising another hand to me.

As soon as I'm sure that Jameel is not coming back, I begin the painful process of making my way downstairs to get a cup of tea. For the first time in my life, I don't feel like eating anything. It's almost a cause for celebration, this sickness inside of me that feels repulsed at the thought of biscuits or cake. Instead, I reach for my usual peppermint tea, wincing as I reach up to take a cup from the cupboard, my arm trembling as another spasm goes searing through me. I have to be brave, I tell myself, as in a few days the bruises will fade, and the incident will be nothing but a memory. Although how I am ever going to truly recover from this mentally is beyond me.

Going through into the lounge, I look around to see if my husband has left his mobile phone behind but, of course, being the smart person that he is, he's taken it with him. I have no idea what to look for, anyway. Something to hold against him in the future, perhaps? Text messages? Call records?

I hug my sides. I think at least two of my ribs are cracked, the pain is so intense. As I sit waiting for my tea to cool, I replay Jameel's last call in my head. Shazia told him that there was a man involved. I say the words over and over, and then a realisation hits me. The man in my daughter's photos from Paris! How could I have been so blind? In every touristy shot that she took, Uzma captured many of her fellow students, but one constant, in every single frame, was that dark, curly-haired art teacher, smiling at the camera... smiling at my daughter.

After finishing my tea, I go back upstairs, taking the steps one at a time which is all my poor legs can manage. I have no idea how soon Jameel will return, but I need to check Uzma's bedroom before he comes back. The effort is exhausting. Never in my life have I found it so painful to move such a short distance, but I need to hurry. There's something I must look for.

Ten minutes later, I've seen all I needed to see. Two photographs pinned to the inside of Uzma's closet speak volumes about her French art tutor. Naturally, Jameel and I have both looked at these pictures before. At first, we only saw a group of happy students and their Parisian instructor. But, on closer inspec-

155

tion, all the tell-tale signs were there, if only we'd been looking.

The man in the centre of the group is much older than the others, his hair unruly and his stature muscular and dark. There's something about the way that he's looking into the camera, and in turn at the photographer, whom I presume to be my daughter, that unnerves me. The students are gathered by the river bank and all are doing the peace sign with their fingers, all except the older man who has both hands pressed together to make a heart-shape, his thumbs barely touching. And it's that one, minute gesture that tells me all I need to know. This man is making a heart for Uzma.

I turn to the second photo and the man has gone from the centre of the group. He's now standing smoking against a wall, watching his students pose for another picture. His hand is extended slightly as he holds the cigarette to his lips and now I can see something red at his wrist, bright in comparison to his white linen shirt. It's a plaited band – a friendship band, I think the youngsters call them – but this one is very specific in its style, having six black beads stitched into the band across the wrist. This matters, you see, as the bracelet is something that I've seen before. It's the very one that Maryam bought for Uzma on her last holiday abroad. Now he, that devil of a tutor, is wearing it.

I take down the photos, half expecting to find some kind of clue written on the back, but my daughter is not stupid. All that's visible is the printer code from where she got them produced. I feel almost triumphant at having discovered something that Jameel has no idea about and I take the pictures downstairs to conceal them while I decide what to do.

The first hiding place that comes to mind is in my box of peppermint tea. Nobody else drinks it and it would be the last place that my husband would ever look, so I lift out the teabags, press the photos into the bottom of the box and then replace the tea on top. By the time I finish this one small task, sweat is pouring from my forehead and the crunch of tyres alerts me to Jameel's return.

"Do we have food for tonight's dinner?" my husband asks, striding into the kitchen as though nothing has happened. "Ali and Tariq will be hungry after their long flight."

"Yes." I nod, and even that small gesture causes me pain. "I'll prepare some chicken. Will six o'clock be alright?"

He grunts, pouring himself a glass of water from the kitchen tap. "Fine."

My skin is prickling at the thought that he might get closer, maybe urged to throw one more punch in my direction, but he just stands there, gulping down the water and staring out into the back garden.

"Do you want something to eat now?" I ask, careful to keep my eyes low.

Jameel shakes his head, pausing for effect before he eventually turns to look at me. "Go and put some decent clothes on, Farida, we're going to the bank."

"What, now?" I can hear the quiver in my own voice.

"Yes, now. We're going to close your account and you're going to pay me back every single penny that you've taken from me."

"But Jameel, please," I try to explain, biting my bottom lip until it bleeds. "Couldn't we wait? I'm not really... I mean, I'm in pain and..."

My husband looks at me in disgust, as though I'm something nasty on the bottom of his shoe. "No, Farida, we're going now. I'll wait for you in the car. Understood?"

I nod my head, twice, three times.

"And don't get any smart ideas," Jameel scoffs, as he heads for the door. "It would be most unfortunate if you were to meet with an accident, wouldn't it, dear?"

I watch him go, afraid that I might actually pee myself and then hurry upstairs to change.

SATURDAY MID-DAY –
SYLVAIN RENO

My mother will have a fit if she sees me hanging around the square today, but I urgently need to speak to Father Francis. I haven't been here long, and I won't be staying, but I suppose curiosity is causing me to look across at the guest house as I make my way to the church. I know that Uzma is inside, but I dare not risk being seen or everything I hold dear will come crashing down.

It was supposed to be fun, our summer liaison and I never imagined that she would actually come here expecting us to have a future together. Pulling my jacket collar up around my face, I take the stone steps two at a time, hoping that my best friend has time to talk.

"Father?" I call, using his title out of respect, just in case there are people inside the church, but on closer inspection I find the pews empty and the building silent.

A door opens and my childhood friend comes out of the vestry, hands tucked in his cassock, head on one side.

"Sylvain, is that you?" he asks, striding towards me with surprise. "What an unexpected pleasure."

We hug, the formalities of priest and parishioner disintegrating, to be replaced by boyhood friendship and mutual trust. I would give my life for this man, so much do I respect him.

"Come, sit down." Francis smiles, sliding onto a hard bench halfway down the aisle. "Are you well?"

I follow, rubbing my hands together to generate warmth, trying not to spurt out my troubles too soon.

"I'm fine," I tell him, "but in truth, I wondered if we could talk?"

My friend's expression doesn't change. He's still smiling, pockets of skin crinkling at the corners of his eyes, but he pulls his hands into view now and presses the fingertips together.

"I'm always here for you, Sylvain," he says. "What's troubling you?"

I spill out everything in a tumble of words –the affair with Uzma, the conversation with my mother and the fact that the girl is now here – hardly pausing for breath as I let out my woes.

"Do you love her?" my best friend asks, raising his eyebrows slightly.

"No, no I don't," I confess, careful to look Francis in the eye so that he can see the truth in my face.

"Did you give her any reason to think that you love her?" he presses, wise to my game.

I shrug. "Perhaps. You know how it is. Sometimes I say things in the heat of the moment. But I honestly didn't think I'd given her any encouragement to come back here."

Francis gets up and paces a few steps down the aisle. He's now every inch the holy man and is weighing up what to advise me to do. No matter what his words are to be, I'll pay heed to them.

"Does Sophia know?"

He drops the words like a bomb, out of thin air, but I should have known the question was coming. As I shake my head, I know that I look ashamed, but Francis is still watching me steadily. He hasn't judged me yet, but there's something brewing under the surface.

"No, thankfully she has no idea." I confess, trying not to think about my beautiful wife or the hurt which this whole situation could bring.

"Why, Sylvain?" Francis pushes, turning to walk back towards me. "You have the most perfect wife a man could wish for and you continue to play around with these... *immature students.*"

He spits the last words at me as though they taste vile on his tongue, and for a second I wonder whether I've made a mistake by coming here. But then Father Francis drops his shoulders and places a hand on my arm.

"Sylvain," he says, squeezing tightly, "You are like a brother to me, but I'm still a man of God and in His eyes, you have committed a sin. I want to understand you, really I do, but I cannot condone your actions."

"I know," I manage to say, amidst my embarrassment and regret. "I promise this will be the last time. I couldn't bear the thought of losing Sophia. I'll change. I've learned my lesson, really I have."

Francis doesn't look convinced, and I worry that he might be re-evaluating our friendship, until finally he sighs and nods.

"It's self-destruction, Sylvain," he tells me, keeping his voice low as if worried about eavesdroppers, "You have a baby on the way now. It's time to be a man and take care of your family."

"Sophia told you?" I smile. "Wow! We've only known for a couple of weeks."

"I'm her priest," Francis reminds me, "and also your closest friend. Of course she would share the wonderful news. Now, what are you planning to do about this... unfortunate dilemma?"

I bite the skin around my thumb and close my eyes for a second, thinking hard. "My mother seems to think I should lie low and hope that the girl leaves," I tell him.

"Well, that's a reasonable supposition," my friend agrees. "It will probably depend upon how much money she has. Paris can be an expensive city for one so young."

"In the meantime, I should stay away." I shrug. "Will you come over for dinner tonight, Francis?"

"I think I should stay close to your mother," he replies, after a slight pause, "in case she needs me. Would you like to use the confessional box before you leave, Sylvain?"

"Of course. Lead the way, Father Francis, I am ready to repent."

My old friend insists that I leave by the vestry door which opens out onto a small side street. I'll need to walk in a wide loop to get home without being seen from my mother's guest house, but I don't have any classes waiting for me today, just a half-finished canvas that is awaiting inspiration.

I hurry home, smoking a cigarette and thinking about my future. Francis is right, as he undoubtedly always is, much to my annoyance. I owe it to Sophia and our unborn child to turn my life around.

As I open the apartment door, a bottle of red wine in one hand and flowers in the other, I can hear my wife softly humming in our tiny guest bedroom. The smell of paint, emulsion if I'm correct, wafts into the hallway and alerts me to her activity. She's painting the walls for our baby's room.

"Hey." I smile, poking the flowers around the open doorway but hiding my face. "Ooh, yellow!"

"Buttercup yellow, to be precise," Sophia replies, waving the wet brush at me teasingly. "Like it?"

"Love it," I lie, wishing that she hadn't chosen my least favourite colour. "How about I paint a mural on one wall? Maybe some trees and some wild animals?"

My wife turns and gives me the half-smile that she has perfected so well as she pretends to consider my proposal. "Rabbits and foxes?"

"Why not?" I grin. "I can't think of a better way to spend the weekend."

A short time later, eating salad and a crusty baguette, I watch Sophia across the table as she sips her mineral water. I take a good glug of wine and reach for her hand.

"This baby is going to be the best thing that ever happened to us," I tell her, tickling her palm with my forefinger. "I can feel it."

"I know," she returns, unaware of what a cad she has married and, in that split second, I feel so nauseous that I could throw up right here. I don't deserve Sophia's love, but I'm going to start afresh from today. My confession to Father Francis has me feeling as though I can turn things around, wipe the slate clean, look after my family.

"Is there something wrong?" her soft voice asks. "You seem different somehow."

I shake my head and touch her lustrous auburn hair. It reminds me of the soft walnut veneer in the priest's vestry, the sheen almost mirror-like in its gloss.

"Everything is perfect, Sophia," I say, praying that it will be as soon as the Asian girl has gone home. "Now, shall we make a start on that mural?"

My wife kisses me, a long and lingering sensation that arouses me instantly. "Mmm, it can wait."

SATURDAY 2PM – UZMA RAFIQ

I'm getting frustrated sitting up here in my room. All the television channels seem to be in French, except for one showing old black and white films, and the battery on my phone is now completely dead. It scares me to think that most of my money is inside the suitcase, together with all my clothes and my laptop, and I still haven't done anything about trying to locate it.

I've been waiting for my only set of underwear to dry on the radiator, having washed them in the sink with some lavender soap, but I can't keep doing this every day. I feel grubby already, having to wear the same clothes as yesterday.

Swinging my legs off the bed, I get dressed, lace up my Converse trainers and make up my mind to stop being a fucking wimp about everything. Madame Joubert might be able to help me and I should have asked earlier instead of sitting up here brooding like a spoilt brat.

At least, not having my phone charged has saved me from the thousands of messages that I know my father will have left there. I dread to think what's been going on at home, but it also makes me feel really helpless not having any outside communication. It would be good to speak to Maryam at least and see if she's heard anything. I bet my dad's been giving her a right roasting.

I check myself in the bathroom mirror and curse that I didn't put a few make-up items in my handbag. I look awful. God, I don't want Sylvain to see me like this. I'll have to buy a few things this afternoon. I pull my comb through my tangled locks but there are too many stray hairs sticking out at all angles for my hair to look tamed. At the last moment, I grab the beanie hat that I bought for Sylvain, pull off the tag and put it on my head. Without my straighteners, my hair feels really messy and a few tendrils hanging down either side of my face looks quite edgy.

As I get to the bottom of the stairs, I notice how quiet the guest house is. No music or talking anywhere. It's almost as though the rest of the world has gone to sleep. Maybe the French are like the Spanish in their habits and take an early afternoon siesta. Tentatively, I ring the brass bell on the desk, which 'pings' loudly, echoing up to the high ceiling, an intrusive noise that embarrasses me.

I hear a rustling sound in a back room and then Madame Joubert appears through a side door. She's dressed in black and looking effortlessly chic, with just a pearl bracelet and expensive watch accessorising her outfit. I wonder whether French girls have lessons in how to look this good, or does it just come naturally?

"*Oui*?" she says, smiling at me but instinctively speaking in French. "Can I help you, Miss Rafiq?"

"I was wondering if you could do something for me, please?" I start, realising that I probably sound as though I'm rambling. "It seems I picked up the wrong suitcase at the airport last night."

The Frenchwoman frowns, placing a manicured finger on her pink lips. "Oh dear. And so, you would like me to telephone the airport for you?"

"Yes please." I nod. "My suitcase has everything inside."

I could kick myself for saying that, it sounded so dumb; of course my case would have everything in it!

"Perhaps you could describe it?" Madame Joubert asks, her pen already poised over the notepad.

"Well, it's just black," I tell her, unable to think of any distinguishing features. "With a *Globe* logo on it. It did have a pink tag, but it fell off..."

I watch her write down the colour and the name, underlining them twice.

"Let me see what they can do." She smiles at me, then punches some numbers into the phone while I wait nervously. I don't know why, but the guest house owner makes me feel quite inadequate.

I wait, unable to understand the conversation fully but alerted to the fact that the landlady is getting increasingly annoyed as she speaks to the clerk.

"*Lundi, à quelle heure?*" she finally says, writing down a number. "*Merci. Au revoir.*"

Turning back to me, she says, "It seems that the lost luggage office is closed until Monday." Madame Joubert sighs sympathetically. "They open at nine. I'm so sorry, but nothing can be done until then."

Feeling the tears well up inside, I take a deep breath and bite my lip. Can nothing go right for me? I think the French lady feels sorry for me, as she comes around from behind the desk and opens the door to the communal lounge, inviting me to sit down.

"Please, come and join me for a coffee," she says and, not knowing what else to do, I follow.

"So," Madame Joubert begins, setting down two cups and a cafetière of hot coffee on the table, "what brings you to Paris, Miss Rafiq?"

Her English is perfect, with just the slightest accent, enough to confirm that she is a native of France.

"Please, call me Uzma," I say, feeling strangely uncomfortable in the woman's presence, but unable to carry my burden any longer. "I've come here to be with my French boyfriend."

The older woman doesn't look surprised at all. Fixing me with her twinkling blue eyes, she says softly. "And this man of yours, where does he live? Perhaps we can call him?"

"He was in the middle of moving to a new apartment," I admit, my voice trailing off as I realise how pathetic this sounds. "We usually Skype, you see, but now my laptop is in my missing suitcase."

"Skype," she repeats. "How very modern. Gone are the romantic days of letter-writing, *oui*?"

I'm not sure why but it almost feels as though Madame Joubert is mocking me. Perhaps I'm just being over-sensitive due to my circumstances. I watch her closely as she pours the drinks.

"Tell me, Uzma, how long have you and your Frenchman been together, if you don't mind me asking."

"Since July," I say, without hesitation. "We met through the art scene here in Paris."

As the woman lifts the delicate china cup to her lips, I see a slight tremble in her fingers which emboldens me to say more. "Perhaps you remember him, Madame Joubert? You see, we stayed here in the summer for a few nights. His name is Sylvain."

I think my words have caught her off guard and some of the coffee spills over into the saucer. She puts her cup back down, avoiding my gaze.

"No, I don't think so," she says confidently. "Although I have so many guests here in the summer, it's impossible to remember them all, especially at my age."

She offers me a ginger biscuit, taking one herself, but I decline.

"He's very tall and handsome," I continue, determined to find out if she might recognise Sylvain, "with thick curly hair and quite tanned skin."

Having quickly recovered her composure, she nibbles at the ginger snap and shakes her head. "No, my dear, I'm fairly certain that I don't know your gentleman friend."

As we finish our coffee, I sit waiting for Madame Joubert to say something. She's been deep in thought for a few minutes now, but I have no idea what's occupying her mind.

I cough politely. "I was wondering..." I begin, shy once more, "would it be alright if I stay an extra couple of nights?"

It would be hard to miss the steely glare with which the Frenchwoman appraises me as I speak and, at that moment, I wished that I could scoop the words back up into my mouth.

"Mmm, well, how long were you thinking?" she asks, tapping her long nails on the empty cup. "I have a lot of guests arriving on Monday. Would just two more nights suit you, Uzma?"

"Great. I mean, yes, thank you," I tell her. "Although, can I pay you when I get my suitcase back? Most of my cash is in there and I think I'll have to buy a few clothes to see me through the weekend."

I feel my face flushing. What an embarrassing situation to be in! If only I hadn't followed my dad's advice about putting your travel money in different places.

"I should think so," Madame Joubert says softly. "How do you plan to spend the rest of your weekend, my dear? I can recommend an affordable shopping centre not far from here."

"I'm going to find Sylvain," I tell her. The words tumble out and I am confident that everything will turn out fine, despite the nagging doubts that are tugging at my conscience.

My host stiffens, pushing herself back into the seat of the chair. "And where do you think would be a good place to look? Paris is a vast city."

"He teaches here in Montmartre, at the art school," I offer, proud that at least I shall have somewhere to look for my beloved Sylvain on Monday. "He should have classes next week."

"Really?" the woman says, putting a hand to her forehead as though she were in pain. "Well, that's good, isn't it? I'm sorry, my dear, but I feel an awful headache coming on. I fear I must lie down."

"Of course. I hope you feel better soon," I say sympathetically, getting up to leave.

Ushered out into the hallway, I thank my host for her kindness and ask if there's anything I can get her to help with her discomfort, but she assures me that a rest will do the trick.

"An hour on my bed should work wonders," Madame Joubert mutters, holding her head and leaning on the heavy oak reception desk. "I'm probably just a little tired."

As I begin my ascent, the French woman calls to me again, something obviously bothering her. "Uzma dear, do you still have the suitcase that you picked up accidentally?"

"Yes, I didn't realise that it wasn't mine until I got all the way here," I admit.

"But you haven't tried to open it?" she asks mischievously, looking all of a sudden much better.

"No, of course not."

"Well, enjoy your day and I hope you find your young man."

Nodding politely, I thank her again and make my way upstairs to fetch my denim jacket. I might as well go for a walk and see if I can find Sylvain in one of the bars or cafés around Montmartre. I feel confident that I can find some of the places he took me to and it seems the obvious place for him to hang out at the weekend.

As I enter the bedroom, the first thing that catches my eye is the black suitcase. It's still locked, untouched, but now Madame Joubert has planted an idea in my head and, in desperation, I make a mental note to buy a pair of pliers. I'm going to open it later.

Then the strangest thing happens. As I tread softly on the thick carpet, locking my door and starting to go back downstairs, I hear someone. Instead of retiring to her room, I distinctly hear Madame Joubert pick up the telephone in the hallway and speak abruptly to someone in French. I stand deathly still, afraid to move in case she catches me listening in.

"*Un problème*," she says clearly and, by those words, I take it that between us drinking coffee and me fetching my jacket, something must have happened.

SATURDAY 4PM – ALI RAFIQ

As soon as he catches my eye across the crowded arrivals hall, my brother rushes to greet us, hugging me tightly and offering to carry our bags. It's great to see Jameel again, it's been far too long, although I sense that he's stressed due to circumstances beyond his control. Perhaps my news will set his mind at rest. But more about that later. We've got all weekend to go over the details.

"You're doing well for yourself, brother," I comment, as he unlocks the Lexus and gets behind the steering wheel. "Nice motor, very classy."

Jameel shrugs, but I can see that he's proud. Life in London suits him and even in his casual weekend clothes, my little brother looks polished and affluent.

"How was your flight?" he asks casually, glancing in the rear-view mirror at my son Tariq. "Did you manage to get some sleep?"

"No, Uncle." My boy smiles. "There were too many great movies to watch."

Jameel nods, concentrating on the road ahead, his fingers gripping the wheel like his life depended on it as he manoeuvres out of the car park and onto the open highway.

"How's Farida?" I venture, thinking of my brother's wife fondly, her excellent cooking skills and shapely figure. "Is she coping alright?"

"*Coping*?" Jameel repeats. "Why? What have you heard?"

I realise then that I need to keep my big mouth shut until we get to the house. I have a lot of explaining to do, which is not advisable whilst my brother is trying to negotiate the motorway traffic.

"You know, with the upheaval of having guests," I quickly say, shooting Tariq a warning glance to say nothing about the events of the last few days. "She must have been quite busy."

Jameel keeps his eyes fixed on the road. "Farida is fine. She'll be preparing a good meal for you."

My stomach rumbles at the thought of my sister-in-law's chicken tikka and her amazing tandoori roti bread. What a talent she has for making a man's mouth water at the very thought of her cooking.

"Excellent!" I say with a grin, eager to avoid all mention of my brother's daughter until we arrive. "So, tell me, how's business in the city these days? Plenty of new cases to get your teeth into?"

Jameel forces a smile and visibly relaxes at the mention of work. "Ali, you wouldn't believe the workload right now. We're getting half a dozen new clients every single week."

I listen intently as my brother begins to tell me about a particularly interesting legal dispute between two neighbours, but I'm feeling concerned at how the next twenty-four hours are going to pan out.

As soon as we pull up outside the house, Khalid rushes out to greet us whilst Farida lingers in the doorway. I can see that my nephew has grown since our last visit and now towers above his mother. Farida, though... well, she's certainly gained a few pounds.

"Uncle Ali! Tariq!" Khalid shouts, opening the car door and hugging me. "Great to see you."

I notice that Jameel takes his time coming around to our side of the drive and a furtive look passes between him and his wife. It's not worry, more like a warning.

"So, you're finally home," Jameel says to Khalid, putting a hand on his shoulder as he helps with the luggage. "About time, too."

"Sorry, Dad." The youngster grins. "If I'd known about Uzma, I would have –"

"Enough about that for now." Jameel hushes him discreetly, but still within earshot. "Let's get inside."

We sit politely drinking tea and I steel myself for the conversation that needs to take place. My brother and sister-in-law are under the impression that they need to confide in me about the whereabouts of their daughter but, for me, it's old news.

"Ali, there's something you need to know," Jameel begins, setting his cup on the table and clasping his hands. "Uzma isn't here. She left last night and –"

"I know," I interrupt, not wanting to drag this out any longer than I have to. "I'm aware of her leaving."

"Dad," Khalid whispers, "I didn't really think she'd go."

Jameel turns on his son, unable to believe that there's been some kind of conspiracy behind his back. His face starts to turn red and I hold up a hand and put the other on my nephew's arm as he sits down quietly beside me.

"Jameel, let me explain," I say, desperately trying to stop my brother from exploding. "Khalid overheard Uzma talking about her plans on the phone to Maryam and he told Tariq. You know how young men confide in each other. It was only after Tariq mentioned the marriage proposal to Khalid that things changed, and I became involved."

"Involved?" Jameel repeats, staring at me in that confused way of his that makes him look like a schoolboy. "What do you mean, *involved*?"

I glance over at Farida and see her watching me intently, waiting for the information to fall from my lips. "Perhaps we should talk about this in private."

Jameel nods and rises from his leather armchair, ignoring his wife completely, and leads me to his study in silence. I take a deep breath and wait for the fireworks to start.

"Jameel, it's a matter of family honour," I say, emphasising my role as head of the family and eldest

Rafiq son. "I knew you'd blow up over this, so I made arrangements."

Jameel sits facing me across a huge oak desk, raising his eyebrows and waiting for me to go on.

"I contacted someone I know here in London and purchased a tracking device to hide in Uzma's case."

"But you've been in Pakistan until today..." My brother frowns. "How could you..."

"Khalid," I explain. "All he had to do was pick it up and push it into the lining of your daughter's luggage. Very simple, but effective."

My brother rubs his face, taking in my words. "But why go to all that trouble? Why didn't you just tell me what was going on, and then I could have –"

"What? Lock Uzma in the house? Make a fool of yourself? Ruin your good reputation?"

Jameel looks at me but says nothing, I'm unsure how to gauge his reaction.

"Look Jameel," I say soothingly, "this way, we find out who she's meeting, and where, and then we do something about it."

"Do what?" he enquires, a touch of sarcasm and disbelief in his voice, "What are you planning?"

I'd sincerely hoped that we wouldn't come to this yet, but it's pointless trying to divert my brother away from the natural conclusion. I sit back, but my shoulders remain tense.

"I've contacted someone in Paris. They, erm, make people disappear."

"*Disappear*?" Jameel mouths the last word, not fully understanding the implications of where this is heading. "You're planning to make my daughter..."

"No, no, no!" I hold up my hands in a peaceful gesture. "For goodness' sake, Jameel, of course not! But they'll take care of this man, the one she's gone to be with."

It takes a few moments for my explanation to sink in and, while my brother thinks, I use the time to take another, much needed, deep breath.

"How much?" he suddenly asks, looking right through me. "What is it going to cost?"

"Twenty thousand pounds," I reply without hesitation. "I have to transfer the funds tonight."

"Ali, I don't know why you think I will go along with this. I'm a solicitor, for goodness' sake."

"It's about Uzma's honour, and the family honour, Jameel," I say softly, taking my brother's hand. "No Muslim will marry your daughter if they find out she's not a virgin. Have some pride, man."

I can see Jameel taking it all in, soaking up the facts and realising that this is the only way forward.

We spend another hour sitting in my little brother's study, churning over other possibilities but always returning to the same scenario. There's no alternative in my mind; this man, the Parisian, has defiled my niece and he needs to pay. I thank Allah that Khalid was so astute in keeping an eye on his sister, and that Tariq had the good sense to confide in me.

Eventually, we come to the same conclusion, Jameel and I. Blood is thicker than water after all.

"I want to pay," Jameel tells me sternly, before we get up to leave.

"Really it doesn't matter," I lie, secretly hoping that my brother can afford to reimburse me for my trouble. "What's twenty grand between brothers?"

"I insist," he replies, taking my hand and squeezing tightly. "I have the money."

"If you're sure," I falter, trying my best to hide my relief. "Can you access that kind of money today?"

"Let's just say my dear wife has been saving a little extra lately," Jameel explains, although he doesn't offer any further clarification and I'm left feeling that there's more to this than meets the eye.

As we step out into the hall, I immediately catch the scent of Farida's cooking and instinctively turn towards the spicy aroma, but Jameel catches my arm.

"The tracker," he whispers. "Is it active now?"

I nod, pointing towards the sitting room. "There's an app on Khalid's phone."

Jameel heads off to speak to his son, leaving me in search of a snack. I hope my sister-in-law is making a substantial amount of food and I feel the saliva on my lips as I push open the kitchen door.

"It won't be too long now, Ali," Farida tells me, keeping her head low and her eyes fixed on the pot that she's stirring. "Maybe twenty minutes."

"Smells great," I tell her, grabbing a spoon and cheekily sampling the curry. "And you, Farida, are you okay? This business with Uzma must be such a worry."

She doesn't look up but continues focussing on the food as if in a trance, so I say her name again. When she does eventually tilt her head upwards, there's something searching in her eyes, as though she wants to confide in me.

"I'm coping as best as I can," my sister-in-law confesses after a pause, "But it's hard, very hard."

I wait to see if she has more to say, but already Farida has turned back to the task at hand, so I deposit the spoon in the sink and compliment her on the food but I'm unable to miss the bruises on her bare arm. They look fresh and painful, but none of my business, regardless of the circumstances.

"Is Farida taking this badly?" I ask Jameel, concerned about the strain that their marriage may be under. "I mean, she seems very quiet."

"My wife knows her place when we men are talking, that's all," he states abruptly, glancing over at Khalid and Tariq who are comparing phones side by side on the sofa.

I don't comment, but instead take the other armchair and take a long look at my brother. His temples are greying and he hasn't shaved today, but otherwise he's still the better looking of us two. Jameel has always possessed a superior air, speaking English with only a slight Pakistani accent which comes and goes, depending upon who he's conversing with. We were both educated in London, but Jameel has a more Westernised manner. I can see that more than ever today as, despite the obvious pain of Uzma leaving, he's still managing to maintain his composure. I guess the British would call it a stiff upper lip.

"Dinner is ready," Farida says meekly from the doorway, looking only at Jameel.

I notice that he doesn't reply, just gets up and holds the door open for the three of us to go through to the dining room where the table is laden with a hearty meal.

"Mmm, looking forward to this, Aunty," Tariq tells Farida. "It smells fantastic!"

We sit, waiting politely with heads bowed as Jameel gives thanks to Allah, and then start eating.

Looking over at Farida, I see that she's pulled the sleeves of her tunic back down over her arms and I'm now unable to see any of the purple skin that was so obviously there a while ago. The frosty atmosphere between Jameel and his wife is unmistakeable, but I can't figure out whether it's due to the stress of their daughter's disappearance or something entirely different.

"Roti bread?" Khalid asks, offering me a basket. "Mum makes the best."

I hesitate, looking at my sister-in-law before tearing off a piece of the deliciously warm dough. As I bite into it, I compliment her. "She certainly does. Farida, this is excellent."

Jameel coughs, keeping his eyes fixed on me as we eat, as if desperate for a change in topic.

"How is college?" I turn to Khalid, making polite chit-chat. "Are you doing well in your studies?"

"I'm top of my class in every subject, Uncle." He grins proudly, boasting and explaining which subjects he intends to take at University.

I allow my nephew to fill my head with his aspirations and dreams, but never lose sight of the fact that my brother and his wife haven't spoken more than three words to each other since I arrived.

SATURDAY 6PM – COLIN FOSTER

Well, hardly the most challenging situation I've ever found myself in but somehow, the deliberation of which tie to wear to the theatre has consumed ten minutes of my time. Thankfully, there are still another twenty before I need to present myself in the hallway to escort Madame Joubert to the theatre. I must say, I cut quite a dashing figure in these new clothes, even if I do say so myself. One feels as though the battlefield is waiting, to be honest. It's impossible to predict whether the outcome will be conquest or victory. Frankly speaking , I'll just be glad to end the evening without egg on my face, so to speak, and a bellyful of a decent vintage.

It's in one's nature to be punctual. I really can't recall an instance when one was late for a rendezvous. Habit, I suppose. When one is employed in my particular profession, promptness is essential to the delivery of one's quarry. And here we come again to my purpose in this rather ancient but delightful city. I am here to commit a murder.

Should one happen upon the definition of my work in the Oxford volumes, the words 'assassin', 'hitman', 'eliminator', 'slayer', 'executioner' and 'hatchet man' would no doubt suffice to describe my involvement. However, I prefer the subtle moniker of 'cleaner.' I tidy away other people's problems, human mostly, and get paid a decent fee. I don't take trophies from the bodies, as some of the more unrefined mobsters might do but, I remember the faces, every single one.

The first was the most challenging, back in the days when I still worked in the 'Gentleman's Club'. Several members of the elite had taken it upon themselves to place bets upon me carrying out certain tasks, as I dwelled on earlier; stealing, pickpocketing, any frivolity that elicited raucous laughter from the members and risk to oneself.

On this particular day, a Russian had been invited to dine with a business associate and later, oiled with a tank full of vodka, the men had got into a dispute over whom should pay the very hefty tab. Naturally, it was part of one's duty to intervene but during the skirmish, the aforementioned 'Hooray Henrys' had gathered together a substantial wager and now dragged me to one side to communicate their intent. All one had to do was make a show of escorting the Russian off the premises, follow him several streets away, and then shoot him. I don't mean with a shotgun in broad daylight or anything so dramatic, just bustle the chap down a side alley and use the pistol issued by one of the club members.

Now, when I say that the wager was large, I mean it was enough to change a young man's fortune quite considerably. Honestly, I suppose it took me seconds to agree to the undertaking and once that mission was accomplished, a quick shot to the back of the head with the silencer fitted tightly, one was hooked. Of course, there were questions but, fair play to my backers, every single one of the gents in the club stood by my alibi that I'd been indisposed and was being tended to by one of our senior members at the time of the unfortunate incident.

And so, is that why I am here in Paris? Of course. Twenty thousand pounds for this 'job' will make it my very last. No more reliance upon the 'bureau' to issue me with targets, no more dirty hands. I don't yet know who my prey will be, but that's all part of the fun. One will find out all in good time.

As I straighten my shirt collar and tighten the bright blue silk tie that I've selected, I wonder for a moment what Collette would make of my purpose here, God forbid that she should ever find out. I've stayed here many times over the years, even having instructions for my peers at 'the bureau' sent here, but I was always careful not to leave a hint or a trace of what I'm up to for the dear guest house owner to find.

Once, after a slightly unfortunate incident which caused blood to splatter upon my shirt cuffs, Madame Joubert kindly took the item away to starch and iron, having noticed that I'd hung it up in the bathroom after washing it. Ever since, I've been doubly careful about leaving my room pristine after exiting, as the smallest of slips may give rise to embarrassing questions.

Time to collect my beauty and there she is at reception, looking splendid in a pale blue gown. Collette is talking to the Asian girl again and I can't help but overhear as I make footfall on the bottom step.

"Oh, I don't think this one will fit my phone," the young woman is saying, looking closely at some kind of cable. "Never mind, I'll have to buy one."

I cough once to announce my presence and both ladies look up.

"Ah, Monsieur Foster." Collette smiles, appraising the cut of my attire. "I won't be a moment."

"Madame Joubert," I respond formally, noting the presence of another. "Anything I may be of assistance with?"

The Asian woman shrugs. "Not unless you've got a phone charger I can borrow," she says sullenly, looking almost as if this were her last-ditch attempt at making contact with the outside world.

"Let me see," I mumble, taking my spectacles out to take a closer look at the mobile phone lying on the top of the polished hardwood. "Yes! It appears to be the same make and model as my own."

For a second, I'm overwhelmed by the thought that the young woman might just throw her arms around my neck and hug me. Her eyes light up as though she's just been blessed with a windfall.

"I'll fetch it for you," I say, slightly peeved that our schedule has now overrun by several minutes and a private taxi has just pulled up outside to collect myself and Collette.

The young woman does a strange, childish little dance, clapping her hands together quickly at the palms and hopping on the spot. I retreat back upstairs and return with the electrical connector, together with an adapter. I notice Collette watching me with silent admiration.

"You have saved the day!" she grins, taking my arm and lifting up a soft woollen pashmina.

"Indeed, thank you so much, Mister..." the Asian girl begins.

"No problem at all," I cut her off. After all, nobody needs to know one on an intimate level.

L'Opera Bastille is sold out and I calculate that Collette must have bought these tickets some time ago. One can't help but speculate as to whether the good lady anticipated my arrival, or whether she had originally intended to invite some other admirer to accompany her to the show. Regardless of the intent, one feels honoured to be arriving alongside such an elegant and well-groomed Parisian lady and we take our seats with relish. All around us, couples are dressed up to the nines, smiling, awaiting some sign that the curtain is about to go up, revealing sights and sounds to entice and entertain.

As the orchestra starts up, with a good deal of relish and pomp, I open up the glossy programme to *Act One* and peruse the order of arias, only just managing to memorise them before the lights go out and the heavy velvet drapes part. Glancing to my left side, I appreciate Madame Joubert's profile for a second or two, her neatly chignoned hair, pale white neck and small delicate ears adorned with tiny pearl studs. This woman is so perfect that my mind wanders away from *The Merry Widow* and begins tricking me again, allowing me to believe that perhaps, in some fortunate circumstance, we could have a future.

"Is everything alright, Colin?" she whispers, placing a slim hand upon my jacket sleeve, perhaps having noticed my lack of concentration on the musical extravaganza before us.

"Yes, my dear, perfect," I tell her, also keeping my voice low. "I'm enjoying tonight very much."

For a moment, Collette leaves her fingers resting upon my arm, but then, as the actors take up their roles, she moves them, grasping her fingers together and pursing her lips in delight.

One wonders about the etiquette of telling a prospective spouse one's secrets. I could hardly blurt out the inner workings of a profession such as mine over the breakfast table, A scenario of impropriety and torture, don't you think?

"I say, dear, would you pass me the butter? And by the way, I get paid to do away with people."

No, that would hardly do. One supposes that the most tactful way to deal with such cases is to say absolutely nothing, which in itself is all very well, unless one happens to talk in one's sleep or is a complete flounderer when it comes to covering up one's past. Many a gangster's downfall has come to fruition after excess pillow talk, and not only in the movies, therefore silence on the matter may be the only possible way out.

It has, on occasion, occurred to me that Collette Joubert may be harbouring indiscretions of her own. Naturally, one has the means to research her history, but it's the not knowing that makes her so undeniably attractive. I know that she wears a wedding ring in memory of her late husband, but I most certainly am unaware of any paramours here in Paris. Is she playing a game with me, waiting for me to show my cards so she can then produce an ace from up her sleeve? Honestly, I am sceptical at best.

I have taken the liberty of booking a delightful restaurant for after the show. Just two minutes' walk from the theatre and serving the most spectacular cuisine in the area, *Hubert's* is an absolute gem. Naturally, one requested a table in a quieter part of the dining room, as no doubt Collette and I will seek each other's opinion on *The Merry Widow's* cast and performance. I feel doubtful at this stage whether my bravery will come to the fore and steer things towards a more personal level. Perhaps Monday's 'business' should be concluded before I seek to complicate my stay in Paris.

At the interlude, I scurry to the bar to order two glasses of wine whilst my beautiful companion goes to 'powder her nose.' I must say that there is no amount of powdering or puffing that could improve upon Madame Joubert this evening. One would be vain to suppose that her efforts are directed towards *moi*, although one has done one's very best to present a smart and affable appearance.

She returns, taking the glass that I offer and smiles at me in that coy way that she has. "Are you enjoying the show so far?" she asks politely, raising a perfectly plucked eyebrow.

"It's superb," I tell her, feeling my cheeks flush warm as I relish her undivided attention upon me.

"Indeed, this is one of my favourite operettas," she tells me, pausing to sip at the wine. "Colin, may I ask you something?"

"Of course. What is it?"

"What brings you to Paris this time? I mean, on a weekend?" she enquires, looking me in the eye.

"Erm, well, I just fancied a few days enjoying my time here before my meeting on Monday."

I'm caught off guard and know that the words exiting my mouth are both clumsy and transparent.

"Ah, your meeting," she grins, toying with me. "What line of business are you in again?"

This is so unlike Collette. We have an unspoken agreement about boundaries and she just stepped into the danger zone. I cough and gulp my drink, thinking fast.

"Quite boring, really," I lie, desperately trying to keep my features neutral. "It wouldn't interest you."

"*Au contraire*, I think it would interest me greatly, my dear Colin."

I was saved by the bell, so to speak, as an announcement requests that we take our seats once more and I usher Collette towards the door to the stalls. Something has changed in her demeanour, a kind of smugness radiates from her as though she's caught me red-handed, but I try to shrug off this most irrational of thoughts. How on earth could this woman have any inkling of my choice of career?

SATURDAY 8PM –
MARYAM

I'm so tired as I've had virtually no sleep since my last shift at the hospital. In truth, I'm worried sick about Uzma. She hasn't answered any of my text messages and if I call, it just goes straight to voicemail. Now, on top of everything, Aunt Farida made me feel so guilty that I've said too much.

Uzma is going to kill me when she finds out. Mum said I've done the right thing, but I feel like I've betrayed my best friend's trust. I don't know what they're planning to do but, if it were my parents, I think they'd be on the next plane to Paris.

There's something else bugging me, too. Khalid has been very quiet. Usually, when there's something going on, he's texting me or putting stupid stuff on Facebook. Today, there's nothing and I know his sister's missing but I feel like the sneaky little shit knows something. It's not like Uzma would confide in him, but maybe she left an address or something in her room and he found it. I'm just guessing, though. It's all I can do at the moment until my friend gets in contact.

Uzma has been gone twenty-four hours now. I'm presuming that she's with Sylvain and, if she is, it's pretty thoughtless of her not to let anyone know she's alright. On the other hand, if something has happened to her, how would we know? All this worry is giving me a headache. I can't think of any other way to contact Uzma without it involving technology. She didn't tell me where this artist lives, and there could be hundreds of Frenchmen with the same first name in Paris. It's so frustrating.

There's a knock on my bedroom door and Mum comes in. She looks tired, too.

"Sweetheart," she says, coming to sit next to me on the bed, "do you want something to eat?"

"I'm not hungry, Mum, honestly," I assure her. "I'm just so worried about Uzma."

Mum touches my hair gently with the palm of her hand, a sweet gesture that only she can do. "You have to eat. I know you're worried, we all are, but I don't know what we can do."

"He's a French artist, the man that Uzma's with," I confide, but then I bite my lip, wondering if my mother is going to dash downstairs and phone Aunt Farida.

"And do you know where he lives? Or how they met?"

I look down and take a deep breath, I can't lie to my mum but it's been a whole day without contact and poor Uzma might be in deep trouble. All kinds of things are going through my mind right now.

"He was the tutor at the college where she went to art classes last summer," I whisper. "Please, Mum, can we just wait a little bit longer before telling her parents?"

Mum lifts my chin and looks earnestly into my eyes. "No, darling, we can't. The whole situation is wrong, she's been very foolish. I will have to talk to her parents and give them this information."

I sit at the top of the stairs while Mum phones Uzma's parents. I'm not checking on her, Mum wants me here in case there are any questions she can't answer but now I'm beginning to feel like a traitor.

"Jameel," my mother says, her voice deadly serious, "I've talked to Maryam and she thinks she might have a couple of clues that are important."

There's silence while the response comes, and I start to bite my nails.

Mum tells Uzma's dad the name and place while I sit and watch. All the time, she keeps her eyes fixed on mine and I can see her blushing slightly.

"I'm fine, really, Jameel," she finishes, before putting down the phone. "We'll talk soon. 'Bye."

"That was quick," I comment, pulling myself up and coming downstairs. "Didn't he ask anything?"

Mum looks flustered and checks her reflection in the hall mirror before answering me.

"No, he said to thank you and he'll deal with it. Ali and Tariq have come over from Pakistan, so as you can imagine it's chaos over there. Jameel said they'll make some calls to the art school."

I'm a bit confused as to why Uncle Jameel would be asking my mother if she's okay. It's not as though she's been ill or anything. Maybe he was just being kind, but it's a strange thing to ask when it's your own daughter that's missing.

"Mum, you are okay, aren't you?" I press, my inner nurse on high alert. It comes with the job, I suppose.

"Of course I am!" She laughs. "Now, why don't you run yourself a hot bath, put your pyjamas on and I'll make you some supper. Hot chocolate and cookies?"

I nod eagerly. Mum always knows how to cheer me up. "Thanks, you're the best."

"And Maryam," she calls as I turn to go back upstairs, "you've done absolutely the right thing, sweetheart. At least now Jameel will know where to start looking for Uzma."

I'm still not convinced. It's as though I've really jumped the gun on this. Maybe I should have waited longer. But then, if another day had gone by, perhaps Uzma really would have needed help.

While my bath is running, I try Uzma's phone again. It's still going straight to voicemail and I leave yet another emotional plea for her to ring me. This time I add that it's urgent, but I don't explain why.

In truth, I hope that I get hold of my friend before her parents do, as it could end Uzma's dreams. We must have talked about the situation with Sylvain more than a dozen times, but not once did I expect Uzma to jump on a plane to go to him. I really hope that the art tutor loves her, but, not having met him, I'm unsure of his plans. Will he propose to Uzma? Is he genuine? Is he just using her?

All these questions hang in the air as I slide into my hot, bubbly bath.

SATURDAY 10PM – UZMA

I'm exhausted. This afternoon I walked all around Montmartre, peering into cafés, searching for galleries where Sylvain might be hanging out, dashing in and out of bars, and generally looking like a tourist with no friends. I did stop to eat at MacDonalds, which I know isn't the most healthy type of meal but it's certainly one of the cheapest. My feet ache, despite these once comfortable Converse and I feel grubby. I went to the market, too and purchased some knickers and a couple of t-shirts which set me back twenty Euros, money that I can hardly afford to spend, but another day spent in the same clothes will have the other guest house occupants noticing. At least it didn't rain this afternoon, but it's quite chilly. Most of all, I'm frustrated at not finding my boyfriend.

Back in my room, my phone is finally fully charged. There are twelve missed calls from home, eight missed calls from Maryam and text messages from my family. I can't reply, not yet, that would be like admitting defeat. I shower and make a cup of peppermint tea. The delicious smell reminds me of my mother. It's her favourite drink, and tears prick at my eyes as I start to wonder if I've done the right thing in coming here. Of course, Sylvain will probably have tried to contact me by now, by Skype I would think, so once I get my laptop back we can finally get together.

Lying on the bed with the television set turned on low, I text Maryam.

I'm fine. Don't worry about me. Hope Mum and Dad aren't giving you a hard time.

Bing! A response comes straight back.

Where are you?

In a lovely little hotel, I type quickly, not really thinking or wanting to give my friend too much detail in case my dad pressures Maryam into revealing what she knows.

Your parents are really upset. Can we talk? Have something to explain.

I'm slightly intrigued by what my best friend might have to tell me but, on the other hand, Aunt Shazia might be there, telling Maryam what to write.

I think for a moment and then respond: *Not today. We're just going out for dinner and I have to finish getting ready. Will ring you in a couple of days, I promise.*

The lies drop easily from my fingers and the reality hurts. Sylvain and I should be going out to eat tonight, this being my first proper night here. How stupid Maryam would think I am if she knew I was sitting here in this bedroom drinking tea, not having seen nor heard from my lover. I need to stay positive, believe that everything will turn out alright in the end.

I've just listened to the messages from Dad. In the first one he sounded worried, but then, as I listen to the rest, I hear him getting angry and frustrated. If I were to go home now, there would be nothing for me. I'd be grounded, and no doubt have to give up my ambition of becoming an artist.

I must have dozed off for a while, as, when I rouse myself, the temperature has dropped due to the central heating going off. I suppose Madame Joubert has to think about running costs, after all. I roll off the bed and go into the bathroom to pee. As I come back into the bedroom, I look over at the black suitcase on the floor and for some strange reason I'm reminded of the guest house owner's crafty smile when she asked me if I'd opened it. Of course, I still haven't as it doesn't belong to me, but I did buy a pair of cheap pliers at a second-hand stall just in case.

Ten minutes later, after another cup of herbal tea to quench my thirst and hunger pangs, I find myself squatting on the carpet, trying to carefully prise open the zip on the case. It takes a few attempts, and I nearly cut myself, but once I've made a hole between the nylon and the stitching, it opens up enough for me to slip a hand inside.

The first thing I touch is soft fabric and then something long and hard, like a folder. I've got the bug now. I'm too nosy to stop and I use the pliers to enlarge the gap a bit more until I can pull a few items out.

First, there are two very crisp white cotton shirts. They look expensive, like the type Dad wears when he's due in court, but the label reveals a designer brand that I know would cost much more. Next out is a man's wash-bag and I find some Molton Brown products that smell astonishingly good, black pepper shower gel and eucalyptus bath oil. I put them to one side, just in case I need to 'borrow' them later.

There's also an expensive-looking bottle of wine wrapped in layers of tissue-paper. Amongst the other items of clothing, pushed carefully between, is the folder that I first put my hand on. It's long and bulky, the texture of cardboard but the colour of blood. I have to slide it out gently to avoid tearing the outer material, but as soon as I do, I feel extremely curious.

Opening up the document wallet, I find two sections. The first holds a stack of black and white photographs. Some of them show people wearing clothes from the 1970s and '80s; I can tell by the flared trousers and wide collars. Others are more up to date. Each picture is just a full-frontal shot of different people. None of them look related and there's nobody else in the image. I wonder whether these are personal photos of the suitcase owner's friends, though it's a strange collection to carry with you on a trip overseas.

I pick up one glossy snap of a man in his twenties. He's got wispy hair and is wearing a leather jacket.

The picture looks as though it was taken with a long lens. I'm no expert, but I like experimenting with my own camera, and these look really interesting, the way that the subjects seem to have no idea that someone is photographing them.

Suddenly, I realise that they're all similar in that respect. Each picture was taken from a distance and not one of the people is smiling for the camera as you normally would. It's very odd, like looking through the private collection of a peeping tom.

I turn over one of the snapshots: *12th December, 1982 – Geneva.*

The writing is in block capitals but extremely uniform, written with care by the look of it.

I flip over a few more and sure enough there are dates and cities on every single one.

3rd June, 1977 – Edinburgh. 25th May, 1994 – Dresden. 18th September, 2003 – Paris.

I look more closely at the photo marked *Paris.* It shows an attractive woman, maybe early forties, wearing a smart suit and high heeled shoes. She's striding along past the Louis Vuitton boutique, an expensive leather handbag on her arm, and doesn't look as though she has a care in the world. I only recognise this as the French capital because the writing tells me so but, on reflection, it could actually be anywhere in the world with busy streets and smart shops.

I push the photos to one side and feel inside the second section of the wallet. Pulling out my treasure, I see a selection of passport documents, driving licences and membership cards.

*Albert Henri, Gregory McCloud, Klaus Reiner, Su-
sannah Nicholls, Julia Beaumont, Jerome Emmanuelle.*

Quickly, I flip over the photos, and sure enough,
it's not long before I'm able to match one document
or card to each of the names written on the back of
the pictures. It's such a bizarre collection of stuff that
I have no idea how it all connects together. At first,
I was thinking that the owner of the suitcase used
these documents as aliases or disguises, but that's too
bizarre. There's no way he or she could change from
male to female, across such a wide age range, too. No,
these are more like souvenirs, but of what?

There's a heavy thud from downstairs as the front
door closes, followed by a woman's shrill laughter.
It's probably Madame Joubert. She went out with
that posh guest, the one that came on my flight. At a
guess, I'd say that they've had fun and a few bottles
of wine, too, by the sound of it. I listen at the door
for a few seconds but soon they're gone, the voices
fading as the pair walk through the hallway and into
one of the main rooms.

As I turn back to the papers on the floor, a rush
of guilt goes through me. What if these photos and
papers are official government documents? Perhaps
I could be arrested for tampering with them. I'm still
really intrigued, though. Gathering everything up, I
push the pieces back inside the folder and gently post
them back through the slit in the suitcase. I almost
replace the other items, too, but something stops me,
and I keep hold of the toiletries and one of the white

shirts. It might be useful if I need something smart to wear. I couldn't bear the thought of Sylvain finding me in these old jeans and cheap top.

Being reminded of Sylvain again starts my tears flowing. I need to find him soon, before my parents work out where I am and come to drag me back home. I don't think there's any way that they could find me here, although Dad does have to do a certain amount of investigation in his work, looking for alibis and evidence, so he might be smart enough to pick up on clues.

But what did I leave that might help him? Nothing, I hope. I was very careful to buy my plane ticket online so there was no paper receipt, and the e-ticket details are on my laptop, which is… well, let's face it, it could be anywhere. I wish I'd convinced Dad to buy me a contract phone; that way, I could have contacted Sylvain and moved out of this place. It would also mean I could get internet access and search to see if there are more art galleries in the area.

I'm so tired. Perhaps tomorrow it will get easier, and hopefully by Monday I'll have my luggage, too.

I lie back on the soft, quilted throw and absently watch a French game show. It appears to be the European equivalent of *Britain's Got Talent*, which I'd usually enjoy, but tonight there are too many questions running through my head.

I drift off, the television in the background a faint murmur. Dreams come… a bird-like man in a pinstriped suit laughing at me, Sylvain running and just out of earshot, Madame Joubert looking exquisite in pearls and an evening gown as she sips from a wine glass. But there are other images, too –passports, photographs and membership cards to exclusive clubs. I see every face clearly but, even though I've never met them, I know that all of them are dead.

SATURDAY MIDNIGHT – ALI RAFIQ

Finally, everything is sorted. The money has been transferred, twenty thousand British pounds. Now all I need to do is make the call. Jameel sits watching me, a glass of orange juice grasped firmly in his hands. I know this is harder on him than the rest of us, but it has to be done.

"Who do you have to phone?" my brother asks eagerly, sitting forward in his chair.

"It's just a number," I tell him, "somewhere in London. No name, no other details."

He nods, and I carefully punch the number into my cheap throwaway mobile.

"Wait," Jameel says, "are you sure this can't be connected to me, or this house?"

"Look we've been over this a dozen times, bro. These are professional people. They're discreet. Besides, as soon as I've made the call, I'll get rid of this phone. Okay?"

"And what about the money, can it be traced?" he presses.

"It's gone to a Swiss Bank account. As far as I know, whoever these people are will pass it on to the... the person doing the... you know, the job."

"I wish there were some other way," my brother whispers. "Doing away with this man is..."

"Too late." I stop him in mid-flow. "We've already paid – well, you have."

I hold up a hand as the line connects and a voice answers.

"Mr Rafiq?"

"Yes," I reply. "The money should be in your account now."

"Very well." The accent is English, a man, upper-class and clipped. "Monday afternoon."

I pause for a second, not quite realising what I'm being told, but then involuntarily nod as the words sink in. Of course, that's when it will happen.

"Will... will we be notified?" I stammer, not knowing what else to say.

"You will know," the person responds. "Goodbye, Mr Rafiq."

Jameel stares at me. We both know that there's no going back now and we sit in silence for a while. We've been keeping our voices low for the past couple of hours, not wanting to alert Farida or Khalid.

"Tea?" my brother finally offers, getting up from his chair. "And then we should try to sleep."

I nod and give him a faint smile. Always the practical one, my brother.

As Jameel busies himself making our hot drinks, I realise that I owe a lot to my nephew. If it hadn't been for Khalid, I never would have found out about Uzma and the Frenchman and my brother might still be in the dark as to her whereabouts. Poor Jameel, He might be the smarter one, but he's far too trusting, I can see that now.

It turns out that Farida hasn't exactly been the model wife, either. She might know how to make a man's heart leap with her biryani, but she's a sly one, too. I can't believe that she's managed to stash away twenty grand without my brother knowing. If she were my wife, I'd have kept a tighter rein on our finances. How Jameel decides to deal with this is not my affair, although I do consider it family business and my sister-in-law should be punished. Perhaps he will prefer to wait until Tariq and I return to Pakistan, then issue the retribution in private.

But what now of Uzma? My slut of a niece has tarnished herself. She is unfit now for a wholesome Muslim marriage in the eyes of Allah. Does the Quran not tell us that '*Unclean women are for unclean men*'?

Word will undoubtedly spread throughout the community and no God-fearing Muslim family will now welcome Uzma into marriage. It would be a disgrace. Jameel's best chance at saving face may well be to send the girl to Pakistan. Tariq is still willing to take her as his bride, on condition that she accept

208

a lesser role should he wish to take a second wife. Although they are cousins, the eyes of God will still permit such a union and I would not stand in the way. My brother is more than capable of providing a handsome dowry for his daughter and the money would help in setting up my boy in his own home.

"Here we are," Jameel murmurs, setting down two mugs of tea. "Are you hungry, Ali?"

I wave a hand at him. "No, no. Farida fed us well tonight."

My brother grunts on hearing his wife's name but, having heard about her recent antics, I'm not surprised and make no comment.

"Tariq would still be willing to marry Uzma, you know," I offer gently, "and he's a good man."

Jameel raises his eyes to meet mine, his forehead furrowed. "I know, Ali, and I appreciate that, but right now I just want to get my daughter back home. We can talk about wedding plans when she's safely returned."

"I understand," I tell him softly, still very aware that Farida may be trying to listen from upstairs. "But these things have a habit of getting out. It won't be long before the gossiping starts. How are you going to hold up your head when the Iman gets word of this, huh?"

My brother nods, a blush rising in his cheeks. "I know. I have never been so ashamed in all my life, Ali, but she's still my baby girl. I need to think long and hard about sending Uzma away again."

I let the matter rest for now and sit in silence, allowing my brother to gather his thoughts.

Time passes and Jameel tells me that he's going to get some rest. I should probably do the same, but I'm too wired to sleep. As the living room door closes, I'm alerted to the sound, a few seconds later, of my brother's study door opening and closing. He's obviously too vexed with Farida to share a bed with her and I cannot blame him.

There's a creak on the stair, just seconds after Jameel shuts the door to his sanctuary. Is it possible that Farida has been listening, anyway? Would she dare to come so close and risk her husband's fury? Perhaps it was just one of the boys going to the bathroom. I'm getting too jumpy tonight.

Sitting here in my brother's comfortable lounge reminds me of what could have been and it's hard to reflect upon so many painful memories. We both had the same start in life, middle-class with hard-working and caring parents. They're still wonderful. Dad is a proud man, involved in many local groups, both political and educational. It's no wonder that Jameel and I both followed the same career path. Mother is the matriarch of the family, strong, but obedient to our father, never putting a foot out of place but always there to support him. It seems that my brother and I have yet to fulfil their dream of bringing good women into the fold, even after all these years.

When I was nineteen, I knew that I would marry Rana. She was everything a man could ever want and our wedding day was the happiest of my life. Losing her in childbirth just two short years later turned me from a care-free newlywed to a bitter and resentful widower.

I've always cared for my son, but it was my mother who took on the role of nurturing Tariq. She was the one who helped him with his reading after school, soothed his head when fever struck and sewed name tags into his uniform. I wouldn't say that I have failed my boy, but perhaps I took too long to grieve, taking my sadness out on the child who was the cause of my Rana's death. I love him now. We are like best friends and I'm very proud of everything that Tariq has made of his life.

High up on the wall, four pairs of eyes look down on me – Jameel, Farida, Uzma and Khalid. I look at this photo every time we visit. It's the epitome of family life, successful father, beautiful mother, sweet and innocent daughter and cheeky son. My goodness, how a person's perspective can change in a matter of just a few hours! The successful father is now torn between love for his daughter and family pride, the mother is no longer young and slim and keeps secrets from her husband, the daughter has been led astray, giving her chastity to a stranger and as for the son, young Khalid... I can see the stress etched on his face as he struggles between loyalty to his sister and the sins which the Holy Book has taught him are so wrong.

It's so ironic, sitting here looking up at them. For so long, I have envied all that my brother has garnered, only to see it crumble before my very eyes. Jameel is lucky that he has me here to help. I will set things right. I will take care of him.

SUNDAY 2AM – KHALID RAFIQ

At last, Uncle Ali has gone to bed. He has been talking to my father for hours and even after Dad went to his study, my uncle continued to sit alone. Dad nearly caught me sitting on the stairs a while ago, but luckily, I'm quick and made it back to my room before he realised anyone was there.

I've been listening to them. I could feel the fear prickling my neck as they spoke. Uncle Ali has sent money to someone, and it had something to do with Mum having a secret bank account. I'm really confused. How could she possibly put money away without Dad knowing? It must have been a lot for him to get so angry. I could almost sense my father's gritted teeth as he told Uncle Ali about it. But here's the issue… I know they've sent it somewhere, but it honestly sounded as though they were planning to hire a hit-man for someone…

Holy shit, it's Uzma!

I might be young but I'm not stupid. They're going to arrange one of those 'honour killings' that I've heard about on the news! I thought that only happened in rural Pakistan, out in the sticks where men far outnumbered women and men paid other people's wives to sleep with them. I can't believe my dad would go along with something like this, but he's a proud man. Maybe he's really ashamed of what my sister is putting us through.

I have to do something. Uzma might be carrying on with a foreigner, but she doesn't deserve to die because of it. How could my father even consider doing that? And who would carry out the act? Maybe my uncle has some Mafia mob contacts here in London, although in truth I can't imagine it. He always seems like such a gentle man.

It's the early hours of the morning and I think France is an hour ahead, so that makes it 3am there. I know Dad's been trying my sister's phone too many times to count, but maybe I should warn her, give her time to get away.

Oh no! I put the tracker in her suitcase! I'm the one to blame for them finding out her location. If only I'd kept my mouth shut! I scroll down to my sister's number and hover my thumb over the green 'call' symbol. She'll never speak to me again when she finds out that it was me who told Tariq about her French boyfriend. If it wasn't for me, nobody would know where she was and Uzma would be safe.

Shit, shit, shit, who can help?

Maryam is on night shift. I could try her on the off-chance that she answers. Yes, that's what I'll do.

"Hello? Khalid, why are you calling me in the middle of the night?" she demands. "Is it Uzma?"

"Yes, kind of," I admit, huddled outside in our garden shed to ensure that nobody can hear. "Listen, I need to explain something. I think Uzma's in big trouble."

I hear Maryam's breath as I tell her the truth, the full confession, my heart beating so fast that I feel as though it will jump out of me at any second. My sister's friend lets me finish before saying anything, although now I can hear the sobs coming thick and fast.

"Khalid, why?" she cries when I'm done. "How could you? What the fuck has your sister ever done to you?"

"I made a mistake, I'm so, so sorry." I'm crying now, too, but I'm also afraid that someone will come outside and find me here. "You need to warn her, please, Maryam. She'll pick up the phone to you."

"Okay, let me think," she says firmly, more in control than me. "I'll see what I can do. I've already had one text message from Uzma, so hopefully she'll pick up if I ring her. You go to bed now, Khalid, and act as if nothing's happened. Can you do that? If anything happens to Uzma, it's on your head."

I promise Maryam that I can keep what I've heard to myself. It's like a bad dream. I still can't believe what Dad and Uncle Ali are planning. It's like a ritual from centuries ago.

As I close the back door, the kitchen light comes on and Dad is standing there, still fully dressed. He's just as surprised to see me as I am to see him, and we blink awkwardly at each other.

"Where have you been?" my father asks suspiciously. "Smoking?"

I feel relieved that he's jumped to the wrong conclusion, but embarrassed that he thinks I've got such a dirty habit.

"No. of course not," I tell him. "I just needed some fresh air."

Dad leans forward and sniffs my mouth, obviously smelling for nicotine or drugs. Satisfied that I'm telling the truth, he steps back and reaches for the kettle.

"Go back to bed now, Khalid," he orders wearily, turning on the tap, "And next time, open your bedroom window like a normal person. Do you hear?"

"Yes, Dad. Sorry if I woke you."

"Hah! There's no chance of me sleeping, not at the moment. Now, go to bed."

I retreat upstairs, grateful that my father didn't notice the bulge of a mobile phone in the pocket of my jogging bottoms. I can't look at my old man in the same way now. Knowing what he's plotting, how can I? And what about Mum? Is she in on this, too? I notice that my parents didn't speak to each other at all over dinner, which was weird, even to the point where my mother had to ask Dad to pass his plate over to her when he'd finished. Usually, he'd be the one hurrying to get the dishes removed from the table. Maybe she knows and is too upset to talk to him. Maybe they're all in this together?

Lying back in bed with the duvet pulled right up to my ears for warmth, I say a silent prayer for Uzma and then another for my own mistakes. I know the Holy Quran well and must punish myself for my sins.

'*You shall behold the wrongdoers aghast at their own deeds,*' I recite in my head, '*for then Our scourge will surely smite them. But those that have faith and do good works shall dwell in the fair gardens of Paradise, and shall receive from their Lord all that they desire.*'

I have no idea at this moment how I can atone for what I've become involved in. My sister might never forgive me; that's if she comes out of this alive. I hope that the Frenchman can protect her, keep her safe, take Uzma to some place where nobody can get to her. Most of all, I hope he loves my sister.

It's impossible to sleep. I keep the phone next to me inside the covers, watching the screen in case Maryam phones or sends a message. I'm keeping the ringer off, can't risk Dad hearing as he paces the rooms below. If I were Uzma I'd never want to speak to me again.

How can such innocence spiral out of control and turn into something so scarily dangerous? I wish I could turn back the clock. This time yesterday, I was playing X-Box at my mate's house, keeping ourselves awake with cans of energy drinks and chocolate bars, oblivious to everything that was happening at home.

It's funny, one of my teachers once said that everyone has a secret, but sometimes you never get to find out. She said many people make confessions on their deathbed, or they write letters saying how sorry they are, or regret doing stuff, and I reckon she's right. Other people, according to my wise old tutor, never tell, but they hold in their secrets, living with hurt and anger instead of letting it out.

I think I'll be like that. If my sister dies, I don't think I could bring myself to tell my children about my part in it. How their grandfather and great uncle arranged the murder of their lovely aunt. How could I? Wouldn't my own children be scared of me, knowing such terrible things? Would they think their own father capable of doing the same should they ever step out of line?

When I do eventually start to fall asleep, my eyes unable to focus on the phone any longer, I dream of myself as an old man with a long, wispy beard and white hair. I'm lying on my bed surrounded by my four children – yes, I can count them clearly, one, two, three, four, all staring down at me. My lips move, confessing the tale of what happened to my sister, the beautiful Aunt Uzma that they never got to meet and even as I try to stir myself from the nightmare, the wet tears on my cheek are very real, dripping down quickly, one after the other, sorry for what I have done.

SUNDAY 4AM – JAMEEL RAFIQ

At last the house is silent and I can be alone with my thoughts. For what it's worth, my head is knotted, like one of Farida's tangled balls of wool, waiting to be unravelled. I have no idea if, or indeed when, life can return to normal after this. I'm involved in something much bigger than I can handle and so much is riding on the consequences, should my part in this ever come to light.

My daughter, precious though she is, may never speak to me again were she to discover the truth behind the Frenchman's... what? Murder? Such a final and damning word, but I suppose, in all honesty, that's exactly what it is. I have no idea how or where it will happen, only when, and the hours are going to drag by until it's over.

There's no guarantee that Uzma will come home afterwards. We're depending upon her grief to prompt her to reach out to her family for support.

None of us know if she has other friends in Paris, so little are we aware of our child's inner circle. Nor do we know anything relevant about the man whose fate we have sealed – callous of us, but a necessary evil. The Quran teaches, *You shall not kill any man whom God has forbidden you to kill, except for a just cause.* What better cause than the preservation of my daughter's chastity, albeit perhaps too late, and vengeance upon the man whom has committed sins of the flesh upon her?

When I think about the two of them together, my daughter in his arms, a tightness grows in my chest and bile rises in my throat, so devastated am I by these circumstances. If Uzma had any inkling of her impending marriage to Tariq, at least that would have been recompense, a reason for running; but this way, eloping with a non-Muslim, is unforgiveable. There are religious rules that we live by in our culture. The lines are very clearly drawn and every year of my children's lives, I have made it my duty to steer them along the correct path, reciting the teachings of Allah, explaining His reasons for following certain cultural criteria. Now, my daughter is sullied, second-hand goods, tainted, a whore. Nothing can return her purity, no hours of prayers, sorrow or forgiveness. She is lost to me.

I've thrown cup after cup of coffee down my throat tonight. I sit here trying to justify my brother's actions, and mine, too, based on the strong beliefs of our faith, yet unbeknown to Ali I am the biggest hypocrite of all. In the eyes of our law, it states: *The adulterer and adulteress shall each be given a hundred lashes.* Shazia and I are the guilty ones, we deserve to be punished.

Perhaps this is God's will. He has taken my daughter from me because of my foul deeds. Only I can be blamed for what has happened. It's almost as though this is some kind of Holy plan, to punish my wickedness. For all my degrees, knowledge, superior schooling and high-standing in the community, I am a weak man. I have allowed my feelings of lust and carnal longings to consume me. I have sinned and must be punished severely.

If Allah wishes to take our daughter from us, in whatever way, so be it. I will shoulder the responsibility alone. Shazia must be protected at all costs, and to ensure her safety I must end this now. No more will we continue to meet in secret, under the pretence of business meetings – or, in her case spa treatments – all for a few hours of lovemaking in a suburban hotel room.

Khalid is the only innocent one in all of this. My boy has tried his best to appease both parents and sibling. I don't blame him for not coming to me with information about his sister. A boy should respect the relationship between himself and his loved ones. I just hope that this does not affect his future. Even tonight, in the early hours, I caught him coming in from outside, his skin pallid from the cold, as though he had been out there for a while. I couldn't detect smoke, there was no whiff of cannabis on his clothing, but why else would my son be up in the middle of the night, unless up to no good? See now, I am beginning to doubt my own boy. What a distrustful father I am.

I switch on the computer, type in my secure password, and immediately the screen brings up the last search: flights. Paris, naturally. There is nothing available today. I'm guessing that there are many Parisians returning home after a weekend break in London, or people setting off for business trips, ready for a bright and early start on Monday morning. I sit back in my chair and try to think clearly, although my brain is fuzzy from too much caffeine and a guilty conscience.

If I travel to Paris, how would I be able to stop this... this contract, this agreement? And if I allow it to go ahead, and find my daughter, would she know that I was involved? Would she guess? I don't even know if the young man is to meet his end in a river, pushed from a building, in a secluded wood... there are no details. I could deny everything, hold my Uzma in her grief, but I fear my own emotions above all. Might I confess in time? And then what?

Reluctantly, I close the tab, shrinking the airline information to the bottom of the screen. If we as a family are ever to continue any semblance of normality, life must continue the way it's always been. I cannot risk losing my career, my son, all that I hold close, because of my daughter's mistake.

I will wait until tomorrow. Only then will I attempt to bring Uzma home. We know of her location, thanks to the tracker in her luggage, so it should be easy to find her, and from then, back on British soil, a flight will be booked for her to fly to Pakistan with Ali and Tariq.

Do I trust my brother not to beat and mistreat my eldest child? A nagging doubt tells me not to, but then doesn't my belief also remind me that Uzma should receive her due? If Tariq is to make a good wife of her, the girl must learn to behave respectfully, in a traditional environment, with her grandmother to show her the light. God forbid that my parents should ever find out what has occurred. I would never again be able to show my face in my homeland, so deep would be their disgust.

I know that Ali has always prayed for a virtuous and beautiful bride for his only son. It's such a pity that Tariq won't be blessed on all counts. No woman should enter into marriage tarnished by another's hand, let alone that of a foreigner, and it cannot be forgiven. I am not even certain that I will be able to look my child in the face again, so dishonoured do I feel, and so there I have lain to rest my own indecision.

Uzma shall go to Pakistan, and never return.

There is movement upstairs. A thud on the floor as my overweight wife rolls out of bed. Farida is a matter that also needs my attention, but that particular retribution will need to wait.

I'm not aware that I've been a miserly husband. The children have always been clothed and provided for, smart for every occasion, well-fed and educated, and my lack of compassion towards my wife's scrimping is justifiable. Twenty thousand pounds! Enough money to start a new life in Pakistan. Perhaps that was always her plan, running away from responsibility, from me. I suspect that Farida was going to wait until the children had moved to their own homes. It's just an inkling, but isn't that the way it usually works in these circumstances? In my profession we call it 'marital breakdown', or 'irreconcilable differences'.

Hah, we're different alright! I'm a man of ambition, I take pride in my home, my offspring, my career. Farida doesn't even look after her own needs these days. I can't remember the last time she presented herself with neatly shaped brows or unbitten nails. I no longer know what I feel towards my wife. It's a mixture of disgust and pity. I'm revolted by her appearance and conclude that she is unable to recognise herself, or the proud woman she used to be. Farida is like a butterfly, although now, with time, the intricate patterns on her wings have faded and all that is left is an unattractive brown moth. Why can she not see that for herself?

It's pointless sitting here, waiting for the house to stir. To see the tiredness in my brother's eyes, the alarm in Tariq's, the fear in Khalid's, and to watch my spouse fumbling around the kitchen in her old-fashioned quilted dressing-gown, fussing over food, her only decent faculty being the ability to feed our guests and avoid talking about the desperate situation in which we find ourselves.

I send a short message to Shazia. We can meet for coffee early tomorrow morning, on the pretence of a chance meeting; she is after all a family friend. This is going to be so difficult, but completely necessary. We always knew this day would come. Time has been kind to her. Shazia can carry on just the way she was before we began the affair, nothing needs to change. We will both be slightly broken inside, but after a while the shards will heal. They must.

I think I love her. I can admit to those feelings now that it's almost over, a yearning that I've never had for my own wife. Maybe it was the temptation, forbidden fruit, another man's woman, all of the things that a legitimate relationship cannot provide. One day, we will both look back, wondering what might have been had we met at a time when we were both free, and hopefully a smile will pass our lips. I unlock my desk, open the bottom drawer, reaching down to remove a stack of legal documents and then feel right to the back with trembling fingers.

Here is the only photograph of my lover, grinning widely at the camera, a shot no doubt taken by her devoted husband. Was she laughing at something he said? Because his actions made her laugh? Or at something else entirely? It would be so wrong of me to ask. I bend my head and kiss the glossy paper.

Goodbye, my love. No regrets.

SUNDAY 6AM – COLIN FOSTER

I've always been an early riser. "He's up with the lark again," mother used to shout sarcastically, when she heard me desperately trying to prepare my own breakfast with as little noise as one could manage. Somehow, I seemed to earn a clip around the ear most days for clanking milk bottles or leaving the water tap to drip, despite my valiant efforts not to disturb the sleeping ogre.

Pulling back the curtains to reveal yet another dull and rather dark morning, the sun not having the decency to stir at this early hour, I hear the pitter-patter of raindrops on the guttering above my window. It puts me in mind of my first years at St. Julian's Junior School, when the mere forecast of a storm would be enough to rouse the bullies, chanting at my expense, intimidating me with my own, in this case, rather misfortunate surname.

"Doctor Foster went to Gloucester in a shower of rain," they would sing, sneering and encircling me as they did so. "He stepped in a puddle, right up to his middle, and never went there again."

It was after one of these gruelling tortures that I threw my very first punch. Martin Nolan got my fist right smack-bang in the middle of his nose, if memory serves correctly. After that, I was given a week-long detention – such is life. It did, however, spur me on to seek solace in a local boxing club, a place where I could indulge my frustrations by beating the guts out of a straw punch bag. Those lessons have served me well in my chosen career, especially on the odd occasion when strength has been to my advantage in the disposal of rather troublesome cadavers. Some might say it comes with the territory, others might very well see it as one's downfall.

Before going out to take the Parisian air, it has become a habitual necessity of mine to check the room. One might call it 'OCD', should a label be required. For myself, it's merely being cautious. Taps need to be turned on and off three times, the last turn tighter, ensuring no leakage. Lights must follow the same process, off, on, off again, leaving the room in darkness. Finally, the lock, door closed, double lock, open again, repeat process. All finished and satisfactory, I can now venture outside.

It's rather fitting that today is wet, the street spitting puddles onto the usually dry walkway, as I feel somewhat like a flamingo. Not in elegance – no glamour, long legs and dramatic plumage – but a flamingo nevertheless, with one leg lifted, the other submerged in a watery grave, afraid to put down that second appendage should one step upon some unsuspecting bottom feeder. Naturally, one doesn't mean that literally, or a step would never be taken during the autumn months, but metaphorically, my feet being the cause of upset and Madame Joubert being the rather elegant fish beneath my toes.

It's all on account of our most peculiar evening, I suppose, a night that could have ended prematurely, with me taking offence at her innuendos and inquisitive digs, but instead, thanks in part to us being slightly intoxicated, a lingering kiss sealed our date and gave one hope that all is not lost.

Shortly, after just a few minutes' walk, I find a café. Most welcome at this time on a Sunday morning, filled only with a couple of sleepy pensioners and the aroma of freshly baked *pain au chocolat*.

"Monsieur?" the waitress enquires, approaching the table with caution as she side-steps my dripping umbrella. "English? Something to drink?"

I order an espresso and one of the warm pastries, my mouth watering as the proprietor reaches forward with silver tongs to deposit my breakfast on a white china plate. The coffee is excellent, nutty and strong, and I order a second, immediately feeling my senses perking up.

No doubt Collette will wonder at my missing *le petit-dejeuner* at her establishment, but I've always upheld the belief that one shouldn't be too overbearing in courtship and the old adage, 'absence makes the heart grow fonder', will bode well for us. It's not as if we'll be apart for long, of course, but I still have a delicate 'errand' to undertake tomorrow and mustn't take my eye off the prize.

Of course, one must wonder whether it was imprudent of me to come to Paris prematurely but, under the current circumstances, it appears to have been a most affable move. I permit myself a slight snigger at how matters are panning out and it causes the café owner to turn his head. Time to depart, I suppose, to spend one final day employing my time as a tourist.

"*C'est combien*?" I ask the waitress, as she veers towards me with the bill, "How much?"

I leave a mediocre tip, nothing too meagre nor substantial. Should tomorrow's outcome ever lead to the police tracking a murderer, I neither want to be remembered for my miserly ways nor my generosity. It's a tactic, you see. Make yourself practically unrecognisable by not leaving visual traces. The human brain will retain information that it finds unusual – too large a tip, vibrant clothing, a facial disfigurement, a disability – therefore my role is to blend in. Over the years, I've lost count of the number of identical suits, crisp white shirts – un-monogrammed, of course – and plain Oxford brogues that I've purchased, all to the same end, to create an 'invisible man'.

Those who see me in the street may describe me as a 'City Gent', a man on his way to conduct business, a person who is memorable only for the few seconds it takes to pass by. Arrest me, put me in a line-up of similarly dressed gentlemen and chances are not one of us would stir a positive identification. That's the beauty of my work, and the secret of its longevity. Nobody ever suspects the smartly dressed man in a suit, slightly past his prime and far too well-spoken to arouse doubt.

All of our lives, we are told that criminals come from disadvantaged backgrounds, poor council estates, broken homes, failed parenting and on all of these counts I tick the boxes. But give a man the means to nurture those same shortcomings and he shall become king of his own destiny. Had it not been for my mother's neglect, I never would have learned to fend for myself, nor seek employment far above my station at the 'Gentleman's Club', and neither would I have had the bravado to take up those same Hoorah Henrys on their insanely rewarding butchery. And so, as I walk away from the bistro café, nobody turns to see my destination and, in a few seconds, they won't even remember the colour of my hair, such an impression the invisible man has left.

I walk in the opposite direction to that by which I approached the café, a habitual trait, I suppose, and the pavement takes me along the far side of the park and down a side street, the road sloping downwards and allowing a partially visible view of the Seine. There are few pedestrians, possibly due to the time, a little after seven, but most probably because of the disagreeable weather. In milder months, my raincoat does a substantial job of keeping one warm and dry, but unfortunately, due to the inadequacy of this umbrella borrowed from the guest house hallstand, cold globules of rain persistently roll down the back of my neck and it isn't long before I'm forced to seek refuge in a nearby building.

It appears that I have stumbled across a gallery of some sort, the advertising posters announcing an upcoming folk music festival and, naturally, a few choral events leading up to the festive season. There are sounds of furniture being dragged across the upper floors and voices, as someone instructs on where to move the items to. I wonder whether this might be a good distraction to while away a few hours later on, and I go in search of information.

At the far end of the entrance hall there's a low table, graced with a red velour cloth and covered in neat piles of leaflets, each colourful and announcing a different event. I note that the organiser has had the foresight to stack each bundle in date order, the first event being today, as luck would have it. My French is far from fluent but, from the illustrations, verbs and nouns, I'm able to quickly ascertain that this afternoon's activity will be a display of watercolours by local artists. Perfect. I may even be able to find a piece to gift to Collette or, on second thoughts, she may wish to peruse the works for herself. I select a leaflet from the top of the pile and fold it carefully before slipping the paper inside the rather watery pocket of my damp raincoat.

Having now walked full circle, the familiar church steeple comes into view as I approach the little park adjacent to the guest house. The rain is letting up a little and I hesitate, wondering whether to stay out a while longer, but the uncomfortable clamminess of my attire requires me to seek the warmth of my room. Besides, it's not many more hours now before instructions should arrive.

No doubt Madame Joubert will raise an eyebrow at my having a special delivery arrive on a Sunday afternoon, as most other times I have stayed fell on a weekday. Still, there are many ways to dispel the inquisitiveness that may be stirred within her. I am, after all, a successful businessman in her eyes. I rarely feel any nervousness at these times; why should I? A man of my years and experience is simply itching to have the job done, a sign of swift and timely efficiency.

Of course, as is human nature, one is rather curious to know the subject of my task. I know not whether it will be male or female, young or old this time. Perhaps my quarry is a local, maybe even a tourist. One would hope that it won't be necessary to trail across the city in this blasted weather, but neither should it be too close to one's lodgings. Still, no doubt all will be revealed in good time, and even now the clock can't tick fast enough. The sooner the deed is done, the sooner the money will be safely in my account.

It's still early and, as I return the sodden umbrella to the stand, I hear very little sound coming from the open dining room door. However, just as I remove my raincoat, I hear footfall upon the stair.

"Good morning," I greet the young Asian woman. Collette has mentioned her name several times but for the life of me it still can't be easily recalled.

"Hello," she says tiredly, looking as though a sleepless night has troubled her. "Is it raining?"

This is our first proper interaction and I sense an awkward exchange on the girl's part. I suppose small talk with a man old enough to be her father is the last thing she expected at this time of day.

"Oh," I remember, pulling out the leaflet from my pocket. "Perhaps this might interest you, if you're looking for a way to pass the time today. It's only a few streets away."

I pass the glossy sheet to her, noticing that the damp edges have already begun to curl, and she reaches out slender fingers. I notice that they are bereft of rings.

"Yes, thank you!" the youngster says eagerly, studying the text with a strangely zealous interest. "Oh, my goodness!" The latter words fall from her lips in a faint whisper, obviously unintentional.

"Yes, I thought it looked rather interesting," I enthuse, hoping that she might return the leaflet in order for me to show it to Collette. "It's starts at two, if I'm not mistaken."

"I'll, erm, yes, I'll go." The girl stumbles on her words, leaving me slightly perplexed. I hadn't expected such a keen reaction and there's something quite odd about her attire, now that I look more closely.

This visitor, she's wearing a crisp white shirt, almost identical in cut to those I order from Saville Row. Admittedly, it's hard to be certain of the make, but the stitching is exquisite in quality and the buttons embossed with the initials of the tailor shop. I try to look more closely without appearing to stare at the woman's chest, and thankfully, she's still reading the information on the art gallery advertisement.

I note that the ends of the shirt are tied in a knot at her waistline, just below the top of her jeans to save modesty, and the sleeves rolled up over her wrists, but by Jove, I'm certain that the shirt is from Bennett and Moss!

"Are you from London?" I enquire, as casually as my startled persona will allow. "By any chance?"

"Yes, I am," she replies, lifting her head to reveal long lashes and red-rimmed dark eyes. "You?"

"Yes," I admit, unused to revealing much about myself. "I noticed the shirt, Saville Row."

The young lady blushes, looking down at her chest. "Oh, I borrowed this from… a friend," she tells me. "My suitcase got lost at the airport, so I…"

I feign disinterest and tell the girl to hurry to breakfast whilst the coffee is fresh and the bread warm, although inside I think I now know where my suitcase is.

Upstairs, I try to figure out a way to swap the luggage, but this isn't going to be an easy task. One also needs to factor in that the Asian girl has obviously opened my case. Now, that is a whole new problem in itself. If, indeed, I have her suitcase, it remains intact. I haven't even tried to break the combination lock and feel certain that nothing inside would be of any use to me.

The portfolio, damn it! Inside my suitcase is the folder containing the faces of every single life that I've extinguished, spanning decades and continents. Those are the people whose very existence had made my fortune feasible... the men and women who crossed a line in the eyes of their loved ones and business associates... those who fell at my hands.

In all honesty, I'm a fool for carrying the blessed folder with me, but it serves as a constant reminder that I'm the best in my field, slipping undetected from city to city, tracking my prey. Perhaps one would expect to feel a modicum of remorse, given the methods employed to 'remove' my targets, but, after all these years, I have become immune to the grief and will admit, on this, my very last mission, that it's the satisfaction that has always driven me.

So, what to do? One can hardly enter another guest's room and swap luggage, especially not in the house of Collette. I must sit it out, wait for the right opportunity and hope that the girl doesn't meddle with any more of my belongings. The wearing of one's shirt is distasteful enough, but the very thought of her looking through my precious documents is unthinkable. And what of Madame Joubert? Can I trust her? Could I possibly confide my fears in her that the young woman is in possession of my case? Surely a word in her ear might pose more questions than resolutions.

Finally, I take a long shower. I am at my best under the heat and pressure of running water. It seems to wash away my indecision and bring clarity to my foggy mind. One should never jump too quickly, for one never knows what lies beyond the void, I tell myself. For the clever man, it's a waiting game.

It wouldn't be the end of the world should I lose the portfolio, for negatives exist in my safety deposit box at the bank. So, too, would it be no loss to order more shirts from Bennett and Moss. I have upon my person everything one needs for identification purposes – passport, debit cards and phone – therefore undue panic need not prompt me into action just yet. There is time. A few more hours and I shall receive my instructions, and once the task is complete I shall slip out of Paris without trace, the only fragment remaining being my proposal to Collette Joubert.

SUNDAY 8AM – UZMA

Sitting alone in the pretty breakfast room, I realise that I'm still holding the glossy art leaflet between my fingers. It's almost as though that strange man in the business suit has given me a clue as to where to look for Sylvain. I'm sure he'll be there. Why wouldn't a local artist be at a local gallery display? I need to tidy myself up and sort out my hair. I can't have him seeing me looking like this, wearing someone else's shirt and without make-up. He'd run a mile! Still, I have time.

I glance at the delicate flowered wallpaper and antique furniture. This is such a comfortable place to stay. When Sylvain and I were here, we didn't stop for breakfast, but sneaked out at dawn so that I could slip back into my lodgings unnoticed. There are two large watercolours on the main wall, vibrant and detailed, not unlike my boyfriend's work. I look more closely. It would be absurd to think that he'd sold some paintings to the guest house owner. Unless she'd bought one when he was out in the street... Now, that would be a really weird coincidence, especially as Madame Joubert says she doesn't remember Sylvain!

"Good morning, mademoiselle." The housekeeper startles me as she sneaks through a side door, smoothing down her starched apron with one hand and carrying a coffee pot in the other.

"*Bonjour,*" I reply, fumbling for something more adequate in French, but my brain won't comply. I wish the basics would roll off my tongue more easily. Perhaps in a few months they will.

"Coffee?" She smiles, raising the cafetiere and filling my cup as I nod.

"Thank you."

The door swings open again and Madame Joubert glides into the room, looking elegant and chic in a knee-length black dress with a string of pearls around her neck.

"Ah, Uzma," she says, gently touching the back of my chair. "I hope you slept well, my dear."

"Yes, thanks. The bed is really comfortable."

I don't even know why I said that. My head is so full of stuff since reading Maryam's text earlier. The woman must think I'm such an idiot.

"Perhaps you would like some smoked salmon and eggs this morning?" she continues. "You need to eat properly. Maybe a bagel to go with it?"

"Yes, please," I reply, finally admitting to myself just how hungry I am. "That would be great."

I have only eaten smoked salmon once before, at Aunt Shazia's birthday dinner, but it was quite tasty despite the slippery texture. Besides, I don't want to inconvenience the cook this morning, so I'll take whatever's on offer.

"Great," the guest house owner repeats quietly as she follows the other woman back into the kitchen. It's just loud enough for me to hear, her voice sounding a bit odd and with a tinge of sarcasm in it. I wonder whether I've just accidentally insulted my host in some way without realising.

As soon as I'm alone again, I pull the phone out of my jeans pocket and scroll down to reread my friend's message.

Your dad knows where you are. Be careful. Tell your boyfriend to stay away.

I don't get it. How could Dad know where I am? I didn't even tell Maryam where I'm staying.

I type: *How does he know? Is he coming to Paris?*

I hit 'send'. It's a few minutes before a response comes and the time drags slowly. I have to stop myself from sending more questions, trying to give my friend enough time to write her answer.

We need to talk. Khalid overheard them. I think your dad and Uncle Ali are planning something.

I think for a few seconds, feeling panic setting in and then choose my reply carefully.

Planning what? Can't ring, will use all my credit. Don't worry, I'll warn Sylvain. Am moving from here 2mo.

Almost immediately, a reply pings back: *I don't know what, just be careful Uz, please. XX*

239

So cryptic. Maryam must know more. In fact, she's the only one that knew I was coming to Paris.

OK. Will text later. X

I don't know what else to tell Maryam. Should I even trust her anymore? Perhaps my mum and Aunt Shazia are sitting next to her while she messages me, looking for clues or something. I'll never forgive my friend if she's grassed on me, not after all the promises she made. Of course, there's also her own secret relationship that she wants to keep hidden, so the risk of me blabbing about that should have kept her quiet.

Just as I push the phone back into my jeans, Madame Joubert reappears with my breakfast.

"Here we are," she says with a smile, setting down the hot plate. "Now, can I get you anything else?"

I shake my head, looking at the delicious food in front of me. "No, that's perfect, thank you."

The woman stands for a moment, gazing down at me as if expecting more.

"I think everyone else is enjoying a... what do you call it in English, hmm? A Sunday 'lie in'?" she says.

"Yes, that's right. Maybe they were out late last night."

A faint smile passes across Madame Joubert's face. At a guess, she's recalling her own evening out with that funny man. I wouldn't put them together as a couple, but you never know.

"So, what are your plans for today?"

I lightly touch the leaflet on the table next to me with my fingertips. "I think I might go and look around this exhibition. The gentleman guest said it's not far from here."

Madame Joubert looks a bit startled as she leans over my shoulder to see the glossy paper.

"Oh, I don't think it will be very exciting," she tells me, putting a hand to her cheek. "Just a few local artists, quite amateur, really."

"Like me," I say. "I'm an art student, and besides, my boyfriend will probably be there."

The Frenchwoman coughs, moving a beautifully manicured hand across her lips, and excuses herself from the dining room. "Sorry, my dear, I've just remembered, I need to make a phone call. *Excusez-moi.*"

She exits the room twice as fast as she entered, leaving me alone to eat my breakfast. Sometimes the French seem so dramatic. I wonder what was so urgent.

As I return to my room after breakfast, Maryam's text is still on my mind. Today's priority is to find Sylvain and explain everything to him. It sounds as though my dad and Uncle Ali might be on their way over here. I know that my uncle had a bit of a reputation as a hothead back in the day and I can imagine him coming here to break us up and cause a scene. My dad wouldn't throw a punch, that's not his style, but I'm sure he would do everything in his power to drag me back to London. The best thing might be to get out of here, although there are loads of hotels and guest houses in Montmartre and it would take them ages to try them all.

241

I'm still clutching the art gallery leaflet and I pray that this exhibition will lead me to Sylvain. I'm sure he'll be displaying his paintings there. After all, this is the area in which he always hangs out and the college isn't far away, either. Suddenly, it dawns on me. That's why Sylvain didn't answer my Skype calls on Friday, he was busy getting ready for this exhibition! Now it all makes sense. He was just really busy. After all, he wasn't to know that I'd be coming over this weekend. I feel lifted slightly, sure that today will be the day that we're reunited. I just hope that my dad isn't on his way, too.

I start running a hot bath and pour in some of the lavender salts that are on the shelf. It looks wet and cold outside, so at least I should warm myself up before getting ready to go out. I don't have much option but to put my black sweater back on as the tops that I bought look too cheap but, if I put this soft white shirt underneath, at least I'll look half decent. There's a hairdryer in the dressing-table drawer but I don't have my good hairbrushes or straighteners, so I'll have to manage as best I can with a comb. Maybe I should braid my hair into a long plait like Mum used to do for me.

After my bath, I'm still feeling tense at the thought of Dad coming to Paris, but now I'm more confident that I can find Sylvain and together, we can hide somewhere safe. He'll know exactly what to do. Still, I can't help thinking that Maryam has betrayed me. She's the only one who knew where I was going.

How could she do that? We were supposed to be best friends! And Khalid, how has he become so involved that he's been talking to Maryam about me? At least she tried to warn me and, thanks to my brother, I can be alert.

I never thought it would come to this. Mum and Dad were supposed to believe my note and think that I'd found a job in Germany. What a mess! I have visions of Uncle Ali charging around every guest house in Paris, pushing open doors, frightening the occupants and waving a photo of me to see if I've been spotted.

I'll have to track down my suitcase as soon as I've located Sylvain. All my money is in there and I can't survive much longer without my clothes – or decent make-up for that matter, I note, looking closely at myself in the bathroom mirror. I look so haggard. There are dark lines under my eyes and my skin looks as though it's going to break out in spots any time. What a sight I must look.

Having dressed, pulling on the posh shirt again and tucking it into my jeans, I look guiltily at the opened suitcase by the end of the bed. Whoever owns it would be absolutely furious to see their belongings used in this way, but I'm so desperate. Perhaps I should take it back to the airport, when my own case eventually turns up. I could even put a note of apology inside with some money to compensate for the shirt. I bet it cost quite a bit, though. I doubt if I could afford the price of a new one.

I've got quite a few more hours to kill before the exhibition opens, although I could always hang around outside for a while, as the artists must get there early to set up their work. I don't have much cash but I really need some foundation and lipstick to make myself look presentable. Perhaps Madame Joubert will feel sorry for me and lend me some makeup if I ask politely, although it's a bit cheeky. What a situation to be in!

And then, wandering around, who knows if I'm going to bump into my father? Maryam didn't even say if they'd got a flight yet. I can feel butterflies stirring up in my stomach now. Just the thought of Dad's anger makes me nauseous. Pulling my denim jacket on, I take a deep breath, but it's too late and I rush for the toilet, spewing salmon and eggs down the bowl. I just want this to be over.

SUNDAY 10AM – COLETTE JOUBERT

As if this morning wasn't tense enough with having a meeting after Mass, now I need to phone Sylvain to warn him about the girl. If he's stupid enough to put his paintings on show today, the game could very well be over, and she'll find him in broad daylight.

I cannot risk the Asian woman seeing my son, his whole future would be ruined. Just now, I heard her being sick in the bathroom as I passed. What more evidence of a pregnancy do I need? My stupid boy, he's really got himself into trouble this time. Still, the girl is not showing any bump yet. There could still be time for a miscarriage, or a trip to the clinic should she finally see sense.

I retreat to my private quarters, many unwanted thoughts rushing through my head, leaving Maria to finish clearing the breakfast plates. I've paid her a little extra for helping out this morning, as I have too much to do and cannot be late for my appointment.

A fleeting thought briefly crosses my mind as I reach for the phone; the Black Sparrow missed his *petit-dejeuner* this morning, so he must have found sustenance elsewhere. Colin and I shared a very enjoyable outing last night, so how strange that he hasn't shown his face yet. Perhaps my teasing broke that icy exterior of his.

Through my lounge window, I hear the bells of St. Pierre already tolling, signalling the start of service and I fear I shall have to sneak in at the back of the church, tiptoeing over the tiled floor and hopefully not disturbing Father Francis's sermon. I pull back the voile panel and peer at the gloomy skies. Such a miserable day for an even more sorrowful task.

The telephone rings three times in my son's apartment.

"'*Allo*," a woman's sweet voice says immediately.

"Sophia," I answer, quickly going through the motions of asking how she is and making small talk.

"*Je suis fatiguée*, Mama," she confides. "I'm tired."

I tell her to go and rest, to take the phone off the hook in order to get some peace. It is Sunday after all. Then I finish with, "*Ou est Sylvain?*"

"*Une galerie d'art en Montmartre*," she tells me. "*C'est cinq minutes à pied.*"

My worst fears are confirmed. He's already at the gallery and I don't have time to meet him.

Quickly reassuring my daughter-in-law that there's nothing wrong and that it was just a mother's

Sunday morning call to her son, I promise to take them both for lunch the following week and hang up. I feel for Sophia. She's been in the dark about Sylvain's tricks for the past three years and it's time that he stopped playing around. I want a solid future for my son, with a woman deserving of his talent and charm.

I sincerely hope that the Asian girl can be persuaded to return home as soon as possible. Perhaps, when she finds her cash running low, and my rooms fully booked for the coming weeks, she will take the hint and give up on her futile search for what can't have been more than a summer fling.

My black cashmere coat is hanging on the back of the door and I quickly pull it on before grabbing my house keys and some loose change to put into the church's bottomless collection plate. With the cash that goes into the upkeep of our local church every week, Father Francis should be able to afford a new roof gilded with gold leaf and diamonds before long, I muse.

The streets are bereft of pedestrians. No doubt the church is already full with those who have walked this way. I will miss the first half hour of the service and go to find my son. It's imperative that I speak with him before the gallery opens this afternoon.

Hurrying quickly along in my sensible Sunday shoes, I arrive at the historic building within five minutes, slightly out of breath and a little damp from the ceaseless drizzle. It doesn't take me long to find

Sylvain, charming a female volunteer as he sets out his artwork on the far side of the upper floor.

"Mama!" He grins, turning unexpectedly as he hears my footfall. "*Quelle surprise.*"

"I need to speak to you urgently," I tell my son, speaking in English to avoid the inquisitive ears of the young woman writing out price tags for Sylvain's work. "Let's go downstairs."

I lead the way, with my child, as I still think of him, trailing behind.

When we reach the main door, I place a hand on his arm and lower my voice.

"The girl, Uzma, she's planning to come here this afternoon, you need to cancel your display."

Sylvain laughs, tousling his hair nervously with one hand as he always used to as a young boy. "Surely not. How could she possibly know I'm here?"

I appeal to his mature side by looking directly into my son's eyes. "She has one of the gallery leaflets, I saw it at breakfast. She told me that her boyfriend will be here."

Finally, Sylvain stops smiling and looks up at the ceiling as though asking for divine intervention. "Jesus!" He grimaces. "Shit! Sophia will be here later, I can't risk Uzma making a scene."

"So, withdraw your paintings," I tell him, "pretend you feel unwell."

"I can't," he groans, through gritted teeth. "There's a high-profile dealer coming to see my work, it might mean a lot of money if he likes what he sees."

We quarrel for a few minutes, me mostly pleading and Sylvain making excuses. It angers me how my son never treats serious situations with the gravity they deserve. Finally, I compromise and agree to follow the girl, to act as a distraction if necessary. I'll think of something.

"And Sylvain," I say as my parting shot, "don't you dare let Sophia get wind of this."

As I slowly push open the creaking door of Saint Pierre, the priest is in full flow, warning of the evils of temptation in today's society, and urging an honest path upon his congregation. I sit in the closest pew to the door, accompanied only by a scruffy-looking old man who looks as though he's only here to seek respite from the drizzle outside. He removes a very worn beret from his head as I make myself comfortable and our eyes meet momentarily, both of us on edge but glad of a dry place to sit and contemplate the future. I feel him inappropriately appraising my legs and pull my long coat around me, purposely staring ahead. It's going to be a long day.

By eleven-thirty, most of the worshippers have made their way to the door, shaking hands with Father Francis and telling him what a wonderful service it was, as they do every week, before dropping their Euros onto the brass collection plate.

As the last stragglers make their way down the church steps, I glance over at the priest. He holds up a finger, indicating that I should wait a moment, and then comes back inside, closing and bolting the heavy oak door, his rubber-soled shoes squeaking loudly as he strides towards me.

Silently, the Catholic priest points a finger at the confessional, pulling aside the curtain and allowing me to step inside. I notice droplets of rain on the shoulders of my son's best friend and resist a motherly urge to brush them away with my hand. I sit down and wait. It's the same routine every time, but rarely on a Sunday.

It's only a minute or so before I hear footsteps approaching, the click-clacking of good quality leather on the cold stone floor, making their way towards me, stepping to the opposite side of the box.

I draw in my breath and wait, suddenly feeling a few degrees colder than I have all morning.

"Colette?" a deep voice enquires, as one of my employer's men settles into his seat, shuffling slightly.

"*Oui,*" I say softly, wondering if Father Francis is standing nearby, silently listening.

"You need to give Foster his instructions at two this afternoon."

I've known that it would be soon, but my own personal worries have distracted me somewhat and I simply say, "Alright."

We converse in English, the bureau employees' language of choice, an unspoken rule.

"Does he suspect you?" the man presses, breathing heavily against the wire mesh separating us.

I smell the faint aroma of tobacco and wish that I had a cigarette at this moment. My hands shake.

"No, of course not. I have been discreet, as always."

"You seem to be getting quite... close," he wheezes. "Is it getting personal?"

I'm taken aback. Has someone at the bureau been watching us?

"Monsieur Foster and I have known each other for many years now," I say, choosing my words carefully. "It's only natural that we should socialise together occasionally."

"Of course," the man murmurs, giving nothing away. "You know that the boss doesn't approve of employees fraternising together? Except in the course of... business."

He draws out the last word, as though pulling it on a piece of string from inside him. I know the rules and, as far as I'm concerned, I haven't overstepped the mark. Yet.

I try changing tack. "Who's the target?"

"No need for you to concern yourself, Colette. Everything that Foster needs is in the package, all you need to do is tell him he's had a special delivery. You can do that, can't you?"

"Naturally," I confirm. After all, it's not the first time that I've had to liaise between the bureau and the Black Sparrow. "Two o'clock."

I hear something being shaken and then pressed at the same moment that the man in the other confessional takes an even deeper breath. The agent is sucking on an inhaler.

"Colette?" he manages, now speaking without constriction in his chest. "Is there something that you're not telling me? You know they have ways of finding out... eventually."

Despite his puff of medicine, the voice is still slightly raspy, but now carries a menacing tone.

"Foster is planning to retire," I tell him. "This will be his last job."

Silence. Then a slight thud as the man's shoulders lean back against the wooden panelling.

"I see. And he told you this when, exactly?"

"Last night. I think he might ask me to... to go with him."

A snort, something between laughter and disgust.

"Well, well. And what do you think about that, Colette?"

He pronounces my name like the cluck of a chicken, purposely stretching the vowels.

I sigh, resigned to my loyalty to the bureau. The income is too much to lose, and I know what would happen should I try to resign.

"I think it's an impossible idea. Monsieur Foster has fanciful dreams."

I listen for the next few minutes as the agent delivers my final instructions. I still have no idea whom Colin Foster is here to assassinate, but I hope that tomorrow comes and goes quickly.

"Colette? Have I made myself clear?" the rasp presses.

"Yes, Monsieur," I affirm, pressing my palms together in prayer.

"Father Francis has the instructions," the voice hisses through the wire. "Wait five minutes until I have gone before coming out. There will be something extra in your bank account by Tuesday. Our boss thanks you for your... compliance."

The last word hangs in the air like a bad aroma, distasteful but hard to dispel. I start to thank him but he's already on his feet, click-clacking away towards the vestry door.

I look at my watch and wait seven minutes, just to be sure, before pulling back the curtain. Father Francis is sitting in the front pew staring at the altar. As I approach, he hardly stirs, silently handing me a crisp, rectangular white envelope and then bowing his head in prayer.

I sit in the pew behind the priest and cross myself, focussing my eyes upon the huge golden cross that adorns Saint Pierre's altar.

"Are you alright?" Father Francis asks, after what seems like an age.

I tighten my grip on the package and avoid the question. "It will soon be finished."

"You can stop this if you really want to," he tells me, turning slightly in his seat.

"That's not possible," I retort, far too sharply. "I have orders to follow and, if my son and his family are to have a decent future, I need to leave them a good legacy."

He sits silently, contemplating my response, so I add, "What about your involvement, Francis? Why do you allow the meetings to take place in the house of God?"

The priest sighs, looking every inch the frightened child that Sylvain used to bring home for supper night after night. "Your employer donates very generously to the church. Without his funding, there would be no 'extras'."

"You mean he's lining your pocket, too," I mutter sarcastically. "I guess the arrangement suits us both then, doesn't it?"

I stand up to leave, giving a subtle shrug of my shoulders as I move away.

"Madame Reno," Francis calls, "wait!"

I turn, surprised by the name that has just come from his mouth and desperately check that there is no-one still here in the shadows of the church pillars.

"Francis!" I hiss, keeping my voice low. "Don't use that name again. How many times have we been over this? I am Madame Joubert to everyone, including you. Colette Reno no longer exists."

I slip the white envelope into my coat pocket and head outside into the wet morning. The streets are as silent as a funeral parade and only a few dog-walkers now brave the November weather. Inside, I'm still reeling. I need more time to deliver on the promises to my employer.

As I sidestep the deep puddles on my way back home, I resolve to take each hour as it comes. I have until two o'clock to feign surprise at the Black Sparrow receiving a special delivery. I know all the correct noises to make by now, I've certainly had enough years of practice; slamming the front door, faking interest at the envelope in my hands and remarking upon the fact that it's rare to see couriers out on a Sunday afternoon.

My employer's other request bothers me, though. Something unexpected and quite out of the ordinary. I don't doubt that I'm up to the task, but I rather suspect that there will be regret afterwards.

Placing my front door key into the lock, I look up at the building in front of me. This house holds so many memories, tragic and beautiful at the same time, but I wonder whether it's now time to let it all go. What would my late husband tell me to do? Would he have me tied to the bureau and their dark affairs for the rest of my days, or would he tell me to run for the hills?

I don't doubt that he would be proud of my loyalty to the organisation that he helped to create. My Emil was a rogue, but a smart one. He was the 'big boss' all those years ago when a much younger Colin Foster entered the fold, vying for attention and challenging the bureau to give him more and more assignments.

Of course, Colin never met me then. We lived in a much grander house on the other side of Paris, moving in affluent circles, but none of our so-called 'friends' were quite sure how Emil made his money. Moving to the guest house after my husband's death was a way of keeping a closer eye on Foster's movements when he came to France, as the bureau was always careful to recommend him to stay in modest accommodation. Naturally, I was reimbursed handsomely for handing over the reins to a more energetic and younger team, the reward for keeping my mouth firmly shut.

Closing the door, I think of the Black Sparrow, no doubt sitting in his room waiting for a delivery. Not once have I seen evidence of remorse after his task is done. Undoubtedly, there will be none tomorrow, either and it intrigues me slightly to think how cold Monsieur Foster really is. Nothing like the man who laughed openly over dinner, or the kind gentleman kissing me goodnight, eager to promise me the world should I choose to follow.

Heavy clouds are gathering overhead, and a migraine is threatening to penetrate my thoughts.

SUNDAY MID-DAY – TARIQ RAFIQ

It's quiet in the house, apart from the faint sound of Khalid playing on the X-Box in his room. Dad and Uncle Jameel have gone out in the car. My guess is that they want to talk about things without Aunt Farida overhearing.

The atmosphere is really strange, like somebody has died, except there's no corpse. Auntie is carrying on as usual, chopping vegetables in the kitchen and listening to an Asian radio show, but she hasn't said a word since breakfast.

Dad told me that things will be sorted in a few days. He's going to see if we can find early flights home, but first he might have to go to Paris with Uncle Jameel. Uzma has got a lot to answer for.

I ease myself off the bed and pull on a sweatshirt. It's so cold over here and it's not even winter yet. The central heating makes the rooms stuffy and I long to be back in my own country, breathing the warm air and feeling the sunlight on my face. We were supposed to be staying for three weeks, but there's no point now. There won't be any wedding celebrations, not if I can get Dad to listen to me.

Sneaking into Uzma's room, I gently close the door but listen carefully, in case Khalid or my aunt hear. However, I think they're both too wrapped up in their own worries to even think about me. It's dark in here. Auntie has left the curtains closed and I need to turn on the bedside lamp. I'm not quite sure what I expected, but it's just a 'girly' room, nothing different. The bright pink bedspread is a stark contrast to the pale blue wallpaper depicting birds sitting amongst cherry blossom branches. It feels warm and smells faintly of stale perfume.

Running a hand along the dressing-table, I look at all the bottles lined up in a neat row, perfumes, nail polish, and a white liquid that says 'eye make-up remover' on the label. I find it amusing how much 'stuff' Westernised girls seem to need. Back home, it's all about magazines and music.

The bed is springy and dips suddenly under my weight. I sniff the pillow and smell the same faint perfume that hangs in the air like the pollen of a dying flower. There's nothing under the mattress. I check cautiously and quickly, although I'm sure that my uncle has already been through here with a fine toothcomb. Getting up again, I check through the drawers of the bedside cabinet. There are books, brushes, hair clips and tissues, nothing to indicate that my cousin has secrets.

I was half expecting to find a diary, but in hindsight that was just wishful thinking. Uzma wouldn't be stupid enough to leave clues about her boyfriend. I feel a stirring of jealousy as an image of them together comes into my mind, but I don't despise her, as long as she's happy. I think it's a pity that Uzma couldn't choose to be with someone of our faith, but times are changing, and things are much different over here.

Picking up a stuffed panda from the group on the bed, I realise that my cousin is still a little girl. She's not ready to marry me, the Frenchman, or anyone. This room is a part of her personality, not the bedroom of a mature woman. Something wells up in me, a kind of sorrow. Maybe they're being too hard on Uzma. Perhaps she should have a chance at happiness. Doesn't everyone deserve that?

Retreating downstairs, I push open the kitchen door and catch my aunt in the act of rubbing her lower back. She looks in pain and, as she turns on hearing me, I can see that her eyes are red again.

"Tariq, you startled me," she says, faking a smile as she takes her hand from her spine.

"Sorry, Aunty, are you okay?"

"Yes, yes, of course, just a bit of arthritis, that's all."

"Maybe you should see a doctor, if it's really hurting," I suggest, as she reaches for the kettle.

"I'm fine, really. Tea?" Aunt Farida asks, already pulling two mugs from the cupboard.

I ask for coffee instead and sit at the breakfast bar, wondering how to broach the sudden, irrational idea that jumped into my head on the way downstairs. My aunt has her back to me, busying herself over our drinks, which makes it easier to ask.

"Aunty, I was wondering, do you think it would be a good idea for me to go to Paris? To look for Uzma?"

She turns quickly, a look of hope flashing across her face. "Tariq. I... maybe. But how would you find your way around? It's a huge city and you don't speak any French..."

"Aunty, I'm twenty-three. Old enough to travel to Europe by myself and with a map, how difficult could it be? I think I might be able to get her to see sense."

Aunt Farida stands still, her left hand stirring the coffee incessantly until she realises what she's doing and stops suddenly, throwing the spoon into the sink.

"How would you know where to look?" she queries. "She could be anywhere."

Obviously, Uncle Jameel hasn't told her about the electronic tracker. I fear that something in my face must have given away my thoughts, as my aunt brings the coffee over and grips my arm.

"Tariq, please, do you know something?"

As much as I love my aunt, I can't risk betraying Dad, he'd go berserk and never let me forget about it.

"No, I don't know anything," I lie, "but it makes sense that Uzma would head for the art colleges, or places where artists hang out, wouldn't she? I mean, she still wants to paint, doesn't she?"

My aunt has brightened suddenly, looking at me intently, seeing logic in my words. "You're right, Tariq, that's exactly where Uzma would be."

"So, could you help me? I haven't got enough money here to book a flight, maybe you could lend me..."

As soon as the words have left my mouth, my aunt looks completely deflated, as though her whole world was on the up but now it's just collapsed again.

"I don't have access to any money," Aunt Farida confesses, looking truly embarrassed. "Nothing."

I'm confused. How does she do the weekly shopping, or buy clothes, if she doesn't have money?

"Nothing at all? I'm sure I could get a cheap flight with one of those economy airlines."

"Tariq," she says earnestly, switching her gaze to the floor, "your uncle controls our finances."

"Okay," I tell her, still slightly confused as to how this could be. "I'll figure something out."

The front door opens and closes, the voices of my father and uncle rise higher than the sound on my aunt's transistor radio and they come into the kitchen.

"Turn that racket off," Uncle Jameel says sternly to my aunt, pointing at the radio.

"Of course," she replies timidly, fumbling over the knobs and blushing.

"Son, come into the living room, I need to talk to you," my father whispers, nudging me gently.

I slide off the high stool and leave my aunt and uncle alone, although the atmosphere is frosty, and I feel that things aren't good between them. Maybe it's all the stress over my cousin.

"Right." Dad sighs, pushing his hands into his trouser pockets. "It looks as though I need to go to Paris with your uncle. We're going to go as soon as flights are available, find Uzma and bring her home."

I nod, waiting for him to go on. This information comes as no surprise.

"So, I've been doing a great deal of thinking. Do you want to go ahead with the wedding?"

Just the fact that I'm being given a choice comes as a great relief to me and I think my father can see the answer etched on my face.

"Not really, if I'm totally honest," I tell him. "I don't think either of us is ready, especially after what's happened. I mean, what if people at home found out?"

I don't care about gossip, there are always those who say negative words about a new bride, like she's too fat, not pretty enough or can't cook, but I know this is what my father wants to hear. He's the one who has the concerns.

"Well, I'm leaving it up to you, Tariq. You're mature enough to know your own mind."

I feel release and it washes over me like a tidal wave, urging me to step forward and hug my dad.

"Hey, what's all this?" He places both hands on my shoulders, grinning. "You're sure, right?"

"Yes, definitely. Uzma's still a child and I can find a good wife back home."

We chat for a while, just ten minutes or so, and then there's a knock on the door. Uncle Jameel's head appears and my father beckons him in.

"Everything alright?" he asks, looking from Dad to me and back again.

"Yes, and I was right, Jameel. Tariq and Uzma shouldn't get married, it's not fair on the boy."

I feel my face reddening. They're doing this for me, so where does that leave Uzma? I have visions of my uncle sending her away to join a Holy Order somewhere in rural Asia.

"Sorry, Uncle," I begin, but he puts up a hand to stop my explanation, although his features are soft.

"It's alright, Tariq, it's understandable in the circumstances. I'd feel the same in your shoes."

Dad rubs his palms together, as if he's expecting a windfall. "So, as soon as Uzma's safely back home, I'll book our flights back to Pakistan. Okay?"

"What about Uzma?" I question, genuinely wanting to know how my uncle will deal with her.

"Don't concern yourself, it's up to your uncle how he decides to deal with his daughter." My father frowns. "I'm sure Jameel will find an appropriate punishment, with the guidance of Allah, of course."

As we sit around the table eating lunch, I can see that Aunt Farida is completely in the dark about Uncle Jameel's decision to go to Paris. I'm also puzzled that they're not going straight away. They could go by car, although I know that they've arranged some kind of warning for Uzma's French lover on Monday. Dad didn't go into detail, but I get the feeling he's going to get a beating. As long as my Dad's not involved in throwing punches, I'm not bothered. After all, the man has defiled my cousin, and deserves his come-uppance.

My aunt has prepared a light meal, vegetable samosas and onion pakoras, with a bowl of crispy spiced potatoes to accompany them. I can see dis-approval on my uncle's face as his eyes go darting over the dishes, one by one. Obviously, he expected something different.

"Too much starch," he tells Aunty, as he spoons a couple of potatoes onto his plate. "I hope you will find time to prepare us a proper meal tonight, Farida."

I want to interrupt, tell him that his wife was up early, praying at the Mosque, cleaning the house, but I know my place. I'm just a guest here and sit silently, eating my food. My dad seems oblivious to the disharmony around the table, which makes me wonder if this is how all couples behave after twenty years of marriage. Maybe I've had a lucky escape. Uzma and I could have ended up like Aunt Farida and Uncle Jameel, miserable, uncommunicative and bored.

Glancing over at my father, I give him a faint smile and he winks. I have a lot to be thankful for today. Things could have turned out so differently and now I can see a future without having the burden of a second-hand wife. I'm going to show my gratitude to Dad. He's one in a million.

SUNDAY 2PM – SYLVAIN

Standing outside the back door of the exhibition hall, I take a deep drag on my cigarette as I think about my mother's word of warning. She's right, of course. Mama is always right.

I know it's risky being here but, as soon as the gallery owner has been to look at my work, I'll make my excuses and leave. Thankfully, Sophia is at home resting, but I can't risk Uzma finding me here.

When all this started in the summer, I told myself that this would be the very last affair. Sophia being pregnant has changed my life beyond belief and I need to grow up, stop chasing rainbows and face my responsibilities. I don't suppose I was completely honest with Uzma, though. She had such a fit body that it was too hard to resist temptation. I never intended to hurt her, it was just going to be a fling, for fun, but the longer time went on, the harder it became to tell her. Our Skype chats have given me something to laugh about, Uzma is really funny, but it's no excuse. I know that now.

I run back upstairs, taking the stone steps two at a time. A few visitors have started to wander in already. They look enthusiastic about the art, but then again, perhaps the exhibition offers a welcome respite from the dismal rain. My friend Ragi has the spot next to mine, set up with portraits and charcoal sketches. The guy is so talented.

"Hey, Sylvain," he smirks, "we've only been open five minutes and you're off smoking already!"

I shrug and splay my arms. "I know, my friend. Old habit. I really must give up."

"Look out, trouble coming this way!" He grins back at me, jerking his head sideways. "God's disciple."

I turn and see Francis walking quickly towards me. He's still wearing a white dog-collar under his black shirt but has changed into a pair of black chinos and a heavy wool coat.

"Hello there, so glad you could come," I say, holding out a hand.

"Well, couldn't miss an opportunity to see your latest masterpieces." Francis smiles, gripping my fingers tightly. "Now, there's a beauty. I recognise Saint Pierre's bell tower in the background."

My friend releases his grip and leans forward to study the work carefully. It's one of my most recent watercolours, painted as the leaves were turning yellow and red a few weeks ago.

"Have you seen your mama today?" he continues, eyes still fixed on the artwork.

"Yes," I tell him, pushing my hands deep into my pockets, "she was here earlier. Why?"

"No particular reason. I was just wondering how she is."

I instinctively know when Francis is lying, he's so terrible at it.

"Wasn't she at church this morning?"

My friend bites his thumbnail and nods. "Yes, but we didn't get chance to..." He stops, finally turning to look at me.

"What is it? Francis, is my mother in trouble?"

He stands still, not answering and then points over my shoulder.

"Sylvain, there you are! Oh, I thought I might over-sleep and miss the exhibition!" Sophia is panting and red-faced. She's carrying a wet umbrella.

"Sweetheart, what are you doing here?" I ask, reaching for a chair for her to rest upon.

"You don't think I'd miss your display, do you?" She winks as I stoop to kiss her. "I'm so excited. Has the gallery owner arrived yet?"

I shake my head, keeping one eye on Francis who still hasn't explained why he's asking about Mama.

"Not yet, but he should be here anytime. Shall I get you a bottle of water? You look hot."

Sophia smiles sweetly, brushing my hand with hers. "Yes, please."

I leave Sophia chatting to my best friend and dash downstairs to the small café for refreshments. It's not terribly busy but several local people recognise me and strike up a conversation. When I return to the exhibition hall, Sophia is talking to a slim, dark-haired young woman. I can't hear the conversation, except for the odd word in English, but I recognise the pert backside and slender shoulders of the woman with her back to me. Shit, it's Uzma!

I back-track a few steps, eager to keep out of sight but desperate to stop the two from talking. Goodness knows what Uzma might say. She can only be here looking for me, and it would break Sophia's heart to find out I've cheated on her. I can almost hear the pounding of my heart in my ears, such is the intensity of its beat. I don't think I've ever experienced such raw panic in my whole life.

Tucking the bottle of water into my jacket pocket, I do the only possible thing that I can do right now. I call Francis. Hopefully, I can get him to separate the women, using his genius. The phone rings at my end but my friend doesn't pick up. His phone must be in his pocket, out of earshot. I can see the priest's head, he's laughing with Ragi, but the pair are oblivious to my plight and don't look over.

For a few seconds, I stand watching Sophia and Uzma talking. Thankfully, Uzma hasn't looked at the art behind my girlfriend, or she would see my signature, but it's literally a matter of seconds until she does. I stand open-mouthed, unable to shout in case Uzma turns around, but also transfixed by how the two young women are talking so casually, each oblivious to the other's identity. My head feels as though

I'm trapped inside a bubble, watching a TV show, so unreal is the scene in front of me.

Suddenly, she's here at my elbow. Mama has arrived. She follows my gaze across the room, her eyes wide and disbelieving, but there's panic in her face. Mama can see what will inevitably happen.

I start to speak, asking her what to do, but she holds up a finger.

"I will get the girl out of here," she whispers, looking around conspiratorially. "And as soon as I have, you get Sophia and go home. I'll ask Ragi to take care of your paintings."

I'm confused by my mother's quiet voice until I notice a tall, well-dressed stranger standing behind her. He looks at me inquisitively and nods a greeting.

"Colin," my mother is saying to him, tugging at the man's sleeve, "I need a huge favour. Could you take the young Asian girl, Miss Rafiq, down to the café on the ground floor? It's rather urgent. I'll meet you there in a few minutes, but I must insist on her going now, if you could..."

The stranger looks over at where Uzma is standing, still close to Sophia, and nods. "Of course, Colette, but is everything alright?"

"Yes, yes," mother fusses, "I'll explain later. Please just do it quickly."

I have no idea how Mama knows this man, or how she can wield such influence upon him, but the stranger asks no further questions, just strides purposefully across the gallery floor.

Mother immediately turns to me and scowls. "I told you not to come," she hisses, baring her perfect white teeth. "When will you ever learn?"

We step into a side room, startling the young volunteer who is sticking price tags on souvenirs.

"Monsieur Reno!" He gives me a friendly grin. "How's the exhibition going?"

"Bonjour, Val," I reply. "Great, thanks. I just need a quiet word with my mother... erm, in private, please."

The teenager takes the hint and disappears out of sight, pretending to sort stock in a cupboard.

I hang my head, waiting for my parent to continue her tirade of frustration but when she doesn't, I look up into her tired eyes.

"I really needed to sell some work today," I plead with her. "It was such a great opportunity."

Mama clicks her tongue and says nothing, I can tell that she's beyond furious.

"Right, they've gone," my mother finally says, peering around the doorframe. "Get Sophia and leave."

I obey instantly, dashing across the oak floorboards as fast as my feet will carry me.

"We need to leave," I tell my beautiful wife. "I don't feel well, an upset stomach."

Sophia looks concerned and is soon asking me lots of questions, which I avoid as best possible.

"Please, can we just go?"

"But what about your exhibition?" She frowns. "You can't just leave your paintings here."

271

I turn to Ragi who, being my most sensitive friend, instantly knows that something is not quite right.

"Hey, no worries, man," he tells me, before the question is even out of my mouth. "I'll load them into my van. Francis can bring you any money from sales."

I look at the priest sheepishly. Francis can see through me like one of his blessed stained-glass windows. He's sitting on a stool with his hands in his lap in true religious fashion.

"Go on." He waves at me dismissively. "We'll sort things out here, won't we, Ragi?"

Outside, having quickly ushered Sophia into a side street, I catch my breath for the first time in what seems like hours. The rain has stopped, and I rub my hands over my face.

"Oh, you do look a bit green," Sophia murmurs, holding my arm tightly, "Let's get you home."

We walk in silence for a while, until I pluck up enough courage to ask, as casually as possible, "Who was that young woman you were talking to?"

My wife pauses to think. "An art student from London. She's just moved here, said her boyfriend's a local artist, but they'd lost touch. I was just about to offer to help find him for her when a strange Englishman came up and insisted on taking her for a coffee."

"I see." I pretend that I'm not very interested, but I can't help myself, "What's her boyfriend's name?"

"We didn't get that far. As I said, that strange man interrupted us."

I put my arm around my wife's shoulders and hug her to me protectively as we continue homewards. Nothing can come between us, especially not some summer fling. I owe my mother a great deal. Today, I was seconds away from being found out. All the lies, secret conversations, the sex, everything would have come out should Uzma have seen me.

What the hell have I done? I just want this all to go away. Perhaps it's time for Sophia and I to make a fresh start somewhere else. Just me, her and our precious baby.

SUNDAY 4PM – COLIN FOSTER

Really, what a palaver! Goodness only knows what motives Colette had for involving me in her strange contrivance. The young artist that she spoke to had familiar features but I'm certain that I haven't met him before. Perhaps he is just a local acquaintance of hers. It was certainly puzzling that she wanted Miss Rafiq removed from the exhibition hall without explanation. I do hope one shall get to the bottom of it later. Life is so very full of surprises.

Back in my room, I put the kettle on and remove these impossibly tight Oxford brogues, flexing my toes inside warm woollen socks. On my arrival back here, I found a small white envelope on the carpet, no doubt having been pushed under the door by the housekeeper whilst we were out at the art exhibition. The front is blank, no name nor room number, and I ponder at how the deliverer of such an item should know to whom it should be conveyed. I am in no hurry to open the correspondence. I am aware of what it will contain.

Sipping hot tea, I lift the envelope with my right hand and then set down my cup on the dressing table.

The words are typed in bold black ink and are exactly what I expected.

ASSIGNMENT CONFIRMED.
MONDAY 4PM.
TARGET DETAILS & TOOLS TO BE DELIVERED MONDAY 2PM.
20K TRANSFERRED UPON COMPLETION.

I strike a match and watch the thick card burn, carrying it to the bathroom sink before the smoke sets off the fire alarm. Confirmation feels strange. Naturally, one was expecting to complete this final job before advising my superiors of my intention to retire but, now that the time draws close, I can't help but wonder how life will be without this solid foundation upon which I have built my career.

I will no longer be 'Colin Foster Hit-Man', although the title does make one snigger, so preposterous does it sound to one unaccustomed to the term, but one will find it necessary to conform to the guidelines of 'Retiree, Man at Leisure' or, heaven forbid, 'Pensioner.'

I finish my tea, sitting on the edge of the bed pondering my future. There are times when one completely forgets the dangers and dire consequences of one's profession, and everyday distractions, such as the odd fiasco with Colette this afternoon, draw one into a sense of normality that is so far removed from one's true personal life that one perceives a glimmer of hope for one's future.

Being here in Paris has given me the opportunity to explore the possibility that one is indeed capable of loving another human being. Sadly, restraint has to be observed, for the time being at least, although I have only this evening to test the water with Colette and perhaps make a suggestion that we begin a more intimate relationship. The question is, do I really know her well enough to gauge her reaction?

After washing my cup and setting it back in its place on the tea-tray, my gaze falls upon the black suitcase, now propped up against the far wall. Having seen the Asian girl wearing that shirt this morning, I'm convinced that she has my luggage and I hers. It repulses me to think of someone wearing my very best tailored shirts and, worse still, freely rummaging through my belongings. A raw anger wells up inside me. There are certain unspoken rules in life that should be abided by, and discretion is one of them. How dare that sullen miss take the liberty of staking a claim on my possessions!

Taking my new nail scissors from their case, I drag the suitcase into the centre of the room and begin cutting a hole in the side of the stiff fabric, pushing harder and harder until the plastic lock gives way at one side, allowing me to force the zip open. I gain no satisfaction from defiling another's belongings, only a slight feeling of retribution. An eye for an eye and all that, but in this case the violation of luggage.

Pushing the flapping lid of the case open to reveal the contents, I'm underwhelmed by the interior. A vast amount of clothing is folded neatly across both sides, some still bearing tags from the various high street stores from which they have so obviously been recently purchased.

Between the layers nestles a middle of the range laptop and next to that, various electronic chargers. I push my fingers into the clothing on the other pile and find a book. If I'm not mistaken, it's an Urdu version of the Holy Koran. My travels have put me in good stead to identify the scripture on the cover.

Poking out slightly from the lining is an envelope and, as I retrieve it from the hiding place, I can visibly count more than four thousand pounds. This young madam really has planned to run away, then. There's more than enough cash here to keep her at the guest house for a few months!

At the very bottom of the case is a plastic folder containing prints and artwork. The pictures are vibrant and show promise. Perhaps they are the work of a budding artist. Flicking through, I stop at a charcoal sketch, the style much more intricate and accomplished, deftly drawn by one with an eye for detail. I am in no doubt as to the subject. There, lying horizontal upon a bed with just a sheet covering her nether regions, is Miss Rafiq, her small, rounded breasts exposed, her facial expression shy and naïve. Searching the corners for a signature, I find the artist's moniker: *S.R.*

I get up off my knees and sit on the edge of the bed, rubbing my legs where they've started to go numb, and cast a glance over the young woman's pitiful chattels. Not much to show, really, but she still has her whole life ahead of her. The money puzzles me greatly. It's such an odd amount. Has she stolen from someone, or simply withdrawn teenage savings? But then, what youngsters save these days?

I'm drawn back to the case for a second snoop, my criminal instincts bearing me in good stead. There could well be more money hidden in the lining. Systematically spreading the contents upon the bed in order to return them exactly as one found them, I empty the suitcase completely.

To an untrained eye, the slit in the fabric would be virtually invisible, so neatly has it been cut, but, to my unfaltering gaze, the tiny gap is like a beacon flashing a warning sign. It takes just a small amount of wriggling to insert two fingers through the gap, and what an interesting find I pull out! If one is not mistaken, the gadget is an electronic tracker, similar to those used by myself in the past. A tiny red light indicates that the device is now active, which opens up a whole new line of questioning.

It's plainly obvious that Miss Rafiq has been tracked. However, the pursuer hasn't made a move yet as she's still here and oblivious to the fact that someone might be watching her movements. So, I ponder, what are they waiting for? Is it perhaps the young woman's father, trying to catch his daughter and her lover red-handed? If the person who hid the tracker were indeed in Paris, one surely would expect them to have revealed their intentions by now, or at the very least appeared at the source, which just happens to be my room, not hers.

I make a split decision. If the device remains in my hands, whoever is looking for the girl will no doubt find themselves knocking upon my door. At this stage in my current proceedings, an unfortunate situation could well have a negative interference upon tomorrow's task and naturally, like a domino effect, could cause all kinds of complications. The tracker must be moved.

Shrugging on my overcoat once more, I step out into the darkening street, the electronic device blinking away inside my pocket like a tiny beating heart. I pick my way through the myriad of cobblestones and puddles, walking quickly away from Madame Joubert's and heading towards the church, then onwards to my chosen destination. The afternoon is cold and dull, a stark reminder that my trip to Paris might almost be at an end but my business is far from concluded.

Arriving at the very same café that I breakfasted at this morning, I take a corner table and order a cup of Orange Peko. The last customers of the day are quietly finishing their refreshments and the waitress regards me with an air of contempt as she prepares my drink.

"We are closing soon, Monsieur," she tells me, spilling hot tea onto the saucer in her hurry to finish clearing up the other tables. "It's almost five o'clock."

I nod and take a gulp of hot liquid, the back of my throat flinching at the scalding heat.

"I won't stay long," I assure her. And certainly that is true; just long enough to use the washroom and drop my blinking friend into the waste paper basket.

SUNDAY 6PM – COLETTE JOUBERT

I feel sorry for the girl. She has been lied to and used. I saw the look in Sylvain's eyes when he noticed her at the gallery this afternoon, like a wolf salivating over a young lamb. His expression was exactly the same as the one that used to linger on his father's face, as he appraised the young secretaries and office juniors who came and went in a never-ending procession through his company doors. They are two of a kind, father and son, having their fun and never staying around to face the consequences. Casanovas, Romeos, cads.

I still haven't been fully enlightened about Uzma's situation, and whether there could be an unwelcome pregnancy on the horizon. I might be a protective mother, but I'm still a woman and therefore not immune to the maternal instincts that take hold in these circumstances. The poor girl's hormones will be causing her a lot of distress, if she is with child.

Perhaps I can help to diffuse the situation, or remove it altogether. I have plenty of money, should she need to procure a termination.

Climbing the stairs, I knock gently on Miss Rafiq's door, an elderly laptop and some fresh clothes in my arms. I can hear an old movie playing on the television set and she switches it off before greeting me.

"Madame Joubert!" she says, surprised to see me. "How are you? Are you feeling better?"

I can see that the young woman's eyes are red, but I am not knowingly the cause of her agitation.

"Yes, thank you, I am," I tell her. "May I come in for a moment, my dear?"

Uzma opens the door just wide enough for me to slide through and my gaze immediately falls upon the open suitcase on the floor. We share a look, a moment, but don't mention it.

"Thank you for escorting me home with Monsieur Foster this afternoon," I continue, as casually as my steely nerves will allow. "It was so good of you."

The guilt that I feel for feigning sickness lies far below the surface, but she isn't to know.

"Really, it's fine," she says quietly, her demeanour of folded arms and furrowed brows showing me that it was the last thing that she wanted to do today. I'm aware that her mission was to find Sylvain.

"I've brought you some fresh clothes," I tell the girl, as I lay the items on the bed. "Just a warm dress and some thick tights, and the offer of an extra night here, free of charge of course, if you so wish."

There's an almost inaudible gasp as Uzma sucks in her breath and thanks me.

"Plus, the use of my laptop," I continue, moving across the room to plug in the device. "I thought perhaps you could use it to Skype that elusive boyfriend of yours."

Tears well up in her eyes and I reach for Uzma's hands. They are warm, but her stiffness relays a mistrust, so I rub the back of her fingers with my palms, trying to soften her icy aloofness.

"Thank you for your kindness," she eventually whispers, the invisible barrier slowly falling down between us. "It's just I thought that today would be the day I would find Sylvain. Rushing away like that, with you and Mr Foster, it stopped me from..."

She's crying again and I pull her closer, although still managing to avoid a full embrace. I adopt a motherly tone, not difficult considering the bond that we share with my rascal of a son.

"Let's sit down. How can I help? Tell me about this man, this Sylvain."

Uzma Rafiq spills everything and within a quarter of an hour I am enlightened about my son's escapades and his promises to this foolish young woman. I don't dislike her, and I do feel a certain empathy towards her plight, but tugging at my conscience is sweet Sophia and my unborn grandchild.

I tread carefully when Uzma has finished speaking, choosing my words slowly.

"Perhaps this is a delicate question, my dear," I begin, tilting my head away from her to appraise the girl's honesty. "Do you suspect that you might be pregnant?"

I know the answer before Uzma has even opened her mouth. A mix of shock and amusement crosses her face as she struggles to comprehend my probing.

"What? No! Why would you even think that? Do I look fat?"

"I heard you being sick," I confess. "I thought that maybe...."

She breaks into a smile then begins laughing. In my desperate relief I join her, satisfied that my son has not sown his seed this time.

"A baby is the last thing that I want," Uzma tells me. "I had a bad stomach from something I ate. I feel absolutely fine now. No way could I be pregnant, we were really careful."

I nod, a slow, knowing gesture, allowing my guest to see that I believe her, and this time I do.

"Try the dress on," I urge, changing tack and assuming a more friendly approach. "Let's see how it looks."

The girl is shy and dashes into the bathroom to change, leaving me to inspect Colin's mislaid suitcase. It seems that the man has been unnecessarily careless, for there, on top of the pristine white shirts, is a collection of photographs that belong far from prying eyes. Is the man really so egotistical that he carries souvenirs of the dead around with him? A killer's portfolio!

I tear my eyes away and see a white cotton Saville Row number lying crumpled on the chair, and at that moment I feel glad that Uzma has defiled one of his precious shirts. Such a blatantly foolish move as bringing these photos here could cost the bureau, and myself, dearly.

"What do you think?" Uzma interrupts my train of thought, twirling in the soft jersey dress.

"A little big perhaps, but easily fixed with a smart leather belt," I say, removing my own and fastening it around her waist. "There, perfect."

She walks to the mirror and almost smiles. "This is the best I've looked all weekend."

"Now, I have entered the password," I assure Uzma, tapping the laptop keyboard. "Feel free to try to contact Sylvain, and good luck. If you need anything, anything at all, just give me a shout."

"Madame Joubert, you're amazing," she gushes, immediately sitting down to begin her search.

"Colette," I murmur, retreating from the room, but the long, glossy hair is already hanging forward as its owner types quickly, in a desperate attempt to locate my son.

Downstairs, I cross paths with Colin and stand rigid for a few seconds, unable to contemplate normal conversation with him given the discovery of his indiscretion.

"Ah, Colette." He grins unashamedly, oblivious to my mood. "Would you care to partake of a bottle with me tonight? I've taken the liberty of purchasing a rather cheeky Burgundy."

I stare at the bottle in his hand, blinking as I run my tongue over dry lips. "Yes, that would be delightful. But later, as I have a few errands to attend to. Shall we say ten? In the lounge?"

"Spiffing," Colin replies excitedly, in his upper-class way. "See you later, my dear."

I watch my lodger traipse upstairs. He takes care not to touch the banister as he goes, probably another obsessive-compulsive trait about germs or suchlike. I suppress an overwhelming urge to call out after him, to disclose who I am and what I know, to assert my authority as a force higher up the bureau food chain than he'll ever be. But, there will be time for retribution later, and enough hours to contrive a worthwhile penance. As his broad shoulders disappear from view, I turn away.

I head to the drinks cabinet and pour myself two fingers of brandy, throwing it back hastily. There's another conversation that I need to have right now, just in case my son is under any delusions that he can continue upon the perilous path that he has been so irresponsibly treading so far.

I am still not ashamed of my boy, it's impossible for a mother to feel that way about an only son, but a lesson must be learned if he and Sophia are to live happily together. Anything else can wait until later. Colin Foster, the bureau, that sad woman upstairs, all of them can be postponed. For until Sylvain is back on track and away from Paris, my mind won't be able to settle, and everything will be in turmoil.

"Sylvain, it's Mama," I say gravely, hoping that he picks up on my no-nonsense attitude.

"Hey, are you okay?" he asks, speaking in hushed tones, no doubt to conceal our conversation from Sophia.

"Not really," I confess, slowly melting inside as my heart invisibly reaches out to my son. "Uzma is going to try to Skype you, so make sure that you keep your computer off."

"Too late." Sylvain heaves a deep sigh. "It's off now, but I already had three missed calls from her, not that long ago in fact. Sophia almost answered the last one, but I got there just in time."

"You can't go on lying," I plead. "I saw your face to-day, Sylvain, full of lust and longing when you caught sight of that girl. You're your father's son, there's no doubt about it, but this has to stop."

"I promise you, Mama, it's over. I have too much to lose to mess around again. And I'm sorry."

"I want you to leave Paris. Take my car and go down to the old cottage in Bordeaux, take Sophia with you."

Silence. My boy is thinking carefully. So I press harder, eager to force upon him the right decision.

"Sylvain, you can still paint down there. Take your easel. Perhaps you will feel even more inspired there. Then, in a few months, when we're sure that Uzma isn't coming back, you can think about coming home."

"What will I tell Sophia?" he questions, always the pessimist, never the thinker.

"You'll think of something. Besides, it will be warmer down there and peaceful, too."

I hear the sound of my boy whistling softly through the gap in his front teeth, just as he did as a child, and that's the moment when I know I've got him and a plan is coming together.

"I'll talk to her tonight," Sylvain sighs, an admittance that Mother knows best. "If Sophia agrees, I'll meet you tomorrow to get the keys. But just for a couple of months, though, Mama."

"But you still need to be careful, do you hear me?" I start, wanting to caution him that Uzma is searching, but I hear a woman's soft voice behind my son and he hurries to finish the call.

"See you tomorrow, Mama, goodnight, thank you for ringing to check on us."

Standing with the receiver in my hand, I look down at where my son's voice has just cut me off so sharply. Now, he is no doubt turning to his beloved wife to tell her that his mother is fussing again.

I hope he has learned, sincerely I do, but the only way to be sure is to find out if Uzma's calls were answered. She'll tell me if they were; she'll be eager to break the news that her lover is once again on the radar. I sneak to the top of the stair to listen and within a few moments, I glean confirmation. Sobbing, loud and unashamedly unhidden, tells me that Sylvain is finally telling the truth.

SUNDAY 8PM – FARIDA

"Why are you saying this?" I plead with my son. "Is it your idea of a joke?"

Khalid looks at me, his face serious, and my gut tells me that this is the truth coming from his mouth, but I can't stop listening, no matter how much I want to cover my ears.

"I found out accidentally," he tells me in a low voice, no doubt worried that his cousin might over-hear. "Uncle Ali asked me to go and fetch the tracker to put inside Uzma's suitcase, but I thought I'd better make sure it worked first, so I slipped it into Dad's jacket pocket."

"What exactly did you see?" Curiosity starts rising rise to the surface where my anger bubbles.

"I told you. Dad and Aunty Shazia, kissing in his car."

"In the supermarket car park?"

Khalid nods, his cheeks flushing red as I ask him to repeat what he's already confessed.

"The very far side of the car park, in the corner. I suppose they were trying to keep out of sight."

"And you're sure they were... I mean, is it possible they were just talking?"

My son lets out a heavy sigh and pulls his mobile phone from a pocket, flicking through until he finds what he wants, or needs, me to see.

The photograph is a bit grainy but I can make out a car the same as Jameel's, a dark saloon. There's a woman with long hair in the seat nearest the camera and someone has their hand on her face.

Khalid takes the phone back and zooms in on the shot, frustrated with my inability to fathom anything even slightly technical.

"There, do you see now?"

The top of someone's head is obscuring the woman's mouth. They are in an obvious clinch, and now I can make out the red and white scarf around the woman's neck, the very same pattern as the one that I gave my best friend on her birthday. I can also see the cluster of little brass bells hanging from the car's interior mirror, the ones that my husband has transferred from car to car over the decades, an heirloom from his father.

Khalid takes the phone back and gently presses his fingers on the screen to show me the car parked next to Jameel's. It's Shazia's red Nissan Cherry.

I can't speak, because I can't breathe. Pressure is welling up somewhere inside me and my son's voice recedes further and further away as I start to go light-headed.

"Drink this," a familiar voice urges, lifting a glass of cold water to my lips. "It'll be okay, Mum."

Slowly, I control my breathing, in through my mouth and out through my nose, just as the doctor told me to do when I first admitted to my panic attacks a few years ago.

"I'm so sorry," Khalid whispers gently, kissing my forehead. "Please don't say anything yet. Dad'll have a fit if he knows I've told you. You know how he'll be..."

It takes all of my effort to nod and agree. I know exactly how Jameel will be; the bruises on my body bear witness to his anger and cruelty. But how am I going to keep this in?

"Rest for a while," my son tells me, forcing me to sip again and then setting the glass down on the coffee table. "Dad and Uncle Ali won't be back for another hour. Tariq's gone with them."

I put a trembling hand on Khalid's arm, stopping him from sneaking away. "When did you find out?"

I need to know this. My eyes search his.

"Four days ago, but I couldn't tell you, I didn't know how. And then, with all the fuss over Uzma..."

"It's alright," I assure him. "It's not your fault."

I've been lying down for a while now, trying to put my thoughts in order. As soon as I think up a possible way to confront Jameel, the memories of last night's beating come flooding back and I know that I have to stay tight-lipped. All sorts of pictures come into my mind. Some make me nauseous, like the image of my husband fondling my so-called friend, but others just fill me with hatred. The deceit, the lies, all of it building up brick by brick to create our sham of a marriage. No wonder Uzma ran away.

Sitting upright, I retrace my movements over the past few weeks. I've visited Shazia's house at least seven times and not once has she ever acted with guilt or shame. Blatant mockery is what it is. She was no doubt laughing at poor fat Farida behind my back whilst arranging lurid meetings with my husband.

I realise that I don't care why. Reasons for adultery are mostly sexual and that side of marriage to Jameel was never anything to write home about, but the shameful thing is that I told my friend about our love-less sex-life. I confided in her. Could that be the opportunity she needed to seduce unsatisfied Jameel?

I don't know why, but suddenly I think about the old lady on the bus again. I suppose she's having a good roast dinner with her brother's family before putting her feet up with the cat for company. It seems like a very tempting existence from where I'm standing right now, the solitude a blessing.

But who am I fooling? Things won't change, no matter whether I challenge my husband about the affair or not. We'll go on, day after dreary day, hardly speaking, oblivious to the other one's needs. I'll pander to his everyday demands, providing freshly ironed shirts, carefully prepared meals and limited conversation. This is nothing to be proud of, my pathetic situation. People will find out eventually. It's no use asking an excitable seventeen-year-old boy to keep a secret like this. He's probably already told at least half a dozen of his friends. I need a way out.

The front door slams and I hurriedly dry my eyes, stuffing the damp tissue into my cardigan pocket. Male voices fill the hallway and I get up to put the kettle on.

"Tea?" I call from the kitchen, my voice croaky and tight.

"Yes," Jameel snaps, standing in the doorway with his arms folded defiantly. "Make yourself useful, and prepare us something to eat, too, would you? I expect Ali and Tariq are starving."

He doesn't even notice my red eyes – or, if he does, he has assumed that I've been crying over Uzma.

Ali and Tariq gesture politely from behind my husband's tall frame, before going into the sitting room.

"Jameel?" I say, testing myself, seeing whether I'm brave enough to spill the beans.

"What now, Farida?" He sighs heavily, rubbing at a mark on his shirt cuff, not even meeting my eye.

"Chicken korma." The words fall from me as though they've been sitting on my lips just waiting to drop off. "Twenty minutes."

Jameel shakes his head, and moves off to be with his brother, the conversation over before it's even begun.

"This is great!" Tariq grins, tucking into his second helping of curry and lifting another chapati from the plate, which he neatly cuts in two with a knife. "You should open a café, Aunt Farida."

I smile faintly but can't defer my gaze from the sharp tool on his plate. I have an overwhelming urge to pick up the knife and drive it right into my husband's heart, twisting until he draws his last breath.

"Farida?"

Ali is asking me something, but my mind is elsewhere, still stabbing Jameel.

"Wouldn't that be a great idea?" he repeats. "You could make a fortune selling these."

My brother-in-law waves a curry-laden chapati in my direction, feasting his eyes on the juicy meat and thick, orange-coloured sauce.

"I don't know," I say curtly. "What do you think, Jameel? A new career prospect for me, perhaps?"

"Don't be silly," my husband retorts sharply. "You barely manage to keep the house clean, without going out to work as well. Your job is here, looking after my house."

The words 'my house' are not lost on me and it's a stark reminder that, without that man to whom I am betrothed, I would have nothing, not a single penny. In fact, some of the savings that I did manage to hide have been taken by my darling daughter and the rest confiscated by my husband.

There's a rattle of spoons and plates as the men finish off their meal. Only Khalid has noticed that I haven't eaten anything, but he's too sensible to say anything and we exchange glances.

"Superb," Ali says, sitting back in his chair and displaying a full stomach.

I find it quite ironic that the meal receiving so many compliments is straight from the freezer, the last of a batch that's been stored away for months. Typical men, oblivious to the pinging of a microwave for the quarter of an hour it took me to reheat everything.

I collect the plates and my son follows me to the kitchen, his cousin a few steps behind.

"I'll clear up," Khalid says kindly, reaching past me to run the hot water tap.

"And I'll help him," Tariq joins in politely, already rolling up his sleeves.

"You'll do no such thing," I reprimand. "You're a guest, Tariq, Please go and sit with your uncle and father. Khalid and I can sort this out."

I watch as my nephew reluctantly retreats, throwing Khalid a half-smile as he leaves.

"Have you decided what you're going to do?" Khalid presses, once Tariq has gone. No doubt he is anxious to find out whether he'll eventually encounter his father's wrath.

"Yes," I sigh, searching the drawer for a clean tea towel and avoiding his look. "Yes, I have."

"So, are you going to tell Dad that you know?" he whispers, watching the door guardedly.

I shake my head. "No, I'm not."

"But Mum…" he starts. I hold up a finger.

"Please, Khalid, let it be. You're too young to understand adult relationships. Your father and me, it's much more complicated than you think. Things aren't just black or grey in this world."

"White," he corrects me, "it's black or white."

"Well, that too," I relent, keeping myself busy, tidying, drying plates.

"So, you're just going to let him get away with it then?" my son says incredulously, looking wide-eyed.

I shrug, there's nothing else to say.

"And Aunty Shazia?"

I can feel a hot flush coming at me, rising from my toes and climbing my legs like poison ivy.

"Oh, don't worry. Aunty Shazia will be sorry for the day she ever set eyes on your father."

The men are settled, including Khalid who was secretly itching to watch some music competition on television. It's what teenagers do, I suppose. They watch these programmes and dream of becoming rich and famous. I can faintly hear the sounds of the singers' voices rising up through the floorboards as I run a hot bath in our family bathroom, up here, out of the way.

I don't take off my shalwar kameez, there's no need, but I roll up the sleeves to reveal my chunky wrists. There's a large purple bruise on one. It must have been where Jameel grabbed me during the interrogation. It doesn't matter now, nothing does.

Slipping into the hot water, I flinch. It's hotter than I can usually bear but it seems fitting for tonight.

A slow wave glides over my shoulders as the fabric in my clothing gets saturated, the yellow hues turning golden as they darken with the water. I slide my head under, too, wanting the heat to envelop me completely. I want to know what it feels like.

On the side of the bath is my tool of choice, a single razor blade taken from Jameel's wash-bag, the one that I have never opened before but has revealed its secrets to me this evening in the form of a packet of condoms. 'Sensitive', the label says; apparently that would mean something of a sexual nature, but doesn't cause more than a blink of my eye.

When I'm ready, which really doesn't take long as I only need to mentally prepare, I take the shiny new blade between two fingers and carefully cut where a distinctive blue vein protrudes, repeating the action on the other wrist before I lose my nerve. The blood oozes quickly and I watch for a few seconds as it discolours the bathwater like a swirling pot of overturned paint.

I haven't said goodbye to my children. That's the only thought that causes a second of panic, but then I lie back and let the light-headedness take over. They'll be fine. Without me, Jameel need never find out that his only son has betrayed a secret. He'll be okay, Khalid is a good boy. Uzma will be fine, too. She's probably hiding somewhere with her gorgeous French artist, planning for a future away from the confines of this house and its rules.

I close my eyes, dreaming lucidly of my family in Pakistan and the childhood laughter of happier days. If only someone had told me how things would turn out... if only I'd known. But if I'd shunned the hand of Jameel Rafiq in favour of some country boy back home, then what? Who's to say life would have been better? I can only blame myself.

I feel warmth on my face, almost like morning sunshine, and there are voices, I'm sure. Although they're all talking at once and the words won't come together as one, they're calling to me. It won't be long now. Freedom is enveloping me like a cloak, warm and safe. I can no longer feel my body. I couldn't raise my arm if I tried, so limp do I feel, but I'm sliding, down, down under the water like a mermaid discovering the depths as my hair fans out behind me. It doesn't hurt. Nothing hurts anymore.

SUNDAY 10PM – COLIN FOSTER

She's different tonight somehow, guarded, yet full of bravado, a fake smile, a glinting eye. Something has shifted within Colette. The sexy, sophisticated pussycat is watchful, and one can easily guess upon whom her sharpened claws are preparing to swipe. As I watch her deftly pour us a second glass of claret, swathed in a jersey jumpsuit, dressed to kill, there's a definite aloofness in her composure. Maybe the incident this afternoon is connected. She still hasn't explained why it became necessary for me to escort Miss Rafiq to the cafeteria.

I decide to probe, forcing a jaunty air into my enquiry.

"Are you feeling completely recovered now Colette?" I venture, taking the proffered glass of wine. "You seemed most unwell this afternoon, almost as though you'd seen a ghost, my dear."

She stands poised, the crystal goblet half way to her thin red lips.

"Yes, it was just a chill I think, but thank you for asking. At our age, it's best to be cautious." She lets out a short giggle, but it's artificial and doesn't belie the slightest pleasure.

"And the young woman, Uzma? What was so important that you required me to take her from the exhibition? Was it something to do with that artist fellow that she so desperately seeks?"

Colette's eyes shoot downwards, as if feeling the urge to inspect her immaculate leather loafers, and I can see that a raw nerve has been exposed. I may be advancing in years, but my intuition is still very much intact. It took very little consideration upon my part to connect the necessary dots.

"In a way," she finally replies, biting her bottom lip. "I just can't bear the girl to get hurt."

She forces a nod, although this is the second untruth within seconds. One is sensitive to these things.

I'm confused. "My dear, why on earth would Miss Rafiq get hurt? And surely the situation with her young man shouldn't become a burden to you? Don't worry yourself. Young love doesn't always run smoothly and maybe the couple are not destined for each other."

Colette regards me with slight amusement, as though one is talking utter tosh and, given one's continual singledom, the dear lady could well have a point.

"Well anyway, it would be a shame, that's all," she tuts.

There's more to it, much more, but she doesn't reveal it and I'm forced to let the matter lie, for now.

"Tell me," Colette begins, taking the comfortable leather armchair opposite, "what will you do once your business trip to Paris is concluded?"

"I rather fancy that I might travel a little." I smile, attempting to be open with my friend. "Although venturing off to pastures new can be lonely for a single traveller…"

I allow my response to trail off, hoping to provoke a reaction, but Madame Joubert simply studies me carefully, her piercing blue eyes glistening playfully.

"It's been my plan for a while, that I might retire early." I find myself continuing without provocation, irritated that alcohol invariably loosens one's tongue. "Do you ever consider a life with a tad more freedom, Colette? A longing to see the world, perhaps?"

She shifts, uncrossing her left leg and lifting the right one over the top, like a graceful feline stretching its limbs.

"Sometimes." She shrugs. "But I have many reasons to stay in Paris, so…"

I wait expectantly, eager to hear what tethers this beautiful lady to the city, but she closes like a clam and reaches for a grape from the fruit bowl, pressing it to her mouth hungrily. I change course, wondering whether Colette might be more easily… opened up, shall we say?… with a different topic, for at the moment, even the sharpest of shucking knives couldn't penetrate this pretty oyster.

"Do you realise that I've been coming here to your guest house for almost a decade now?"

The question hangs in the air until she plucks at it, momentarily amused.

"Really? So long! And in all that time we haven't really dug deeper than the surface, have we?"

She's toying with me again, perhaps trying to embarrass me or extract a confession.

"Maybe now is the time to be open," I urge. "You know that I admire you very much, Colette."

Admire. God damn my verbal incompetence when it comes to the female species. One admires paintings, poetry and scenery, not women! She's holding in a smirk, I can see it quite visibly. How ridiculous one looks at this moment.

"Have you never been married, Colin?" she suddenly asks, leaning forward to better hear my answer.

"Always a bachelor," I confess, setting my glass on the table between us. "Unfortunately."

One tries to read Colette's eyes, but there's nothing beyond the inquisitiveness with which she continually regards me. I anticipate some form of reflection and it comes.

"I can't imagine a life without love," Colette sighs, in her romantic Parisian way. "I loved my Emil with all of my heart. We had a wonderful life together."

This is the first time I've ever heard Colette use her husband's name and I mentally note the information. I stay silent, waiting, but she clams right up again, drifting into an inward swoon, obviously thinking of better times, of days when entertaining a middle-aged Brit would have been an unthinkable bore.

Colette excuses herself and disappears to powder her nose, leaving me to sit, and indeed contemplate, whether my original plan of suggesting that we take our friendship to a new level, should actually be thrown to the wolves.

Casting a seasoned eye around the parlour, I notice that the bureau drawer has been left slightly open and for several minutes I resist the urge to go over and close it. That is, until my OCD goes into over-drive and nags me to get up and attend to the task, the untidiness of anything left partially ajar setting my compulsive urges on edge.

Therein lies the beginning of a greater issue. You see, for one as particular as myself, a drawer cannot simply be closed, it must be slid out upon its edges quite fully to ensure that no contents become crumpled or creased and then gradually, slowly, shut three times, the magic number required to ensure completeness. This I undertake quickly, keeping a sharp ear for Colette's return.

A few papers are sitting untidily and as I am smoothing them down before making the initial closure, I notice a passport lying there, almost blinking at me. Curiosity peaks and I lift it out, turning quickly to the identity page, and see a picture of my beautiful friend. The name reads *Colette Reno.*

"Did you find anything interesting?" a familiar voice whispers like a ghost behind me.

"Colette, I…"

Unfortunately, I am still grasping the passport, unable to give a plausible account of why I'm doing so.

"I suppose it's only natural for a man such as yourself to snoop and pry," she sneers, as I turn to look at her. "I think it's time we said goodnight, don't you, Monsieur Foster?"

"Please, let me explain," I say feebly, desperate not to end our evening on such a bitter note. "I only meant to close the drawer. You see, it was open slightly and I…"

"You couldn't help yourself?" Colette teases sarcastically. "Why would I expect anything less?" She arches a brow with the natural ability of a seasoned actress.

"Please, Colette, I wasn't prying, just mildly curious perhaps…"

"Goodnight, Monsieur Foster."

For the second time, Colette uses my title and one instinctively knows that a fragile situation can only be made worse by trying to back-pedal one's way out of it.

I place the document in the drawer and push it shut, only just resisting the urge to repeat the process another two times. All the time, Madame Joubert is watching, like a wounded animal.

"Very well, goodnight," I acquiesce. "I do apologise, my dear. Perhaps we can talk in the morning."

Colette is holding the door wide now, waiting for me to pass through. Time to leave the stage.

Back upstairs, I curse aloud. Such a petty mistake to make and now I have been branded a snooper, a common peeper, a meddler.

I prepare a cup of tea... anything to distract oneself from this embarrassing scenario. As the little kettle bubbles away, I reflect upon the passport once more. *Colette Reno*, very definitely not *Joubert*, printed in the holder's details. Has the dear lady changed names?

Something niggles at me, like a pin-prick at first, but then develops into a deep splinter as suddenly I realise where I've heard that name before. Emil Reno! Colette called her late husband Emil, and Reno must be her married name. Oh my goodness, how can one have been so stupid for so long! A sickness washes over me like a damp shadow.

Emil Reno ran the bureau when I first came to be enlisted. Essentially, the man was my boss, although our paths never crossed in the real world, only via message, phone conversation and the occasional bank transfer for services rendered. Drat! Colette must know everything about me. She's been playing me at my own game. What happens now, one must ask? A termination of tomorrow's contract? Surely yes!

I want to race downstairs, to confront that woman and her hidden secrets, but to what effect? I can be sure that Madame Joubert is fully aware of one's purpose in Paris, both now and in the past. She would have been privy to so much at Emil Reno's side.

I sip the tea, uncertain of my next move for fear of a checkmate situation. Common sense is telling me to cut my losses and get out of Paris, but compulsion, the side of one that insists upon neatness, the tying-up of loose ends, orders one to stay and see this through. Colin Foster is not a runner.

Vigilance must now be the order of the day. I try to figure out if and how Colette could still have connections to the bureau without her late husband, but the answer eludes me.

One is destined for a sleepless night, lying in bed with one eye upon the door.

SUNDAY – MIDNIGHT – UZMA RAFIQ

Eight hours. That's how long I've been trying to get through to Sylvain via Skype. I think for at least four of those hours I've been crying, too. I haven't eaten since breakfast but just the thought of food makes me feel sick. I swear that tomorrow I'm going to try to find him. Once the airport staff have tracked my suitcase, I should be able to use the cash inside to pay someone to help me. A niggling doubt has started to set in, though. I mean, it's odd, but could Sylvain possibly be avoiding me?

The most rational explanation is that he's simply had a busy weekend. Perhaps he's had a student group this weekend, or maybe he's just been out with his friends. Either way, I need to stop overreacting. Even though I told him that I intended to come here to be with him, the flight was last minute and supposed to be a complete surprise.

I stop myself mid-thought. How was it now? Did I tell Sylvain that I wanted to be with him in Paris, or was it him who asked me? I've been so excited, and in love, for the past couple of months that I can't recall exactly how this plan came about.

I was sure that this afternoon would be the time and place to find my boyfriend. There was an exhibit of artwork very similar to Sylvain's style, colourful street scenes in vibrant shades, but the woman who was standing there said they were her husband's paintings. I didn't catch her name, but she seemed to want to help me – well, that is until stupid Mr Foster dragged me away to have coffee with him.

And all that fuss with Madame Joubert feeling ill, too. It seems as though the whole world is conspiring against me sometimes. Strange, though; Madame Joubert seems to be completely recovered tonight. I heard the two of them, her and Foster, clinking glasses and talking earlier.

My phone buzzes again, the sixth time in the last two hours. Four text messages from Dad and two from Khalid, all of them asking me to phone home urgently. I'm not falling for it. All they want is to talk me into going back but it's not going to work. I've made my mind up to stay in Paris and no amount of arguing or pleading is going to make me change my mind.

I'm quite surprised that Mum hasn't been at it, too – emotional blackmail. She's usually the first one to use her tears on me. I'm not even sure if I can fully trust Maryam at the moment, and it's risky telling her too much in case my parents force her to 'fess up, but she hasn't been in touch at all today. She's probably at work on a late shift again.

It's lonely without my parents and Khalid. On a normal Sunday night, we'd all be watching a film or Dad would be interrogating me and my brother about this week's lessons and whether we'd finished our homework projects. Sometimes, when Dad's working on a big case, he'd be holed up in his study. On those evenings, Khalid would sneak upstairs to play on his X-Box, leaving me and Mum to watch catch-up episodes of our favourite soaps. Dad goes mad if we try to watch them in the week, he says it's the kind of trash that turns sensible youngsters into tearaways. Honestly, he's so old-fashioned.

I'm tempted to text Khalid back but I'm not sure if he's just messaging me because Dad told him to. He's not a bad brother but he's easily led. He wouldn't hurt a fly – a spider, maybe if I screamed loud enough – but he's got a good soul. Dad wants him to become a solicitor, naturally, and I think he'll be good at it. Khalid has a lot of compassion. He's a bit sensitive sometimes, but he's a good kid.

I'm guessing that Mr Foster will want his charger back in the morning, so I plug my phone in to give the battery full strength overnight. I can't wait to get my stuff back. It's been unbearable without the bare essentials and I'm in dire need of clothes. It was kind of the Frenchwoman to lend me a dress, but it's not really me. I feel older, and frumpy. My hair is a mess, too, without straighteners, decent shampoo and styling mousse.

I must remember to take the charger down at breakfast time, just in case the old boy needs it. He's a funny bloke, very particular over things, such as how his breakfast is cooked, from what I noticed yesterday. He's a bit odd, too, fiddling about with the cutlery as though the table hasn't been laid correctly and he has to neaten it up. I suppose older people can be like that, though – picky.

I think I'm too wired to sleep tonight. There's not much on TV and even less in English, unless you want to watch reruns of *Doctor Who*, and I don't have anything to read. I've already looked at the magazine three times and know the features off by heart now.

The rest of the house is deathly silent. There was music playing downstairs earlier, I think it was opera, when Madame Joubert was with Mr Foster, but it stopped a while ago. She doesn't invite any of the other guests to join them, so they must be quite close. It seems like a strange match in my opinion, though. She's far too good for him.

Looking around for something to do, I pick up the glossy black and white photos from the stranger's suitcase. They're interesting, especially the names and dates. I wonder if they could all be related somehow. Curiosity gets the better of me. It's time to do a little research.

Madame Joubert's old laptop is still fifty percent charged, so I log in, wondering if I can find anything. It's not the quickest computer I've ever used, but the internet connection is strong and it doesn't take long for the browser to open.

Picking up the top photograph from the pile, I glance at the handsome young man staring back at me, dressed in a smart light-coloured suit, his teeth perfectly straight in a flawless face. I start typing the information from the back of the photo into the search engine, quite unprepared for what it reveals.

Albert Henri, Geneva, 12th December, 1982.

The laptop whirrs into action and several seconds later, a series of news articles appear on the screen. I can feel myself biting my lip as I read.

The body of multi-millionaire playboy Albert Henri was washed ashore on the edge of Lake Geneva yesterday. Police suspect foul play although there are currently no leads. Post-mortem pending.

Gosh, poor man. I scroll down, looking for updated news and a cause of death.

Coroner reports reveal that playboy millionaire Albert Henri was murdered. A post-mortem has confirmed that the man was suffocated before being thrown into the lake. Family are flying out to Switzerland today and a full police investigation is ongoing.

I search for the announcement of an arrest or someone being charged, but there's nothing more. Perplexed, I pick up the next photo and find myself looking at a glamorous older woman, perhaps in her sixties. She's wearing heavy gold bracelets around both wrists and her coat looks like it's made from real fur.

Susannah Nicholls, London, 18ᵗʰ September, 2003 is neatly printed on the back.

Again, I type in the information and wait.

Police have launched a full-scale inquiry into the murder of businesswoman Susannah Nicholls after her body was found by her husband on Monday. Stuart Nicholls returned to the couple's home from a week-long business trip to find his wife had been shot through the head at close range whilst sleeping.

I put my hand over my mouth. There's something not quite right here. As I pick up the next picture, of a much older man with white hair wearing a kilt, I'm actually dreading what I'll find.

Gregory McCloud, Edinburgh, 3ʳᵈ June, 1994. I type the details and wait.

The poor man was found with a bullet wound through his heart, out on a remote Scottish farm. Once again, reports show that the case went unsolved and nobody was convicted.

After typing in the fourth name, *Klaus Reiner, Dresden, 25ᵗʰ May, 2012*, I feel sick.

Every single person from this pile of photographs so far has been murdered in cold blood, each case still open, the murderer free to kill again. I plough on, with the need to know whether all of these people are victims, and if they all met their end alone. They are, and they did.

I don't know what this means, but I'm damned sure that it's not normal for someone to have this kind of information in their luggage. It almost looks as though they have been collecting trophies. I'm beside myself now, stressing and scared stiff.

I lay the photos out on the dressing table, noticing for the first time that they're numbered on the back. Looking at the dates, I can see straight away that they relate to the chronological order in which the murders were committed. I feel a strange sadness wash over me. I didn't know any of these people, some were killed long before I was born even, but they all look very real now, staring back at me from their black and white snapshots. Scanning the faces, the clothes, it seems that whoever murdered them in cold blood was indiscriminate about age or gender, although each of these people looks well dressed and successful.

I can hear a thumping in my ears and realise it's the rapid beating of my heart. What should I do with the information? I'm here in a strange country, holding evidence that might well be vital, but I have no idea where to turn.

I'm parched and reach for a bottle of mineral water from beside the bed. Taking a couple of long sips, I look back down at the strangers' faces, some smiling for the camera, others looking off into the distance. But they all seem to have one factor in common – they're all dead.

Maybe I'm just over-thinking this. The suitcase might, and please let it be true, belong to a detective charged with solving old crimes. What do they call them? Cold cases? Maybe that's why the information is here, like this. But then where are the files? Surely, if you're investigating something you'd also have a folder full of details, wouldn't you?

I feel really confused, but also a bit afraid. Supposing this case, and the photographs inside, belong to the person who killed these people. What then? Would he, or she, go crazy if he found out that some random person was looking at them? The only trouble is, I can't un-see the information now... or can I? Maybe I can pretend that I never saw the pictures, and that I never read the information.

Ten minutes later, I'm downstairs putting the laptop on the reception desk. I quickly grab a yellow Post-it note and scribble *Thanks* before sticking it on top and returning to my room. As I push the key into the lock, a door opens and closes downstairs but then everything is silent again.

Shit. I didn't clear the search history in the browser.

I doubt very much if someone of Madame Joubert's age is very technically savvy, but it's not worth taking any risks. I don't want her thinking that I'm some kind of nut job who reads up on murder for kicks, so I dash back downstairs as quietly as I can, mostly to avoid any snooping residents, to retrieve the laptop again.

Too late. It's gone. Madame Joubert must have heard me come down the first time and seen that I'd brought her computer back. Aargh! Everything has turned to rat shit today.

MONDAY 2AM – KHALID RAFIQ

Police, paramedics, coroner's office, they've all been here this evening, but the house is empty now, except for me and my family. I feel hollow, can't speak, nothing to say.

Mum's body has been taken away. I think it will be at the mortuary, or wherever it is they take the dead. I still can't believe she's gone and I'm one hundred percent certain that it's my fault. If I hadn't told Mum about Dad's affair with Aunt Shazia, she wouldn't have had a reason to kill herself. She must have really loved my dad to be so upset about what he's done. I should have kept it to myself, not shown her the photos, not opened my big mouth.

I can't get the picture out of my head. Mum lying there with her eyes closed, her hair floating around her face like strands of seaweed, and the red, the deep red of the water. We don't know how long she was lying there, alone and dying, but Dad says that the bath water was cold, so it must have been over an hour. If Uncle Ali hadn't needed to use the bathroom at the same time as Tariq, it might have been a lot longer before we found her.

Not long after Uncle went upstairs, he shouted, that water had seeped into the carpet on the landing. Dad and I went up. The bathroom door was locked. Dad shouted to Mum but she didn't answer. Well, she couldn't, could she? He banged for a few minutes, but she still didn't respond, so he fetched a screwdriver and broke the lock. I don't think Dad realised that I was still there, right behind him, but I was, and I saw her. She looked so peaceful, but it was the blood that made me scream. So much red.

Dad is still downstairs with Uncle Ali. He's in shock, apparently. I want to shout at him, explain that it's all my fault, and his, but I'm afraid of what he'll do. I don't think he'd ever forgive me.

I go into Uzma's room and sit on her bed. My bedroom's next to the bathroom and I can't bear to think about what happened in there just a few hours ago. Why didn't Mum just confront my Dad? That's what women in TV dramas always do, they shout and cry and threaten divorce. Mum must have thought there was no turning back. She must have been so deeply hurt by what I showed her. I hate Dad and Aunt Shazia for this. They disgust me.

I tap in another text message to my sister. I don't think it's right to tell her that our mother is dead in this way, so I just ask her to call me, urgently. I can see that the text has been delivered but I wait for ages and she still doesn't answer. Probably asleep in her French boyfriend's house.

I don't blame my sister for any of this. I reckon that Dad and our aunt have been carrying on for a while. It's horrible to think about people of their age sneaking around behind their partner's backs, meeting up in car parks, snogging the face off each other. If this is how life is, I'm never going to get married. I'll stay single forever, go travelling, make loads of money and build a massive house to live in, alone.

Poor Mum. I think about her all over again. She's all alone in a strange place. Someone should be there. They zipped her into one of those huge black body bags that you see on police programmes.

Everything is the same in Uzma's room. I guess both my mum and my dad have been in here since Friday, looking for clues, turning everything upside down. But Mum's neatened it again, the bed's made properly and the wardrobe doors are closed. I don't want to touch anything. I'm scared now that something might happen to my sister. After all, I haven't got anyone else to talk to.

I wonder how long it will be before Dad starts telling everyone? People will need to know about Mum and most of the neighbours have already been up at their windows watching the blue lights arrive and trying to get a glimpse of what the paramedics were doing. The gossip will start in the morning.

When something like this happens, people always ask why. Why did she do it? Why was she so upset?

Why did she lock the bathroom door? Why didn't she go to someone for help?

I can answer a couple of those questions, but I don't think I will. The fingers will point at me if I do. I won't ever forget the look on Mum's face when I told her what Dad was doing. She looked shocked, naturally, but there was something else, almost a look of defiance, as though she wouldn't let it beat her, that she could get through it.

If I'd have thought for one moment that Mum would take her own life, I would have kept the secret, deleted the photos, never spoken about it. But I honestly thought she deserved to know. Uzma and I are both old enough to cope with our parents splitting up, it wouldn't have been so bad. I can't even face Dad right now, though. I'm going to stay up here out of the way.

He comes upstairs looking for me, his feet thudding heavily as he heads to my room.

"Khalid? Where are you?"

Dad opens the door and finds me sitting on the floor next to the radiator in Uzma's room.

"What are you doing in here, son? You should try to get some sleep."

I sit still, a big fat tear welling up in the corner of my eye.

"Come on, how about I make you a hot drink? I know how you must be feeling."

How can he know? He can't have loved my mother or he wouldn't have been messing around.

"Khalid, come on."

Dad wraps his arms around me and heaves a big sigh, I think he's going to cry at first, but he holds on.

"Let's go down to the kitchen," he says quietly, easing me up onto my feet gently, hooking my arm in his. "A warm drink might help us both."

The tear escapes, rolling down my cheek and landing on my top lip. I quickly lick it away. I don't want to go with him, but I don't know what else to do, so I get up slowly but leave my head hanging. We shuffle down the stairs, side by side, although there's not really enough room for us to walk comfortably together and I'm squashed up against the wall for a moment or two.

Dad finally starts boiling milk, searching every cupboard for a pan and the drinking chocolate. It's obvious that he doesn't know where anything's kept, evidence that Mum did absolutely everything around the house. I sit silently on a stool at the breakfast bar and wait for him to say something.

"The next couple of weeks are going to be difficult," he finally blurts out, both hands shaking as he grabs mugs and spoons. "We have to be strong for each other."

I nod, but I'm not convinced that he's as upset as he's trying to make out.

"Did your mother talk to you? Did she seem upset about anything?"

"No. I don't think so."

The lie pops out before I even have time to think about the question, but I quickly add, "Of course she was upset about Uzma leaving, but not enough to... you know."

I can't keep the tears from flowing, and I'm scared that Dad will prise the truth out of me in a minute. Luckily, Uncle Ali comes in and Dad turns his attention away from me.

"You're still up," my uncle states, rubbing my back. It's a strange gesture but I suppose he doesn't know what else to do under the circumstances. I sit perfectly still.

"I can't sleep," I confide. "I keep thinking about her, my mum."

Uncle Ali hugs me to his chest for a few seconds. "I'm here for you. We all are."

Dad pours the hot chocolate, spilling some on the work surface. The drink tastes awful, he's forgotten to add sugar and hasn't put enough powder in it. I take a sip, not to make him feel better, but because I'm genuinely thirsty and can't be bothered to open a can of pop. Dad briefly smiles at me.

There's a white printed card on the kitchen worktop and I pull it towards me, reading the name.

"That's the Coroner's number," Dad tells me, "I have to ring them in the morning, to... erm, you know, sort things out. I'll probably have to go and..."

"Jameel, I can do that, if you need me to," my uncle tells Dad, but my father shakes his head and says that it has to be next of kin.

"I suppose the police will have more questions, too," Uncle Ali continues. "Are you sure you can face it?"

Dad shrugs. "What choice do I have? There's nothing to tell them, though."

I shoot a look at my Dad and words tumble out. "Surely we'll have to tell them about Uzma going to Paris? Won't we? They might be able to find her."

Dad looks at Uncle Ali. "We need to wait until the day after tomorrow."

"Why?" I demand, confused by the glances they're giving each other. "What difference will it make?"

"Nothing to worry yourself over," my uncle tells me. "Now, maybe you should get some sleep, Khalid."

"I'm not a child," I protest. "What's going on? Why can't we tell the police about Uzma yet? Maybe they could help to find her. Maybe they could contact detectives in Paris."

"We'll talk about it in the morning." Dad sighs. "It's late and we all need to rest."

"But, Dad..."

"Enough, Khalid. We're all upset. And tomorrow is going to be a long day."

Back in my own room, I undress and get into bed. I pull the duvet over my head so that I'm totally enclosed, and type another text message to my sister: *Where are you? Please call, need to talk to you.*

Again, it shows as sent but nothing comes back.

I can't close my eyes. If I do, I'll see Mum.

Only now do I realise that she was wearing her favourite shalwar kameez. Grandma's gold bracelets, too, and the heart-shaped gold locket with mine and Uzma's photos inside. I try desperately to think back to our conversation in the kitchen, the very last time that we talked to each other, thinking about what was said. Mum didn't seem so upset that she'd take her own life because of what I told her, but she was most definitely shocked. Maybe she felt more betrayed by Aunt Shazia than Dad. Men do have affairs sometimes, you read about it all the time, but my aunt was supposed to be Mum's best friend. I guess that's like a slap in the face, when your bestie does the dirty with your husband.

I lie awake, now and again drifting, but not quite sleeping. Mum was such a kind person. It's so sad that she died alone, in that cold water, with nobody there to talk her out of it. I want to blame my dad, he's the one who was unfaithful, but I can't. I'm the one who broke the news, I spilled the secret, I told her. My mother is dead and it's my fault. I caused her to take her own life, to slit her wrists, to lie in the bath with the water filling her lungs, nobody else. It was me.

MONDAY 4AM – SYLVAIN RENO

It's freezing out here and the smoke from my recently discarded cigarette lingers for a while before slithering off like a well-camouflaged snake. I rub my gloved hands together and pull another from the packet, inhaling deeply to keep warm, but not taking my eyes from Mama's house for one moment. The ground is crisp with frost, glistening on the cobblestones, reminding me that it's slippery underfoot. I must tell Mama to take care and wear sensible footwear and several layers when she goes out.

It's stupid of me to be so close, but force of habit took me in this direction. I wanted to see if Uzma had gone home yet, back to London, but it's impossible to tell as the lights are off and each window shrouded by tightly closed shutters. What if she's still there, anyway? There's nothing I can do. Mama is right again, of course. The sooner Sophia and I leave for the countryside, the better.

I turn away from the familiar building and head for the Church of Saint Pierre. Francis has kindly agreed to meet me, despite the ungodly hour. I need my friend to do something for me, the only favour that I will ask, and then this afternoon we will leave, straight after my wife's clinic appointment – the check-up that will confirm the sex of our child, to tell us that everything is going well.

"Sylvain?" Father Francis calls out as soon as the heavy oak door creaks open. "Is that you?"

"Yes," I answer, closing the latch firmly behind me. "Where are you?"

The church is lit by just a few candles laid out along the altar, and I pick my way carefully down the aisle, my winter boots clicking on the flagstones as I move forward, eyes searching the darkness for the priest. Everything echoes, it seems, even my hurried breath. I call out again.

"Over here," the priest calls from the vestry. "I have the heater on and some decent brandy."

I turn towards Francis's voice, skimming my fingers over the pews for support in case I trip.

"Hey!" I hug my friend. "Thanks for coming. You're a star, you know that, right?"

Francis shrugs. I can see by his face that he's wondering in what capacity I called him out in such bitterly cold conditions, priest or confidante. In truth, I need both his friendship and his guidance.

"Here," he offers, pushing a flask of brandy at me as I enter the little room. "Take a seat."

There's a small electric heater warming the space, but it does little to take the chill out of the air and I notice that Francis still wears his padded jacket and woollen hat. No dog-collar or clergy's robe today. I ease myself down into one of the brown antique leather armchairs, which creaks under my weight.

We regard each other for a few seconds, each waiting for the other to speak. I decide to go first.

"Sophia and I are leaving this afternoon. We're going down to the cottage in Bordeaux for a while."

My friend takes the brandy flask from me and swigs hard, swallowing in one gulp.

"Your idea? Or your mother's? Running away from a messy situation, eh, Sylvain?"

"Mama's suggestion," I confess. "But I think it's the best thing to do at the moment, don't you?"

"Is your mother going with you?" Francis questions, leaning forward slightly in his chair.

"No, why would she? I mean, the guest house has bookings still…"

There's a twitch, something niggling at the priest and I put my hand on his arm.

"What is it? Francis, tell me."

"I'm worried about your mother." I can sense by the sigh he gives that the admission is reluctant.

I pause, aware that pushing my friend may cause him to close up, his professional head clouding as he decides how much I need to know and which parts to confess.

He hesitates briefly. "She's involved in something," he tells me. "It's connected to that Englishman."

I'm confused. I'd asked the priest to come here to help with a delicate matter, not to talk about Mama. I sit waiting patiently as he tells me about the meeting with my father's old colleague.

"Who's the target? Do you know?" I ask, after having listened to what Francis has to confide.

He shakes his head. "No, but apparently a courier will deliver details this afternoon."

"Shit." I thought my mother had given up playing at the spy games, that she'd buried bureau business with Papa. How can I not have realised that she is still on the payroll?

"The Englishman, he's planning to retire after this one," Francis adds, almost as an afterthought.

"Fuck the Englishman!" I shout, running my fingers through my hair. "I don't give a damn about him."

"But somehow that's important, too," my friend explains calmly. "Your mother made a point of telling the contact when they met. He didn't seem too pleased. I think it's significant."

I'm confused. So what if that stuck-up Brit isn't coming back; isn't that a good thing for Mama? She won't have to put up with him fawning all over her again like a love-struck teenager.

Francis and I sit in silence for a while, each lost in our own thoughts.

"Do you want some more brandy?" he offers, breaking the mood after a few minutes.

I shake my head. "Better keep a clear head. Who knows what today might bring."

Francis watches me steadily. My face must be plastered with worry lines and frowns. He takes a short sip, licking his lips as the heat of the alcohol warms his throat, and screws the cap back on the flask. He looks weary. Maybe the burden of all these secrets is taking its toll.

"Why did you ask me to come here at this hour?" he murmurs, raising his eyes slowly upwards.

I'd almost forgotten my purpose and it seems like a ridiculous request, now that I'm aware of the danger that Mama might have found herself in. Being mixed up with a hired hit-man is not what I'd imagined for my dear mother and Papa would turn in his grave if he only knew. Foolish woman.

Still, I dig deep into my coat pocket and take out an intricately designed golden pendant.

"What is it?" Francis queries, pressing it gently into his palm and then holding the object up to the light.

"Apparently it's called an 'Ayat al Kursi' charm," I explain, tracing the pattern with my forefinger.

"Pretty," my friend comments, rolling it carefully between his cold hands, "And quite heavy."

His eyes search for mine, confused, awaiting an explanation. I swallow hard, uneasy.

"Uzma, the Asian girl, she gave it to me. It was her grandmother's, some form of protection, I think."

Francis has assumed the role of priest and advisory again, I can tell by the way his shoulders have straightened and his fingers start tapping. He gently passes the shining pendant back to me.

"I need you to give it back to her," I tell him, "and to say that I'm truly sorry for everything."

A low whistle comes out from between the priest's shining white teeth and his head goes back, eyes raised to the low vestry ceiling. A flush begins to redden his cheeks, though I can't be sure whether it's caused by anger or alcohol. It takes only seconds for his blood to boil, for me to find out why.

"So, I am to be your scapegoat? Is that it? Your simple errand boy? Your what, your cleaner?"

His voice has a sharp edge. He's wounded that I would force such a distasteful task upon him.

"No!" I snap, a little too harshly. "But can you imagine how she will be if I go myself? Please Francis, as my closest friend, I need you to do this for me. To let her down gently. She's just a young girl."

"A woman. A woman whom you seduced, Sylvain. Not a girl. You had an affair with her. You had sex."

The insult smarts, like a slap. I hadn't expected my friend to feel so bitter about my mistakes.

We regard each other closely, neither wanting to throw harmful words that cannot be unsaid.

Eventually he nods, holding out his hand for the pendant and I pass it over to him.

"This is the last time, so help me God. You are pushing our friendship to the very limit, Sylvain."

I place my hand over the top of Francis's smooth knuckles, swearing to him that these circumstances will never occur again during our lifetime. This will be the last mistake on my part. I am certain of it.

"So, what time are you leaving?" he mutters quietly, raising himself from the comfort of the chair.

"Sophia has a clinic appointment at three," I explain, "so we should be able to pick up Mama's car around four. We can be in Bordeaux by late this evening. I'll call you when we arrive."

"Don't hang around," he warns. "Leave as soon as you can. I'll talk to Uzma, I'll be gentle."

"Thank you. I don't know what I would do without you, my dear Francis. I'll never forget this."

Francis laughs, a bitter, nasal sound, reminding me that a man of God still inhabits his mortal body.

"Go now," he says. "You'll have my soul for this. Goodbye, Sylvain and take care of your Sophia."

We hug briefly before I head back out into the dark November morning, thanking my lucky stars.

I slip back into bed beside my wife, careful not to chill her with my cold feet as I slide under the covers. It's doubtful that I'll sleep now, but at least the closeness of Sophia's body is a comfort on such a freezing morning. She stirs slightly, rolling towards me and I feel the curved bump of our unborn child.

"Hey, where have you been?" she whispers, nuzzling fondly into my neck. "You're so cold, Sylvain."

"Just for a walk, I needed some cigarettes. Go back to sleep, it's still too early to get up."

"You should give them up when we get to Bordeaux," she teases tiredly. "Enjoy the fresh air instead."

I nod. "I will give up absolutely everything for you, Sophia. Anything you ask me to. *Je t'aime.*"

We lie together, me listening to my wife's shallow breathing, the beautiful woman next to me easily falling back into a contented slumber. I close my heavy eyelids, urging dreams to come quickly.

I imagine Father Francis walking towards the guest house, the golden pendant weighing heavy in the pocket of his cassock, his face taut and serious, striding purposefully towards Mama's home.

Uzma is there, watching him from an upstairs window. I don't know why, but she's all dressed in black, her face pale, eyes red and tearful. She follows the priest's progress as he navigates the cobbles and then disappears around the front of the building. In my dream, there's a bird on the window ledge. It looks like a common sparrow, but its feathers are black, not brown as they ought to be. The bird pecks at the glass of the window-pane, menacing the woman who stares out, trying to get her attention.

There's a loud bang, almost as if someone had fired a gun.

I wake with a start, perspiration beaded across my brow. I'm alert now. The noise must have been one of the other tenants banging the front door on their way out. Everything is still here, and my wife lies undisturbed. I resign myself to an early start and disentangle myself from Sophia's long limbs, the cold floor bringing me back to my senses.

I wander into the bathroom and gaze at the tired, unshaven face looking back at me. But I also hear tapping, the noise of a small, black-feathered companion, chipping away at the windowsill outside.

MONDAY 6AM – JAMEEL RAFIQ

Just as I'm about to put on my overcoat, Ali comes dashing downstairs waving his mobile phone at me.

"I've just had a text message," he hisses, his face a strange combination of alarm and excitement.

For a moment, I don't comprehend what my brother is telling me, and I just stand, gaping at him.

"The thing, you know, the hit-man," he whispers, looking quickly behind him to ensure that neither of the boys are listening. "It's really happening. Four o'clock this afternoon."

I rub a hand over my brow, wondering if, after everything that's happened now, we should call it off.

"Cancel it," I say, the icy words sounding as though they belong to someone else. "Call it off."

"What?" My brother laughs incredulously at my comment. "It's too late to go back now, Jameel."

I can't deal with this now. What difference will it make, anyway? My daughter has lost her mother.

Why make the heartache worse by getting rid of her so-called French boyfriend as well?

"Call the airport," I tell him, "see if we can get a cancellation to Paris today. I need Uzma home."

Ali stands staring open-mouthed while I search in my coat pockets for the car keys.

"Are you serious? Jameel, where are you going? Wait, I'll come with you."

"I'll be back soon," I snap. "Just get that flight. There's something I need to do now."

The drive to the twenty-four-hour café is the longest of my life. It's as though my whole body is going through the motions on auto-pilot while the voice of reason in my head drifts in and out of various emotions. Fatigue, grief, love, anger, self-pity, disbelief. I need to pull myself together. I have to focus.

When I arrive, Shazia is already sitting in the far corner booth, hugging a mug of frothy coffee. I order a tea and then slide across the seat on the opposite side of the table. This isn't going to be easy.

She smiles and reaches for my hand under the wooden surface but I don't reciprocate the gesture.

"Hey there, my love. You look tired. Haven't you slept, Jameel?"

I shake my head, trying to push the sentences together in my brain, to tell her what needs to be said.

"Shazia, listen. It's Farida," I begin. "She's –"

"Is she ill?" Shazia interrupts, her brows furrowing slightly. "Can I help?"

"Please, let me speak," I murmur, lowering my voice as the waitress brings my drink. "I need you to listen and please don't say anything, not a word, until I've finished."

My lover watches my lips moving as I tell her of how my wife has taken her own life. Shazia brings both hands up to cover her mouth. Perhaps she's afraid that she might shout, or cry.

"Poor Farida. But why? Jameel, why would she do such a terrible thing?"

"I don't know. Maybe she convinced herself that Uzma wasn't coming back..." I say hopelessly. I don't believe that this could possibly be a good enough reason to commit suicide, but then I guess I never really did know what was going on in my wife's head. Obviously, nobody did.

"You don't think she could have found out about..."

Typical woman, I think to myself, always thinking about themselves, forever conniving.

"No, she couldn't possibly, we've been so discreet, so cautious."

Shazia glances around the room as though she's willing someone to see us together, just to disprove me. I sip my tea in silence, allowing her to take in the enormity of the situation.

The silence between us is hanging thickly in the air like a dust sheet. I'm tired and weary, still mystified by my wife's death. Shazia is understandably in shock, they were best friends after all.

"I saw her on Friday," she suddenly tells me, her voice no more than a croak. "Farida was at my house. She was laughing and joking, we had afternoon tea."

"And did she give you any reason to think she was unhappy? Anything at all?"

Shazia shakes her head, "No. We chatted as usual. Everything was fine. Do you think all this business with Uzma tipped her over the edge? Maybe she thought her daughter was gone forever."

I sigh. "I really don't know. She was upset, but I thought we were dealing with it."

After a minute or so, Shazia touches my sleeve with her beautifully painted red nails. "Jameel, don't be angry, but there's something I need to tell you. It's about Farida..."

I don't say anything, allowing her to go on and her open confession is unexpected.

"I think Farida was planning to leave you. She was putting money away in a bank account, an account which I helped her to open. Just a little every week, not much, but she'd been saving for years."

Shazia can tell by my face that this is old news, as I give no reaction, not a single twitch.

"I know. Uzma took some of the money to set herself up in France."

She's shocked, I can see it in my lover's eyes. She is searching my eyes for answers, excuses.

"Maybe that's why Farida... I mean, perhaps it ruined her plans. She must have been upset about it."

I turn my face away, gather my thoughts, try to quell the rising emotions.

I stop her in her tracks. "For goodness' sake, we may never know the reason. I have to focus on bringing Uzma home now, making sure that she's safe. I've obviously failed my wife, so the very least I can do is take care of my only daughter. Be reasonable, please."

Shazia lays her prettily hennaed palms flat on the table between us, breathing steadily. I'm not ready for what's next. She's getting desperate. Talk about coming at me from left field.

"Jameel, in a few weeks, or months, after the funeral and when Uzma's back home, I'm going to tell Sanjeev about our affair. I'll leave him and we can move away, somewhere new, make a fresh start."

The words buzz at me as though they're coming from an old, crackly radio. What's this she's saying? Am I hearing correctly? No, this isn't the way it's supposed to go at all. This is a really bad idea.

In a split second, my decision is made. My only concern is for my children, the two people in my life that I'm solely responsible for. Their mother is gone, so now they have to be able to fully depend on me.

"Shazia, it's over," I murmur softly, taking her hand in mine to soften the blow. "You and I, it can't be. Too many people will get hurt unnecessarily and I owe it to Khalid and Uzma to be there for them."

She looks panic-stricken, eyes wide, not blinking. "No, Jameel, no. Please, think about this. Given time, they'll get used to us being together. I can help them to get over Farida's death. Don't push me away."

This is so hard. I love this woman. Shazia is funny, beautiful, slim, everything a man could wish for, but suddenly it's not enough. Something shifts inside me. I need more than this. I realise that I crave for what I've already lost. I need a faithful and diligent woman, someone who will look after my home and my children, not one who will embark on an illicit affair and bring shame upon her whole family.

I need someone pure, true to their strong Muslim principles. I need Farida.

"It will never work," I whisper, levelling my voice and keeping my head low. "This, what we had, what we've meant to each other, it was great, but it wasn't meant to last. I'm so sorry, Shazia, truly I am."

She's crying now. Big, round, fat tears stream down Shazia's cheeks in an unstoppable torrent. People are starting to look curiously in our direction and I'm beginning to feel embarrassed by the situation.

"Come on," I urge, "let me pay the bill and we'll get out of here. Perhaps we can sit in the car for a while, at least until you feel calmer and able to make the short drive home."

Shazia claws gently at my sleeve again. "But can we at least talk about this, Jameel? Please?"

Her pleading is the last thing that I need right now. It's too much. I have enough to deal with already.

"Shh, please. My wife is hardly cold and we're sitting here being selfish. How do you think that news of our relationship will affect our children, eh? Not just Khalid and Uzma, but Maryam, too. And what about Sanjeev? He's given you a decent roof over your head and works hard. Sanjeev's a good man, Shazia. Please, come on, be rational."

"*Rational*?" she spits. "Were you being rational when you were having sex with me in those hotels?"

This is getting out of hand now. I knew that sitting here in full view of the public was probably not the most ideal location. I gesture curtly to the waitress and pull a ten-pound note from my wallet.

"Keep the change," I tell her briskly, sliding out from the booth and buttoning my coat.

"Is everything alright?" the woman asks, regarding Shazia and I with interest. The tears and trembling hands are a good indication that we are not, in fact, in the best of spirits at this moment.

"My wife is suddenly feeling unwell," I say abruptly. "We should be getting home."

Shazia follows me outside. I don't look back at her, but instinctively feel that she must be trying desperately to control herself, to keep calm, to stop crying. I've broken her fragile heart.

Sitting in her compact car, I wait for the woman I love to berate me. I can see the anger building in her.

"All this time, you've used me," she accuses, banging her hands heavily on the steering-wheel.

I take Shazia's hands in mine, afraid that she may hurt herself and sorry for the emotional pain I'm causing her.

"My darling, no," I whisper, pulling her to me and allowing her head to rest upon my shoulder. "I do love you, but my children have just lost their mother and this changes everything. It has to."

I'm unable to resist stroking her soft curls. This woman is so deliciously tempting and fragile.

Shazia looks up at me, desperation and hurt in her huge brown eyes. "But Jameel, maybe in time..."

"No," I utter, taking my hand from her soft, shiny locks. "Shazia, it's over. Really, it's over."

I don't know how long we've been sitting here. It's far longer than I had planned, that's for certain, and rain has begun to pelt down onto the windscreen, providing us with a modicum of privacy. Shazia has been silent for quite some time and I'm hoping that she's coming to terms with my decision. At least she still has Sanjeev, a decent Muslim man, hard-working and good-natured, if not the most handsome.

"I have to go," I say gently, sliding my arm out from round her back. "Ali and I are going to try to get a flight to Paris today, to find Uzma. Will you be okay? Are you alright to drive?"

Shazia nods, but her jaw is clenched as though she's holding back a torrent of poisonous words.

"Go then," she tells me sharply, reaching into the glove compartment for tissues. "I'll be fine."

I feel the urge to leave her with a kind gesture, to show that this hasn't just been about the sex, although I have to admit that I'll miss her incredible body, so I kiss the very top of Shazia's head.

"Take care," I whisper, before opening the car door and setting foot out into the rain. Behind me, I can hear the sobbing begin again but I don't turn or look back, I won't allow myself a last glimpse.

Clambering into the driver's seat of my saloon, I notice that the rain has penetrated the bottom half of my trousers where my overcoat didn't quite reach. I turn the ignition and switch on the heater, all the time trying not to let my eyes rove back towards Shazia's car, which is parked a few bays away.

I allow warm air to take the chill off the sodden fabric for a couple of minutes before clicking on the windscreen wipers and pulling on my seatbelt. It's then that I finally look up and notice the car parked directly in front of mine. A sporty convertible BMW, silver with a black soft-top.

The engine is running, and a couple sit inside. I can just make out their faces through the dripping rain. The man, a complete stranger, is red-haired and wears a dark jacket; the young woman, I already know. Maryam stares straight at me and then glances over at her mother's car, shock and confusion written on her young face.

I drive out of the car park, heading for home. The only thoughts in my mind now are speculations as to how long Maryam has been sitting there, how much she saw and what exactly she has taken from it.

I'm over the speed limit for this part of the city and gradually ease my foot off the accelerator as I weave my way through the housing estate, beads of perspiration studded along my forehead. I'm panicking. I need to calm down and think this through rationally. What a start to a tough day.

Whatever Maryam was doing there, sitting in that car, with that man, it looked as secretive and inappropriate as my meeting with her mother. She must have a Western boyfriend, perhaps someone from the hospital. It's almost as bad as what my Uzma is doing. Young women have no morals these days. But then, isn't that 'pot, kettle, black', as my English colleagues would say? Haven't I just flouted every rule in our Holy book by sleeping with another man's wife, a friend's wife?

As I swing the car back in through the open double gates of my driveway, I let out a shout, finally. Everything has been bottled up so tightly lately, I need to focus on going one step at a time to bring my children back together, to save what scraps of a family unit we still have left. My first priority today must be to get to Paris, to locate my wayward daughter and bring her home where she belongs.

I run up to the house, the rain and wind buffeting me hard as I enter the porch. There's still a nagging issue, one that I cannot resolve. I just hope that Shazia has the sense to make up some tale to tell Maryam about our secret get-together. Is she smart enough to do that?

A slight relief washes over me. Of course she can do that. Her best friend has committed suicide, Maryam has lost her Aunt Farida. My former lover has a reason to be upset today. I was delivering the news in private and comforting her. Perhaps I am saved from shame after all.

MONDAY 8AM – COLETTE JOUBERT

I am totally exhausted this morning. The confrontation with Colin last night brought me a night fraught with unease and restlessness. I suppose that now he is aware of my identity, as the wife of his former employer, there will be many questions, most of which I am unprepared to answer.

Still, he cannot be avoided completely, and will no doubt be checking out this afternoon once his final mission is complete. I will miss our little soirees. The trips to the theatre were very pleasant and he did make a companionable dining partner. *C'est la vie!* Such is life, everything must inevitably go on.

As I enter the warmth of the dining room, the pompous Englishman is already sitting there studying yesterday's *Sunday Times* newspaper that I ordered especially for his perusal. The colour supplement lies discarded on a side table and I make a mental note to pick it up, something to occupy my mind later while waiting for events to unfold. I honestly do enjoy reading in English, It keeps me alert and enhances my language skills, although the English fashion articles are a cause for occasional amusement, as it seems that only French and Italian women know how to dress appropriately for their age.

"Good morning, Colette." The familiarity of his greeting stings me like a wasp as I swiftly make my way to the kitchen. "I must say you look a little peaky, my dear. A sleepless night, perhaps?"

There is subtle irony in his voice and despite the red-painted smile upon my lips, I would very much like to slap him across the face. This man knows how to rile me.

"I am perfectly well, thank you, Monsieur Foster," I reply through firmly gritted teeth, as I come to a halt next to his table. "Now, is the lovely Maria seeing to your breakfast?"

He nods eagerly, never a man to play down the importance of mealtimes. "Oh yes, indeed she is. I've been promised Eggs Benedict. Quite a treat. I'm rather famished this morning."

"In that case, I shall see how preparations are going. Please excuse me."

I glide through the double doors to the kitchen, holding in my breath and feeling confident that the tone of my voice has put paid to any ideas Monsieur Foster may have had about whisking me away into the sunset. It's ridiculous how perspectives change, really it is. If Colin had asked me to go travelling with him a week ago, I would have been upstairs looking through my wardrobe for beach hats and sarongs. But now, circumstances being as they are, my professional head has won the game and I will see through the task that the bureau has entrusted me to do.

"Maria, are these eggs for Monsieur Foster?" I ask of my housekeeper, as she carefully plates up two perfectly poached ovals. "They look impressive."

The plump woman smiles at me and gives a knowing wink. "The only guest allowed to dictate what he eats every morning, Madame. Monsieur Foster is very special, *oui*?"

"It pays to keep him happy," I tell her. "You know how fussy these middle-aged men can be."

My housekeeper gives a little chuckle and carries the plate through to where the Black Sparrow is hunched over the financial pages, looking every bit the professional city gent.

The reception desk bell rings twice, creating an echo in the darkened passage.

Leaving Maria to attend to our hungry Japanese guests, I go out into the hallway to see who it can be. A courier stands there, in neon cycling shorts and an orange safety helmet, with a white envelope, a large package and a clipboard in his hands.

"*Bonjour*. A signature please, Madame," he grunts tiredly, itching to leave. "*Au revoir*." The door bangs shut behind him.

I am left clutching the two items tightly to my chest. The bulky parcel is for *C.FOSTER*, the other is addressed to me.

344

I know exactly what they are. The first contains instructions and a weapon to enable Colin to remove his target. The second is probably a receipt regarding the bank transfer that the bureau will have deposited into my overseas account. I am surprised at them arriving together, though, as I rarely receive payment before an assignment has been completed.

Pushing the large package under the desk with my foot, I pocket the other envelope and return to where my antagonist is grinding black pepper onto his breakfast plate.

"Everything to your liking?" I ask sarcastically, keeping the smile rigid for effect. "Perhaps I can bring you another cafetiere? Blue Mountain roast, wasn't it?"

Colin turns his steely eyes towards me and purses his lips for a second. "Thank you, that would be most agreeable. And the eggs, they're perfect."

Returning with a second coffee pot, I wander around the other tables and check that everyone is happy. It seems that they are. A moment later, the door swings open and Uzma enters the dining room, still looking pale and tired.

"Come and sit here, Miss Rafiq, by the window," I tell her, knowing that Sylvain will be exceptionally careful to stay away from me today. "What would you like to eat?"

"Some coffee please." She smiles faintly. "And just a croissant."

"Wouldn't you like an omelette?" I ask kindly. "Eggs are a wonderful way to start the day."

She nods, looking at me from under heavy lids. "Okay, that would be nice, thank you."

I encourage the young woman to help herself to cereal and yoghurt but she makes no attempt to move from her spot at the window and sits gazing sadly out. It looks as though there are three of us who haven't slept, and I'm partially to blame for two of those insomniacs.

I have done my damnedest to keep Uzma from locating Sylvain and Colin has been given a lot to consider after finding my passport last night. The next few hours are going to be very long, for all of us. Never before have I wished a day to pass by so quickly.

Having cleared the breakfast tables and left Maria to attend to the dirty dishes, I go back out to Reception to check how many guests will be departing, or arriving, today. I have three groups checking out, not including Monsieur Foster, and no more arriving until Wednesday, an ideal situation. We will have plenty of time to change the bedding and replenish the store cupboards. Excellent.

As I make a few notes in the heavy desk diary, I suddenly remember what lies close to my feet. The package is tucked out of sight but its presence is drawing me close like a magnet. I reach down and pull it towards me, carefully tugging at the heavy-duty tape that covers the seal. I know that what I'm about to do breaks all of the bureau's rules of confidentiality, but the intrigue of the situation is powerful. I need to see who it is that the Black Sparrow will be eradicating this afternoon.

Inside the parcel, a bulky, bubble-wrapped item is the first thing that my fingers encounter. I know exactly what will be inside; the weapon of Monsieur Foster's choice, a handgun with an effective silencer attached. The bureau chiefs are excellent at keeping their hired killers well-equipped. I don't need to touch it. Only the identity of the target will quench my thirst for knowledge. Besides, I wouldn't want to be stupid enough to put my fingerprints on the gun. Foster has already shown that he can be careless, carrying those blessed photographs around in his suitcase. I wouldn't want to run the risk of him leaving the weapon at the scene of the crime and leading the police to my door.

There's a white envelope with a card inside it. This is what I'm searching for. My fingers tremble slightly as I expertly navigate the seal with my sharp letter-opener. Then I read.

SYLVAIN RENO.

I cannot read the next line, although I know that it contains my son's address. It also states that Sylvain will be coming here at four o'clock to collect my car. My head is swimming and the air is being sucked out of my lungs as though I've been delivered a heavy blow to the chest.

I sit, quickly gripping the sides of my desk chair as the printed white card quivers in my hand, a photo of my handsome son attached to it with a flimsy paper clip.

No, not my Sylvain! How can this be? Who would want to have my boy killed?

"Madame Joubert?" a voice calls. It sounds distant, as though my head were underwater. "Are you alright, Madame Joubert?"

I blink, lifting my head slowly to meet the dark eyes that look down upon me. I cannot speak.

"Shall I get you a glass of water?"

I nod and Uzma Rafiq runs quickly towards the dining room.

During the minute or so before her return, I manage to hide the package in my desk drawer and take a few much-needed breaths.

"Here you are." Uzma smiles as she offers a glass tumbler. "Drink this."

I sip gently, not taking my eyes from her, grateful that she was here to help me regain my composure.

"Did you need something?" I manage to murmur. "Were you looking for me?"

She shakes her pretty head. "It doesn't matter now, you're obviously not well."

"It's fine," I insist. "Please, what was it you wanted?"

"My suitcase," she confesses, a little embarrassed at bothering me. "I wondered if…"

"Ah, yes." I smile weakly. "I promised to phone the airport. You need to find your suitcase, as does Monsieur Foster."

"Don't worry if you're not… Mr Foster has a missing case, too?"

"Oh, yes, perhaps you weren't aware. Monsieur Foster's luggage was misplaced on the same flight as yours. I'll ring them right now."

Something flickers in Uzma's eyes, a tiny light, a glimmer of insightfulness as she takes in my words.

"*Non, ce n'est pas necessaire. Merci, Monsieur*," I tell the luggage officer a few minutes later, as both Uzma Rafiq and a very curious Colin Foster stand watching. "*Au revoir*."

The latter has stopped in his tracks on leaving the dining room, sensing, quite correctly, that I am trying to trace the missing suitcases. He does a hop from one foot to the other as he listens.

"Any joy?" he jumps in, before the telephone receiver is even cold in its cradle.

Taking a deep breath, I look from one to the other, wishing that they had worked it all out for themselves by now. Surely the mix-up is as clear as the sky on a summer's day.

"Apparently, both suitcases arrived at the correct carousel, neither were left at the airport, therefore the authorities can only conclude that the owners of each case have them mixed up."

"But, that means…" Miss Rafiq stares at me openmouthed as realisation suddenly dawns.

I nod and gently shrug my shoulders. "It would appear that you may each have the other's suitcase."

"But that's absurd!" Colin protests. "The possibility of such a coincidence must be a million to one!"

I note that the man's cheeks are glowing. He's probably thinking through a scenario where Uzma has rifled through his perfectly pressed undergarments. The thought adds a little amusement to my otherwise stressful morning. I stand very still, choosing my words carefully.

"The only way to settle the matter, to be certain, is to swap the cases over. Wouldn't you both agree?"

Both nod their heads, but I can see anguish on each of their stricken faces.

I know what they've done. Foster has searched through Miss Rafiq's personal effects and the young woman has likewise been through his, although I'm sure that Uzma's belongings were a lot less incriminating than the set of photographs she found in the hit-man's suitcase.

"In that case..." I smile. "Oops, excuse the pun. I will leave you to do the necessary exchange."

Foster looks at me with narrowed eyes as he quickly follows the Asian woman upstairs. I watch him go, silent as a deadly spider and swift on his feet for a man of his age. Everything about Colin is wrong, too perfect, the manicured nails, smart clothes, not a hair out of place on his head. But now I see it, the clue that allows me to see into his soul, the ice cold eyes, the fixed mouth, his sharp and viper-like tongue ready to criticise at the drop of a hat. Colin is every inch the deadly assassin.

The Black Sparrow is unaware that he is supposed to murder my son in cold blood this afternoon. I have no idea if it would make any slight difference for me to tell him that the target is my only child. In ten years of coming here, Colin has known nothing of Sylvain, and to that end I can imagine he would feel only the chilling indifference of a paid gunman. To him, it is just another job. His last one.

On the other hand, poor Uzma is probably just as uninformed. If she had the faintest idea of a plan to kill Sylvain, why would she be here searching for him? I cannot be sure, but I fear that his death was perhaps to avenge their liaison, some form of bizarre honour killing paid for by her family. You read of such things in the newspapers, protested about by Human Rights activists, but never in my wildest dreams would I have expected such a wicked plot to emerge on the streets of Montmartre.

Voices come from upstairs, both raised, slightly angry. A door slams and I hear footsteps. I stand at my station, wishing to remain neutral. No doubt the owner of each suitcase has discovered the treachery of the other now, the forced locks, the broken zips. It's a laughable, piteous matter compared to the tragedy that I must prevent from happening this afternoon. So what if the young woman has worn one of Foster's shirts? And does it matter that he has discovered her stash of cash? Neither has been totally innocent in their discoveries and the matter is closed as far as I'm concerned. I have a much more serious matter to attend to. It concerns the life, or death, of Sylvain.

As I turn to go to my private quarters, I slip a hand into my trouser pocket and immediately my fingers touch upon the envelope. Inquisitive as to why it has arrived now, I tear open the seal. The words stamped there are not at all what I was expecting. I, too, have been given instructions. With a slightly shaking hand, I hurriedly slip the note away out of sight. Suddenly, nothing that has happened in the last two days makes sense.

On the other hand, I have just made a vital decision. I know exactly what I need to do to save my son.

MONDAY 10AM – ALI RAFIQ

I've been scouring the internet for hours, flight scanner pages, travel agents, airlines, but there are no seats available on any Paris flights until tomorrow afternoon. I've been scribbling notes of times, prices, airports, and still nothing, unless we drive all the way up to Birmingham. It's unbelievable that so many passengers are flying to France tonight. It's probably still not as chaotic and crowded as the departure lounges in Pakistan, though. It always makes me laugh when I think of all the shouting going on about oversized baggage, lack of travel documents and haphazard queuing. It's like a cattle market with human cargo.

I bring my thoughts back to the task at hand. Jameel's out of his mind with worry now. He just wants to bring Uzma home, which is completely understandable. The poor girl doesn't even know about her mother's death yet, although goodness knows how she'll feel when she finds out. Surely it was because of her daughter's actions that Farida took her own life, otherwise life was good, wasn't it?

And when we do finally get my niece home, there will be a funeral to arrange and goodness knows how much questioning and arguing. I think Tariq and I might have to stay in London a while longer. There's nothing pressing that can't wait back home. I'll just need to make a few phone calls to the office, get them to shuffle things around until I know when we can get back.

Tariq comes trudging into the kitchen, his slippers scuffing the floor tiles noisily. He's closely followed by Khalid. Both look tired. I suppose we all do. It's been impossible to rest with everything that's happened and poor Jameel must be devastated. I've only seen my brother briefly since he came back in, with no mention of where he's been or why, and now he's shut in his study. I can't help feeling that he should be out here, comforting his son.

"Hey," I say trying to lighten up the heavy mood, "you boys should get some breakfast. Toast?"

"I'm okay with coffee," Tariq replies, going over to switch on the electric kettle. "Khalid?"

"Huh?"

My nephew is exhausted, probably hasn't slept a wink, I pull him towards me in a tight hug and we stand connected for a minute or so before he pulls away. He smells like a typical teenager, a little bit sweaty and sweet, like old candy. I'm guessing he's avoiding the bathroom because of what happened in there. In all honesty, I think we all are.

"You need to eat something. Have some coffee and biscuits if you don't want toast," I say softly.

Khalid nods and grabs a packet of shortbreads from the cupboard, offering them to me and Tariq.

"You two share them," I tell him. "We'll sort out some take-away food for lunch."

I watch the boys take a biscuit each and bite down hungrily. My stomach is doing somersaults this morning after last night's events. What a sickening sight. Poor Farida.

"What are you looking for?" Khalid suddenly asks, nodding at the screen on my iPad.

It's no use keeping anything from him, so I turn the information for the boy to see clearly. "Flights to Paris. It's important that we go and find your sister, to bring her home quickly and safely."

"I've been trying to call her," Khalid tells me in a weak voice, "but she's not answering. I've texted loads of times, too. I need to tell her about... you know."

I look over at Tariq, but my son is busy at the sink so I lower my voice to question my nephew.

"Your dad's been trying to get hold of her, too. Have you had any contact with Uzma over the week-end? You really need to tell me, even if it was just a text message."

Khalid hesitates, then shakes his head.

"And the tracker?" I remind him. "Where does it say that she is now? Let's have a look, shall we?"

The teenager pulls out his phone and, after a few taps, shows me the map, a blinking red dot flashing wildly. At least the detector is still working, Jameel and I should have no problem finding the girl.

"Bring it up close," I instruct, pressing a finger down to enlarge the area, "What's the district?"

"That's odd." He frowns. "She's been in the centre of Paris, in Montmartre since Friday, but now this shows her in an area outside of the city. What's this place, Uncle?"

I take the phone and zoom in properly, immediately seeing an industrialised zone. "No! This is a waste disposal area, a rubbish dump. How can this be right?"

Tariq stops stirring his coffee and turns to face me. The three of us look from one to the other, all thinking the same thing; Uzma has outsmarted us.

"I've got a plan," Jameel tells me, rushing into the kitchen with a notepad in his hand. "We'll go by car, on the Eurotunnel, we can get tickets at the station. I reckon we'll arrive by late afternoon if we leave now."

My brother is animated, filled with an unnatural energy. He's unshaven and wide-eyed.

"We're coming, too," my son tells us abruptly. "More eyes to look for Uzma. Don't even try to stop us, Uncle."

Jameel thinks for a second but then agrees. "Okay, okay, go and pack a few clothes, enough for a couple of days. I'll grab us some snacks and drinks from the cupboard."

Both Tariq and Khalid are running up the stairs before my brother has time to change his mind, their noisy chatter and heavy footsteps vibrating around the house.

As soon as we're alone, I break the news to Jameel.

"We have a problem," I disclose. "It seems that Uzma, or that boyfriend of hers, has found the tracker and got rid of it."

"What? I thought it was hidden in the suitcase lining. Maybe it's just not working," my brother suggests, desperately looking for a solution.

I pull Khalid's phone across the breakfast bar and open up the screen to where the tracker is still giving a strong signal. "No, it's definitely working, look here. There are three possible scenarios that I can think of. Either she's found the device and thrown it away, got rid of her suitcase, or they've moved, and that Frenchman lives near the rubbish collection site."

Jameel has been holding his breath and lets it out in one loud puff. "Can this situation get any worse?"

"Look, we've already had confirmation that the 'disposal' will go ahead," I tell him, choosing my words carefully, "so the hit-man, whoever he is, must have Uzma's boyfriend under surveillance by now."

"Ali, this is turning into my worst nightmare," Jameel says tearfully, thudding down onto a stool. "I can't lose my daughter, I've already lost my wife. How am I supposed to cope on my own?"

I can't provide the answers that he needs, so I say nothing for a while, letting my thoughts unravel in the hope that the best course of action will reveal itself.

We're almost ready to leave, with a couple of rucksacks and two carrier bags in the hall, when there's heavy knocking on the front door. I look at Jameel but, if he's expecting a visitor, he's keeping it to himself. He makes no attempt to answer it, just looks at me blankly.

"Expecting anyone?" I enquire. I'm unaware of what arrangements have been made with the authorities over the release of Farida's body but, I reason to myself, it's too soon for them to be calling.

My brother shakes his head, still looking solemn, broken.

"I'll go." I quickly push past him, planning to tell whoever it is that the household is in mourning.

"Jameel Rafiq?" a squat middle-aged man in a brown leather jacket demands to know. Behind him, a taller and younger man stands peering in through the open doorway. They look every inch like police. I smell good cop, bad cop.

"I'm his brother, Ali," I say calmly. "I'm afraid this isn't a good time."

"It's never a good time, Ali." The man shrugs and pulls out a laminated identity card. "Detective Inspector Hadfield, and this is Detective Constable Robinson. May we come in, sir? It's about Mrs Rafiq."

So, I was right. I automatically open the door wider, allowing the men to pass through, I note that they both wipe their feet on the doormat. Courteous, given the dismal wet weather outside. I suddenly remember the Coroner saying that the police might need some more details and they obviously don't waste much time. With a bit of luck, they'll just be tying up loose ends. I don't suppose Jameel will be able to tell them very much. Neither of us knew what was going on upstairs last night.

"Please come through to the lounge," I suggest, and then louder, "Jameel, it's the police!"

Introductions over, I watch as the older detective, the one in charge, narrows his eyes at my brother.

"What state of mind would you say your wife was in yesterday, Mr Rafiq? Any unusual behaviour?"

"No, I don't think so," Jameel replies, glancing swiftly across at me. His look tells me that we're not going to tell them about Uzma. I give a discreet, conspiratorial nod.

"Any arguments?" the younger police officer asks, appraising the room as he speaks.

"No," my brother answers a little too quickly, "it was just a normal Sunday, until..."

There's silence as we wait for the senior detective to tell us why they're here. Judging by the look of shock on Jameel's face, it's not what either of us are expecting.

"We'd like you to come down to the station if you would, Mr Rafiq, for further questioning."

Jameel looks worn out and I wonder whether this is absolutely necessary. I begin to feel irritated.

"Officers, Detective Inspector, my brother has just lost his wife. Perhaps in a day or two..."

D.I. Hadfield blinks hard, dismissing my weak protest and continues to look at Jameel. "I think you should get a coat, Mr Rafiq. We might be a while and it's pretty wet outside."

The men haven't sat down and now all four of us are standing in an untidy circle.

"I told the Coroner everything I know, and the policemen that were here last night," Jameel tells them, obviously as confused as I am about being asked to go with them. "What else do you need to know? My wife committed suicide, I have no idea why."

"The Coroner has since examined your wife's body," the younger detective confides, looking sheepishly at his superior, perhaps wondering whether he should have spoken out.

"And?" Jameel demands. "What difference does that make? She cut her own wrists! I would have thought that cause of death was bloody obvious."

"It's not quite as simple as that, there were other unusual findings," the young man confesses.

Detective Inspector Hadfield gives a short cough before playing his trump card. "Farida's body was covered in bruises, Mr Rafiq. Her arms, legs, stomach. It appears that she was badly beaten the day before her death. Would you happen to know anything about that? Sir?"

A sudden terror washes over my brother's face and he sinks down into the nearest armchair, rubbing his hands through his hair and shaking his head. I stand looking at him, full of confusion. Is my baby brother being accused of beating his wife? Of causing her death?

"Hang on," I tell the officers, kneeling down to comfort Jameel. "Surely that's not right! Did Farida have a fall yesterday? Think, Jameel... Could she have slipped on the stairs?"

D.I. Hadfield flips open a notepad. "The bruises are inconsistent with a fall, Mr Rafiq. It's more likely that someone used their fists on her. A very nasty beating it must have been, too."

He pauses for effect, raising his bushy eyebrows. "Now perhaps, if you don't mind, we'll continue our discussion at the station. Here's my card, Mr Rafiq, just in case."

The detective passes me his details between two fingers but doesn't take his eyes off my brother.

As Jameel is escorted to the waiting car, I stand helpless in the porch of his home. The boys are right behind me, asking questions, demanding answers, but I can't fill in the blanks, not yet.

"There's been some kind of mistake," I tell Khalid, with a fake cheerfulness that any amateur actor would be proud of. "Your dad will be home again soon, I promise."

"But I don't understand! Why can't they just ask him what they want to know here?" Tariq wants to know. "Why does Uncle need to go down to the police station? And how long will he be? Are we still going to Paris?"

So many questions, flowing like a bubbling stream. What can I tell him but the truth?

"I have no idea," I mutter, watching the car pull away, my brother sitting in the back with his head down, looking every bit the grieving widower in his dark clothing.

"I heard them say that Mum had bruises all over her."

"You shouldn't listen in to other people's conversations, Khalid."

"It's true," Tariq pipes up. "I saw purple patches on Aunt Farida's arms and she was rubbing her back as though she was in a lot of pain."

"You didn't say anything," I say sharply. "When was this?"

"Yesterday," my son confesses, "She told me not to say anything."

I hear myself letting out a heavy sigh. This house is a den of secrets. But then I think yes, I, too, saw the purple welts on my sister-in-law's arms. I, too, said nothing.

"Come on," I coax the boys. "All we can do is wait until he gets back."

"The police think that Dad beat up my mum, don't they? And you do, too."

Khalid's voice is little more than a squeak. It's heart-breaking to hear him so full of emotion.

"Of course not," I lie, slipping an arm around his shoulders. "I should think this is pretty standard procedure after such a death. As for the bruises, there must be a reasonable explanation. Your mum obviously had a nasty fall but didn't want to worry any of us."

My words seem to pacify the boy but I wish they could have such a calming effect on me. None of this makes sense. Farida didn't seem to be depressed, she was cooking and chatting as normal yesterday, and now these marks on her body... Something is definitely not right.

Gently closing the front door, I begin to wonder whether I need to make a phone call. Should I contact one of Jameel's partners at the law firm? What would he do if our roles were reversed? What happened to Farida? Has my brother done something unspeakable?

I stand with my back against the wooden frame, wondering what happens next. What do I need to do?

MONDAY MID-DAY –
KHALID RAFIQ

The hot water drenches me as I turn my face upwards to the shower head in Mum and Dad's en-suite bathroom. Uncle Ali said it would be a good idea to come in here. I don't think any of us fancy using the family bathroom. I feel bad for Dad. He had to scrub the bath this morning to get rid of the bloodstains. It makes me want to retch, just thinking about all that pinkness on the tiles.

As soon as I think about my mum and what's happened, the tears come again. No matter how hard I try to control them, they fall steadily down my cheeks. I've always thought it was uncool for someone of my age to cry, but you never expect to be in a situation like this, do you?

Switching off the water, I dry myself on a fresh towel. It's really quite weird being in here, because despite living in this house all of my life, I've hardly ever been in this room. I can recall a handful of times when I was younger, with Mum putting me in the bath here while she sat at the dressing-table pinning up her hair, the door wide open so that she could keep an eye on me.

There are lots of things in here that remind me of her; a pair of pink flowery pyjamas hanging on the hook, pretty perfume bottles, bottles of different coloured bubble bath, and her wedding ring, discarded by the side of the sink. I think the ring is the strangest thing. I don't ever remember her taking it off before.

Going through to my bedroom, I pull on some jeans and a sweatshirt, casual clothes and warm, too, as we're supposed to be walking around Paris to search for my sister later. Although my uncle doesn't seem to have any idea how long Dad's going to be at the police station. I guess we just have to wait.

As I reach the top of the stairs, planning to watch a movie with Tariq until Dad gets home, there's a heavy knocking on the front door. It can't be the police, so I head down to answer it. Uncle Ali gets there first and as he goes hurrying into the porch, I see Maryam through the glass, her hood up against the pouring rain and I then tiptoe down a couple more stairs. I quickly press a finger to my lips, urging her to say nothing until we can speak to each other in private.

Maryam ignores my gesture and demands to know, "Is Uncle Jameel here?"

My uncle isn't quite sure how much to say but he recognises Maryam from previous visits. "No, he's,

365

erm, out at the moment. Is there anything I can help with? You're Shazia's daughter, aren't you?"

I'm right behind my uncle now and I beckon to Maryam to come in. "It's okay, Uncle, Maryam is like family. Come on in, you're soaking."

She takes off her wet raincoat and stands looking at me. For the first time, I notice her red-rimmed eyes and puffy cheeks. I immediately wonder if something has happened to Uzma.

"Have you heard from her?" I beg. "Please tell us if you have. Is she okay?"

"Who?" Maryam frowns, puzzled for a few seconds. "Oh, you mean Uzma. No, nothing today."

Uncle Ali leads the way into the kitchen. "You'd better come through, I'll make us a cup of tea."

"So, if you haven't heard from Uzma, I'm guessing you've heard about poor Farida?"

My uncle keeps chatting as he takes mugs from the cupboard. "Milk and sugar?"

Maryam pulls out a stool and climbs up, her legs too short to touch the floor once she's sitting down. A single tear rolls down her beautiful face and I see the distress that she's in for the first time.

"Maryam, it's okay," I tell her, reaching over and putting my hand on her arm.

She shakes her head, thick dark curls tumbling around her shoulders. "No, it's not."

I wait for her to carry on, while my uncle stays on the other side of the kitchen looking kind of awkward.

"Do you know why your mum..." She pauses for a moment. "Do you know why she did... what she did?"

Glancing at my uncle, I tell her that we have no idea why. Then she continues.

"It was because of your dad!" she spits angrily. "And what he has been doing with my mother!"

"Now, hang on," my uncle jumps in, starting forward, "just what are you trying to say?"

I lower my eyes quickly to avoid Maryam's accusing stare, but I'm too late and she picks up on it.

"You knew!" she yells at me. "God, Khalid, how could you not say anything?"

I mutter that I'm sorry, but I know full well that it's not enough to appease her, so I try to explain.

"I haven't known long," I confess, "but I told Mum about their affair yesterday. How did you find out?"

Before Maryam can explain, Uncle Ali has me by the shoulders, his face full of disbelief. "Tell me this isn't true! It can't be! Jameel and Shazia? What the hell...?"

A while later, we're all sitting in silence, each with our own thoughts, every one of us in a state.

"Have you spoken to your mum yet, Maryam?" Uncle Ali breaks the stillness in the room.

She blows her nose loudly on a tissue and says that yes, they've had a huge argument.

"Listen to me, both of you," my uncle insists. "We have to keep this amongst ourselves for now, just until we know what the police are talking to Jameel about. Understand? It's very important."

"But Uncle…" I protest, "this is why Mum killed herself!" My voice trails off as the sobbing threatens to start all over again, so I stop speaking. The last thing I want to do is cry in front of a girl.

"They should know," Maryam demands. "Khalid's right. Aunt Farida would still be here if it hadn't been for that pair sneaking off to hotels together and having dirty meetings in the car park, of all places!"

The anger is, of course, natural, but my uncle is a quick thinker and tries to calm the situation.

"If you go spilling everything out, Jameel could be in big trouble," he says seriously to both of us. "For the moment, we just have to wait patiently until we know what's going on. Okay? Got that?"

Maryam is thinking, obviously unhappy with being dictated to. "Why is he at the police station?"

Uncle Ali shoots me a stern look over the top of Maryam's head, obviously warning me not to say anything about the Coroner's report, so I shrug and let my relative do the talking.

"You know how it is," he explains, much more softly now. "Paperwork has to be filled in before the Coroner will allow us to make funeral arrangements. Jameel just has to sign a few documents."

Maryam seems to accept my uncle's account and doesn't add anything further.

We finish our tea, which has been getting cold during the shouting, and I can see Uncle Ali plotting.

"Maryam." He smiles kindly. "What do you know about Uzma's boyfriend? We really need to find her, you know... tell her the tragic news about her mother and try to persuade her to come home."

She doesn't respond immediately but when she does, there isn't any enlightening information.

"Not much. He's an artist that she met at summer school. He was the tutor on her course."

"Her tutor? Wow, how unethical is that?" my uncle questions out loud. "And who paid for this course?"

"Dad did," I interrupt. "Uzma brought home an advert about an overseas art course in Paris."

The wheels are turning in Ali's head and we wait patiently until he's connected all the dots.

"Knowing your Dad, he would have kept a receipt of payment, wouldn't he? He's meticulous in that way."

"Probably," I say, looking blankly at him. "What difference would that make?"

My uncle is on his feet before I can figure out what he's thinking and both Maryam and I follow him out into the hallway and across to the door of my father's study.

"Aha, Jameel didn't have time to lock it!" he announces, more to himself than us. "Let's see if we can find that piece of paper, shall we? Now then, where could it possibly be?"

By now, Tariq has come downstairs to investigate the commotion and follows us into Dad's study. None of us know what we're supposed to be looking for, but my uncle's methodical mind soon puts us all to work. It's like a precise military operation.

"Maryam, you check the desk drawers. I'll take the top two drawers of the filing cabinet. Tariq, you take the bottom two. Khalid, you look in the waste paper basket and on top of the desk."

We look like a bunch of amateur spies, rummaging and searching, but nobody dares say a word. Finding this receipt might just be the best chance we have of locating my sister now.

We keep on looking for half an hour before Maryam suddenly waves a piece of paper, a faint smile on her pink lips. "I think this might be it! Sylvain Reno, artist, 1696 Rue de Lyon."

Uncle Ali carefully lifts the receipt from Maryam's outstretched fingers and gives a low whistle. "Three thousand Euros? Wow, this guy must be rolling in cash."

"It was a six-week course," Maryam offers defensively. "Five days a week, full-time."

My uncle does a quick mental calculation. "That's still a hundred Euros a day, per pupil. Imagine if he had twenty students? That's a lot of money to learn how to paint."

"I don't suppose he was shagging them all though, was he?"

The words are out of my mouth before I can stop myself. It's sounds crude and my uncle turns quickly.

"Khalid, stop that!" he snaps back, narrowing his dark, beady eyes. "That won't help."

I really wish Mum were here, I think desperately. She'd make me feel better and wouldn't judge.

Just ten minutes later, Uncle Ali is snatching up Dad's car keys and heading out through the door.

"I'm going to bring her home," he promises, looking at the three of us with determination. "Tariq, you're the eldest, so you're in charge of everything until I get back. I'll phone you from Paris."

"What shall we tell Uncle Jameel when he gets home?" my cousin queries.

"The truth," his father says solemnly. "But it might be a while until he's back, if my gut feeling is right."

Maryam slips her arm through the crook of mine but then lets go again. I can tell she's had an idea.

"Ali, let me come with you," she pleads. "Uzma will listen to me, she's my best friend. Please?"

I watch my uncle's face, where indecision giving way to reason. "Okay, maybe you're right. Perhaps Uzma needs another female to get her to see sense. Boys, you take care of each other."

Tariq puts a firm hand on my shoulder as we watch my father's black saloon reverse out of the drive and into the wet, deserted street. The rain is pelting down so hard that the driver and passenger's faces are just a blur. I have an urge to see Maryam's face clearly before they drive away.

"Shit, Maryam's forgotten her coat," I murmur, turning back inside the house and seeing the damp navy waterproof hanging limply from a peg. "She'll get soaking wet."

MONDAY 2PM – COLETTE JOUBERT

Running my fingers along the seal of the package to ensure that it looks perfect, untampered with, I take a deep breath and look in the mirror. My features will give nothing away should anyone happen to meet me upon the stair and, for all intents and purposes, today could very well be just an ordinary day. I know that what I am about to do is wicked, heartless even, but I have no other choice.

I'm aware that Colin sits in his room waiting for his instructions, the very details and equipment that I now hold firmly in my grip. Taking the stairs upwards, I keep my eyes fixed on the landing above me.

Two knocks, quick and in succession, before I quickly retreat along the passage to hide myself from view whilst he opens the door. I can feel my heart beating rapidly, there's a heavy lump in my throat, but I'm safe now. Foster isn't quick enough to catch the messenger.

I return to the lounge by the back steps, a winding turret that is used mostly by Maria these days, carrying laundry and cleaning materials up to the guest suites, and sit, holding my breath.

In my mind's eye, I can imagine the Black Sparrow carefully opening up the parcel, inspecting his weapon of choice with those delicate long fingers of his, and then eagerly eyeing the card and photograph to see who his final target will be. I can see how shocked Monsieur Foster will be. Who wouldn't be? He will encounter the pretty Uzma Rafiq looking back at him, her name printed clearly in bold black letters, and the location written underneath:

PASSERELLE DE LA RUE BELHOMME – 4PM

I have chosen the little bridge crossing the canal for a reason, but Colin will not know that.

The Black Sparrow's own fate lies in his success, or failure, to complete the task at hand. I am sure that he will not disappoint. After all, retirement is calling him.

I wait for a while, ensuring that I can keep calm and collected, and then walk around the corner to the church. If I'm lucky, Father Francis will be there, preparing for this evening's Mass. I feel that I owe it to him to break the news that Sylvain and Sophia are going away for a while. After all, they are best friends and the priest will be worried, given all that has happened of late.

Inside Saint Pierre, he is kneeling in prayer, a solitary figure hunched over, knees on a cushion as he counts off his rosary beads. I wait until Francis has finished before stepping out of the shadows, but the sound of my heels tapping on the flagstones has already alerted him. He turns slowly and smiles.

"Colette, how lovely to see you. Is everything okay?"

"Yes." I smile faintly. "But I need to tell you about Sylvain."

Father Francis stops me mid-sentence with a shake of the head. "No need to explain. Sylvain came to see me, he confessed about the girl, and I totally understand."

I'm a little taken aback, although hardly shocked that Sylvain has been so open with his best friend.

"So, you know they're going to Bordeaux this afternoon?"

A smile flickers across the clergyman's face and he takes my hands. "Yes, and I think it's for the best. I have offered to go and see the Asian woman, to break her heart, I suppose, but gently."

"Really?" I'm surprised that my son would be so tactless as to ask Father Francis to do his dirty work.

The priest takes out a disc-shaped pendant from the deep pocket in his cassock, holding it out in the palm of his hand. "Apparently this is hers, so when she sees it, she will know that I speak the truth."

I run a nail across the surface of the gold and it's as if a bolt of lightning hits me when the idea strikes.

"Francis, I am happy to undertake this difficult errand on your... well, Sylvain's... behalf. Besides, such harsh news may best be broken to her by another woman, someone she trusts."

"You mean…" the priest starts.

"Yes, my dear Father Francis," I whisper, taking the shimmering item from his hand. "Let me tell her."

There is very little hesitation whilst the tall, dark man thinks through my offer, an undertaking that he so obviously has been dreading. "Are you sure, Colette?"

I put a finger to my lips, thoughts whirling around in my mind as I turn to leave. "Yes, no problem at all."

I tuck the amulet into my purse and head towards the main doors, leaving the priest to thank his saviour that today has been his lucky day.

I return to the guest house full of determination, the final part of my plan now complete. It's been a burden these last few hours, working out how to convince Miss Rafiq that I've located her lover, but now, with evidence of our paths crossing, I will be able to lure her to the site quite easily.

Touching up my lipstick and adding a dash of rouge to my cheeks, I mentally prepare what I will say and then trot back up the winding staircase to knock on Uzma Rafiq's door.

"Yes?" she calls before opening. "What is it?"

"Uzma, it's me, Colette," I say sweetly. "Would you care to join me for a cup of tea?"

The door swings open and tired brown eyes look back at me. She nods and comes downstairs.

The pot is barely brewed before I brace myself for the joy that will flow forth from the young woman's heart. I clench my hands together on my lap and break the news.

"My dear," I begin, pasting a fake smile upon my visage, "I do believe that I have some good news for you. I have asked around the local artists in our community and we have managed to locate Sylvain."

A hand goes up to Uzma's mouth as she tries to contain the shriek that threatens to escape from her lips. "Seriously? Where is he?"

"Well," I explain, pulling out the gold pendant, "he asked me to give you this, as proof that I genuinely have found him, and he's eager to meet you this very afternoon."

Miss Rafiq is on her feet, the cups of tea sitting forgotten and only one thing on her mind now. She takes the charm from me and touches it gently.

"It's my grandmother's 'Ayat al Kursi'." She smiles faintly. "Where is Sylvain now?"

"Well..." I sigh, preparing my best fake smile. "He wants to meet you by the canal, a romantic spot for two young lovers to reconcile, in my opinion, at four o'clock sharp. So, my dear, I suggest you go and get changed, put on your face and get going. The bridge is called Passerelle de la Rue Belhomme."

I push a detailed map of the area across the coffee table and mark an 'X' next to the spot.

Within seconds, Uzma is heading towards the door, pendant clutched to her chest and the widest of smiles stretching right across her face. But then she stops, faltering, a question at the ready.

"Madame Joubert," she ponders, "why couldn't Sylvain just come here?"

I think rapidly, a gift which luckily I am truly blessed with.

"I think he wanted your rendezvous to be as romantic as possible," I lie, ushering her out into the hallway. "Now, go and make yourself look the very best you can, and I'll call you a cab."

"Thank goodness I have my clothes and make-up back now," she witters, doing a little jig before grabbing the handrail. "I've only got an hour, so I'll need to hurry."

The smile doesn't fade from my face until the young woman is safely upstairs, prettifying herself. I feel guilty for doing this but, to save my son, it must be done. With Uzma Rafiq out of the way, Sylvain will be free to live his life in the Bordeaux countryside, with his beautiful wife and my grandchild.

It's a pity, really, that there's no other way. I've started to feel a fondness towards the Asian girl, but everything about her relationship with my boy was doomed from the start – religion, age gap, his attachment to Sophia. But in all of this, her own family have been Uzma's downfall, as they are the ones who ordered the paid assassination of my son.

It's easy to point the finger of blame now, but I know that I'm right. It must have been Mr Rafiq, with his wealth and connections, that ordered the ruination of his daughter's lover. I am convinced that my intervention has done us all a favour.

My tea has cooled beyond saving and I return the tray to the kitchen. A small shot of brandy will serve me better for my own task now. I pour myself one and endure the burning as the liquid trickles down my throat before becoming a scalding ball in the pit of my stomach. On the counter top is the slim white envelope that arrived addressed to me this morning. I am aware of the contents for I have read them several times, but I remove the card from its hiding place once again and stare at the instruction for the final time:

COLIN FOSTER – PASSERELLE DE LA RUE BEL-HOMME – SUNDAY 4:05PM – ELIMINATE.

The years, the months, the weekends, all of our outings and conversations merge together into one. I can hear Colin's voice just by closing my eyes, so well do I know his upper-class tones, and the smell of his after-shave is one that I have often inhaled with great relish.

It will be such a great pity, assassinating the assassin, but unless I rid them of the Black Sparrow, life will be impossible. After all, the bureau knew that Sylvain was coming here to pick up my car this afternoon, which leads me to believe that I am either being followed or my phone is tapped.

Colin is just a pawn in all of this, but his carelessness and obsession with carrying those photographic trophies around in his luggage could well have cost us all our careers. The bureau will go easy on me, once I explain that there was no other solution but to remove the girl. After all, Sylvain is the son of the bureau's founder, and therefore should surely be untouchable.

I call a cab for the girl and pick up my own car keys. With a bit of luck, I won't be out long and my task will soon be over. I just need to ensure that Foster plays his part first. When I return, Sylvain can take the car and begin his new life whilst I clean up here.

The front door clicks shut and I know that Foster has, indeed, already gone out to find the perfect spot by the canal to conceal himself. He's going to go along with it. What choice does he have?

Uzma is ready fifteen minutes later, giddy with love and unaware that her fate is to die today. She looks more radiant and beautiful than I've ever seen her.

I slip black leather gloves onto my slender hands – one cannot take too many precautions – and then slip a few bullets into my pistol. It will be quick, I'll make sure that the Black Sparrow doesn't suffer. I may even shed a tear or two tonight on my return. Things could have been so very different, I muse. Instead of ridding myself of the man who so obviously loves me, we could be heading off over the horizon to a life of sun and companionship.

But that's where my issue with Colin lies. He is incapable of the raw, incessant passion which I crave and sadly, now he will never live to experience such carnal delights. Poor Monsieur Foster, I mouth, before closing the front door. I could have so easily loved you. I take one more draught of brandy before leaving.

MONDAY 4PM – THE END

There were few pedestrians on the wet November Paris streets that afternoon and as Uzma Rafiq slid out of the yellow taxi, she was glad that they would be meeting alone. Every minute of this weekend had been a painful reminder of a distant love, months of on-line plans, snatches of conversation with the man she planned to spend the rest of her life with. But here, today, Sylvain was coming. He should be here any minute, and then everything would finally be alright. She pressed the golden talisman tightly in her palm, closing her eyes and imagining that Sylvain had been holding this close to his heart ever since the day they parted last summer.

From his lookout across the street, Colin Foster watched as the young Asian woman stood gazing out over the murky canal water. It was impossible for him to step onto the adjoining footpath without being noticed, but he was a decent enough shot to hit his target without being detected by passers-by. He

watched intently as she rubbed something shiny between the palms of her hands, waiting, he knew not
why, nor for whom. Bringing the barrel of his gun
up to eye level, the assassin brought it to a halt in the
middle of the woman's back, a little to his right, in
line with her heart.

A couple came running quickly in the opposite direction, hurrying out of the rain, laughing as they huddled together underneath a far from adequate umbrella. Their breath left warm air hanging in the late
afternoon chill as they stepped forward, their feet in
rhythm, blissfully unaware of the rest of the world.
They hadn't planned to walk this way from the ma-
ternity clinic, the path was far from comfortable underfoot and the puddles deep, causing mud to em-
bed itself in their boots, but this way was quicker,
and they were desperate to pick up the car that they
planned to borrow.

Colette Joubert parked her two-door Fiat out of sight
beside a row of closed shops, glad that Monday was
half-day trading in this part of the city. She wore a
man's waterproof trilby pulled low over her face and
crept forth like an alley cat slinking into the shadows
looking for scraps. If the man she sought was here, he
was well hidden, and she stood peering into the trees
for a few minutes, searching for the outline of a man
in dark clothing, or the slightest glint of metal.

Uzma turned, her ears drawn to the laughter coming
her way along the footbridge. There was something

all too familiar about the man, but this wasn't right. He was supposed to be alone! Tears pricked at her eyes, then anger released itself in a torrent of screams and howls as she realised that her dreams were shattered. Here was Sylvain, larger than life, walking towards her and very much in love. But not with her. Not with Uzma. He had his arm tightly around the woman from the art gallery!

The Black Sparrow flinched slightly as the young Asian woman moved out of his line of sight for a second, lurching forward, shouting at the couple on the bridge. He couldn't hear her words, couldn't comprehend the fury with which she rained blows upon the young man's chest, but he had to move fast or his chance would be over. Pulling back the safety catch, he fired, just once and then exited the scene as swiftly as he could without being detected. He didn't see Uzma Rafiq fall into her lover's arms as the life drained out of her, while a bewildered Sophia Reno stood by, horrified.

Colette Joubert was in a state of confusion. What was Sylvain doing here? Why had they come this way when the usual route would come nowhere near the canal? But then Uzma Rafiq was suddenly on her knees, clutching Sylvain's arms as she slid to the muddy footpath. In her panic to stop Sophia from realising who the Asian woman was, Colette stood silent, watching the girl's eyes widen as blood began to ooze slowly from her mouth. The words couldn't come, and thankfully, Sophia would never hear them. A fuzziness... something... began coursing through her veins like a wildfire. Colette clutched at her chest, panicked, believing that she was about to have a heart attack.

Colin Foster turned the ignition on the little Fiat, pleased that he'd been able to pick up Madame Joubert's spare keys from the rack behind the reception desk, a most foolish place to put them. He drove purposely back to the guest house where his packed suitcase stood waiting in his room. He felt no joy at completing this last mission, just remorse at having to slip the crushed cyanide pill into Colette's brandy bottle. Still, he told himself briskly, orders are orders, and the bureau must be obeyed. Twenty thousand pounds would now top up his retirement fund. Minus two hundred and forty Euros, of course. You see, the Black Sparrow had a penchant for tying up loose ends, and today was no exception, he mused, dropping the cash onto Colette's empty desk. A gentleman always settles his debts.

THE END

Dear reader,

We hope you enjoyed reading *Black Sparrow*. Please take a moment to leave a review, even if it's a short one. Your opinion is important to us.

Discover more books by A.J. Griffiths-Jones at https://www.nextchapter.pub/authors/aj-griffiths-jones-traveler-turned-author

Want to know when one of our books is free or discounted? Join the newsletter at http://eepurl.com/bqqB3H

Best regards,

A.J. Griffiths-Jones and the Next Chapter Team

You could also like

Layla's Score by Andy Rausch

To read the first chapter for free, please head to:
https://www.nextchapter.pub/books/laylas-score

About the Author

Having been brought up in a small village in the English countryside, A.J.Griffiths-Jones has plenty of happy memories from which to source information for her novels. However, it's been a long journey. Spanning three decades and two continents, her career & personal life have taken some incredible turns, finally bringing A.J. back to her roots and a promising writing career.

As a young woman, A.J. left the rolling Shropshire hills behind her & headed to London, where she became fascinated in the world of Victorian crime & in particular the unsolved case of 'Jack the Ripper'. Having read every book available to her on the subject, she started her own mini investigation which eventually led to her first non-fiction publication. However, there was a long period of research necessary before A.J. could finally complete her first book and during the intervening years she relocated to China with her husband and took up a post as Language Training Manager for an International bank. As the need for English grew within the company, A.J's responsibilities expanded until she was liasing between two cities and nearly three thousand employees. An initial two year move soon turned into a decade and the couple found themselves in the vast metropolis of Shanghai for a much longer period than they had firstly intended.

Using their Asian home as a base, A.J. and her better half travelled extensively during their time overseas, visiting New Zealand, Australia, Philippines, Malaysia, Thailand and many provinces within China itself At weekends they would jump into their Jeep and set off to remote villages and mountains, armed with little more than a compass and a map set in Chinese characters, photographing their trip as they explored. Eventually the desire to move back to the U.K. prevailed and the couple returned to their native land in 2012. It was at this point that A.J. made the decision to fulfill her lifetime ambition of becoming an author.

Initially embarking on penmanship in the historical crime genre, A.J. felt it necessary to create a balance between research and writing. The long hours of studying census reports and old newspapers were beginning to take their toll and, having a natural ability to see the funny side of everything, she decided to turn her hand to writing suspense novels with a comical twist. This newfound combination of writing styles has enabled A.J. to get the best of both worlds. For half of her working week she creates humorous characters in idealic locations, whilst the rest of her hours are devoted to research in the Victorian era.

In her free time, A.J.Griffiths-Jones is a keen gardener, growing her own produce and creating unique recipes which she regularly cooks for friends & family. Her plan is to create healthy, filling meals which will eventually be compiled into a cookbook. In her free time A.J. still enjoys travelling, although these days she spends her time visiting Europe and the British Isles, and takes regular holidays in Turkey where she has a relaxing holiday home, which also serves as a haven to complete the final chapters in her books with a glass of wine and a beautiful sunset.

Another of the author's passion's is reading, especially books that take her out of her comfort zone and into a different historical period.

Nowadays, A.J. lives in a Shropshire market town with her husband and beloved Chinese cat, Humphrey. She regularly gives talks at local venues and has also appeared as a guest speaker at New Scotland Yard, where her investigative research was well-received by the Metropolitan Police Historical Society. The author's professional plan is to write a series of suspense novels as well as non-fiction publications relating to notorious historical figures.

Books by the Author

Skeletons in the Cupboard Series
The Villagers
The Seasiders
The Congregation
The Circus
The Expats
Black Sparrow
Prisoner 4374

Black Sparrow
ISBN: 978-4-86745-390-2 (Mass Market)

Published by
Next Chapter
1-60-20 Minami-Otsuka
170-0005 Toshima-Ku, Tokyo
+818035793528
28th April 2021

CPSIA information can be obtained
at www.ICGtesting.com
Printed in the USA
LVHW041210110521
687088LV00007B/556